P9-EDV-394

"Excuse me. Are you Liz?" he asked me, pocketing his red yo-yo. "I hear you're in advertising."

"And you've got all your hair!" I blurted like an idiot, thinking about how many guys I knew who needed Rogaine after they turned thirty-five. I consider myself a very verbal person, but his looks robbed me of words. Intelligent ones, anyway.

"Yes, I do, but it's not as nice as yours." He smiled—the kind of smile that radiated kindness as well as humor, a smile with the eyes as well as the lips. "It's so shiny, you could be on one of those shampoo commercials."

I threw caution to the winds. We weren't even properly introduced, but I wanted Jack to touch me; I wanted to know how it would feel to have him run his fingers through my hair. I don't know how to explain it. It was something new for me, something primal. Maybe it was pheromones. "You can . . . touch it . . . if you want to," I offered, in a fit of lust and chutzpah.

The man didn't reach out and tentatively run his palm along the length of my hair. He grasped a handful of it. In one bold gesture. Jack ran his fingers through my hair like he wanted to memorize its texture, color, weight. Instinctively, I found myself leaning backward, toward him. Before I could even consider editing my reaction to his touch, I realized I'd just let out a tiny moan. . . .

Also by Leslie Carroll
Published by Ballantine Books

MISS MATCH

Books published by The Ballantine Publishing Group
are available at quantity discounts on bulk purchases
for premium, educational, fund-raising, and special
sales use. For details, please call 1-800-733-3000.

Reality Check

LESLIE CARROLL

IVY BOOKS • NEW YORK

ALBANY COUNTY
PUBLIC LIBRARY
LARAMIE, WYOMING

Sale of this book without a front cover may be unauthorized. If this book is coverless, it may have been reported to the publisher as "unsold and destroyed" and neither the author nor the publisher may have received payment for it.

An Ivy Book
Published by The Ballantine Publishing Group
Copyright © 2003 by Leslie Sara Carroll

All rights reserved under International and Pan-American Copyright Conventions. Published in the United States by The Ballantine Publishing Group, a division of Random House, Inc., New York, and simultaneously in Canada by Random House of Canada Limited, Toronto.

Ivy Books and colophon are trademarks of Random House, Inc.

www.ballantinebooks.com

ISBN 0-8041-2000-5

Manufactured in the United States of America

First Edition: January 2003

OPM   10   9   8   7   6   5   4   3   2   1

For d.f, who . . .

1/The Contest

Are you perennially single?
Do you want to make $1,000,000.00?
Have your dating experiences been "doozies"?

You could be a contestant on

BAD DATE

The new reality-based TV game show coming to
you this fall from the people who brought you last
season's hit series *Surviving Temptation*.

14 lucky contestants'll share harrowing tales of
their hard-luck laps on the dating circuit.
Our studio audience will vote on who has
the worst date of the week.
If you're the solo single standing
at the end of the season,
YOU WIN ONE MILLION DOLLARS
Plus an all-expense-paid trip for two to romantic
Paris, the City of Lights.

Auditions March 15 in NYC, Chicago, and LA
Phone 1-800-Bad-Date for audition information.

I was the first one to see the ad. It must have been a karma thing, as my roommate Nell would say, because I never read the *New York Post*. I'm a *Times* kind of gal, and these days I read even that on the Internet. Jem, my other roommate, buys the *Post* for the horoscopes. You would think a professor of communications at a local community college, a grown woman with a Ph.D. on her wall and three pairs of Manolo Blahniks (bought retail) in her closet would have more sophisticated journalistic tastes. Not Jem. I know for a fact, though, she reads more than the horoscopes. She reads all four of the tabloid's gossip columns, too.

I'm a sharer, so I thought it would be unfair to my other apartment mates to leave a gaping gash in the newsprint and smuggle the ad into my room. Besides, it wasn't like I was the only "perennially single" woman in the country, let alone in the city, to see it. I was convinced, however, deep down in that unknowable way, that the jackpot was mine, though in the great collective unconscious, that was probably the thought shared by every unmarried person in the contiguous forty-eight states within a three-thousand-mile radius of either coast.

"C'mon you guys, let's audition! I think we're all photogenic enough to be on the show," Nell said. I thought that was mighty charitable of her since Nell is perfect. She even has a perfect-sounding name, Anella Avignon. Nell has the naturally straight honey blonde hair that every movie star on all those awards shows pays a fortune to replicate. She's got a metabolism like a tiger shark and never needs to exercise. She's also got a trust fund. Nell is drop-dead gorgeous and does absolutely nothing all day, but since she pays the rent on time, I can't complain. She could easily afford her own apartment but she says she gets lonely and has a horror of ending up like a modern day Miss Havisham, wandering aimlessly for decades around a warren of overdecorated rooms, so she prefers the company of roommates. Nell is also one of the most generous women on the planet. Witness her complimentary remark about all three of us vis-à-vis this *Bad Date* show. Nell is perfect. A perfect blonde goddess. This morning I started to face it—I've got Venus envy.

"Nell, you don't need the million dollars. Why would you humiliate yourself on national television?" Jem asked her.

"Well," Nell said thoughtfully, gazing into the middle distance, "it's something to do. Besides, Daddy's fed up with giving me something for nothing."

Jem and I gasped in tandem. "What?!"

"Since I've got to eat and pay rent, it means I may actually have to get a job," Nell said sadly. "So if I win the million dollars then I can afford to do nothing. And still give half the money to charity if I want to." Nell got that "epiphany" look in her blue eyes. "That's what I would do. I'd throw charity balls with it. Dress up in an evening gown, meet rich, great-looking guys, and give a bunch of dough to the Fresh Air Fund or something. I could do that. I'm good at throwing parties."

See, this is why I can't hate Nell. She really is such a generous soul despite the fact that she mentioned the chance to dress to the nines as her primary motivation for giving to charity. "I've never quite understood how you can do nothing all day and not get bored," I said.

"Well, I do nothing *now*," Nell insisted. "It's only until I find something I really like to do. I'd rather do nothing than something I don't like." She added, looking straight at me, "I don't know how *you* can do *that*, Liz."

"Because some of us don't have daddies who are CEOs of Fortune 500 companies," I sighed. "And because people actually pay me money to write. Even though half the time these days I have zero belief in the product I'm writing the copy for . . . which makes it a tad hard to promote. And occasionally makes the client a little testy."

"Yeah, well, I can see that," Nell said helpfully.

I used to get a thrill out of coming up with an ad campaign from scratch, writing clever copy that would hook the consumer. Lately, though, I'd been getting my creative kicks by writing a parody of a Regency-era novel called *The Rake and the 'Ho*.

"I feel so soulless now, you guys. When I started copywriting, I enjoyed its creative challenges. There was an alchemy to it. Spinning words into gold. Smoke and mirrors. It was rewarding to know that my public service campaigns were reaching other people and perhaps making a difference in their lives. Maybe one more battered wife would seek help. Maybe one more mother would warn one more child about the dangers of ingesting lead paint. But over the past few months, every day I feel more and more like a charlatan. One of our clients—a *very* big account— household name—launched these little computer screens called 'The *Intel*ligencer,' mounted inside elevators. The screens flash headline news, traffic conditions, weather, sports for the captive audience. A fifteen-word visual bite that changes every five seconds or so. Not even enough time to remember what you read, or enough information to make it truly useful."

"You're on your soapbox, girlfriend. It's just a new form of communication," Jem said. "What's the matter with that?"

"The matter is that I was struck with how useless the product really is. My agency is being paid to pitch something that no one needs or would have even known they wanted if it hadn't been invented. Complete manipulation of the consumer and a totally useless waste of technology."

"So, if *you* won the contest . . . ?" Jem asked me.

"I'd open my own cutting-edge ad agency that specializes in PSAs—smart public service messages for companies with a conscience. A million bucks would pay for the start-up."

"Makes sense to me," Nell said, dog-earing a page in her Victoria's Secret catalogue. "This bathing suit wouldn't make me look fat, guys, would it?"

Jem and I rolled our eyes.

"Honey, it could be down-filled and you wouldn't look fat," Jem answered her.

"Why would *you* enter this contest?" I asked Jem.

Jem may be the most hypereducated woman I know, but she's finally—after years of psychotherapy—coming to terms with her name. "How can a black woman name her daughter *Jemima*?" she used to rant. The true genesis of Jemima's name came when her mother saw the movie version of *Chitty Chitty Bang Bang* when she was pregnant. She fell in love with the name of the little girl, Jemima, in the film. But Jem claimed that she was stigmatized, traumatized, and every other kind of "-tized" for the rest of her life by the appellation.

Jem laughed. "I think it would be a damn kick, that's why. And kind of an interesting experiment to be part of. From a sociological point of view."

"What would you do with the money if you won?" Nell asked her.

"Get out of teaching apathetic college students who are taking my courses merely to satisfy a requirement. Not have to deal with the unwanted sexual advances of a department head who's a self-professed warlock. I'd bank the money so I could afford to teach inner-city first-graders. Mold their sweet little minds; teach them to read."

"You're incredibly noble," I told her.

"I mean it," Jem said.

And that was how we all decided to shelve our dignity in the name of a commitment to community service and audition for *Bad Date*, the reality game show.

2/ The Job from Hell

Gwen, the in-house chef at Seraphim Swallow Avanti, the ad agency where I work in SoHo, decided she was going to celebrate St. Patrick's Day by whipping up a pre-holiday lunch comprised of foodstuffs that were the colors of the Irish flag. Forget those old standbys of corned beef and cabbage; Gwen was paid well to feed us bunny food. Hence, the *plat du jour* was a salad. With Gwen in the kitchen, the *plat* of every *jour* was a salad. Never before have I worked at a job where I spent half the day craving bacon cheeseburgers.

I took another mouthful of my radicchio, pignoli nut, and mandarin orange salad. SSA lured its employees with the promise that there was indeed such a thing as a free lunch. I always thought it was really just a clever ruse to keep everyone from leaving the building for the obligatory—and lengthy—three-martini lunch, still popular in the canyons and caverns of the advertising world.

"Okay, folks, chow down. We don't want to spill raspberry vinaigrette all over the product," chirped Jason Seraphim, one of my bosses.

I pointed to a pile of what looked like fluffy Kleenex. "What is that stuff, by the way?" I asked.

"Snatch," said F.X. Avanti, using one of the cloths to clean the lint from his thick eyeglasses.

"Correction. *Floral-scented* Snatch." Jason rolled his eyes. "And it is our job to make the dustcloth-buying public forget they ever saw the Swiffer and switch to Snatch."

I practically choked into my napkin. "You are kidding me, right? This isn't one of your post–Thanksgiving April Fool's jokes, is it?"

"Would we kid about a thing like this?" Jason asked.

"I, Francis Xavier Avanti, swear on the grave of my maternal grandmother, Nona Rosanna, may she rest in peace, that I would not, nor did not, invent this ad campaign just to make you giggle, Liz."

Jason rattled the ice in his Fresca. "It's actually a British product. Lillian snagged the account and is handling it from the Berkeley Square office, but they want to roll out an American mass-market launch within the next three months, so the New York office was tapped. They have sales totaling five million pounds sterling and they've only been on the market in the U.K. for less than half a year."

It was really hard for me to keep a straight face. "First thing we should do is ask Ms. Swallow if we can change the name for the U.S. market. Talk about two countries divided by a common language. Does Lillian know that *snatch* doesn't exactly mean over there what it does over here? At least I don't think it does." I waved my hand dismissively at the product, wishing I could make it go far, far away. "That box doesn't bear the royal coat of arms on it, does it? I can just imagine Her Majesty's endorsement." I brandished the dustcloth as though it were an Irish linen hanky and launched into my best impression of Queen Elizabeth. "I don't go anywhere without my Snatch. It traps all sorts of rubbish in its fluff and leaves every surface clean as a whistle." I dropped the English accent. "And Lillian wants us to position new 'floral-scented Snatch'? I mean, *come on,* guys!"

"It's pretty funny, if you ask me," F.X. snickered. "But you sounded more like Elizabeth Hurley than Elizabeth Windsor."

"By the way, we're doing print *and* commercials for this one. Think 'out of the box,' you should pardon the expression."

"That's really funny, Jason," I said. "What am I supposed to do with this? Have a nubile teenager dressed in hot pants like Daisy Duke or Daisy Hazzard or whatever her name was, hose down and wipe up the family SUV with the product, smile provocatively into the camera, and purr 'Grab some floral-scented Snatch now'?"

F.X. furrowed his monobrow beneath his Coke-bottle lenses. "That could work," he said. "But you don't wet them to use them. That's the whole point. So come up with something else."

"Aaargh." I took a breath. "Oh. So we want America to be turned on by a *dry* snatch. Just what the free world needs. An opportunity to purchase myriad brands of electromagnetic dustrags. Snatch or Swiffer: You decide."

"Sounds like scratch 'n sniff. Ugh." Jason rose from the long conference table. "The ball's in your court,

Ms. Pemberley. Get something back to me by the end of next week. We've got the client coming into town then. I want a minimum of three campaign ideas."

"Only if I can have Demetrius as my art director," I lobbied. Demetrius was SSA's most talented graphic artist. "Only a gay Rastafarian who roller-skis to work every day is off center enough to come up with some visuals on this."

"Just remember: Snatch is a family-oriented product," snickered F.X.

So you see, I already compromise my integrity for far less than a million dollars. What did I have to lose by auditioning for a dopey game show?

3/The Audition

Jem, Nell, and I sat in a long corridor outside the executive offices for the Urban Lifestyles cable channel with our brown standard issue clipboards in our miniskirted laps. The deeply curved configuration of the orange plastic chair was giving me premature scoliosis, so I shoved my purse between my lower lumbar region and the seat back in order to get a bit more comfortable.

"Hey!" Nell leaned past me to speak to Jem. "What are you putting down under 'race'?"

Jem suppressed a smirk. "Well, it's multiple choice and 'mixed' doesn't seem to be an option, so I'm going with 'other.' " She paused for dramatic effect. "I wrote 'four hundred meter hurdles.' "

"You didn't," Nell squealed.

Jem shoved her clipboard under Nell's nose.

"She did," I said somewhat dryly.

"What did you two put down for 'age'?" Jem asked us.

"Twenty-nine and holding," Nell said proudly.

I read verbatim from my information sheet. " 'Age is a number and mine is unlisted.' I read that in someone's obituary once. Words to live by."

"Shit. I put down my real age. Maybe I should change it." Jem studied her own response and angled the eraser portion of her mechanical pencil toward the page.

A production assistant who looked like she hadn't yet completed puberty walked toward us with the brisk efficiency of someone who wanted desperately to be regarded as a responsible grownup.

"Hi, I'm Tara," she said, introducing herself. "Are you ladies ready?"

We nodded our heads in assent.

"Cool! I'll be taking you one at a time to meet with our producer. It's a really informal thing, so don't be nervous. He'll just talk a little bit with you to get a feel for who you are, so just try to act as natural as possible. There are no right or wrong answers, nothing specific he's looking for, other than people who are comfortable about being candid." Tara looked at her list of interviewees. "Okay, number forty-seven. Liz Pemberley."

"That's me." I stood up and shouldered my purse, noticing for the first time a tall, suntanned man leaning against the opposite wall. Suddenly, I felt as though he'd been watching me the entire time I'd been sitting there. When our gazes met, his was so penetrating that I felt he was drinking me in, somehow managing to learn everything there was to know about me in that single look. Yet oddly enough, his gaze didn't feel intrusive or invasive; it felt warm, comforting in the strangest way. Maybe it was the fact that he was also playing with a red yo-yo, executing the most elaborate tricks without even looking at either his hands or the toy, that made me feel so relaxed.

"Liz?"

"Huh?"

"Hi, Liz. Pleased to meet you." Tara shook my hand. "And you've answered all of the questions on the information sheet as fully as you can?"

I nodded.

"Okay, then. Let's rock 'n' roll."

I turned back to my compatriots and gave them a little smile, which was returned by a thumbs-up sign from each of them. Tara led me down the hall to a glass-walled office. The beige linen vertical blinds were closed for privacy.

Tara rapped gently on the glass, then let us into the room. A young, puppyish man was seated in a large brown leather chair, with his legs extended, feet propped up on the massive desk. There were shiny pennies in his cordovan loafers. "Rob, this is Liz Pemberley," Tara said, then handed him my clipboard and quietly closed the door, retreating into the corridor.

The puppy swung his legs to the floor and rose. He offered me his hand. "Hi. I'm Rob Dick. No jokes about my name or you'll never get on the show. Thank you for coming in this afternoon, Liz." He motioned for me to sit. "I'm just going to turn on this video camera," he said, adjusting the lens. "I need to tape your interview (a) so I can remember it since I've got associate producers taping potential contestants in two other cities today; and (b) so we can see what you look like on camera." Rob switched on the camera and returned to his chair. "So," he continued, "what makes you want to be a contestant on *Bad Date*, Liz?"

Before I could reply, Rob barreled ahead. "We were

going to call the show *Date from Hell* but the religious right got on my ass and the network executives thought it was the better part of valor to go with something a bit less ... site-specific, if you get my drift."

Why did I want to be on the show, whatever it was titled? Good question. Of all the smart mouth things I'd planned to say, I really didn't have an answer for that one. I was afraid that telling Rob that I wanted to use the prize money to start up an ad agency focusing primarily on public service campaigns might not be a compelling enough reason for him to cast me. "Because I'm just your average twenty-first century media whore" didn't sound like the right thing to say either. Besides, that wasn't true.

I crossed my legs. "Well, Rob." I smiled as warmly as I could. "I have led a rich and varied life as a single woman in New York and Lord knows I've had my share of experiences with men. And when I saw your ad, I thought here's my opportunity to share my nightmares with America in the hope that if I can reach just one kindred sister spirit out there, my bad date stories will prevent her from making the same mistakes I did. I suppose they'd have some entertainment value to anyone who wasn't *on* those dates."

Rob stopped chewing his pencil. "Good answer!" he exclaimed.

I felt like I was trying out for the old *Family Feud* show instead. He looked down at my questionnaire. "So, you're a copywriter for Seraphim Swallow Avanti. My sister works for J. Walter Thompson. She's an art director over there."

"They're a worthy competitor," I acknowledged gracefully.

"Nina always complains about them being too 'old school,' though," Rob said. "You guys are supposed to be real cutting edge, according to her. Hey, did you have anything to do with the 'site bytes' campaign for that *Intel*ligencer gizmo? We've got their screens in our elevators here. I love that I can see how the Dow *and* the Knicks are doing before I even get to the tenth floor!"

"That was me. My baby. Thanks, by the way. All the ad copy including the 'site bytes' nickname sprung from my ever-fertile mind." *Unfortunately*.

"Damn!" Rob pointed his pencil at me. "You're the kind of quick thinker *Bad Date* needs to keep the energy of the show flowing. Smart, snappy comebacks to our host's scripted ad libs. Now, this isn't a guarantee, mind you. We're conducting interviews across the country—a three-city marathon. And we're looking to cast a good mix of people from all backgrounds, all colors . . ."

"A veritable rainbow of disappointed singles."

"Exactly! So, have you got any questions for me, Liz?"

I thought about asking him something like "How do you spell the name of the president of Indonesia?" but I decided to play it straight. I wasn't yet sure what kind—or even how much—of a sense of humor he had.

Rob noticed the pause, so he added, "Questions about the show, I mean."

"Well, what's the format?" I asked. I figured I'd give him an easy one to start with.

"The show has been picked up by the network for a thirteen-week season. Half-hour episodes. We're going to cast fourteen singles—seven men and seven women—who each week tell our live studio audience and our TV viewers across the country a sob story—hopefully, one that's tastefully titillating—about a bad date they've been on, past or present. The contestants are hooked up to a monitor when it's their turn to talk about their date."

"A monitor?"

"Finger electrodes. They look like little metal cones that you stick your forefingers into."

"And what's that supposed to do?"

Rob grinned like the Cheshire Cat. "You can't lie! Isn't that cool? The electrodes work like a polygraph, and the graph itself, with all the little lines that go up and down, you know, *zitz-zitz*—" he illustrated by waving his arm up and down as though it were a huge stylus, "—that's going to be displayed on a big screen behind the contestant. See, the show would have no integrity if the cast members were just making up bad dates or our staff writers were feeding them copy. We're going to be the most honest show on television! Except maybe for *60 Minutes*. *Bad Date* has to be *real*. That's what's so exciting. Real people with real horror stories."

"Competing for real money," I added. "So how does someone get the million dollars?"

"At the end of each week's episode, the studio audience votes someone off the show. The person with the least objectionable bad date gets canned. The surviving contestants go on to compete against one another the following week when they give a completely new date-from-hell story."

It was sinking in. "So the person with the thirteen worst dates of anyone, the most pathetic one of all of us—"

"Wins a million dollars! Of course you do get compensated each week you stay on the show. A thousand dollars per week. Which you get in a lump sum cashier's check given to you the night you get voted off the show, in the amount commensurate with the number of episodes you've survived. In other words, if the audience votes you off the show after the seventh episode, you walk away that night with a cashier's check for seven thousand dollars."

Somehow a grand an episode didn't sound like very much mollification for the amount of humiliation involved.

"Did I tell you who our guest host is?" Rob asked.

"Nope."

"Guess."

"Colin Powell," I sassed.

"Nope. But we asked him. Gotcha!" Rob said when my eyes widened. "Our guest host is gonna be—if we can nail down the details of his contract, which I expect the network brass will do this week—Rick Byron!"

"The movie star?" I shifted in my chair and crossed my legs, angling my body to one side so that I would appear thinner and, hence, more potentially castable.

"Yup. It's a perfect tie-in with the movie he's got out now, *What's Your Sign?*"

"That's the one where he signs up with this match-making agency and ends up going on a whole slew of bad dates, right? I loved that movie," I gushed. Actually, it was a total piece of fluff that was less challenging than the box of Dots I munched during the picture. At least the Dots got stuck in my fillings and stayed with me long after the movie plot did. I asked Rob what would happen when it was down to just a few contestants. How would they fill the half-hour program?

"Early on in the game, the contestants only have a couple of minutes each to share their tale of woe. Just a slam, get-in-get-out kind of thing. As we reduce the number of cast members, they'll have more air time to elaborate on their sob story for that week and we'll get to learn more about who they are, their backgrounds, their jobs, whatever they want to talk about. It'll be more like an interview on Letterman."

Rob's enthusiasm was contagious. I was getting the idea and forming a strategy of my own—a game plan for surviving *Bad Date* all the way to the jackpot. But I wasn't about to share it with the show's producer. I smoothed out my mini and smiled at Rob. "I see."

"Well, then," he said, rising from his desk, "just one more thing before you go. Tell me about a bad date you've been on. Don't worry, if we cast you, you still can use it on an episode."

I had had a feeling it would come to this. "No lying, right? Not even an embellishment for dramatic effect?"

Rob shook his head. "The practice will be good for you."

I took a deep breath, debating whether to hit him with one of my absolute worst or just give him a taste of the misery of some of my matchups. "Do you want to hear about the guy who dumped me for my kid sister?"

Rob jumped up from his chair before I could get any further. "That's a great one-liner," he exclaimed. "In fact, that's all I need to see for now. Well! It's been terrific meeting you. And we'll be in touch." He turned off the camera and shook my hand. Tara materialized out of nowhere to escort me back out to the waiting area.

Jem had her head bent over a stack of papers. In a careful hand she was writing a comment on the final page of one of them. I watched her lips move as she turned back to the first page, slid the tip of her violet Pilot marker along the left margin of each sheet, subtracted from one hundred in a muttering tone I knew well, then returned to the first page and wrote a big seventy-nine below the student's name.

"Are you doing what I think you're doing?" I asked her.

"With all this time to kill, I figured what better opportunity to grade midterms?" Jem flipped the exam she'd just finished grading to the back of the stack, then tackled the next one, shaking her head and muttering to herself. "About a half dozen kids make the same error every semester," she griped.

"Which course is that one?" I asked her.

" 'The Pen or the Sword: Communication Through Violent and Nonviolent Means.' Whenever we cover the segment on frontier justice and vigilantism, a handful of students always refer to Shane as the hero of *High Noon*." She sighed, exasperated.

"Well," I said brightly, "I'm glad to see you're taking this million dollar contest so seriously."

Jem grinned up at me, rolled her eyes, and resumed her grading. "At least *I'm* doing something useful," she added, still fixated on the midterm. When I didn't ask to whom she was comparing herself, she explained. "Nell," she said.

I looked across the corridor and saw Nell, her hand caught in mid–hair toss, her head tilting back, her smile a bus ad for Pepsodent. The British call it "chatting up." We Yankees tell it like it is. Nell appeared to be in full-throttle flirt with the dark-haired man who had been so intently looking at me. For some reason, I felt one of those icky jealousy pangs. And I didn't know the guy from Adam.

Tara reviewed her list. "Number forty-eight. Anella Avignon," she said, looking down the corridor.

"Oops! 'Scuse me." Nell treated her new friend to another dazzling glimmer—the effects of several thousand dollars' worth of adolescent orthodonture. She skittered over to Jem and me and grabbed her clipboard. "Almost forgot it," she said, as she straightened her skirt with her free hand, then gave her hair another once over.

"It's a piece of cake," I whispered to her.

"Oh, please. I'm just sorry they called my name already. That Jack guy is really cute. . . . I was just getting to know him. And he can cook! This is such a lark, you two." Halfway down the hall to Rob Dick's office, she was still laughing at the sheer goofiness of our mutual adventure.

4/The Hunk

I sat down to talk with Jem, but Professor Lawrence wasn't interested in anything but getting her midterms graded. She frowned when a shadow crossed our paths, obscuring the light she needed to decipher her students' sloppy scrawls masquerading as penmanship.

"Hey, hey! I can't read," Jem said, looking up at the obstruction.

An extremely nice-looking obstruction, if I do say so myself. The tall, dark, and drop-dead gorgeous obstruction Nell had referred to as Jack.

"Excuse me. Are you Liz?" he asked me, pocketing his red yo-yo. "I hear you're in advertising."

"And you've got all your hair!" I blurted like an idiot, thinking about how many guys I knew who needed Rogaine after they turned thirty-five. I consider myself a very verbal person, but his looks robbed me of words. Intelligent ones, anyway.

"Yes, I do, but it's not as nice as yours." He smiled—the kind of smile that radiated kindness as well as humor, a smile with the eyes as well as the lips. "It's so shiny, you could be on one of those shampoo commercials."

I threw caution to the winds. We weren't even properly introduced, but I wanted Jack to touch me; I wanted to know how it would feel to have him run his fingers through my hair. My scalp is one of my most erogenous zones, so if the guy was courageous enough to comply, the worst that would happen was that I would get a cheap thrill. I don't know how else to explain it. It was something new for me, something primal. Maybe it was pheromones. "You can . . . touch it . . . if you want to," I offered, in a fit of lust and chutzpah.

The man didn't reach out and tentatively run his palm along the length of my hair. He grasped a handful of it. In one bold gesture. It didn't remotely hurt; in fact, it felt quite wonderful, gave me a little shiver at the nape of my neck. Jack ran his fingers through my hair as though he wanted to memorize its texture, color, weight. Instinctively, I found myself leaning backward, toward him. Before I could even consider editing my reaction to his touch, I realized I'd just let out a tiny moan.

"Guys, can you take that elsewhere?" Jem asked, a slight edge to her voice.

"Not a problem. Can I offer you something to eat? Either of you." He steered me over to a vending machine. The machine was a good six inches taller than I was. Jack was taller than the vending machine. "Sugar or salt?" he asked. "Or you can cover more than one of the four basic food groups with such combinations as Reeses or those cheese-stuffed pretzel nuggets. My treat."

"Jem, they've got Sugar Babies," I called out to her, then turned back to face my handsome co-conversationalist. "That's my friend, Jem. Mine and Nell's. Whom you just met a few minutes ago."

Jem waved her hand at us.

"Does that mean she wants the Sugar Babies or she passes?" Jack asked. I was beginning to fall for that warm smile of his. And the best way to my heart is by being nice to my friends. I shook my head.

"Was that a yes or a no? God, I hate women who can't make decisions."

His grin indicated that he was just having fun with us. The high-wattage smile could have lit up the room. It drew attention to his dark eyes, and briefly sounding their depths, I decided to add intelligence to the cocktail of Jack's qualities.

Our new benefactor deposited three quarters into the machine and punched the alpha-numeric code for Sugar Babies. The yellow and red packet thunked to the well inside the glass case at the bottom of the machine.

"I'll get it. I'm built closer to the ground than you are," I offered. I retrieved the bag of caramels and turned to Jem. "Jem! Catch!" She looked up and I underhanded her the pack.

"Nice toss. Ever play softball?"

"Nah. Just a lucky throw. And yes, I *am* Liz, by the way. Liz Pemberley."

"Jack. Jack Rafferty." Instead of shaking my hand, he rested his on my shoulder. It felt warm. "So, what would *you* like?"

Oh, mister, you don't want to know, I thought. I peered at the range of selections. "Oh, yes, my favorite petroleum product. Gummi Bears."

"What a coincidence. Mine too." Jack fed seventy-five cents into the vending machine.

"Do you rob parking meters or something?" I said.

"Why do you ask?"

I wondered if his thick dark hair curled naturally or if he used some sort of gel. "You've got so many quarters."

"I usually save them up for the laundromat, but when damsels are in need of midafternoon sugar-craving satiation, I feel I must leap to the rescue."

When he leaned past me to retrieve my cello-wrapped packet with the pseudo–Brothers Grimm graphics, I found myself breathing a bit more deeply to catch the scent of his aftershave or whatever it was he was wearing. He smelled like those blue water colognes that are supposed to remind you of the sea . . . make you wish you were drifting off to sleep on the deck of a catamaran with an umbrella drink in your hand.

"So, how did you know I was in advertising?"

"Your friend Nell told me you were one of the top copywriters in New York. 'Fastest brain in the business,' she said, as a matter of fact. So I had to meet a woman whose mind goes from zero to sixty in a millisecond."

Well, well, good for Nell. "I pay her to say those things," I kidded. I felt my pupils dilating by the centimeter.

"I asked her what kind of stuff you work on that really rings your bell and she told me your favorites are public service campaigns."

Good grief, he'd practically interviewed Nell about me. "All true."

"Any one in particular that you're proudest of?"

"There are a couple, actually, but I guess I felt the most connected to an early detection breast cancer campaign that ran nationally, which I did a few years ago. My mom died of it." I was shocked at how comfortable I felt sharing this with Jack. His relaxed manner had a reassuring effect on me.

Jack reached out and stroked my hair. Affectionately, this time. "I'm sorry, Liz."

I fought back the tears that come every time I mention the subject. Fifteen years later and I still respond no differently. "It was called 'Life Begins at Forty,' educating women about getting a baseline mammogram at that age." I looked away from him for a moment. I needed to get my bearings back. "We don't even know each other and already we're talking about breasts," I joked feebly.

He gently touched my shoulder. "Hey, there. I didn't mean to upset you." He delicately smudged away a tear that had begun to trickle down my cheek. "I'm sorry, Liz."

"You didn't upset me, Jack. I upset me. Memories are pretty powerful things." I sniffled and tried to smile. "But enough about me. So what do you do, Jack Rafferty?"

"I'm part owner of a restaurant in Miami. South Beach, actually," Jack said. "The silent partner, if you can believe that."

"You're pretty garrulous for a silent partner," I admitted.

"I'm the money man and the business head—for now. The not-so-silent partner is pretty well known in the music business. So the restaurant has nightly

entertainment—mostly Latin, Salsa; it's a good place
for him to front his band and the bands of his friends.
That's primarily what it's known for, not for its food,
to my personal dismay. What are you doing to those
poor little things, by the way?" He caught me wor-
rying two Gummi Bears—a champagne colored one
and a red one—into a sort of sexual 69 with one
another.

I felt my cheeks grow warmer. "Um . . . I . . . uh . . .
like to play with my food before I eat it. Make sure it's
really dead and all that." I popped the trysting jellies
into my mouth. "I can see how the restaurateur thing
fits in. Nell said you cook."

Jack beamed. "Cordon bleu and CIA. And proud
of it."

"What does the Central Intelligence Agency have to
do with haute cuisine? Did they teach you how to fry
stool pigeon?"

His smile faded. "Culinary Institute of America.
And in haute cuisine, we call it squab."

"I don't cook . . ." I started to say, when Jack
turned around, momentarily distracted by the sound
of heels click-clicking down the corridor. Tara was
ushering Nell back to our butt-killing orange seats.

"Cool. That was fun! Thanks, Tara," Nell said,
then announced she was going to the loo, in case I
wanted to join her.

"I think I'm up next," Jem said, as Tara checked her
roster. Jem reluctantly put her stack of midterms on
my chair. "Watch these," she called out to me. "And if
you're leaving the area, then could you just put them
all in my folder and shove them in my carryall? On
second thought, never mind. I'll do it myself."

While Tara expelled a puff of air and checked her watch, Jem meticulously collated her students' exams, slid the clip of her Pilot cap over the open accordion folder, and shoved the file into a huge black leather tote, which she then slipped under her chair—but not before checking to see that the marker hadn't detached itself from the file folder in the process.

"Well, *she's* really anxious to win a million dollars," I commented, as Jem followed Tara down the hall.

"Didn't even check her makeup," Jack observed dryly.

"She doesn't need to. She always looks good. Unlike me who tends to eat lipstick."

Nell returned from the ladies' room and grabbed me by the arm, steering me back to our chairs. "Excuse us, please," I called to Jack over my shoulder.

She pulled me into one of the chairs. "You do realize you were flirting with the enemy?"

"What are you talking about? And hey, wait a minute. When I got out of my interview, I saw *you* flirting with him."

"That was before I realized that he was trying out for *Bad Date* as well. Once I learned that, I just started smiling and tossing my hair a lot."

"What makes you so sure that we're all going to get selected, Nell?" I looked over at Jack. He was watching us. And playing with his yo-yo again.

Nell lowered her voice, looked past my shoulder at Jack and smiled. "You just never know."

"I thought we weren't taking this audition seriously."

"*I'm* not . . . but in case *you* decided to . . . I don't know . . . I mean, it just doesn't seem like a good idea to, you know, fraternize with the competition. He *is* really cute, though."

"Definitely," I agreed.

"Besides, Liz, he's going home to Miami after his interview. He's got a 6:45 flight out of Newark this evening."

"So we'll also probably never see him again."

"So it's a waste of time to really try to get to know him."

"Right." I tried not to look disappointed. I realized I wanted to get to know Jack a lot better. I wanted to find out what was behind his dark eyes, what made them twinkle, what made him tick.

Jem's interview seemed to go more quickly than Nell's and mine did. "We're running a bit late," Tara said apologetically, as she shuttled Jem back to her orange chair. "Don't worry, Ms. Lawrence, I'm sure your tape is great and you have a terrific personality. . . . It's not really the length that matters. Just what you do once you get inside."

The poor girl apparently had no clue what she'd just said, but I gave a quick glance around the room just to make sure that the other three adults in the vicinity were trying not to blush . . . or laugh . . . as much as I was.

"That said—" I began.

"It's a myth." Jack winked at me, then I caught Tara looking in our direction. "I have a feeling my number is up, so . . ." He retrieved a monogrammed silver card case from his breast pocket. "I hope we meet again, Liz; but in case we don't . . . if you're ever in the Miami area, just give a shout. I'd love to hear from you."

"Jack Rafferty," Tara announced. "You're up next. I hope you don't mind if we move things along a bit quickly." She started down the hall toward Rob Dick's office.

"Story of my life," Jack quipped under his breath. "Or should I say, my relationships?" He looked back over his shoulder and waved at the three of us as he headed down the corridor.

"He's got a sense of humor like yours, Liz, but I think we can forgive him for that. Actually, he's a really nice guy," Nell said after we were sure Jack was safely out of earshot.

I slipped Jack's business card into my jacket pocket. "Yeah. He even overlooked Jem's incivility and bought her a bag of candy."

"I have to return these midterms by the end of the week. I couldn't waste valuable time flirting."

"You were just being an ice queen, Jem. And since when is flirting a waste of time?" I posited. "Except when you don't want the guy."

Nell shook her head. "That's okay, too. You just do it for the practice. To keep from getting rusty. So when one you really want comes into the picture, you'll be ready for him. I didn't want Jack, but it was fun to talk to him."

It was hard to believe what I was hearing. Nell can get any guy she wants. And she invariably does. "You . . . what? I thought you said he was very cute."

"He is. From a purely aesthetic point of view. Like I can appreciate the beauty of Michelangelo's David, but I wouldn't want a copy of it in my living room."

"In fact, because I couldn't help overhearing it, most of Nell's conversation with Jack consisted of talking *you* up, Liz," Jem said, as she shouldered her huge tote bag.

See, this is what I mean about finding it impossible to hate Nell. I admit to having felt weirdly jealous when I thought she was flirting with Jack. How could I have known that as she tossed her perfect blonde hair from shoulder to shoulder, she was telling him all about *me*?

5/The Pitch

It was D-Day at Seraphim Swallow Avanti. Time to deliver a ninety-five-mile-an-hour pitch for Snatch. I spent the entire lunch hour fiddling with my food. We were celebrating the acquisition of another new account, a foreign automaker that would bring in big billings, so instead of grazing on her usual greens, greens, and more greens, we were treated to a fish dish (albeit swimming in a "spinach reduction"— whatever that is), that Gwen proudly named Saab Turbot. It was the first attempt to feed protein to the hungry hoardes in weeks, but I had no appetite. Gwen feared that I might be watching my girlish figure and eschewing anything but salads. I assured her that I loved real food as much as the next person, but that my anxiety at pitching my ad campaign to Lord Ian Kitchener, a real-life British nobleman, was giving me butterflies.

At three P.M., I entered the conference-slash-lunch-room with Demetrius. He hadn't bothered to dress for the occasion. His dreds looked rattier than usual and he was wearing an old Jamaican Olympic bob-sled team T-shirt. On the back of the shirt, he had created an addition of his own, a beautifully hand-lettered

"Colonize *This*!" In my humble opinion, not exactly the best selection of haberdashery when you're making an important presentation to a member of the English aristocracy.

F.X. and Jason were seated at one end of the long, burled, blond wood table, flanking the nearly equally blond man who sat at its apex. He was attractive in a doughy British sort of way.

F.X. made the introductions, informing Lord Kitchener that I was SSA's top-flight copywriter. "Right! You're the 'site bytes' chick!" Kitchener said enthusiastically. As if the pressure weren't already on, now I really felt I had something to live up to. I prayed that the client would go for my ad campaign ideas.

"So pleased to meet you," I said. He was too far from me to shake hands with him without my running around the table. Since he didn't extend his own hand, I thought I had better keep my place, not knowing the proper etiquette of it all. *Wow,* I thought. *A real life royal.* "Lord Ian Kitchener, Knight of the British Empire: Likkbe, for short," he joked. "Sounds like I've got a head cold and I'm begging for oral sex."

Super. An English nobleman with the coarse sense of humor of your average loutish soccer fan. His attractiveness quotient dipped precipitously.

"*I* would do him, mahn," Demetrius muttered to me under his breath in his thick Jamaican accent.

"Oh, you're gross," I whispered back. We both giggled.

Jason explained that we had a few different Snatch campaigns to present, adding that over the past ten days or so, Demetrius and I had been working late into the night to come up with three rock-'em-sock-'em ideas. Some of that was true. I can't presume to speak for Demetrius, but I'd spent several sleepless nights wondering how the hell to promote a dustrag.

I told Lord Kitchener what an honor it was to be working for him, took a deep breath, and wound up for the first pitch. "I like to call this idea 'Scrubbing Bubbles meet the Energizer bunny,' " I began.

His Lordship grinned in approval. "I love those bubbles—with their brush mustaches! They all look like Teddy Roosevelt."

This raised my confidence a notch, inasmuch as I felt that the client was at least in a jovial mood. I asked Demetrius to display the storyboards. "We've got these computer-generated dust bunnies, you see," I said, pointing to the board. "And the voiceover is delivered by someone with a really sexy, throaty voice, someone like Kathleen Turner or Lauren Hutton." I read the ad copy to them. " 'Everyone knows that bunnies, uh . . . *multiply*, well—like bunnies. Especially dust bunnies.' Then we see a shot of lots of these adorable gray dust bunnies of all sizes, getting larger and larger as we get to the area under the bed. 'And some parts of your home can be a real warren!' Then we go to a close-up of a couple of really large dust bunnies poking out from beneath the dust ruffle. 'But now there's a way to keep dust bunnies from growing . . . and growing . . . and growing. With new floral-scented *Snatch*, dust bunnies are eliminated as fast as a jackrabbit!' Then we see the sexy woman on her knees by the bed, and go to the close-up of the woman's hand holding the product, and we watch her sweep up the dust bunnies in a single swipe. Now we go to a super-tight close-up of the product, covered with schmutz. 'With Snatch's space age electromagnetic properties, dirt, dust, and stray hairs remain trapped on the cloth.' Demetrius, may we go to the next card?" Demetrius flipped up the storyboard and I continued reading.

" 'And with Snatch, you don't even have to stoop to conquer.' And we show the woman fitting the Snatch rag onto the moplike thingy and securing it. 'With Snatch's patented telescopic Magic Wand, cleaning those hard-to-reach locations is a snap. Snatch fits snugly and securely on the wand's spacious head.' Then we have the woman demonstrate how the wand unfolds, segment by segment, like those old-fashioned vaudeville canes. 'From a mere six inches, Snatch's Magic Wand becomes a full-sized industrial tool. And storage is a breeze. Just toss your used Snatch in the trash, and shrink the wand to its original pocket-size dimensions.'

"So," I added, pointing to each of Demetrius's drawings on the board, "we follow the woman's step-by-step demonstration, of course. She puts everything away in her broom closet, and we zoom in on the box of product and go to the voiceover tag line, 'New, floral-scented Snatch. Grab some today!' "

I looked over at F.X. and Jason. Jason was rolling his eyes, but he was smiling. A very big smile for the benefit of Lord Kitchener. I couldn't tell if F.X. was rolling his eyes because his thick lenses appeared to be fogged up. He, too, was grinning at the client.

"Right!" Lord Kitchener concluded, rubbing his palms together. I hoped that meant he was pleased. Frankly, it was difficult to tell. Sometimes when Brits exclaim "Right!" it just means "Let's get on to the next thing."

"Wait 'til you hear Liz's second idea," Jason prompted. I probably paled. Demetrius removed the storyboards from the conference table and stacked them against the wall. He lifted up a second set of renderings and placed them on the table. "You know, I'm less crazy about dis idea, mahn," he whispered to me.

"Keep it under your dredlocks," I hissed in his ear, and flashed the client what I hoped would be read as a radiantly confident smile. "Picture yourself in the Olympic Village," I began, pointing to the first storyboard. "Or at the weight-lifting world championship match. The final round. We hear the voiceover announcing very *sotto voce*, like sports commentators do when an athlete is about to do something very difficult, 'The clean and jerk requires immense concentration. Alexeyev has managed to lift 570 pounds. Can the Bulgarian beat him, for the medal?' Then we see this humongous world champion weight lifter guy approach the barbell on the floor. The commentator says, in voiceover, 'Will he be able to do it? This is becoming a very dirty competition.' And we see the guy squat down to lift the bar. We see him huffing and puffing and groaning. 'Nope, I'm afraid Putzin will have to settle for the silver,' the voiceover continues. Then we see the guy pull something out from his little red leotard-thingy. And the commentator says, 'Oh, oh, what have we here, folks? It looks like Putzin has located a bit of Snatch.' And then we see the weight lifter using the Snatch rag like a hanky and placing it on the bar of the barbell. And suddenly, he can hoist the free weight over his head like it's a Tonka toy. And we hear the crowd go wild and the announcer is all excited, saying, 'Well, well, it just proves that a patch of dry Snatch will pick up anything.' And we see the grinning Bulgarian with the barbell high over his head, and he releases it to the floor with that sort of bounce it makes, then takes a bow. And the announcer's tag line is 'And you won't have to carry the weight of the world on your shoulders.' "

I wished there had been an in-flight barf bag in the SSA conference room, because I was ready to throw up on the spot. Never have I come up with such a lousy ad campaign that made even *me* want to puke. It sucked. As far as I was concerned, there was no disguising this factor. I'd even forgotten to include the phrase 'floral-scented,' which was kind of an important omission, since it was the name of the product. Not just Snatch but *floral-scented* Snatch. I looked over at Demetrius, who shrugged. F.X. and Jason were staring at me with the dismayed expression of parents who have come home from a lovely evening at the movies only to discover that their much-trusted babysitter has just shaken their infant twins to death. Lord Kitchener did not look especially enthusiastic. He didn't say, "Right!"

Did I dare tell them the awful truth? The last thing I wanted to hear at that moment in time was "Well, let's see your third idea." I heard those dreaded words and couldn't provide an answer. Because there wasn't one. Instead, I mumbled something vague about needing to leave, headed right to my office, grabbed my jacket and purse, and walked straight past the conference room and out the door. When I got down to the street I went directly to the nearest Starbucks for a caramel mocchiato and contemplated my next steps. I figured the sugar and the caffeine rush would flush the fuzz from my brain. I felt like a spin doctor who has run out of suture material.

As I sipped the mocchiato, it occurred to me that I had better get my act together and stop fighting my assignments, or that would be the last $3.62 cup of coffee I would be having for a long time. I fished in my jacket for a Kleenex and pulled out a fistful of clean but crumpled tissues, along with a tortoise shell hair barrette, a taxi receipt, an ancient stick of Juicyfruit, and a scrap of card stock, which I almost tossed in a nearby trash can with the gum, but something made me look at it first. It was the business card Jack Rafferty had handed me at the *Bad Date* auditions. For a moment or two I stopped obsessing about my disastrous Snatch pitch and started wondering what Jack might be up to . . . if he was enjoying his day. I ran my finger over the raised lettering on the card, imagining my touch would work like some sort of voodoo charm, and that wherever Jack was, he would feel it.

I slipped his card inside the coin purse of my wallet and decided to savor my coffee.

6/The Envelope, Please

I meandered home, stopping first to clear my head by trolling through a farmers' market near the office. I unlocked our mailbox, as is my usual habit on returning to our apartment building, only to find the box empty. Nell must be home, I figured. Jem teaches late on Wednesdays, so unless we were experiencing a synchronistic meltdown, she was busy showing community college students how to communicate and Nell was . . . well, who knows what Nell does with her time? I've occasionally considered taking a mental health day so I could discreetly follow her around to see how she fills at least eight hours of daylight.

I put the paper bag of green market goodies, provisions for the three of us, on the kitchen counter. Nell was in the living room, surrounded by clouds of pink tissue paper and a stack of Victoria's Secret boxes. She was wearing a blue terry bathrobe that made her eyes seem even more cornflower colored than usual. "Ooh, a popsicle!" she exclaimed, noticing the Frozfruit I was nibbling on.

I walked over and offered her a bite. She took a tiny nibble and looked enraptured. "Here, take the whole thing," I told her.

"Coconut. My favorite," she cooed. "Thanks, Liz. That's just what I needed. Hey, look what I got," she exclaimed, lifting an identical robe in a shade of Navajo turquoise from one of the boxes.

I looked at her in her lapis colored wrap. "But you have a robe already. Are you buying one for every day of the week?"

"They were two-for-one at Vicky's Secret," Nell replied. She tossed me the turquoise bathrobe. "This one is for you. I thought it would be perfect with your skin tone. And I got one for Jem, too." From another box she removed a third robe, identical to ours, but the color of an ice blue sky. "I thought we could all wear them when we open our envelopes." She gestured to the dining table, where she had artistically arranged three fat envelopes from the Urban Lifestyles Channel, addressed to each of us. "Isn't it like college?" she giggled.

I went for my envelope. "I guess after three rounds of interviews and auditions, we made it in, since the fat ones usually mean you got accepted, while the skinny envelopes are 'ding letters,' so let's just find out now."

Nell threw her arms protectively over the envelopes. "Nope. We wait until Jem gets home. But we can have a drink to pre-celebrate, if you want. That is, if you don't think we're jinxing it by assuming we got picked to be on *Bad Date* before we actually open our letters."

I followed Nell into the kitchen where she started whipping up a yogurt-and-mango smoothie, then opened a bottle of champagne and poured an ounce

or two on top of her concoction to give it some
sparkle. I rinsed some of the strawberries I'd purchased at the farmers' market and handed a couple to
Nell. She popped one in her mouth and dropped another in her glass. "Want one?" she asked me. "I call it
a 'Culture Cooler.' "

"Sorry, but I always find yogurt gross. It tastes . . .
already eaten to me somehow. How 'bout you hold
the yogurt and the mango and just give me the cham-
pers?" I took the bottle of Moët from Nell and filled a
flute for myself, adding a strawberry, watching it
wobble through the fizz to the bottom of the glass.
"Pre-cheers," I said, clinking glasses with Nell.

I suck at delayed gratification, and Jem didn't return to our apartment until close to seven-thirty. As
soon as she walked through the door, I jumped up
and, taking hold of one of her wrists, dragged her to
the dining room table. Nell started frantically waving
her arms and presented Jem with her terry bathrobe,
then insisted that we cut off the tags and wear the
robes to open the mail. I made a drum roll sound on
the table top and handed out the envelopes, which we
ripped into with such excitement that we practically
tore the contents. I hate to admit it, but once our
hunches were positively confirmed, we started jumping
around the apartment, whooping it up like a bunch of
drunken sorority sisters.

"Yee-hah! I felt this way when I got accepted to
Mount Holyoke," Jem said.

"That's just what I was saying to Liz before," Nell
remarked, bubbling with enthusiasm. "That it's like
opening your college admissions envelope."

"It's better. These days you have to give the *college* a million bucks; this is the other way around," I added somewhat dryly.

For three women who had started off thinking the idea of auditioning for a dopey reality television show was just a lark, we'd become pretty wired. I think I could hear our collective hearts pounding as we perused our contracts.

"We should probably each see a lawyer," Jem finally announced, scrutinizing the papers. "There's a ton of fine print here. And especially as we all live together."

"You think we're gonna screw each other over?" I asked her.

"No. But if there's a media feeding frenzy about *Bad Date*, the first thing they'll do when they learn that three of the contestants just happen to be roommates is start poking around as to whether we all signed a pact before the first episode or something."

"Or formed an alliance," Nell snickered. She looked through the contract with an increasingly puzzled expression. "It's in here already. At least I think it is. There's something about making no deals to share the money with other contestants, or 'something, something, something' in legalese, which I totally don't understand."

"Wow," I said, reading the fourth paragraph on the third page of the eight-page contract. "We have to agree not to turn anyone else's dating experiences—including our own—as revealed on the show, into literary or dramatic fiction, screen or teleplays . . ."

"Oh, screw it. You're right. Who's going to do that

anyway? It's probably like the online Citibank thing, where you used to have to click 'I agree' before you could access your own account. What would they do if you clicked on 'disagree' instead? By the way, this celebration calls for a Bloody Mary," Jem said, heading for the kitchen.

"I'll take mine with V8," Nell said.

She drinks the most disgusting things.

"So, guys, now we have to wrack our brains for all the bad dates we've ever been on and lived to share the tale." I leaned against the butcher-block counter top and watched Jem work one of her mixological miracles.

"I think *all* my dates have been bad," she ruminated, as she chewed on a stalk of celery. "I just never know what to say once you've both gotten past the preliminaries."

Nell took a "churchkey" to her can of V8, squinched up her eyes, and regarded Jem. "I never heard of a communications professor who couldn't communicate. But, speaking of college, it was definitely much easier back then. I mean, it was 'Hi, my name is Nell; what's your major? Hi, Nell, *my* name is Bob; what's *your* major? Wanna fuck?' You know, God *has* to be a man, because no woman would have invented guys as we know them."

"And now times have really changed, haven't they? Now it's 'Hi, I'm Liz, I'm in advertising. Hi, Lizzie, I'm Bob, I'm a Wall Street dork. Wanna fuck?' "

"Thanks," Jem said, handing us our drinks. "To both of you."

"Were you toasting us or being facetious, Jem?" I

stirred my Bloody Mary. "I think part of our problem isn't simply a failure to communicate. We're just meeting the wrong guys in the wrong places."

Nell nodded her head. "I had a sorority sister who used to steal all her best friends' boyfriends. She said at least that way she knew where they'd been!" Nell reached for the pitcher and topped off my glass. "Mary Frances Connolly," she said slowly, letting each syllable roll off her tongue. "M.F.C. The Tri-Delt girls used to say that her initials really stood for 'Mother-blanking-you-know-what.' "

I began to ruminate on my own boyfriend history. I always seemed to find the pick of the litter. More like I picked litter. Two of the guys I went out with between the time I graduated college and the time I turned twenty-seven were advised to attend anger management classes by a couples therapist we visited in an effort (my idea) to salvage the relationship. And to think I would have married either one of them. My mother could never fathom my penchant for the "bad boys" and "angry young men" of this world. No wonder I had such rotten luck with guys. I had rotten taste.

I contributed my two cents to the M.F.C. discussion. "Well, if Nell's friend had wanted to steal my old boyfriends, she who steals *my* man steals trash. By the way, Jem," I said, changing the subject, "you make a mean Bloody Mary. If you wanted to, you could go into business with these if you ever decided to give up teaching. For some reason, your cocktails always make me horny."

"Don't look at me," Nell teased.

The phone rang, almost intrusively. We looked at each other and before the answering machine could pick up, I reached for the receiver.

"Hey," the voice on the other end said.

"Hey, yourself," I replied.

"Do you know who this is?"

"Napoleon? Leonardo DiCaprio? I really hate it when people say that on the phone. Do I know who it is? If I did, would you have to ask me? It's rude and arrogant."

"Well, there's no mistaking that I've got Liz and not Jem or Nell on the phone. Any more acid in your voice and you could make etchings with your tongue. It's Jack, by the way."

"Jack?" I asked. "Jack Frost? Jack Nicholson? Jack-O'-lantern?" I could feel my heart begin to pound and wondered if my roommates could tell.

"Jack Rafferty. I called to see if you got accepted onto *Bad Date*." His voice sounded nice. Pleasant and upbeat without seeming forced.

"Yes, Jack Rafferty, I did. In fact we all did. Nell and Jem and I are just celebrating. By the way, how did you get our number?"

"You're one of a kind," he responded. "At least in Manhattan, 4-1-1 only has one Liz Pemberley listed."

Was I blushing? I placed my hand over the receiver and turned to my roommates, mouthing "It's Jack Rafferty" to them—as if they didn't already know. I swear, the man made my brain fuzzy. Or maybe it was the alcohol.

"Look," Jack said, "this may sound really goofy to you, but I wanted to thank you for letting me touch your hair the other day in the waiting room. I'd considered just reaching out and touching it, but I was afraid you might freak out. So I'm glad you made the offer. Your hair is really beautiful, Liz . . . it's like brown velvet."

"Thank you." I smiled and felt my cheeks grow warm, but of course he couldn't see them.

"I'm a very tactile person," Jack continued. "I love crisp cotton sheets, the rich softness of my cashmere blazer—and, well, your hair . . . I felt this chemical 'thing' happen when I first noticed you."

I looked over at my roommates who must have been wondering what the heck was going on, since I wasn't doing all the talking. "Yes . . . I did, too," I said. "The same thing, actually. Which is why I . . . reacted the way I did."

"You moaned," Jack said. "I remember."

"Yes, I did do that." Jack and I shared a laugh. "Since you're so tactile," I added, "did you . . . feel anything earlier today?"

"Like what?" Jack asked.

I was thinking about the business card I'd stuffed in my wallet. "Oh, I don't know . . . like a"—I lowered my voice significantly—"tickle or something."

"What did you just say, Liz? Your voice came out muffled. I'm on my cell. Can you speak up a bit? I must have lost you for a second there."

I raised my voice a tad. "I said, like a—"

"What does he want?" Jem hissed suspiciously.

This was not the best time to continue this phone conversation. Jem and Nell were staring hawklike at me, so I thought I should alter my tone of voice, which

I hoped would indicate to Jack that I couldn't get any more personal at the moment. "Never mind. So, hey, Jack, thanks for the congratulations. Will you be joining us as a contestant, too?"

"Yup," he said. "I'd like to take you out to continue the celebration, if you're up for it."

"Me specifically, or all three of us?" I queried.

There was a brief pause on the other end of the line. "Well, you specifically, if that's all right. Not that I don't like your roommates. Because I do. I just want to get squared away on that issue. They both seem to be very nice women, but . . ."

I furrowed my brow. "Where are you?"

"Miami. At the airport. I should be arriving at JFK in about three hours. I'll catch a cab into the city and pick you up, if you give me your address."

It was my turn to pause. I did a few mental calculations and indicated to my roommates that Jack was sort of asking me out, trying hard not to let on that I really wouldn't mind accepting his offer. Jem started to mutter under her breath about Jack's rudeness—busting up our party of three to take only one of us out. She said something about it being bad for the group dynamic. Nell agreed that it was bad karma for him to try to come between us.

"Jack?" I said into the phone. "You're not flying in to New York just to ask me out, are you?" *God, how romantic would* that *be?*

"Oh, no. I've got a business meeting in the morning and I figured you might be up for getting together this evening."

So much for romance. I was strongly considering

saying, "Yes, what the hell," but I figured Nell and Jem probably had a point. Regardless of our powerful mutual attraction, Jack Rafferty was practically a stranger. Why should I run out of the apartment in the middle of a "school night" to meet him? There were any number of valid reasons to decline. "By the time you get here, it'll be nearly eleven P.M.," I told him. "I really don't think it's a good idea."

"Are you sure? What about a raincheck?" he asked.

I found myself agreeing to one, and ended the phone call. "You're right, guys. I shouldn't rush out on you. This is *our* night to celebrate. Blowing off best friends just because a cute guy calls is definitely uncool."

Jem nodded. "Liz, don't you think there's something suspicious about this guy's ringing up right away to ask if we got chosen for the show? Sounds to me like he's fishing for something."

Nell laughed. "Jem, you never trust a man's motives. And Liz . . . I know I was the first one to try to dissuade you from getting together with Jack, but it's true that I did talk you up to him that day we all auditioned for the show. He was into meeting you just from the stuff I told him, and then you guys really did seem to hit it off right away. Maybe Jem is right that it's kind of weird that he called you up tonight; but on the other hand, he could just be trying to be friendly. I hate attributing sinister ulterior motives to a guy right off the bat." Nell poured some more V8 into her glass and held it out to Jem for Tabasco and vodka.

Jem refreshed Nell's drink and put the vodka bottle back in the freezer. "Well, maybe he just thinks Liz is hot and his motives are pure. But if he's just another skank of the species, then he probably figures Liz is the weakest link of the three of us and he wants to infiltrate to see if we have a game plan."

"How could we have a game plan if it's up to a different studio audience each week to decide who stays and who goes?" Nell asked.

"Who knows?" I said, feeling protective of Jack's feelings as well as my own, and consequently not ready to share with them the more personal aspects of the phone call. "Maybe he does think we're all huddled together making lists of all our dreadful dating experiences and trying to rank them in a certain order and figure out which story we're going to tell each week based on that. On the other hand, maybe he does actually think I'm cute. He seems to have a thing for my hair. And my brain. I'd say that definitely makes him a head case."

"By the way, Liz, I forgot to ask you why you got home so early today," Nell remarked.

"Yeah, well . . . I wondered what it would be like to be a lady of permanent leisure. I have a fantasy about being able to have a job I actually like going to in the morning, and where I can come and go as I please, dividing my free time equally between being creative and going shopping." I told them about bailing in the middle of the Snatch pitch. "Much as I bitch about the assignments these days, I really hope I have a job to go back to when I walk back into SSA tomorrow. I've started to daydream about getting that million bucks on *Bad Date*, though, and telling them all what they can do with their Snatch."

"We've all got our dreams, girlfriend," Jem said, and raised her glass.

"To dreams," Nell said, saluting us with her drink.

"To girlfriends," I said, putting an arm around each of them and pulling us into a group hug.

7/Crunch Time

There was a yellow Post-it note stuck smack-bang on the center of my computer monitor when I went in to work the next morning. I anxiously read it, crumpled it, tossed it in the wicker trash basket by the edge of my desk, and walked down the hall to Jason's office. He and F.X. were waiting for me. They motioned for me to pull up a chair and F.X. poured me a cup of Gwen's freshly brewed chicory coffee. That stuff is so strong you could stand a spoon in it. I knew something was coming—I would have had to have been totally clueless not to surmise that there would be no fallout from my little performance yesterday afternoon. I just prayed that I still had a job.

"Let's start at the very beginning," Jason said, folding his arms on the desk and resting his torso against them as he leaned toward me.

"A very good place to start," I sang, to the tune of "Do-Re-Mi" from *The Sound of Music*, a nervous attempt at levity that I immediately regretted.

"We may see the humor, but Lord Kitchener was not amused," F.X. said. "He told us he considered it the height of unprofessionalism to walk out in the middle of a presentation."

"Do you have anything to say for yourself, young lady?" Jason asked prissily.

"Yeah, actually"—I took a sip of coffee—"not that I gave it too much thought at the time, but it occurred to me that bailing after the second ad campaign idea was somehow preferable to my admitting that I had nothing to offer for an encore."

F.X. removed his glasses and squinted at me. "Are you saying that you didn't have an idea for a third Snatch campaign? You do recall that your mission was to come up with not two, but a minimum of *three* separate and distinct campaign ideas."

I nodded. "Oh, I knew what you expected. But I didn't even have a clue for a third campaign—and it wasn't for lack of trying, believe me. I spent many sleepless nights agonizing over how to sell that electromagnetic dustrag with the dirty name to the American consumer. And clearly I made something of a miscalculation by not confessing to you guys in advance of the pitch session that I'd hit a brick wall. I guess I was hoping for some eleventh-hour divine intervention in the inspiration department."

"You've had tougher assignments," Jason said. "Your 'Am I Blue?' campaign for the Second Opinion Home Pregnancy Kit is a perfect example."

"Jase, did we neglect to tell Liz that Lord Kitchener is Lillian's lover?" F.X. asked his partner.

"I hate it when you call me that. My name is Jason. Liz, did we neglect to tell you that Lord Kitchener is Lillian Swallow's lover? As in the man who sleeps with the other partner of Seraphim Swallow Avanti advertising?"

If they were implying that I should have done an

extra terrific job on the Snatch ad campaigns, it still wouldn't have made my ideas any better. Frankly, I kind of liked the first idea I had pitched to Kitchener.

"Does that mean that I blew the entire account for you guys?" I asked.

"Let's put it this way," F.X. answered, absentmindedly twirling his eyeglasses by one of the ear stems, "it's safe to assume that the only reason Kitchener is letting us still hold onto the Snatch account is . . . well—"

Jason interrupted him. "Because Lillian's letting him hold on to her—"

"I get the picture, gentlemen. In Technicolor. So what's the next step? Am I fired?" I asked with tremendous trepidation.

"Jason is going to handle the Snatch account and write all the copy on his own from now on. You're too valuable to let go due to this incident alone—"

Jason interrupted F.X. again. "But we've got to put you on some kind of probationary period, because, well, Kitchener told Lillian about what happened in here yesterday afternoon and Lillian gave us hell for it. The guy's got money up the yin-yang, Liz. Queen Elizabeth knighted him back in the mid-nineties because his product empire contributed so greatly to the upswing in the British economy. We understand that not every commodity is going to be your favorite kind of thing, or one you would necessarily buy or use yourself. I can't believe I'm even giving this speech to such a seasoned veteran of the profession, but this is your job and we hired you because you're damn good at it. Liz, you could sell Stouffer's frozen entrees to Martha Stewart. You're a terrific copywriter and we don't want to lose you, but . . . well . . . basically, F.X. and Lillian and I are warning you to get your shit back together. We've got something else for you to work on. A print campaign for a new low-calorie snack food."

Jason swiveled his chair to face the credenza behind him and brought out a colorful box, which he handed to me.

"Numbers Crunchers," I read.

"It needs new copy on the box as well," Jason said. "Something catchy, of course."

"What's the demographic?" I asked him. "Kids? Teens? Barflies?"

"Funny you should mention that," F.X. replied. "The client envisions the product everywhere. As an educational tool in school lunchrooms, in vending machines at gyms and fitness centers, behind the counter with the peanuts and crackerjacks at ball games . . . you name it. So come up with some slogans by next Monday." F.X. rose and opened Jason's door.

"Back to work, now," Jason said cheerily.

I let the two of them know how appreciative I was of the second chance they were giving me. It had been extremely unprofessional of me to walk out of a pitch session. No one expects a copywriter to have a vested emotional interest in the products she writes about. And sometimes the most creative element of the job is to come up with memorable things to say about something you find thoroughly useless, in order to convince the consumer that they can't live without it. I took the box of Numbers Crunchers back to my office and placed it on my desk where it would remain perpetually in my sight and, therefore, always on my mind.

* * *

After work, feeling somewhat euphoric that I still
had a place to work at at all, I headed up to the
Chelsea Market to treat myself to some fresh bread
from one of its several gourmet bakeries. I had an in-
explicable craving for a cheddar-and-fennel loaf.

The Chelsea Market is wonderful, like a giant food
court for gourmet palates. Bakeries, butchers, con-
fectionery shops, and one of my favorites—a kitchen
supply place with wholesale prices for everything
from pots and pans to stemware, the culinary equivalent of a penny candy store. On today's excursion I
found some martini glasses with a zigzag stem that
looked sort of like a lightning rod. I've only had one
martini in my life, and it was too strong for me to
finish, but these cocktail glasses were stunning. And
only $4.25 per stem. A steal. I placed a half dozen of
the zigzag glasses in my red plastic shopping basket,
and stopped enroute to the cash register to admire
several different pairs of lacquered chopsticks. They
were too pretty to eat with, but I figured they'd make
terrific hair ornaments.

I was ready to pay for my purchases, but found the
narrow aisle to the register blocked by a tall man with
a jar of prepared salsa in each hand. He seemed to be
comparing the labels, ingredient by ingredient. "Excuse me, mind if I get by?" I said to the man's back.

The man turned around. "Very little gets by me.
Hey, hey, it's you!" Jack exclaimed. "I hope you
weren't offended just now. I've been told my sense of
humor is an acquired taste."

I barely remembered what he had just said. He
could have been speaking in tongues for all it mat-

tered to me at that moment. I was too busy staring at his face—his dark eyes and his dazzling smile. He really was quite gorgeous. "Jack Rafferty, hi! Well, it certainly is a small world. What the hell are you doing here?"

"That's kind of a rude question, Liz. I could ask the same of you."

"But you're not a New Yorker, so this isn't an obvious place to run into you."

"And you told me you don't cook. So ditto."

"Touché, I suppose." I bit my tongue. "But what *are* you doing in this store?"

Jack showed me the two salsa jars. "This one," he said handing me the jar he'd been holding in his right hand, "is my product. My restaurant's house brand that's now being sold all over the country. It's my own recipe. This other one, and I apologize if I sound like a commercial, is the northeast's other leading brand. My meeting this morning was with my distributor up here; we were figuring out how to market Tito's, so we can overtake the competition." He put the other jar of salsa back on the shelf and surreptitiously moved jars of his own product in front of it so that all you could see on display were jars of Tito's Famous South Beach Salsa, the *caliente*, *mas caliente*, and *muy caliente* varieties.

"Look, I'm sorry about last night," I said. "I really did want to see you again, but we would have ended up getting together so late by the time you actually made it into town, and I had to be up early for work." I didn't feel it was somehow right to mention the little fact that my roommates thought it was the worst idea since Little Red Riding Hood admitted the wolf into her grandmother's cottage.

"Well, you did agree to my offer of a raincheck, so whaddya say we do dinner this evening? How do you feel about lobster?"

"Do you mean from a moral standpoint? A dietary one? I'm not kosher if that's where you're fishing," I told him as I paid for my purchases.

"Are you always this literal, Liz? I was only asking if you liked lobster."

"I was kidding, Jack. What girl could resist the offer of a lobster dinner with you?"

"Terrific!" he said, relieving me of my package from the cookware store, tucking it under one arm. He stood still for a few moments regarding me, his countenance a mixture of sweetness, curiosity, and amusement. "I feel like I want to hold your hand," he said finally. "May I?" I offered mine to him. "Did you know that the very first Oreo cookie was made right in this building?" Jack asked me. "In March of 1912, to be precise."

"I had no idea," I laughed. "So how does a non–New Yorker know such local trivia?"

Jack grinned. "It was a *Jeopardy* question a few months ago. I have a weird memory when it comes to food facts." He led me across the tiled concourse, and I smelled our destination before I saw it. The scent of Superior Seafood permeated the entire atmosphere at its end of the market. The store didn't have a door; it was in a corner location that opened entirely onto the concourse. I could see that the owners gated it shut at night. Wooden display tables painted a deep shade of forest green supported mounds upon mounds of shaved ice, on which rested the catch of the day: whole fish, their silver scales glinting in the fluorescent glare of the overhead fixtures, their eyes and mouths gaping open as if the fisherman's hook had caught them by surprise. I don't like to look at whole critters on my plate. That's when I tend to agree with Nell, who is an ovo-lacto vegetarian. She doesn't do critters at all; not even fish as some vegetarians do. I prefer my fish to arrive already filleted so I won't choke on any nasty little bones and so I can pretend that that's how fish *always* comes—all flat and innocuous salmon pink or sole pale, with a light lemon and white wine butter sauce, instead of bulging yellow eyes, iridescent scales, translucent fins, and those open, indignant mouths.

As I was grossing myself out by anthropomorphizing Superior Seafood's merchandise, Jack was talking in my ear about the best ways to prepare lobster. I have to admit, I wasn't listening too hard. I was too busy enjoying his proximity and the sensation of his warm breath on my neck. I asked him about that high-pitched whining sound they make when you toss them in the pot. He looked a bit annoyed with my question, then assured me that the lobsters were not in fact crying. "Well, I don't see why not," I said. "I'd cry if someone dumped me, alive and kicking, into a pot of boiling water." He was trying to acclimate me to thinking of the thing as dinner as opposed to a Disneyesque pet; so I let Jack talk me into picking out my own lobster. I told him I felt sorry for the culls, the lobsters that only have one claw left. "Are they the ones that get picked on the most in the lobster schoolyard?" I asked Jack. "Or do they lose a claw because they get it caught in a trap and have to chew it off in order to free themselves?" By the time I was done speculating about it, he was ready to suggest we go for cheeseburgers instead.

But we did leave Superior Seafood with two live lobsters in a grocery bag. Jack steered me back to the cookware store. "Why are we going back here?" I asked.

"How am I supposed to cook us lobsters without a lobster pot? Are you going to be okay holding these?"

I nodded. I was lying, but he didn't know it, so he thrust the bag of crustaceans into my hands. In a matter of minutes, while I trailed after him like an infatuated puppy, trying to keep pace with his long stride and determined agenda, Jack had amassed a pot large enough to contain several gallons of water and a couple of live lobsters, an electric hot plate, two metal cracking tools for the shells, a raft of bottles of various seasonings, a container of bread crumbs, a corkscrew, a starter set of melamine plates and flatware, a pair of royal blue placemats and matching napkins, and a couple of wine glasses. White wine stems to be exact. He was a whirlwind of organized activity. Very impressive. I found him quite a pleasure to watch. I love a man with a plan.

In the produce shop toward the other end of the Chelsea Market concourse, Jack selected a couple of lemons and limes, some fresh herbs, and found some butter in the dairy section. Then he zipped across the tiled floor to the liquor store and came back with a chilled bottle of California chardonnay. Meanwhile, all this time I'd been left holding the bag, so to speak, enjoying Jack making Olympic time in the food shopping trials.

It was an exhausting sport, so I decided to rest for a few minutes. I sat on one of the wooden park benches strategically placed throughout the Chelsea Market to wait for Jack to finish making his purchases. After a minute or so, I felt a tapping on my wrist. I didn't realize how loudly I had screamed and that the tile floors really amplified the volume in the marketplace. It's just that one of the lobsters must have figured out his—or her—fate and was trying to escape from the grocery bag. The lobster's contact with my arm certainly surprised the hell out of me, and the creature got its wish, because I was so startled that I dropped the bag and the rosy critters started to make a getaway out of the brown paper and onto the tile floor.

My scream brought Jack running over to my bench. I sat there, paralyzed, watching them try to make a run for it. He handily corralled the lobsters before they had gotten more than a couple of feet away. By now I felt incredibly guilty and was beginning to think that Jem was absolutely right and that my getting together with Jack Rafferty was indeed jinxed in some way.

"We don't have to do this, you know," he said to me.

"I don't think you can return a lobster to the store on the grounds of recalcitrance," I replied. "Its *or* ours."

Jack took the bag of lobsters and handed me back my own purchases from the cookware store plus a safer package: the wine and the produce. He placed a protective hand on my shoulder and steered me out of the marketplace and onto Ninth Avenue, where he hailed a cab.

The driver popped the trunk and Jack deposited all the parcels, including those he'd given me to carry, into the well. Then he held the door for me to get into the taxi ahead of him.

"Where are we going?" I whispered after he closed the car door.

"Where else? We're going back to my place to make dinner." Jack leaned forward to speak to the driver through the Plexiglas partition. "The Waldorf-Astoria, please."

8/The Dinner from Hell

The taxi slowed to a halt in front of the Park Avenue hotel entrance. Jack got out first and went around to the trunk to retrieve our packages, as the driver, his tush firmly rooted to the upholstery, had clearly abrogated any responsibility for coming to the aid of his passengers.

Something about the configuration of New York cabs makes them conducive, when you're the person sitting farthest from the curbside door, to exiting them feet-first. I was in the process of executing just such an ungainly maneuver when a kamikazelike bike messenger sped past the cab. The messenger thumped the open car door with his fist just as I was kicking my leg out, practically closing the door on my foot.

As the bike messenger passed me and raced up the street, I kicked back with greater force—the unfortunate result being that one of my turquoise slingbacks—the ones that refuse to cooperate and stay on my feet in the best of circumstances—went flying past several surprised pedestrians, landing in a decorative stone planter adjacent to the Waldorf's entrance. "Jack," I cried out, wiggling my bare leg and naked foot. Laden with our parcels, he responded to my alarm.

"What the . . . ? How did . . . ?" His baffled look made me laugh out loud. "Where is it?" he asked me.

I pointed to the potted ficus.

Jack looked from left to right, unsure of how best to handle the emergency.

"You wanna pay me now?" the cab driver demanded. Some people have no patience. If he'd helped Jack take all our stuff out of his trunk, he'd have been well on his way ages ago. Juggling the bags, Jack took a bill from his wallet and tossed it at the cabbie. Then he motioned for the doorman to send out a luggage cart. While the hotel staffer loaded up the rolling golden gazebo with our dinner ingredients and accoutrements, Jack lifted me, still half-shod, out of the cab. What a prince he was. I've known plenty of guys who would have made an insulting quip about my impractical footwear and let me limp around on the pavement playing hunt the slipper.

It was silly and wildly romantic, and the gesture sent me into convulsions of laughter. Jack carried me over to the planter and retrieved my slingback, stuck the shoe in his pocket, and we followed our luggage cart into the hotel. I looked for a convenient place to stop so I could sit and put my shoe back on. When we passed a couple of armchairs I pointed one out to Jack and suggested that he'd already been chivalrous enough. "Besides, people are staring at us," I added, still laughing.

"Does that bother you?" He smiled at me and shifted my weight in his arms.

"See, I'm too heavy for you."

"Nonsense, you're as light as a popover."

I confess I was rather delighted that he hadn't yet

put me down. "Are you *sure* I'm not too heavy?" I asked, giving him a second chance to back out. "At least put me down there and wheel me to your room," I suggested, pointing at the spacious platform on the luggage trolley.

"You think people won't look at you then?" Jack said. By now, he was laughing, too. And he'd made no move to put my shoe back on my foot. I liked the idea that he didn't mind the spectacle we were making. In fact, we both were rather enjoying it. And there's nothing like shared laughter to shave the ice off an embarrassing situation. As my Aunt Cecilia—who had an ecstatically happy forty-five year marriage— used to say, "Laughter is the glue that brings people together. You bare your teeth, you bare your soul." I found our mutual mirth very intimate. It was *our* joke, *our* way of communicating to one another a sense of collective ease—not simply about the way we both handled the episode of my flying slingback or even our little secret that we were smuggling live crustaceans into a room at the Waldorf—but an indication of compatible personalities. I had a feeling that life with Jack Rafferty might be an endless string of fascinating adventures.

The uniformed bellhop was so intent on observing the antics of his giggling passengers that he didn't even comment on one of the bags that rested on the cart and gave an occasional wiggle as we sped up in the elevator to the nineteenth floor. Jack tipped him well. The cart was brought directly to his door, and once safely inside the suite, Jack deposited me on the edge of the king-sized bed. "Madame," he teased, removing my slingback from his jacket pocket with a dramatic flourish. I extended my foot and he slipped the shoe on, ensuring that the strap fit snugly around the back of my ankle. Then he deposited a gentle kiss on my bare instep. His lips felt soft against my skin.

"You would have given Sir Walter Raleigh a run for his money, Jack." I reached out my arms to him. "Come here. I want to thank you."

He leaned down and I brushed his lips with my own. "Thanks," I said. "It was gallant of you. And I love the way you didn't mind looking silly."

"My guess is that every guy in that hotel lobby wished he'd been me," Jack replied softly.

We looked at each other; it was that moment that always arrives in every new, blossoming, mutual attraction. That ocean of time where you sort of size each other up . . . where, for some reason, it always feels like an eternity from that moment when your gazes lock and you both acknowledge what's going on to the one-time-only instant when you have that first real kiss. The one that's for keeps. Jack's lips were soft and tasted of spearmint. His kiss was tender and gentle, and although we hardly knew each other, it felt like the most natural thing in the world to be kissing him. In fact, it felt so right, *so* natural that our mouths didn't need to learn one another's lips and tongues.

"Thank you for that, too," I said, enjoying the look of contentment on his face.

"You're welcome, Liz. Very welcome." He regarded me for a few moments, then turned his focus toward our lobsters, which were still hell-bent on survival. "Shall we start working on dinner?"

"I suppose so," I replied, a bit disappointed, thinking another kiss would have been nice.

Jack began to lay the Chelsea Market purchases out on the coffee table. "You can watch or you can help," he told me. "It's up to you. And I promise not to make any jokes or judgments on your lack of culinary expertise, whichever you decide to do."

I elected to pitch in. Jack handed me the lemons and a sharp knife and told me to cut the fruit into wedges. I looked at him. "Where?"

He looked just a teensy bit exasperated. "In the bathroom. On the marble counter top." I regarded him wide-eyed, terrified we were going to end up trashing the place. "Marble is the best cutting surface," Jack said. "When you're done with the lemons, you can mince the herbs."

Mince?

While I was struggling with the lemons—mostly because I was so self-conscious about preparing a meal with a true pro, trying very hard to slice only the citrus and not myself—Jack had mixed up a fistful of the breadcrumbs with dashes of this and that seasoning. He didn't measure a thing; he just seemed to know exactly how much of each ingredient to use. He uncorked the wine and poured us each a glass, then added a splash of chardonnay to his breadcrumb mixture.

My lemon wedges were all uneven, with jagged edges. Jack wiped his hands on the legs of his pants— in the absence of an apron or dishtowel—a gesture that sort of shocked me a bit. He placed his now-clean, warm hands on my shoulders and surveyed my handiwork, leaning over me. He seemed to be breathing in the scent of my shampoo. "Oh, Liz," he sighed, "you're smart, you're funny, and you're very, very attractive, but you're hopeless in the kitchen."

"Better hopeless in the kitchen than clueless in the bedroom," I kidded.

He turned me around to face him and looked me straight in the eye. "Who says you have to be one or the other?" Before I could reply, he winked at me and handed me a plate for my lemon wedges. "Just put those in the minifridge," he said.

I opened the door to the little refrigerator and almost had a heart attack. Jack had stashed the two lobsters in there and as soon as they saw daylight, they tried to make yet another dash for freedom. "Jack," I sort of wailed, "can you put them back?" I could swear that one of them had one of those teeny bottles of Stoli clasped in its claw, no doubt in an effort to blunt the horrible contemplation of his imminent demise.

Jack stuffed the crustaceans back into the fridge and took the plate of lemon wedges from me, carefully placing it on one of the shelves. "Why don't you just sit down for a while," he suggested. "I've got everything under control."

I curled up in one of the armchairs. "Then you've done this before?"

"Done what?"

"Cooked a lobster dinner in a hotel room."

"Actually, Liz, I haven't, but the task doesn't daunt me."

"I can see that."

"You have to know my background. When you've run a noisy, bustling, professional kitchen like it's an army on the march or a well-oiled machine—

where each participant has his place and knows exactly what his responsibility is, and where timing is essential, even crucial—something like this is only a minor challenge."

I sipped my chardonnay. "I'm sorry I blew it. Didn't rise to the challenge."

Jack stopped what he was doing, knelt in front of me, and took both my hands in his. "If it's any consolation, the kitchen help at Tito's don't do any better on *their* first day of the job either."

I felt like such a butterfingers. I had told Jack that I *don't* cook, not that I *can't* cook. I had made a pact with myself a couple of years ago not to go out of my way to cook elaborate meals for my dates because after a while I started to feel taken advantage of by guys who would show up for some good home-cooking, never offer to help pay for the groceries, chow down, and then sit on the couch watching TV while I did the dishes.

Tonight, though, I'd wanted to impress Jack with my dexterity as a chef's helper. I was more than a little intimidated by his cordon bleu credentials, in addition to which I found him so attractive that it was hard to concentrate in his presence.

"So how did you become a chef?" I asked, preferring to put the focus on him rather than on my embarrassing inability to cleanly slice a lemon. "I can't imagine a little boy deciding that's what he wants to be when he grows up."

Jack checked the status of the water in the lobster pot, which took up both burners of the hot plate, and removed the critters from the refrigerator. "I'm going to put them in the pot, now. Don't look if you don't want to."

"Good idea." I went into the bathroom and covered my eyes, even though I was in the next room. Jack started to sing "Home on the Range" at the top of his voice. "What are you doing?" I called out to him.

"Singing. So you won't hear that pathetic whining sound you said you hate when they first hit the water."

"That's very considerate of you," I yelled back. "You didn't answer my question."

Jack poked his head in the bathroom. "All clear. You can come out now."

I returned to the safety of the armchair.

"You're curious as to why I became a chef," Jack said. "Everyone's got to eat and a meal should be a pleasurable experience. It should delight all the senses. My mom was a dreadful cook. I was raised in a working-class household where my father firmly believed cooking was a woman's job, so he never went near the kitchen except to get another beer, and I was a boy who liked to eat—in fact, I was a bit of a porker as a kid. I was also a mediocre student; the one subject I truly excelled in at school was chemistry. I liked whipping up concoctions and testing the results. My parents, and later my friends, were willing to be my guinea pigs because more often than not my creations were a success. A little weird sometimes, I'll admit . . . like the time I did an artichoke leaf and rose petal tart—don't wrinkle your nose, Liz—I know it might sound gross, but it actually tasted pretty good!"

"My roommate Jem is like that. She's a communications professor, but she's also a genius behind the bar. She invents all sorts of wild cocktails. I don't know exactly what she does or how she does it, but there's . . . like . . . voodoo magic in there or something. She's mixed race, got all sorts of island blood as well as Indian blood—as in 'Native American,' I mean—and she swears it's the legacy of her ancestors that she can create these potions that make you feel a certain way, or behave a certain way. Not all of them have the same effect, but every one tastes wonderful."

"And how do Jem's cocktails usually make *you* feel?" Jack asked.

I blushed. "Horny. B-But I haven't had any of her concoctions this evening, so . . . let's not go there," I stammered, when I felt him looking at me. I wondered if he had any additional romantic thoughts beyond that first kiss we'd shared. If he did, he wasn't letting me in on the secret.

When the lobsters were boiled, Jack removed them and placed them on plates, while he drained the water from the pot by dumping it into, of all unromantic places, the toilet. He slit open the crustaceans' bellies and stuffed them with his herb and breadcrumb mixture, then, as unselfconsciously as he'd done earlier, wiped his hands clean on his trouser legs. I wondered if it was a "chef" thing, but I was too embarrassed to call attention to his now-filthy chinos. *Should I get him a handtowel from the bathroom?*

"You're on," he said to me, pulling me out of the armchair.

"Huh?"

Jack motioned to the minifridge. "Go get a couple of your lemon wedges and squeeze the juice onto the stuffing." I did so and he congratulated me on my apprenticeship. I think he was teasing me. He refilled my wine glass and sent me back to the armchair while he placed a lobster over each of the two burners on the hot plate. "Not optimum, but the best I can do under the current conditions," he said, looking at his handiwork. "It's the closest I can get to broiling."

"I'm sure they'll be delicious."

"Now, if you would be so kind as to set the table." He motioned to the placemats, napkins, and flatware. I actually enjoy setting tables and I made the coffee table look as pretty as I could. Too bad neither of us had thought to pick up a couple of candles. I was now thoroughly into the romantic loopiness of this dinner.

Jack smacked his forehead with his palm. "Jesus, what kind of chef am I? I forgot to pick up vegetables. Corn on the cob would have been perfect. And so easy."

"I won't hold it against you," I said, saluting him with my glass.

Once the lobsters were sufficiently "broiled," Jack rested them on our plates, then melted some butter for each of us, pouring it into small ceramic ramekins that he'd picked up at the cookware store. He handed me a cracking tool and a lobster fork, and brought our plates to the table. We dug in.

"This is amazing," I said, tasting the stuffing along with the sweet lobster meat. I raised my fork to him. "Bravo!"

He nodded. "You're welcome."

"I can't believe you were a fat kid," I said. He sure as hell looked amazing now. "How did you take it all off—if you don't mind my asking?"

"First? I stopped feeling compelled to taste everything I cooked. This may become a problem again when I open my own restaurant. I'm seriously considering leaving Tito's once the salsa launch goes national. Anyway, I discovered the joys of exercise. I was never much for team sports, so I started running on a regular basis and took up golf."

"Golf?" I wrinkled my nose. "Golf isn't *exercise*."

"Then what is it?"

"It's a waste of perfectly good park land, that's what it is."

"Watch it, Liz. I happen to love golf. And it's terrific exercise if you walk the course."

I think we'd just hit our first sandtrap. "You really love golf?"

"Uh-huh. You can't grow up in Miami and not play. Love to watch it on TV, even."

There was an awkward silence. I looked down at my plate and picked at my lobster.

"Don't worry, I won't subject you to my plaid pants and white bucks." Jack diplomatically changed the subject. "So, how did you end up a copywriter, Liz? *That* doesn't seem to be something a little kid in the sandbox decides she wants to be when she grows up."

"Did you ever wonder what makes people tick?" I asked Jack. "Why the color blue makes people feel one way and yellow makes them feel another? Why something that costs $99.99 seems so much cheaper than something that costs a hundred dollars? Maybe I'm nuts, but I get a kick out of this stuff. I've always been fascinated with what makes people buy what they buy and use what they use. The power of advertising and marketing is enormous. Think about it.

Would you really buy a *car*, for example, from a TV commercial? But if those ads didn't get people into the showrooms, the automakers would never spend gazillions of dollars to run them. The art of persuasion intrigues me. In school, I found out that I was good at using words as power tools, so I took summer internships at advertising agencies, and when I graduated college, I had a short list of places I wanted to work that were creative, trendy, and cutting edge. I was very lucky, Jack. My first choice liked my portfolio and I've been at Seraphim Swallow Avanti ever since. Of course, who knows how much longer I'll be there."

"What do you mean?"

I told him about the pitch session that I'd fled.

" 'Snatch'?" he asked. "As in . . . ?" He looked like he wasn't sure whether to point to my crotch or his own, just for the sake of gentlemanliness.

"You know of any other kind of snatch?" Then I told him about the Numbers Crunchers assignment. "That one should be less of a challenge. For one thing, the product doesn't sound obscene."

"Sounds like the snack food of choice for CPAs," Jack joked.

"You're not bad at this. Want my job?"

"Got any ideas for the ad campaign yet? You can bounce them off of me. 'Jack Blow, American Consumer.' I'd love to hear them."

My throat seized up.

"It's all right. You don't have to tell me. I didn't mean to pressure you, Liz."

I put my hands on my neck. I couldn't swallow all of a sudden. In fact I could barely breathe. My legs started to itch, too. So did my arms. I looked down and noticed that my limbs were covered with red splotches that seemed to increase in size with every passing second. I touched my right leg. The skin felt blisteringly hot. My stomach seized up with cramps while a simultaneous wave of nausea sent me running to the bathroom. When I returned to the living room, I tried to speak to Jack, but the sound would barely come out. What I managed to say was apparently unintelligible. I bolted up from the couch and grabbed a Waldorf-Astoria notepad and pencil from the desk.

"I think we should get to a hospital," I scribbled as hastily as I could manage. "Something really weird is happening to me." I shoved the pad under Jack's nose.

"Oh, my God!" he exclaimed.

I took the pad away and scrawled two more words: "I'm scared."

9/Where's George Clooney When You Need Him?

Next thing I knew, we were speeding in a taxi toward Mount Sinai hospital. I refused to be taken anywhere else. While Jack stroked my forehead and whispered reassuringly that everything would be okay, I counted how many successive green lights we made in an effort to take my mind off the ever-increasing rash swelling body part after body part. The fact that I could barely breathe or speak because my throat felt swollen shut from the inside made me a lousy conversationalist.

The cab dropped us at the Madison Avenue emergency room entrance to Mount Sinai. I wasn't prepared for the sight. Inside the dirty white waiting room, about half a dozen people, who looked like winos or addicts sleeping it off, were curled in or sprawled over the vinyl-covered chairs.

Jack wrinkled his nose. I wasn't sure if he detected a whiff of piss coming from one of the waiting room denizens (I did), or whether he was reacting to the noxious fumes of disinfectant that stung our nostrils as an indifferent janitor pushed a stringy, filthy mop across the linoleum in front of us.

Jack seemed twice as anxious as I was. "Are

you okay?" I mimed the question. He cracked his knuckles. "I hate that," I started to say, but I was having trouble forming the words.

"Sorry." Jack shoved his hands in his pockets. "Hospitals make me nervous. I hate them. I really, *really* hate them."

I raised my shoulders to ask him why, but he waved his hand to interrupt me. "Forget it," he said, "I don't want to get into it right now. No need to freak out either of us more than we already are." Jack's tone of voice reflected his squeamishness in spades. "Let's take care of you and get the hell out of here as fast as we can," he added.

I pointed to an unstaffed window with a sign that read TRIAGE. PLEASE FORM A LINE. The *compos mentis* people in the waiting room—those who were not already passed out or otherwise asleep—looked as though they had long given up hope of seeing a doctor that night. I started scratching my leg again and Jack tried unsuccessfully to encourage me to stop.

Leaving me at the triage window, Jack started to pace the hall, looking for a doctor, nurse, anyone who could admit me. I noticed another sign inside the little triage cubicle and ran over and grabbed Jack's arm. I pointed to it: IF YOU HAVE A PERSISTENT RASH OR COUGH, DO NOT STAY IN THE WAITING ROOM. SEE THE TRIAGE NURSE IMMEDIATELY. I gestured frantically at my legs and arms. Jack nodded and reminded me that there was no triage nurse to be seen, regardless of my condition.

"Entertain me, Jack," I scribbled on the back of a trifolded brochure I found lying on the floor. "It'll give us something to take our minds off being here."

Jack threw his hands in the air in a semi-shrug. "Like what?"

"I don't know. Tell me a story. I told you about my job situation. What's the silliest one you've ever had?" By now my hand was starting to cramp from writing so quickly, and Jack was squinting at the brochure in an effort to decipher my scrawl.

"Well, I'm not sure this qualifies as 'silly,' but I managed one of the gift shops at Disney World the summer between my college graduation and the start of business school. Every morning before I opened up for the day, I would go around the store and decide to make all the Eeyores smile—the ones I could affect—you know, the stuffed toys where I could take my fingernail and manipulate the stitching around their mouths. There I was, in charge of the largest gift shop at the 'happiest place on earth' and we sold unhappy toys. I didn't want them to be gloomy anymore." He kissed the top of my head, then rose and resumed pacing and cracking his knuckles, despite the desperate look I gave him, hoping he might quit. The manifestation of Jack's nerves set mine even more on edge.

Finally, someone appeared at the triage window. We must have waited for upward of twenty-five minutes, by which time I was so itchy I could have scratched all my skin off with my fingernails, my throat felt even more constricted, and now I was beginning to get nauseous again. Except that I couldn't throw up because I could hardly breathe. Jack tried to explain the situation to the nurse, a Latino with an overworked, harried, but kindly expression. The nurse started asking me questions. I pointed to my throat. "She can't speak," Jack told the nurse. "Her throat seized up. And she's got this rash. Liz, roll up your pants leg and show him. Your sign says we're not supposed to . . ."

The nurse stood, peered out of the little window of his cubicle at me, then motioned for us to come in and sit down. "When did this start?" he asked.

I looked at Jack, who answered for me. "Maybe an hour or so ago. We were eating dinner and suddenly—"

The nurse interrupted him. "What were you eating?"

"Lobster."

"Have you ever had an allergic reaction to shellfish before?" the nurse asked me.

I shook my head.

"It can happen at any time," the nurse told us. "Let's get her inside. Do you have insurance?"

I nodded my head yes. I took my insurance card out of my wallet and showed the nurse several other vital pieces of information, including the phone number to call in the event of an emergency, in this case my home number to reach Nell or Jem.

I was then shuttled to a "payment" window where a woman affixed a plastic bracelet to my right wrist and told me I was good to go.

I felt like I was getting closer and closer to seeing the Wizard of Oz. The next room they made me wait in was at the edge of the ER itself, where they seated me in a spectacularly uncomfortable chair. For what seemed like hours, no one even came to look at me. Jack valiantly scoured the halls trying to attract some attention on my behalf. No one even asked him who he was, what his relationship was to me, or why he was wandering around the ER. Finally, I went to a semicircular nurse's station and pointed at my rash and my throat. "I can't breathe," I tried to tell them. I showed her my bracelet.

A young Filipino nurse, strikingly beautiful, flipped through a series of clipboards at the station. "Well, why didn't somebody say something before?"

My sentiments exactly.

"Come with me, Ms. Pemberley." She took me over to a pale pink vinyl chair that looked a bit like Barbie's Barcalounger. The sweet-faced nurse sat me there and told me a doctor would be right with me. Her voice was soothing as she told me not to worry. I didn't believe her.

I think I waited another twenty minutes or so before someone came over. When I wasn't panicking, I spent the time watching the staff and patients pass to and fro, and assessing the depressing condition of the facilities. In the bay next to mine, an addict appeared to be detoxing. He emitted various unpleasant guttural sounds while in a state of deep repose.

The area was practically as filthy as Shea Stadium's dank cement corridors by the concession stands after a Mets game. The floor of the ER looked like it hadn't been properly washed in a decade. I spied the odd foil gum wrapper and even a cigarette butt ground into the linoleum below the NO SMOKING: OXYGEN IN USE sign.

After what seemed like an eternity, a tall man appeared to me in a white light. Or maybe I just thought that because his lab coat was so bright. He wore his stethoscope with a jaunty air of confidence. He was extremely tall and, from what I could tell, very well built. He also had a way, when he was talking to my pretty nurse, of keeping his left hand thrust deeply into the pocket of his white lab coat, thereby burying the gleaming gold wedding band.

"I'm Dr. Michaels," he said, extending his right hand. "Drew Michaels."

The nurse smiled. "You're in good hands." She beamed reverently at Dr. Michaels.

"And this is Lila." The doctor officially introduced the nurse.

Lila handed Dr. Michaels my admitting chart, which he perused thoroughly. I didn't like his frown.

"Have you ever had any reactions to eating shellfish before?"

I shook my head. I'd already given that information. It should have been on my chart. The doctor read my expression. "Don't worry, it's all here." He tapped the clipboard. His hands were beautiful— surgeon's hands. "I was just double-checking."

I wished that the allergic reaction hadn't rendered me so ugly. Dr. Michaels was the kind of man who made every woman want to check her lipstick.

"We're very lucky that you came right up here. If you don't catch this in time—"

I motioned for something to write on. Lila brought me a prescription pad and a pencil. "I've been waiting in the ER to see someone for about three hours, I think!!" I scrawled.

Dr. Michaels emitted an angry rumble and mentioned something about being woefully understaffed that evening. "Well, you're here now, Ms. Pemberley, and we can nip this thing in the bud with a shot of adrenaline. If you'd gone untreated too much longer, you might have gone into anaphylactic shock."

When words failed again, I wrote them down on the pad and showed the page to Dr. Michaels. "What's that? It doesn't sound pretty."

"It isn't. You could have ended up dead."

My heart must have skipped several beats.

The doctor reviewed my admitting form. "Lila will call your roommates and tell them where you are. I think we should keep you here overnight, just to be on the safe side. We need to give you an immediate injection of epinephrine, which we'll do through an IV. That'll open your air passages and your blood vessels. Then we'll give you a shot of cortisone to halt the progress of the rash, followed by a big dose of Benadryl to stop the itch. If, after an hour or so, it still itches, let us know and we'll give you a second Benadryl injection. The swelling should start to go down by then. I'm afraid you'll have to stay on this very attractive lounge chair; we don't even have a proper bed to put you in down here. We're all full up." He retrieved a thin white cotton blanket from a metal storage cabinet, draped it over the lower half of my body, and placed a reassuring hand on my forehead.

The cortisone coursing through my veins emitted a sharp, almost alcoholic odor when they gave me the medication through my IV. It felt like every pore of my body was giving off fumes. I was in and out of sleep for hours. The Benadryl had knocked me out completely, yet somehow I was still able to hear the sounds of the ER . . . the hum of hushed conversation, the whoosh of the dingy curtains being parted or drawn around a patient, and the squeak of gurney wheels amid the myriad smells that permeated the low-ceilinged, claustrophobic corner of the room. I had no idea what had happened to Jack. Given his visceral adverse reaction to hospitals, perhaps he'd left. Poor guy. If he was still out in the waiting area, he may have needed more reassuring hand-holding than I did. If I'd been able to, I would have gone out there to see how *he* was holding up.

Time has a funny way of passing in the ER. I began to tell the hour by the number of bags of clearish liquid Lila attached to the hat rack–like stand that supported my IV. After a while, I deduced that it took approximately one hour for the bag to empty into my veins. The light never varied in the windowless room. It could have been midnight, dawn, or noon.

I felt a gentle touch on my forearm and opened my eyes. Nell was standing by my chair wearing an expression of extreme concern. "Hey there, girlfriend," she said. She placed a plushy turquoise teddy bear in my hands. "The gift shop just opened."

"What time is it?" I asked her hazily.

"A little after eight-thirty in the morning. Jem is in the waiting room. They would only allow one of us in at a time. Your *majorly* cute doctor told us that you had a really bad scare and it could have been super dangerous, even deadly, but that he caught it in time, and you'll be fine from now on, as long as you never eat anything with shellfish in it." She took a printed list from her pocket and handed it to me. "You can't have anything on here, and if you aren't sure, you're supposed to ask. Like I know you like to order *mee krob* in Thai restaurants. Well, you can't do that anymore even if you pick out the shrimp and don't eat them, because the shrimp are in there to begin with."

"That sucks," I replied, realizing for the first time that I had my voice back. I practiced a swallow or two. Silently, I thanked God and Dr. Michaels. "No more *mee krob* for the rest of my life."

Nell squeezed my hand. "Let's put it this way. You could either eat *mee krob* and maybe end up dead, or you could watch your diet from now on." She looked at her watch. "It's Jem's turn. Time to switch. I'll see you in a bit."

I was exhausted and closed my eyes again for a few moments. I heard the retreating *click-click* of Nell's stiletto heels on the linoleum. What was probably less than a minute later, Jem's appearance at my chair announced itself in a cloud of Thierry Mugler's "Angel," her signature perfume. Her cool hand brushed my forehead.

"Hey, I don't have a fever, Jem." I opened my eyes. "Apparently I had shellfish poisoning and it's permanent."

Jem bent over to whisper in my ear. She was convinced that Jack had deliberately tried to poison me, to take me out of the running on *Bad Date*.

"Don't be ridiculous. We don't even start taping until . . . *tomorrow*."

"Precisely," Jem said. "Imagine if you were laid up here and missed the first episode. Or worse."

"You mean like imagine if I were dead?"

"They'd have to find another contestant at short notice, Liz."

I reminded Jem that Jack knew nothing about how pathetic my personal life had been. You'd have to

know me as well as she and Nell do in order to understand that the catalogue of my hellish experiences with
men is thicker than the Manhattan phone book. I'm
the poster girl for women-who-do-far-too-much-for-
undeserving-men-who-don't-appreciate-them. Yet, I
am compulsive. Liz Pemberley—who loved not wisely
but too well. Nell once described me as the kind of
woman who is naturally one part *Martha Stewart
Living* to three parts Sharon Stone–loving. This is
why: In addition to the great sex, I'll knit a guy a
sweater, cook both gourmet meals and comfort food,
do his laundry, shop for his demanding mother, and
follow the stats of his favorite football team.

Jem touched my hand. "Hey there, you drifted off
to sleep while I was talking to you," she said softly.

I realized I'd been on a dream rant. "I'm not surprised. I'm filled with Benadryl, I think. And who
knows what else has been coursing through my veins
all night? Plus, I didn't really sleep. I didn't nod off on
you on purpose, believe me."

"I'm just wondering if it's all right to take you
home."

"Hi there, kiddo. How're you feeling?" Dr.
Michaels approached my chair. "We can discharge
your roommate when this drip has finished," he told
Jem. "Your other roommate has the list of things Liz
should avoid from now on in her diet. It would help if
you were aware of the items as well."

"So we can be the food police?" Jem smiled.

"You may have to be," I countered weakly. "I have
lousy willpower."

Dr. Michaels dropped his more or less jovial

demeanor. "Well, young lady, last night's episode should have scared you senseless. Not that you could ever have predicted it, because this kind of allergic reaction can strike anyone at any time, but there's no such thing as 'just one' shrimp being harmless from now on." He placed his hand on my leg and surveyed the state of my rash. "Much better. You might want to wear long sleeves and pants for the next couple of days, though. I'll start the ball rolling on your discharge process. The paperwork should take about a half hour at this time of the morning and by then"—he checked the liquid in the bag hanging over my right shoulder—"this should be done, Lila can remove your IV, and you'll be all set." He shook my hand.

"Thanks. You've been wonderful," I said, as I watched him walk away.

"By the way," Jem said after Dr. Michaels had gone down the hall, "Jack Rafferty is out there. At least he was when Nell and I arrived. He was surrounded by Milky Way wrappers, using his jacket as a pillow, and was sound asleep, sprawled across two chairs and practically bent in half like a pretzel when we got here. Nell woke him up and started firing questions at him about what happened. Then Dr. Michaels came out and talked to us and Jack got really upset. He wanted to know why they hadn't bothered to tell him what was going on with you in here as soon as they diagnosed you. The doctor told him that Nell and I were listed as your emergency contacts and it was hospital policy to call the emergency contacts first and explain everything to them—us—when we got here. Jack was pretty pissed off that he'd been waiting all night to find out what the hell was happening and whether you were all right. He thought that someone on staff could have had the courtesy to keep him apprised of your condition."

"I have to admit he's got a point, Jem. He was wandering the halls looking for someone who could take care of me for hours before they finally took me back to see a doctor. No one questioned his presence then."

"They probably hadn't yet looked at your admitting form to see that you had emergency contact names listed. When they saw that you had put down Nell and me, they went back to playing by the rules."

It must have been a big deal for Jack to duel with those hospital demons he harbored and spend the night contorted in a chair in that awful waiting room on my account. It was comforting to know how much he cared for me as a friend, but I felt like I really owed him one. "Is Jack out there now?" I asked. The poor guy had waited there all night with no one giving him any information; then, when my roommates arrive, the girls treat him like a pariah because they've concluded he was trying to kill me to keep me from competing on a reality television show.

"As far as I know," Jem said. "When I came back to see you, Nell started talking to him. He missed his eight A.M. flight back to Miami because he was adamant about not wanting to leave without being sure you were okay. I don't want to tip our hand, Liz, because we've all got to do the show with him, but we don't trust him."

"We?"

"Nell and I. Mostly me, actually."

"Jem, he's a very nice guy. You can't begin to imagine *how* nice. We had a wonderful time last night . . .

before I got sick. And he was an angel afterward, too."

"You shouldn't be friends with him."

"You're jealous."

"Liz, it's in our contract. 'No fraternizing with other contestants.' "

"Obviously, being roommates is fraternizing, too. And the network knows the three of us *live* together." But Jem refused to listen to any explanations or rationalizations. I felt sorry for any of her students who might try to weasel their way out of being downgraded for a late assignment. She was intractable.

When Lila finally discharged me and I went back out into the ER waiting room, seeing sunlight for the first time in hours, all three of them were waiting for me. I wanted to rush into Jack's arms and give him a hug, glad our mutually nightmarish ordeal was over, but I could feel the scowls of my girlfriends burning into my back like lacerations and I had no intentions of subjecting either of us to another earful of negativity from my roommates. But I came as close to him as I felt I safely could and gently touched the back of his hand. I hoped the expression in my eyes would convey to him what was truly on my mind and in my heart.

"You're looking better," he said.

"*You* look like hell," I replied woefully. He was a rumpled mess, his pants totally encrusted with dried breadcrumb-crustacean mixture, and he smelled faintly of a fishing vessel. Small wonder people had been steering clear of him. "Are you all right, Jack?" I asked softly.

"I've had kind of a bad night, Liz. So I guess I'm as

'all right' as anyone can be who's spent several uncomfortable and interminable hours waiting for a doctor's verdict on a friend. I didn't mean to scare you with my own hospital issues, Liz. It's just that there have been far too many times in my life where I've brought friends and relatives in to an emergency room and they didn't make it out." He looked over at my roommates who were straining to hear his words. "I don't want to talk about it anymore; it's too depressing. The point is, you're going to be fine . . . and I'd give you a big hug and a kiss, but your roommates would probably have a fit, you'd never hear the end of it, and you need as little stress as possible right now. Plus, I really need a shower. By the way, you should be pleased to hear that I very successfully substituted stuffing my face with chocolate for cracking my knuckles." He pulled a crumpled Milky Way wrapper from his jacket pocket and tossed it in a nearby trash can.

"I'm surprised you managed any sleep at all, on such a sugar high," I said, smiling at him. "Look, thanks for . . . everything," I whispered. "Sorry I screwed up our . . . date."

"Don't worry," he whispered back.

I felt reassured.

He raised his voice enough to be heard halfway across the waiting room. "It wasn't a 'date.' It's in our contract. No fraternization with other *Bad Date* contestants. It was just a getting-to-know-one-another-better kind of thing."

My empty stomach lurched. Considering he'd just mentioned a hug and a kiss, I hoped he was protecting what had passed between us in his hotel room . . .

although . . . I barely knew him, while my roommates and I had been thick as thieves for years, and I wasn't feeling well enough at the moment to visit the subject from a carefully reasoned perspective. "I'm sorry you had to miss your flight," I said, attempting to match the businesslike shift in Jack's tone.

"Yep. It'll be an even quicker turnaround for me than I'd originally planned. I'd intended to fly home first thing this morning, take care of some business down there; then pack up what I needed for the telecast of the first *Bad Date* episode and fly back to New York sometime after noon tomorrow. It's going to be something of a commute for me for the next thirteen weeks. I've got too much going on with the restaurant to just pick up and move here for the duration of the show." He gave me a quick, passionless peck on the cheek. "Well, I can't tell you how glad I am that you're up and about . . . so . . . I guess I'll see you tomorrow night." He looked over at my roommates and smiled warmly, waving to them as he headed for the revolving door that emptied onto Madison Avenue. "Nice to see you again, ladies."

I felt embarrassed that they did not return his cordiality. "C'mon, you guys, let's go home. I need what's left of the weekend to get some sleep before the broadcast."

Nell started to laugh. "Used to be Sunday nights was reserved for Walt Disney movies on TV. Now, *Bad Date* is going to be the main event. What does that say about our society?"

"Honey," Jem said in a drawling tone. "If you have to ask, you don't want to know the answer!"

We headed for the exit arm in arm, all three of us.

Nell started to do a little jig, pulling us to and fro with her. "Lions and tigers and bears! Oh, my!" Jem and I fell into sync and took up the chant; then we jumped into the same bay of the revolving door. Suddenly, we were like little girls in a playground again, dissolving into giggle fits. I felt like shit, but I was deliriously happy. Happy to be alive.

10/Pre-show Jitters

Nell and Jem were very helpful in outfitting me for the first *Bad Date* episode. What do you wear on live national television when your arms and legs are still dappled with raised scarlet splotches, and yet you want to give the impression of alluring sexuality? Miraculously, my face and hands had remained unmarked by the rash. We settled on a pair of slim black slacks with just a hint of body-toning Lycra in the fabric and a ribbed cashmere turtleneck. Who cares that I might roast under the lights; at least I would look chic. Nell loaned me a goldtone chain belt, which broke up the monotony of the ensemble. With my stiletto-heeled suede booties, I looked like the prototype of a real New Yorker. Nell, with her perfect, chemically tanned coltish legs, chose to wear a vintage Pucci print minidress in various shades of blue that complemented her eyes, no stockings, and a pair of precipitously high pumps. Jem elected to go with a pearl gray linen pantsuit. I have to admit that half the fun of the day was figuring out what to wear. It took our minds off the butterflies in our stomachs. We assumed the other female contestants were sharing similar anxieties, but wondered if the men on the show had given more than a moment's thought to their appearance.

"Are we shallow?" Nell questioned aloud.

"Do you really want to hear the answer to that?"

"Jem . . . ," I warned. I checked my watch. "Five-thirty. The car should be downstairs." We were expected to be at the studio at six o'clock and report straight to the hair and makeup department. *Bad Date* went on the air at eight P.M.

The studio had sent a black limo for us. Its interior smelled of new leather and old money. We felt like VIPs. As soon as we stretched out our legs, marveling at the amount of room, Nell went straight for the complimentary bottle of champagne. "This is so cool you guys! Where do you think they keep the glasses?"

"In the Green Room after the taping," Jem said, grasping the bottle by the neck, removing it from Nell's hand, and replacing it in its leather nesting place.

Nell wrinkled up her nose. "Spoilsport!"

"We need to be sharp for this, Nell."

"I just wanted to take the edge off."

"So do we," Jem said, looking to me for concurrence. I nodded my head. "But let's not give them any reasons to kick us off the show before we get to tape a single episode, by walking in buzzed."

"Then why did they put a bottle of champagne in the limo?" Nell asked. "If not for us?"

"I think they probably keep all the limos stocked with bubbly, no matter where the passengers are headed. There's no sign on the bottle that says, 'Hi, Nell. Drink me,' so we shouldn't assume it was put there specially for us." I finally got her to give up on the booze.

The limo pulled up to the back of the television studio and the driver got out and opened the car door for us like we were celebrities. I rang the bell and after waiting about half a minute, we were admitted by a burly stagehand with a salt-and-pepper crew cut who pointed the way to the hair and makeup room.

We followed a series of hand-lettered signs down an unremarkable and somewhat dark corridor that finally led us to a large room that looked like a beauty salon. The room was a hive of activity with about a dozen individual stations set up with large mirrors rimmed with lights. The counter tops were piled with assorted tools of the trade: brushes, blowdryers, and tackle boxes overflowing with pots and wands and tubes of color. The air smelled of a dozen different colognes.

I was assigned to a handsome, ponytailed hairdresser named Ethan who made a point of telling me that he was the only straight guy on the hair and makeup staff. He wore a white shirt, crisply ironed, unbuttoned just enough to show a thatch of brown chest hair, and, suspended from a length of rawhide, a Native American amulet: a small leather dream pouch that he wore as a necklace. I watched his hands in the mirror as he ran them through my hair, deciding how to style it for the show. On the middle finger of his right hand he wore a silver ring wrought with Celtic knots.

"You can really see how great a color your hair is when I blow the wave out of it. You've got natural auburny-russet highlights in the chestnut." While

Ethan talked shop, I gave myself over completely to his capable hands, which sent tingles along my scalp. By the time he finished and my makeup artist, Gladiola—a woman with a pierced tongue and fuchsia streak in her bleached blonde hair—had worked her magic, I felt very glamorous indeed.

"Listen up, folks!" I looked in the mirror and saw that Rob Dick had entered the room and was clapping his hands for silence. "Hi there, remember me? Just your friendly producer here, to say hello and welcome, and to wish you luck. You all look terrific. Let's have a round of applause for our talented hair and makeup staff!"

We obeyed him like a flock of dutiful sheep.

"We've got dressing room assignments posted on the door here, so take a gander at them on your way out of the room. You can lock up your personal belongings in there for the duration of the taping each week. For the first half of the season until we 'attrit,' so to speak, you'll have a dressing-room mate, except for two of you who will have your own room, since we've got an odd number of each gender."

Rob Dick clapped his hands again to get our attention. "Okay, now, I went over the guidelines for the show with each of you at your auditions and interviews, but let me reiterate that we're on live TV. That means no curse words, even though we've got a seven-second air delay, so we can bleep you if it comes to that. However, let me remind you that *Bad Date*, the most honest reality show on television, is family entertainment and we don't want to alienate any of our sponsors nor do we wish to offend our audience."

I couldn't help myself. "Yeah, we don't want the

kiddies to switch channels from true-life tales of our miserable sex lives to Nickelodeon, now, do we?" I caught Ethan winking at me in the mirror.

"Keep it up, Ms. Pemberley," Rob Dick said.

Shit.

The producer approached my chair. "No, I mean it." I felt his warm breath in my ear as he whispered to me. "I told you at your interview that your quick wit was just the ingredient the show needed to have a natural foil for our host Rick Byron." He patted my shoulder reassuringly, then thought of something else and leaned down to me again. "Just don't go too far."

Rob Dick returned to the doorway and resumed his group pep talk. "Another thing to remember: When you share your bad date experiences, you will be connected to finger electrodes that will monitor your remarks like a polygraph. Behind the head of the speaker will be a big screen that will show the results of the polygraph right on TV. So, if you gild the lily, the world is watching and our studio audience will more than likely liquidate you. Remember, *keep your eyes on the prize and strategize*. There are intercom speakers in each dressing room, so you'll receive updates on how many minutes we've got until air time, plus a real-live human stage manager—oh, here she is now, folks, this is Geneva."

An efficient-looking, young, black woman with fifties-style harlequin eyeglasses had just poked her head in the door and whispered something to Rob Dick. She showed him the time on a large stopwatch that hung from her neck on a woven lanyard, the kind you make in arts and crafts at day camp. She waved at us, whispered something else to Rob Dick, and left the room.

"So, that's Geneva," the producer continued. "She will knock on your door to let you know your calls, just in case the sound system is a little wonky. We've got an after-show party in the Green Room, which is all the way down the hall to your left as you exit this room. Dressing rooms are off to the right; the letters are on the door, along with your nameplates, so you can't get lost. So . . . that's all I have to say for now. Just go out there and make commercially viable entertainment!"

No one knew if we were expected to applaud, so we did, just to be on the safe, butt-kissing side.

Now that we were all beautified, glamorized, and pep-talked, we were free to head off to our respective dressing rooms. I checked the assignments posted on the door. Jem and Nell were assigned to share a room. I was paired with someone surnamed Fortunato. I looked at the men's list. Jack got the long straw, his own dressing room. Lucky devil. I hadn't said a word to him since I got to the studio. Nor had he acknowledged my presence, or indicated that he knew Nell or Jem. Was that part of a strategy attributed to him by my suspicious roommates—not to let anyone know that he was already acquainted with three of the contestants? Or was he just being inexplicably rude? Or could his aloofness simply be due to the fact that *he* was just as nervous as we were, and was just putting his "game face" on? Still, I'd have thought at the very least he would have found some way of asking me how I was feeling.

A woman with heavily moussed blue-black hair

wearing a hot pink sweater, leather miniskirt, fishnet stockings, and thigh-high boots was following me down the hall to the dressing room. "Hey," she called out, "you Pemberley?"

I turned around. "I'm Liz Pemberley."

She stuck out her hand. "Candy Angela Fortunato. Do you think they'll make me take my gum out for the show?" She snapped it for emphasis. "You can just call me 'Candy' because the 'Angela' part makes it too long. Looks like we're sharing a room."

We arrived at Dressing Room A. The door was unlocked. At first glance, the décor was impersonal but comfortable. One wall was mirrored and lit in the same way that the hair and makeup room had been. The dressing table stretched the length of the mirror. There was a little sink, a hanging bar for clothes, and a door that led to a toilet. Elaborate floral displays, courtesy of the Urban Lifestyles Channel, greeted us, the enormous rubrum lilies perfuming the narrow room with their pungent scent. A tray of soft drinks and Perrier, with glasses and an ice bucket, rested on a low table between the two armchairs.

Candy sank into one of the armchairs and threw her legs over the side. "Well, whaddya say we kick back until they need us?" She surveyed the room. "I wonder if they can get me a Dr Pepper. I don't drink any of that stuff," she said, pointing to the beverage bottles. "Actually," she added, sliding up her skirt and removing a small silver flask from a black garter encircling her thigh, "this is just what the doctor ordered." She waved the flask at me. "Bourbon. Dr Pepper and a splash of Jack is to die for."

"Jack?" My head was somewhere else. Another

Jack. The one whose business card I was still carrying like a talisman in my wallet.

"Jack *Daniels*," Candy replied. "Whatsamatter with you? You don't drink?"

Candy's Brooklyn accent was so thick you could cut it with a chainsaw. It sounded to me like she'd said "witchyou," instead of "with you." I shook my head, declining her offer. "Not before the show."

"Ya sure?" Candy took a swig.

"Positive. But thanks."

Candy capped her flask and replaced it in its satin holster. She adjusted her skirt in a ladylike manner that seemed oddly out of character.

An announcement over our intercom told us we had ten minutes before we were needed on set. There was a knock on the door and a young man came in to hook us up with body mikes. He tucked the battery pack down the waistband on the back of my pants. I turned around to look at him, somewhat appalled. "Oh, don't worry," the man said matter-of-factly, "no one will see it there."

A few minutes later, Geneva knocked on the door and we joined the other contestants, following her into a holding room just outside the soundstage. "You'll all be seated on set in just a minute, so you'll be in place by the time we actually go on the air. Break a leg, everyone," she said flatly.

I surreptitiously reached for Jem and Nell's hand and gave each a little good luck squeeze. Maybe it wasn't such a bad idea to take a leaf from Jack's book and not act like I knew anyone really well. Studio staffers had materialized to escort us to the sort of chairs that stars have on movie sets, those high captain's

numbers with wooden footrests and canvas backs
that have names stenciled on them. First thing I
checked for was whether mine was correctly spelled.
Once we were seated, the mike guy came around
again to make sure that everything was still copacetic,
asked each of us to say a couple of words as a "sound
check," and then the hair and makeup people gave us
a final once-over. Ethan smoothed one recalcitrant
strand of hair back into place, then pronounced me
"magnificent" and "foxy." Gladiola dipped an enormous brush into a jar of loose face powder, tamped
the handle against the side of the jar to eliminate the
excess, and daubed my face to take down the shine.

I noticed that each of the three cameras had a red
light on top to indicate when it was on. "Don't worry
about playing to the camera," Gladiola whispered.
"He'll find you. Just try to act natural."

Act natural. Yeah, right. The audience was staring
at us as though we were lab rats. I felt a sudden wave
of nausea and that urge to pee that you only get when
you know you don't have the opportunity to go.
Geneva walked to downstage center and stood by
the shoulder of the man operating camera two. She
counted down from "five," splaying her fingers until
she got to "one," when she pointed directly upstage
and there was a burst of horn music. The show's
theme song had begun.

"Welcome to *Bad Date*, America's hot new reality
TV show!" the announcer's voice boomed. "Where
our nation's most pathetic singles compete for a million dollars by sharing their worst experiences, totally
live and totally uncensored! Now"—there was the
obligatory drum roll—"let's meet the host of *Bad*

Date, fresh from his starring role in the blockbuster film *What's Your Sign?*"—another obligatory drum roll—"Hollywood's Reigning Hunk . . . Rick Byron!"

Hollywood's Reigning Hunk bounded onto the stage in head to toe black Armani, all boyish charm and gleaming capped teeth. The crowd went nuts. I couldn't see whether there was an APPLAUSE sign cueing them. Or a sign that said "squeal and act like he's all four Beatles arriving at Idlewild." Or was the New York airport called "Kennedy" by then? I blinked, realizing I was spacing out.

"Hey, hey, hey," Rick called out to the audience. They squealed again. "Welcome to *Bad Date*! Are we ready to rock and roll?!"

He turned his hand-held mike to the crowd to record and amplify their response. "Yeaaaaahhhhhh!" they screamed madly.

I gripped the wooden arms of my chair, feeling like I was on an airstrip increasing speed before takeoff, and thought to myself, *Hang on, girlfriend, it's going to be a bumpy night.*

11/The First Episode

"And we're back, folks!" Rick said after the first commercial break, which came only moments after we went on the air, and during which our faces were repowdered and our hair touched up and teased back to lacquered perfection. "We're going to introduce you to our contestants, now ... ladies and gentlemen ... our *Bad Date* producer scoured the country for fourteen of the most pathetic people on the planet, and you voyeurs in our studio audience will get to hear all about their miserable little love lives and then decide who gets to go and"—he gestured to the illuminated Plexiglas platform on which all of our chairs were placed—"who gets voted off our island!"

The audience cheered.

"First up alphabetically," Rick said, "we have Luke Arrowcatcher." One of the cameras zoomed in for a close up of Luke's handsomely chiseled Native American features. "Luke is an 'aboriginal American,' folks, which means ... he's a real-life Indian!"

I wondered if Rick's banter was scripted. The patter made him sound like such a moron. A politically incorrect moron at that.

"Luke's tribe runs a casino in upstate New York where Luke works as a croupier. Tell us a little more about yourself, *Kimo Sabe*."

Luke didn't crack a smile. "Why waste air?"

Rick was temporarily thrown a curve. I saw Geneva make a looping gesture with her finger indicating he should move on to the next contestant.

"Next we have the—might I say very lovely—isn't she a knockout, folks? Anella A-vig-non."

I stifled a giggle when I heard him mangle Nell's name. "If you were thinking with your brain instead of something else, you'd have gotten her name right, Rick," I said to myself. At least I thought I said the words to myself. Guess who forgot she was miked? All of America and probably a few foreign countries just heard me insult our nation's hottest movie star.

The audience applauded. I hadn't expected that kind of reaction. It made me feel oddly empowered and considerably less nervous. On the other hand, I wasn't in the "hot seat" yet.

"Hey, who said that?" When no one, including me, fessed up, Rick continued to cozy up to Nell. "So how do you say your name, sweet thing?"

"Anella Avignon," Nell said charmingly. "Like the French nursery rhyme." She began to sing. "*Sur le pont d'Avignon—*"

"Hey, cupcake, the only nursery rhyme I know is the one where the guy stuck in his thumb and—"

He was cut off by a paradiddle from the house band's drummer.

"Moving right along . . . but I can't wait to get to know you better," Rick told Nell. "Next, we've got jazz musician Ellis Ellis DuPree. Tell me, brother, what instrument do you play?"

"Licorice stick," replied the contestant. He reminded me of a character from the old *Shaft* movies. Very black and very laid-back and very *baaad*.

"Whoa there, are you telling me you like boys? Not that there's anything wrong with that, as Jerry Seinfeld says."

"A licorice stick is a *clarinet*," DuPree drawled in a rich honeyed tone. "And they call me 'Double-E' DuPree, just in case you care to get on my good side."

"Well, then, I'll just catch you on the fly, Double-E." Rick raised his fist to Double-E in the black power salute. I could feel America cringing.

Down the line Rick went, stopping at the next contestant, my dressing room–mate. "Well, don't you look like the happy hooker," he said, focusing on her breasts, which were practically spilling out of her top, thanks to a remarkably strong push-up bra.

"Thanks." Candy snapped her gum and pumped Rick's hand. "But I'm not a hooker, I'm a stripper. A former stripper, actually. Now I'm a fashion designer. I'm Candy Angela Fortunato—from Bay Ridge, Brooklyn—in case you couldn't tell, and I have a line of stripwear out on the market—my very own personal creations—called 'Snap Out of It!' "

"Well, Candy, maybe you can model some of your designs for us on the show."

Candy simpered a little. "I'd be honored."

"And who have we got here?" Rick approached an older, somewhat heavyset woman with short steel-gray hair and a tattoo on her forearm.

"Diz Larrabee," the woman said in a voice that was

no stranger to straight sour mash and unfiltered Camels.

"And 'Diz' is short for . . . ?"

"It's short for nothing." She bared her right arm and the camera operator zoomed in for a close up of a large tattoo. "This here's my favorite bike. FXSTC Softail Custom."

"I'm a Harley rider, too," Rick said enthusiastically. "I've got three of them at my place in Malibu. Maybe sometime we can get together and talk bikes."

Good grief, for the first time since Rick Byron had been on the air, he sounded sincere. He hadn't even seemed genuine when he was flirting with Nell! Clearly, in his little discussion with Diz he was deviating from the prepared text.

He moved down the line to Jem. "Damn, woman! Anyone ever tell you that you look like Halle Berry?"

"All the time, Rick," Jem answered cooly.

"Jemima Lawrence," Rick read from his card. "A professor of communications at Chelsea-Clinton Community College. I've got two questions for you, Jemima: was the college named for the daughter of a former U.S. president, and will you make me stay after school?"

The audience laughed. It sounded forced. Or coerced.

"4-C, as we like to call it—"

"4C, like the bread crumbs?" Rick interrupted.

"*Just* like the bread crumbs, Rick," Jem said, like ice on steel if you knew her as well as I do. "Chelsea, and *Clinton*—which used to be known as 'Hell's Kitchen' and is still often referred to that way— are adjacent neighborhoods on the west side of

Manhattan. The college is located right on the border of the two areas. Hence the name."

"*Hence.* Big word," Rick bantered.

"It's only got one syllable and five letters," I heard myself say.

The laughter from the studio audience sounded authentic this time.

"Moving right along now! We've got Allegra McGillicuddy, a Los Angeles native who is a feng shooey consultant? What is that, Allegra?"

Allegra looked like an illustration in a book I once owned of Sir Walter Scott's Lady of the Lake. She was dressed in filmy garments of blue and green, her long, straight blonde hair parted in the middle and flowing all the way down her back. "It's pronounced *fung sh-way*, Rick," she replied in a tinkly, musical voice that reminded me of a set of windchimes my grandparents used to have on their terrace. "It's an Eastern system of arranging the objects in your home or office according to the energy they carry, so proper placement is absolutely essential to ensure the right kind of karma."

"And people *pay* you to do this, Allegra?" Rick snickered.

"Why not? People pay *you* to act." The words flew out of my mouth. The studio audience erupted.

"H-Hey, that's a good one," our host stammered.

Oops. I think that's what Rob Dick meant about "going too far." I was probably off base with that remark. I mean, if Rick Byron had been Anthony Hopkins, then the quip wouldn't have sliced so close to the bone, although in his defense I figured Rick couldn't be nearly as untalented in person as he seemed from the tacky banter the show's writers had crafted for him to say on the air. Suddenly, I felt sorry for him. In the right film roles, he was charming and occasionally even adorable. It shows how far a charismatic personality and good dialogue can take a person.

Rick gamely barrelled on. "Our next contestant is a personal injury lawyer who has made two unsuccessful runs for the California legislature. And he was first runner-up in the 1974 George Hamilton Malibu Tanning Classic, let's meet Millard Milhaus!"

Millard had orange skin and looked like an iguana who had undergone reconstructive surgery to make him look almost human. His silver hair was slicked straight back giving his head the look of a Brilliantined ball bearing. His heavy gold cuff links glinted in the light. "I only lost my second bid by forty-five votes, I want you to know," he said, looking straight into the camera. "It was the district's most closely contested campaign in the last seventy-three years. If I had avoided that unfortunate incident on Hollywood Boulevard, I would have swept the election."

Rick was clearly ready to move on. I was up next. I felt my heart begin to race.

"She said she was eighteen," Millard continued, not letting go of the bone. "And that 'she' was a woman. How was I to know the scarf around her neck concealed—"

"Liz Pemberley!" Rick interrupted, effectively turning Millard into yesterday's news. "You remind me of the pretty one on the old *Charlie's Angels* series. What was her name?"

"Jaclyn Smith," I said.

"Although you're dressed like the smart one."

"Kate Jackson. It must be the dark hair. I don't think I look like either of them," I said.

"So, Liz, what do you do? In real life?"

"What's *this*, Rick?" I joked. "An out-of-body experience? I have no real life. I write advertising copy for a living. My job is to convince people to buy things they never thought they wanted or needed."

"Ouch! I can just see our sponsors pulling the plug on their commercials as we speak. So, you're the one who's been giving me grief all night, Liz. You're really busting my chops out here, ya know?"

I smiled at him. He really was very cute. It wasn't his fault that (a) he was no Einstein and that (b) the writers compounded the matter by making him seem like a cocky jerk on the air. "They're *nice* chops, Rick," I purred.

He winked at me and gestured a "gotcha" response with the stack of index cards. "We'll talk later." He moved down to the contestant on my right, a young blond in a Vero Beach bright yellow muscleman T-shirt. "Ladies and gentlemen . . . and especially the ladies," Rick said, "meet Travis Peters. Travis, it says here that you're a professional cabana boy at the Beverly Hills Hotel."

"Uh, yeah." The kid made Rick Byron sound like George Bernard Shaw.

"Ever had any ambitions beyond that, Travis?"

"Uh, yeah. I would really like to be your body double in your movies."

"Dream on, dude," Rick said.

"Because, you know, I really think I could be good at that."

"You think you can do what I do, Travis?" Rick turned to the studio audience. "He thinks he can do what I do." There were derisive hoots from the house. "Yeah, right," someone yelled. Rick looked back at the contestant. "Okay, Travis, tell you what. Stand up."

"Huh?" The boy was as thick as two planks of wood.

"Get out of the chair, dude," Rick coaxed. "C'mon, let's see what you're made of. Ladies and gentlemen, Travis Peters is going to host the show for the rest of the evening, while I just take his seat and have a little chat with Liz, here."

Travis didn't budge. He stared at Rick like a deer caught in the headlights of an oncoming pickup.

"See, folks, this job ain't as easy as it looks!" The crowd rewarded Rick with a spontaneous burst of applause. "Now, we come to . . . Milo Plum. Milo, that's a very interesting outfit."

"My lover made it for me."

"I thought everyone on this show was supposed to be uncommitted. Hey, where's the producer?"

"He was my lover last week," Milo corrected. "He sews fast."

"It's a wonderful suit. What do you call that color, Milo?"

"Mulberry. And the ascot is chartreuse."

"What have you got in the bag? It's wiggling." Rick pointed to the Burberry plaid carryall on Milo's lap.

"Oh, this is Basil," Milo said airily, lifting a Chihuahua from the bag. "This is his Indian Chief outfit, but he has one for every member of the Village People."

"Tell us about what you do, Milo."

"What I do, Rick? Oh, you mean my profession. I run an alternative lifestyles bookshop and gift emporium on Christopher Street in Greenwich Village. It's called Phallus in Wonderland. You should stop in sometime. I'll give you some almond and patchouli massage oil. I blend it myself."

"I'm sure you do," Rick said, and grinned at the audience. "Our next contestant, Jack Rafferty, is a restaurateur and entrepreneur from Miami Beach. Whaddya say, Jack? Can you tell us the name of the restaurant?"

"It's called Tito's Famous and it's in South Beach. We're known for our salsa—the music and the sauce. In fact they're selling my sauce up here in New York now." Jack glanced over at Milo. "It's *my* own recipe, too."

"So, Liz," Rick said, startling me. Since I was no longer in the hot seat, I'd started to relax and let my guard down. "Liz, if Jack brought you his salsa, could you write an ad campaign for it? Or is it one of those products no one realizes they want or need until you tell 'em?" Needless to say, I didn't like the question, nor did I appreciate being put on the spot.

"Yeah, Liz," Jack chimed in.

I could have killed him. It was like being sandbagged by a tag team. I fanned myself with my hand. "Is it hot in here or is it Tito's Famous South Beach Salsa?" I asked, attempting to muster as much confidence as possible.

Rick looked at me somewhat incredulously. "How did you know the name of his product?"

My turn to look like a deer in the headlights. *Cover for me, Jack,* I prayed.

"That's a very good line, Liz. May I use it?" Jack asked.

"It's yours, buddy." *Please, oh please, let me off the hook now.*

"Gee, I'm sorry, we'll have to pick this up another time; we've got two more contestants to meet," Rick said, responding to Geneva's hand signal to pick up the pace.

Thank you, God. And Geneva.

"Hey, there, pretty lady. Folks, meet Rosalie Rothbaum."

Rosalie beamed at the audience. "Hiiiii," she whined. "I'm from The Five Towns."

Rick looked taken aback. "But Rosalie, you're so thin. How can you be from five towns?"

"Haaanh, haaanh," Rosalie laughed nasally. "You're so funny. There are five towns that make up The Five Towns and of course you can only be from one of them, really, but we say we're from The Five Towns because . . . ya know something, I don't know why we say it. We just do."

"And what do you do, Rosalie?"

"I'm a personal shopper at Nordstrom's over in New Jersey. I help women put together ensembles—including accessories—and help guys pick out nice things for their wives or their mistresses or their secretaries."

Rick grinned and shook his head, then, somewhat relieved, came to the last contestant. "And, last, but certainly not least in the heft department . . . I'm talking about your *weight*, buddy, is Chad Wilkins.

Chad, it says here that you were an all-American
quarterback from Boston University."

"I sure was, Rick. But I got a rotator cuff injury,
which played hell with my throwing arm and pretty
much ended my career. What can I say? Now, I sell
insurance."

"Ever miss the old gridiron?"

"Every Sunday, guy."

"Well, folks," Rick said, walking across the stage.
"You've met our fourteen contestants. And quite a di-
verse group they are. We're going to take another
break and when we come back, we'll get a quick sentence or two from each of these guys and gals about
one of the worst dates they ever had . . . and then,
you, our studio audience, will decide who gets to stay
and play for another week, and which single just
didn't have it so bad after all. So keep that dial right
where it is! Back in three!"

And we were off the air for another commercial in-
terruption. My next thought terrified me. I'd suddenly
started to actually care about *Bad Date*. My adrenaline was pumping, I felt the little germs of ruthlessness
begin to invade. I have no idea what Jem or Nell or
Jack were thinking then, but sandwiched between the
McDonald's "You deserve a break today" slogan and
Nike's "Just do it," Liz Pemberley, bitten by the competitive bug, decided to go for all the marbles.

12/The First Round

"Welcome back to *Bad Date*," Rick said, "as we head into the part of the show you've all been waiting for!" Rick bounded upstage to a device that was set atop a waist-high platform, similar to the apparatus they use on lottery telecasts, where little Ping-Pong balls spin around in a giant gumball machine. "Here's how this works," he explained. "On each of the balls currently spinning inside this machine is the name of one of our contestants. I'll push this big red button and one of the balls will be spit out by the machine. I'll read the ball and whichever contestant's name is on it will come up here," he added, bounding onto a spooky-looking black platform, "into the hot seat." Rick gestured to a contraption that looked like a high-tech electric chair. It gave me the creeps. Dangling from the gray armrests were various wires attached to little metal cones. Behind the chair was a big screen that currently bore the words "Tell the Truth."

Rick explained that the contestant would be seated in "what we like to call the 'cone throne,' " where he or she would be hooked up to the electrodes that would record the veracity of his or her statements on the screen above the chair. He told the members of the studio audience that they were free to make notes on the scratch pads provided in front of their seats but that they would be unable to tabulate their votes electronically until every contestant had shared a sob story.

"So, now," he said, hopping back to the gumball machine, "let's get ready to play *Bad Date*!" He pressed the big red button and the machine ejected a ball into the well. The house band played music that was intended to add tension to the atmosphere. It worked. "The first name up is ... Luke Arrow-catcher! Step on up here, Luke."

Luke ambled to the chair and slid his fingers into the cones, as we'd each been taught to do at our final audition for the show. He laconically shared a poignant story about a girl who refused a second date with him because he was too nonverbal for her. This was followed by Rosalie Rothbaum's anecdote about the boyfriend who dumped her because she was too garrulous and kept interrupting him.

Then it was "Double-E" Du Pree's turn in the chair. "I probably never should have done this," he began, "but I wasn't much more than a youth and I'd smoked a little weed, and there was this singer in a joint I was playing and she was *fine*. So I asked her out for a cup of coffee after the show, which in those days was a kind of euphemism for something else. I was driving this old beat-up blue Chevy to the only nice place in town to get a drink, and I pulled over to the side of the road because she was getting kind of ... *amorous*. So I was thinking *better now than later*; and when she put her hand in my lap, I just kind of exploded, if you catch my drift, and she just laughed right in my face.

She kept laughing and laughing, so I told that bitch to get out my car. I didn't care where we was; she was gonna have a long walk home." The crowd rewarded him with a big round of applause. By now, I figured they were supposed to clap for everybody.

"Anella Avignon!" Rick called and practically escorted Nell to the cone throne. "You can call me Nell," she said, beaming at our host. Once hooked up to the electrodes, she made a big production number of crossing her legs. "A few years ago, I was taking an art class," she began. "Life drawing. And there was this majorly cute guy in the class who stopped me one day as we were leaving and told me he wanted to paint me in the nude."

The audience went wild. Some family entertainment, I thought. I could see that Nell, whatever she said, was going to be a crowd favorite.

"So we get to his place and I thought he was going to put the moves on me, so I got all naked and seductive and it turned out that he really did *just* want to paint my picture. It totally sucked."

Chad was up next and told a story about a blind date who turned out to have more chest hair than he did.

I could feel a wave of sympathy issue from the audience. Then I heard *my* name. *Shit, shit, shit, what am I going to say?* The walk to the cone throne felt like a journey to the gallows. Where had my confidence gone? Give them a good one, I thought, but save the bigger ammo for later in the season. We were a little less than halfway through the round. Five down, and eight to go after me. So far, the tales of woe had been pretty good. I hoped Rob Dick and his staff were pleased with how willing we were to humiliate ourselves.

"When I was in college, I had a huge crush on this gorgeous grad student who became a professional actor," I began. "And a few years after we were both out of school, I went to see him in a Broadway show and I went backstage to say 'hi' afterward. The dressing room was filled with people, including a couple of pretty famous actors and actresses who had also gone back to congratulate my friend on his performance. And in front of all those people, Geoff invited *me*, little, insignificant, unfamous me, to go out for a drink with him. So after everyone left the dressing room, he let me stay there while he showered and dressed. I was in heaven. He kissed me and we started making out on his couch. And then he suddenly jumps up and says it's time to go for that drink, and we head out of the theater and down the street, and where does he take me—but to a strip club! And from that point on, he totally ignored me and spent the whole time leering at the strippers. He didn't even look away when I told him I was going home."

I heaved a huge sigh of relief. I was past the first hurdle. Well, I wouldn't know for sure until all of us had been given our chance in the cone throne. I couldn't look at either of my roommates or even at Jack for that matter, because the camera followed me until I returned to my seat and the red button was pushed, ejecting the next contestant's ball. Rick announced the name. "Jemima Lawrence!"

Jem strode cooly up to the platform, took her time seating herself, then stuck her fingers in the cones and began her anecdote. "I went to dinner with this guy once who told me that he had to go out with me because he thought I was so beautiful. And for the whole date, he kept asking me what I was. I didn't know what he meant. What I *was*? I'm a teacher, I said. I'm a Democrat. I'm a Christian. 'Well, but what *are* you?' he kept asking. 'Are you white? Are you black? Are you an Indian?' and I couldn't figure out why it would make any difference to him if he knew what my ethnicity was. And in truth, my answer was 'all of the above,' but that wasn't good enough for him. He had to have me narrow it down to one thing, and there seemed to be a right answer as far as he was concerned, but I didn't have a clue what it was and I wasn't into playing his head games. So I walked away and left him with two plates of food and a big check in front of him."

Only Jem could silence a room like that, but the audience had been paying attention. I watched their faces as Jem spoke and they clearly thought her date had been an asshole.

Allegra was up next. "I had sex on the beach," she said in her lilting voice.

"Do you get the point of this game, Allegra?" Rick asked her. "It's called *'Bad' Date.*"

Good. She was providing some much-needed comic relief after Jem.

"I know," Allegra said. "It was with my first cousin."

"So?" Rick asked.

"Her name is Julia."

"Well, well," Rick grinned and shook his head. "Did anybody take any pictures? You know, for the family album." He ejected the next ball and read the name.

The butch-looking Diz loped up to the cone throne and talked about confessing her attraction to the guy who was her best buddy when they were in the navy together. His unedited reaction had been one of total and insulting shock because he'd assumed she was a lesbian.

Diz returned to her own seat and was replaced in the cone throne by Travis.

"I had sex on the beach, too," he said. "But it turned out that the woman was the trophy wife of some really rich financier guy who was staying at the hotel, and I ended up getting demoted to washing towels for half a year. You can't get any tips washing towels."

"I hear ya, dude," Rick commiserated. I figured the film star had never washed a towel in his life. "Next up is Jack Rafferty," Rick said, reading the ball that had just popped out of the machine.

Jack walked up the platform to the cone throne. He cut such a fine figure it was hard not to stare at him. His bearing was presidential, in the best sense of the word. Regal. Assured. He wore a pale blue shirt and a custom-tailored navy blazer that enhanced his telegenic appearance. "You said short and sweet, Rick, so here it is: a woman I once took out on a date in San Francisco tried to run me over with her car after I insisted on paying the check."

"Whoa, there. Some women's libber," Rick quipped. "Or was she off her medication? Okay, folks, we're in the homestretch now." The machine popped another ball into the well. "Milo Plum, come on up!"

Milo strolled with feline grace to the hot seat and slid his long fingers into the metal electrode cones. "I grew up in a very conservative small town, and they were ready to run anyone out on a rail if they even painted their house an unusual color. So of course I was expected to take a girl to the prom, and I invited the ugliest girl in my class because I knew none of the straight boys were going to ask her and I felt terrible that she might have to suffer the humiliation of going alone, or worse, staying home because she was too embarrassed to show up dateless. So I took this girl—Cornelia Winthrop—and she was so happy, she just blossomed on that dance floor and told me that she thought I was the best dancer in the class and how much she really liked me but she was always too afraid to approach me. Then she tried to kiss me and I didn't want to disappoint her, so I kissed her back but I realized I just couldn't keep up the charade. So I gently took her hands off me and sat her down and told her that I was gay. It was the first time I had come out to anyone, and it ended up being with this misfit girl who liked me for who I was until I burst her bubble. And she didn't know how to deal with it and I didn't either and we both burst into tears and just sat there looking at each other and crying."

I felt really bad for both of them as well. Nowhere in the *Bad Date* ground rules was it written that all our stories had to be funny. We were supposed to be pathetic losers anyway, so our studio audience and the rest of the show's viewers could feel smugly superior.

Milo returned to his seat and the machine ejected the next little white ball. Rick read it. "Candy Fortunato!"

Candy sashayed up to the chair and plugged herself in. "First I just wanna say to Liz that I hear ya about that thing with Geoff. Guys shouldn't bring their dates to a strip club unless it's consensual. Anyway . . . so here's my story. There was this guy, Tony, I had a date with."

I couldn't believe she still had her gum in her mouth.

"And he wanted to go to this restaurant which I wasn't so crazy about on account of because I thought the clams there were lousy, and I preferred to go somewhere else, like maybe Chinese instead. But my father started giving me grief about it. So me and Tony go there, and then just before dessert—I remember I ordered the tartufo and he went with the zabaglione—I had to go to the little girls' room, so I excused myself and went to take a wee, and when I got back, the back of Tony's head wasn't there no more. There he was, face down on the tablecloth like he was takin' a nap, with his brains spilling out into his zabaglione."

Candy had an interesting life; I had to give her credit. Finally, it was time for the last contestant to share his tale of woe. Millard Milhaus installed himself in the cone throne and looked earnestly into the camera. "There have been many versions of this story, but I want to set the record straight," he began. "On the night of August fourth of last year, I was driving my white Lexus down Hollywood Boulevard, when a damsel in deep distress flagged me down."

The polygraph line began to wiggle above Millard's head. It was the first time the thing had moved all evening.

"She told me her feet hurt, so I offered, in the name

of chivalry, to let her sit in my vehicle to rest her tired tootsies. I asked her, in the name of making light conversation, what she did and she told me she was an eighteen-year-old student."

The polygraph line began to zigzag.

"She asked if we could take a little drive because she needed to get some sundries at a local drugstore, so I put my car in gear and we drove off. Next thing I know, her face is in my crotch. I am a good father and a model husband—well, I *was* a model husband; I'm divorced now—and the soul of citizenry."

The screen showed the needle on the polygraph going crazy.

"At no time before her lips were on my zipper was I ever aware that this person was not a woman."

The screen looked like a giant Etch A Sketch. Millard returned to his chair. A bell rang.

Rick took center stage. "Well, folks, we've come to the end of Round One. Now, it's time to vote. Which contestant will you choose to liquidate?"

The band played some more heighten-the-tension music. The camera panned across our faces, one by one. "Who will stay . . . and who will go?" Rick asked ominously. "We'll find out when we come back!"

We went to the final commercial break. Back on the air, Rick announced that the votes had been tabulated. If there was a ranking system, we weren't privy to it. The only information divulged was the name of the person who had received the most votes. Not surprisingly, it was Millard Milhaus. He was the only one who set the polygraph-thing off. Also, because he was the last contestant to speak, he was the one who was foremost in the audience's memory. Luke

Arrowcatcher could have said practically anything, I realized. The viewers probably barely remembered it. Something had to stick out in a bad way for them to vote someone off. Lying was the most obvious example. Otherwise, in this first round, everyone but Millard had a pretty good tale of woe. I watched him leave the soundstage, waving his arms as though he'd scored a victory instead of an embarrassingly ignominious defeat.

Jem passed me in the hall on our way back to the dressing rooms. "Let's blow off the after-show party and catch a drink down the street instead," she whispered in my ear. "Meet you over at Pinky's on Fiftieth Street. It's on the south side of the block." She gave a furtive look around to see if anyone had overheard her. "I'll let Nell know, too."

We smiled at one another, as though we had jointly overcome an obstacle. Yet, it didn't feel entirely genuine. I wasn't so sure that we three were a team anymore. Something had happened in the past half hour that changed everything. And I wasn't at all sure it was for the best.

13/A Toxic Shock

I walked into Pinky Moran's with my two room-mates. None of us had said a word to one another since we'd left the television studio. Pinky's was one of those New York theater district pubs that had with-stood the Times Square area's gentrification by mass market conglomerates like Disney and Starbucks, the invasion by cutesy theme restaurants catering to sports and rock music fans, and the sea change in ac-ceptable tavern fare from steam table corned beef and cabbage to personal pan pizzas. The walls were stained from decades of tobacco smoke. Out of curi-osity I stole a peek behind a framed print of Ebbets Field just to see the difference the discoloration had made over time. Even Pinky's nonsmoking area smelled of stale smoke.

The bar had an earthiness to it, which was why Jem and I tended to like it. "Real" people went there. Teamsters; stagehands and supporting cast members of Broadway shows, actors making the Equity mini-mum; journalists, especially sports writers; and the crowd of regulars who routinely grouped themselves at the curve of the long bar near the entrance. Those were the veterans of wars and of life who habitually came in for their first beer sometime around ten A.M.

Five minutes after we were seated, I pulled a lock of hair toward my nose and noticed that it no longer smelled of the Aqua Net Ethan had used on me at the studio, but it now reeked of cigarette smoke. Jem lit up. She only smokes when she drinks outside the home—that's how she manages to control her nicotine jones. I have never seen anyone more in control than Jem. This is not a woman who throws shrill tantrums when she loses her temper; she gets real quiet instead. And she's the only person I know who didn't cry when E.T. had to go home.

Nell started to fuss about the cigarette smoke. She's convinced it darkens her hair color. Jem promised to stop after two and find out if we could then switch to a table in the no-smoking section.

Something else about Nell and Jem . . . Ordinarily, Nell is extremely tolerant. In fact, she once scolded me for complaining about Jem's smoking, saying we should support those around us who were unable to stand up and defeat their addiction. Jem had rolled her eyes at the time and snapped, "I don't have an addiction; I just like to smoke." Tonight, Nell had gotten cranky the minute Jem took her lighter from her purse. Also, Jem usually asks us first if we mind sitting in the smoking section, even though Nell and I always accede. This evening she just told the hostess we wanted a smokers' table. Clearly, I wasn't the only one who had walked off the *Bad Date* set feeling somewhat altered by the experience. The first episode seemed to have had an odd effect on my roommates as well.

"Well, what do you think, guys?" I asked them. "I guess we should be relieved to have survived the first episode. One down, twelve to go. It's time to start thinking about next week."

"I'm not sure what I'm going to say yet," Jem said, looking into the middle distance. I thought she was deliberately avoiding eye contact with me. "After all, we've got a whole week to come up with something."

"Me neither," Nell chimed in. "I mean, me, too." She could be flaky sometimes, but never evasive. She, too, stared off into space.

"Well . . . this is really fun," I sighed. "I was under the impression, Jem, that you wanted to celebrate our surviving the first round. Speaking of first rounds . . ." I flagged down our waitress and we ordered a round of draft beers.

Once the drinks came, Jem tamped out her first cigarette and waved her hands for us to all put our heads together. We leaned inward, forming a sort of huddle. "Okay, then," Jem said. "What *do* we think?"

Nell blinked. "About what?"

"The contestants, silly. Who do you think the weak links are and who do you think are the favorites? Now is the time to start handicapping."

"How can we do that?" I asked. "There's a different studio audience every week so we don't have the chance to become their sweethearts. Each episode becomes a whole new ball game." I shared my theory about the possibility of the producers rigging the show since the cameras didn't show the name of the contestant on the balls as they popped out of the giant gumball machine. "Rick Byron was wearing an ear-piece thing, so how do we know he wasn't getting names fed to him by the producers who wanted the contestants to appear in a certain order?"

Nell was certain she had the answer. "Don't you remember our interviews? Rob Dick gave us the whole spiel about honesty and truth-telling and being above-board, above suspicion. And we've got clauses in our contracts that prevent us from anything resembling collusion. I mean, we're probably not even supposed to be here talking about the show. It's like we're jurors, practically."

You've gotta love Nell. "Just because *we* had to sign something promising to remain honest doesn't mean *they're* doing so," I insisted.

"Liz, do you really think they're playing games with us?" Jem lit her second cigarette.

"Let's just say I don't believe everything I read in the papers." *Hmmm.* We seemed to still function as a trio as long as we weren't discussing our own strategies, assuming we had any.

"Okay," Jem said, thunking her glass beer stein on the table. "Who do we need to watch out for and who's toast?"

"Travis," Nell posited.

"Toast," we three said in unison.

"I mean he's majorly cute," Nell added, "but he's such a dope. I would hate to go out with him. I'd thank him for a lovely evening and he'd probably be stuck for an answer. I like 'em blond and built like the side of an Iowa barn, but they've got to have something going on upstairs."

"Chad, then," I said. "He's sort of blond and sort of built, too. Going to pot a bit around the edges, though, now that he no longer plays college ball. And while he doesn't strike me as the kind of man who can take Nell to the Whitney Museum and discuss the merits of modern painting, he can probably get her a good rate on life insurance. Of course the question is whether he's got more dates from hell than we do and are his stories very entertaining. Do we think he can make it very far?"

"Toast, probably," Jem replied. "Let's run down our impressions of all the guys first and then tackle the rest of the women."

"I like Milo," I said, looking into my beer. "He's kind of neat. And 'Double-E' DuPree is . . . well . . . he's something else."

"Then there's Jack," Nell said. "What about Jack?"

"What *about* Jack?" he asked, appearing through the haze of cigarette smoke, rocks glass in hand, collar unbuttoned, tie slightly askew. He started to pull up a chair. "Mind if I join you ladies?"

"Yes," Jem and Nell said in tandem.

I felt uncomfortable about the abruptness of their response. "That was really rude, guys," I told them. "Although it's true that Jack—who seems to be doing his best Dean Martin impression at the moment— didn't bother to say a word to us the entire time we were in the studio, even though he knew that I almost died the other night and he hadn't seen me since I got out of the hospital. So, I guess we really don't need to extend him our hospitality if we don't want to." His snubbing me this evening smarted all the more because of the intimacy we'd shared during the lobster debacle. How could he have kissed me the way he did Friday night in his hotel room and have been such an angel at Mount Sinai and then ignore my existence this evening . . . until now? "We were having a private conversation," I said rather pointedly to him.

"Girl talk," Nell said.

"So scram," Jem added.

Jack scraped the floor with his chair as he pulled it away from the table. He loped over to the bar. I saw him order another Scotch. His behavior just now had upset me. Just when I'd started to really like him and feel entirely comfortable in his presence, he'd gotten weird and pulled way back. And now he had the presumption to think he'd be welcome at our table. "Why do guys think they can do that? Just barge in on a bunch of girlfriends having a heavy discussion. We wouldn't do that to *them*."

"Jem would." Nell reached for the pack of Virginia Slims. "Can I have one?"

"You don't smoke, Nell," Jem said, pushing the box across the table.

"I know. I'm not going to put it in my mouth; I just like to hold it."

"That's what my wife always says," heckled a burly guy who had overheard us.

Nell flipped him the bird, then giggled at her own gutsiness.

Suddenly, I was no longer in the mood to rehash the episode, contestant by contestant. It was just forty-eight hours after I'd had the allergic reaction to the lobster and I wasn't yet back in fighting shape. I fished through my purse for a vial of pills that had been prescribed by Dr. Michaels. I probably shouldn't have been drinking a beer, but what the heck? I swallowed the capsule with a swig of Sam Adams. "I need to get some sleep, you guys," I told my roommates. "I got through the first episode on sheer adrenaline."

Nell and Jem looked at each other. "We're going to stay a while longer," Jem said. "I could use another round."

I got up, tossed a few bills on the table, and started to head for the door. The smoke had begun to get to me anyway. Jack reached out and touched my sleeve as I walked past the bar. "Leaving already?" he asked me.

"I'm beat."

"Mind if I walk you home?"

"Yes. And I'm taking a bus. I live two and a half miles uptown."

"Then, can I ride with you?"

"It's a free country, Jack." I left Pinky's without waiting for him. He had a drink to finish and lot of nerve to presume that I desired his company right now. Thinking about it as I walked alone to Eighth Avenue to catch the bus, I'd been angry with him ever since he'd told me that our little lobster dinner wasn't a "date." In my head, I assumed it was. And why shouldn't I have done so? He'd extended the invitation, paid for everything, carried me up to his hotel room like my White Knight . . . and then . . . there was that kiss. On my planet, all that definitely adds up to a date. I couldn't think of anything else on the bus ride home. Jem feels that no one should leave it up to men to make the rules, because they keep changing them! For example, they pursue us and as soon as we allow ourselves to be caught, they back off. I wonder if there is any other species in the animal kingdom that behaves the same way.

It was a short walk from the bus stop down Seventy-sixth Street to our apartment building. When I heard footsteps behind me, I naturally accelerated my pace. The footsteps at my back increased their speed as well; they clearly belonged to someone with much longer legs than I had. I didn't even want to take the time to look back to see who was following me. I clutched my purse to my chest and started to trot, but it made the rash on my legs start to throb a bit, so I gave up.

My pursuer caught up with me, and spun me around by my right arm. Before I realized what was happening, Jack's arms were around me, his tongue was doing amazing things to mine, and I was responding with an intensity that matched his own. My body wanted his so much that my mind forgot I was angry with him.

Suddenly, my brain switched into high gear and I stomped on his left foot with my black suede stilettos. Taken completely off guard, Jack ended up biting his own lip. He yelped in pain. "What the hell did you do that for, Liz?" He pulled away, totally stunned by my response.

"Because you're a nut. You were stalking me!" I said, out of breath, adrenaline pumping. "What did you do? Follow my bus in a taxi?" Jack nodded. "How do I always manage to attract the nuts?" I said, turning and starting to walk away.

"Liz, wait! Stop. I won't touch you. I'll stay right here, I swear."

I turned back. "Then you want to let me know what that was just about? You tell me in the hospital lobby in front of my roommates that we weren't on a 'date' on Friday evening. Then, you completely ignore me until you try to horn in on my conversation with Nell and Jem in Pinky's tonight—and now you follow me home and just grab me in the middle of the street and kiss me. What the hell is your deal?"

Jack stood there, shaking his head. "You think *you* attract all the nuts in this world? Every woman I seem to have ever been wildly attracted to turns out to be a toxic bachelorette. I thought when I met you, I'd finally broken the cycle. You seemed to be so 'together.' I guess I was mistaken."

"You're wrong on both counts, Jack." I kept my distance from him. He looked at me as though he expected me to expound, so I did. "First of all—and this should come as no surprise—I'm not nearly as 'together' as you seem to believe. Secondly, I'm not 'toxic,' and I resent that categorization."

"Well, you could have fooled me," Jack replied. "You were so much fun the other night. And those kisses weren't exactly . . . dispassionate. Then, tonight, it's like you're another person. At Pinky's—and then just now, you stomp on my foot, for chrissakes! I try to do something nice for a woman . . . maybe I should just become an asshole, because you women seem to find that more attractive!"

Was steam coming out of my ears? "Okay, Jack, drop the 'you women' thing. This is not about paleolithic archetypes. It's about you and me. I was about as vulnerable as I could possibly be the other night, all helpless and hospitalized. You were so solicitous, so caring—and then *you* turned on a dime. My reaction tonight . . . was a reaction . . . to your reaction." By now, I was as confounded as he was. "So what kind of game are we playing here? Do you actually care about me or even *like* me, or are you acting out a revenge fantasy against every woman who's ever wronged you, and you decided to place the target squarely over *my* heart?"

Jack flattened his upper lip into his lower one in an expression of grim determination. He looked at me, then looked away as I tried to hold his gaze. He exhaled deeply. "I do like you. In fact, I'm extremely intrigued by you. Your effervescence, your sense of fun, your warp-speed brain. Plus, I think you're gorgeous." He paused. "But . . ." I could see that 'but' coming a mile away. "Listen, Liz. I realized that I would be creating potential problems for us on the show if I pursued my interest in you. And since I somehow got off on the wrong foot with your roommates, I didn't think it was such a good idea to take you home from the hospital and tuck you in and sit by your side until it was time for me to catch a cab to the airport—which is, in fact, what I wanted to do then. I would have kissed you as much as you would have let me. At the studio this evening, it seemed like the right thing to do to keep my distance—because of the no-fraternization clause in our *Bad Date* contracts. And then tonight at Pinky's, the atmosphere was none too conducive to conversing either. But I wanted to tell you that I'd like to see you again—and God's honest truth, I really wanted to kiss you again. And I couldn't do that in Pinky's. I'm not into exhibitionism."

"So that's why you accepted a role on a TV reality game show. You *are* a nut case, Jack Rafferty." He looked so earnest, yet I had a hard time believing him.

"On the day of the *Bad Date* auditions I was in town to judge a yo-yo contest. So that's what I was doing in New York and when I saw the ad in the paper, I decided on a flight of fancy to see if they had any appointments left. They didn't, but once I visited their offices I refused to take 'no' for an answer and said I'd wait until they would see me." Jack took the red yo-yo from a pocket in his blazer and executed an intricate trick. " 'Man on the Flying Trapeze.' This is my lucky yo-yo; I had it with me tonight and you saw me with it the afternoon we met. Back in my misspent youth I won the Florida state championships with it four years in a row as well as two national titles. I love toys and games. It's really sad when you meet someone who looks like they never get any fun out of life— or haven't done so for decades. *You're* fun—when you're not jabbing a spiked heel through my metatarsal. Your fun-ness is one of my favorite things about you so far." He did another spectacular trick. "That one's called 'Double or Nothing.' I wanted to appear on a reality TV show for two reasons. First, because game shows are my trashy passion. I won the *Jeopardy* college tournament when I was a senior at Florida State, and I still watch the show whenever I get the chance. It helps me unwind from a busy day. That's how I knew the Oreo question, remember? I'm a *Match Game* fiend, too." Jack put the yo-yo back in his pocket.

I wasn't sure what to make of him and he'd

probably regard *me* as a nut job if I confessed that I'd been carrying his business card around like a lucky charm—the equivalent of his yo-yo. "So, what's your second reason for airing your romantic dirty linen on live television?"

He smiled and ran a hand through his hair. His eyes glinted. "Free publicity. Every on-air mention of Tito's Famous South Beach Salsa is worth a suitcase full of advertising dollars."

"As an adwoman, I could view that as taking the bread out of an agency's mouth."

"Or you could view it as smart marketing." He grinned at me. "Want to hear my bonus round reason?"

"Bring it on."

"I'm only half-kidding when I tell you that I had this wacky notion that if I met a great lady through the show who's had really bad luck with men, then we'd be a perfect match for each other."

I laughed. "Perfect!"

Jack laughed, too, and shook his head.

"Look, I'm not a toxic bachelorette, Jack. Quite the opposite, in fact. But my two best friends are convinced that you're attracted to me because you want something. And I've known Jem and Nell for so long that experience has taught me not to dismiss their theories out of hand . . . despite evidence to the contrary. You seem to win at every game you play or any competition you enter; so already I feel like a wishbone—with you and my attraction for you tugging at one arm—and Nell and Jem on the other. And I don't know whether to follow my instincts or my libido."

Jack took my hands in his. "Your roommates are right about me, Liz, I *do* want something."

I broke our connection and pulled my hands away.

He tried to grasp them again, but I shoved them in my pockets.

"Did it ever occur to you that the 'something' I want is to get to know you better? I'm just trying to figure out how to do that without busting our *Bad Date* contract. If we'd all gone to the after-show party in the Green Room, we could have chatted and pretended that we were just getting to know one another in a fellow cast member kind of way. It was sheer coincidence that I ran into you tonight; I was planning to hang out in the Green Room but I wanted a good Scotch, so one of the stagehands sent me over to Pinky's. The fact that you and Jem and Nell share an apartment was a fact that existed before the Urban Lifestyles Channel came up with the concept for this show. No one at the station can reproach roommates for sharing a beer outside the studio after the telecast, although I think the three of you might want to consider whether Mr. and Mrs. America know that you're roommates or whether Rob Dick and company are keeping it under wraps, since it's technically in violation of their own contract."

He shook his head in frustration. "However once I saw you in Pinky's, I took the chance on 'fraternizing' with you. I was happy and high on the fact that we'd hurdled the first episode. But the main reason I couldn't talk to you in the bar was because you and your friends shooed me away from your table. I took the risk that I'd be seen chatting with you all because I want to get to know you better, Liz. And after two

Scotches, I cared a lot less about what the producers might say, if they even had cause to."

"So when we sent you packing and you went to the bar . . . ?"

"That was my third Macallan you probably saw me order."

My two roommates came skipping tipsily down the street toward us, their purses swinging from their shoulders. Considering we'd just been discussing their opinions of Jack and my conflicted emotions about all of this, he and I quickly dropped hands. It was the better part of discretion.

"With the thoughts I'd be thinkin', I could be another Lincoln, if I only had a brain." Their voices were unmistakable. We girls always sing stuff from *The Wizard of Oz*, especially when we've had a lot to drink. "Liz, don't you think you should be getting upstairs? After all, you said you still weren't feeling well," Jem said, shooting a glare at Jack.

"Excuse us, please." Nell wrinkled her nose at Jack and slipped her arm through mine.

Jem took hold of my other arm. "I'm afraid that prescription Dr. Michaels gave you clouds your judgment, Liz."

Nell feigned sympathy. "He told us that might be a side effect."

"See? Wishbone," I said regretfully to Jack, then turned to Nell and Jem. I was really annoyed with their behavior, but short of breaking out of their arm-lock and causing a scene in the middle of the street, I didn't know what to do. "You two are full of . . ." I began to say. I looked back at Jack standing on the sidewalk as my girlfriends steered me into our lobby. His expression was grim. It certainly felt like he and my roommates had started a tug of war for me. And it was already driving me crazy.

14/By the Numbers

"Welcome back to our little celebrity!" Jason Seraphim chirped as he thrust a split of champagne into my hands. I'd just walked in the door, ten minutes late, and was greeted with a round of applause. "Happy Monday!" F.X. said, shaking my hand. "I hope you haven't grown too big for your britches."

I laughed. "I made it through one episode, guys. It's probably a bit too early for bubbly." I looked at the bottle in my hand.

"It's a new client," Jason said. "A Long Island sparkling wine. We'll talk about that later." He pulled me over to my desk and backed me up so I was sitting on the desk top. "I want all the dirt. What's Travis Peters like in person?"

"As thick as a dictionary. On the air, anyway. I didn't have an actual one-on-one conversation with him, so for all I know he may be an Einstein once you get to know him. I would have thought Milo would have been more your type."

Jason looked me straight in the eye. "Oh, puh-lease, Liz."

Demetrius came into my office and seated himself

at my desk, putting his size fourteen Converse Hi Tops on my blotter. "So, what is dis Travis like?"

I could not understand the mania for Travis. "He's practically nonverbal and he's probably not much older than twenty-one. He's a boy!"

Jason looked at Demetrius. "Exactly!"

I shook my head. "The guy's only got one helix in his DNA. What would you two creative, educated, intelligent guys have to say to a man like that?"

My colleagues regarded one another and dissolved into peals of laughter, leaving me out of their loop. "Fuck me!" Demetrius said.

F.X., having overheard the conversation, entered my room. "I always come in during the best parts," he said grinning. "Speaking of . . . *you* know . . . I wonder if Candy Fortunato charges by the hour."

"She's not a hooker, she's a stripper," I said. "An ex-stripper, actually. And you've got a wife and kid, so what do you care? Unless you want to buy your wife an erotic outfit to play dress-up in from Candy's 'Snap Out of It' line. She showed me her catalogue while we were in the dressing room."

Francis Xavier Avanti's eyes seemed to bulge out from behind his thick eyeglass lenses. "You share a dressing room? Can I come visit?"

I ignored his question. "And she's got a Web site, too, so you can buy her fashion designs online. She models them herself."

F.X. turned on his heels and wheeled out of my office. "I'll be back!" he announced. I'm sure he scooted back to his office to fire up the Internet. Browsing Candy's domain should keep him occupied for most of the day, I figured. People had the strangest taste.

In the "strange taste" department, today's lunch was really weird. Gwen served a carpaccio, which is raw something, but I'm not even sure what, with a brown sauce that tasted slightly fermented. When I asked her what we were eating, she told me that it was raw beef sliced very thin with a sauce, in my honor, made from—guess what—bad dates! She assured me that we weren't being poisoned from what I was afraid was rotten fruit.

When Jason and F.X. popped 'round to my office after lunch and asked "What have you got for us?" I had no idea what they were talking about. F.X. reminded me that my Numbers Crunchers ideas were due. After the Snatch debacle, I didn't think it was the best idea in the world to admit that I had totally forgotten about the snack food assignment. The box of crispy treats had been staring me in the face for the past few days, but after the first hour or two on my desk, it had begun to blend into the general chaos of my office. "Give me a couple of hours," I told F.X. and Jason, closing the door behind them. I remembered our conversation about the client's demographic—everybody, basically—so I sat down and scribbled some notes. Lucky for me, Demetrius hadn't yet smoked his two P.M. spliff, so he was still on planet Earth and thus managed to whip out some terrific artwork. By three-thirty, I'd almost convinced myself we'd been working on the project for the past week. If our presentation to the bosses went over well, I was ready to take the Rastaman up on his offer to share the joint. Maybe I should have indulged beforehand; I would have been considerably mellower. I buzzed Jason and F.X. over the intercom and they came down to my office.

"Okay," I began after they had installed themselves on my white leather couch. "You said the client wants to position the product just about everywhere. We've got a poster for gyms and fitness centers." I motioned to Demetrius to show them the mock-up, wherein a terrifically fit young woman in workout clothes is delicately aiming one of the crunchies toward her mouth; the poster reads "Counting calories has never been easier with Numbers Crunchers."

My poster for ball parks and sports arenas where a teen at a baseball game was keeping a box score by using the crunchies, read "Know the score with Numbers Crunchers." The ad targeted to kids showed a couple of happy first-graders in a school lunchroom, wearing the crunchies on their fingertips. The copy said "You don't *have* to count on your fingers with Numbers Crunchers . . . but it's fun to, anyway!" The tag line on each ad read "Numbers Crunchers: There's no accounting for taste."

"I like it!" Jason exclaimed. "Nice work, Liz. Demetrius, I love the art. Great stuff."

"It shows what you can do when you apply yourself," F.X. added. "This is the old Liz we know and love. We don't know what you did with the Snatch Liz, but please don't bring her back."

Jason and F.X. were pleased enough to take the campaign to the client without sending me back to the yellow legal pad and Demetrius back to the drawing board. "Thanks, pal, I owe you one," I told Demetrius.

"Dat's okay, Liz. You can fix me up with dat Travis guy on your show."

"I think he's too dumb for you. Besides, given the anecdote he related on the show last night, he's straight. Bi at the most."

"I'll settle for dat restaurant guy den. What's his name again?"

"Jack Rafferty, and he definitely doesn't play on your team, trust me. Are you sure you don't want me to put in a good word for you with Milo?"

"Oh, no. Too pooffy."

"Just thought I'd give it another shot." I fired up an Alanis Morrissette CD, kicked my shoes off, and lay down on my leather couch, shoving a throw pillow behind my head. I checked my watch. "Okay, a twenty-minute, much-needed, self-congratulatory meditation period, then it's back to work."

Demetrius went around to my desk and sat in my chair like a CEO. "I hope you don't mind, mahn," he said, lighting up his ganja spliff right there in my office. He offered it to me, after taking an enormous toke.

"No, thanks," I said. "I'll take my illegal thrills vicariously." I closed my eyes and inhaled deeply of his secondhand smoke. The weed had a funny effect on me. I kept visualizing my own music video version of Barry Manilow's "Copacabana," with Candy Fortunato as Lola and a pencil-mustachioed Jack Rafferty as the greasy Rico-who-wore-a-diamond, with jars of Tito's Famous South Beach Salsa floating, gravity-free, through the air.

When my private line rang, I jumped, startled out of my semistoned daydream. "You want me to answer it, mahn?" Demetrius asked lazily. He took another drag off his massive reefer.

"Sure, why not."

He indolently picked up the phone and answered it, trying not to let the potent smoke drift out of his mouth. "Liz Pemberley's line. I hope you know her if you have dis number." He listened intently for a few moments. I was not in the mood to get up off the couch. The whole world would be a better place—at least America would be—if we all still had nap times after lunch, followed of course by milk and cookies, preferably Double-Stuff Oreos. "You looked very good last night, mahn," I heard Demetrius say into the phone. "Was dat Armani a custom job or you buy off de rack?" He was quiet for a few more seconds, but he nodded his head as though whoever was on the other end of the line could see him. "Oh yeah, Liz is a very special person, mahn. Yes, very talented. Dey don't make dem better." I love listening to Demetrius's island lilt, but I was dead curious by now to find out who the heck he was talking to. I motioned to him to ask who was on the phone. My art director waved his hand at me to indicate that he would share such intelligence in a minute . . . or when he got around to it, whichever came later, knowing Demetrius.

"Okay, I put her on de phone, now. Yeah, it was great talking to you, mahn. You take care, now." Demetrius held the receiver in the air, still very much at home in my desk chair. This necessitated my rising from the couch and walking over to the desk to take the phone from his hand.

"Hello," I said, pleasantly mellow.

"Hey, Liz? This is Rick Byron here."

"Yeah, right." It didn't really sink in.

"I'm not kidding. Why wouldn't you think it was me?"

"Because major movie stars don't often call me on my private line at work. Okay, who's this? Is this Jack? If you're playing a practical joke on me, you caught me in an uncharacteristically good mood for a Monday afternoon."

"Who's Jack? Liz, it really is Rick. How can I convince you?"

I thought for a moment. "What was the name of your private acting coach for *What's Your Sign?*" There was a silence on the other end of the phone. "Gotcha! Whoever you are."

"I didn't have an acting coach."

"Then you're not Rick Byron," I replied smoothly.

"Wait—how do you know about that?"

"Your acting coach is a friend of a friend. What's the person's name, Rick? I'll give you a hint. You won't find it on the movie credits."

There was another silence. "Promise not to tell anyone?"

"Rick, I'm one of the God-knows-how-many-people-in-New-York who know that you took some private lessons to get you through that movie. It's an open secret."

"Okay. Her name is Kathryn Lamb. But she calls herself Kitty. My manager read in the *Times* a few weeks ago that she got engaged to the guy who was running that matchmaking service. That's how we—I mean they—met."

"Okay, you're Rick Byron," I said, realizing that I had a smug smile on my face. "And now that your identity has been properly verified, why on earth are you calling me?"

His voice grew muffled. "I'm calling from a pay phone," he said. "So it's harder to trace."

"Are you currently doing research for your next movie, Rick? An unnecessary remake of *The Goodbye Girl*, or an espionage thriller, perhaps?"

"See, this is what I like about you," he said. I could hear the coin drop in the machine in response to the recording requesting an additional deposit. "You're fast, fast on the draw. I need you to do me a *very* big favor. I'll pay you whatever you want; my ass is in a sling over this."

I was certainly intrigued. Why a movie star would call me from a pay phone was a puzzlement.

"Look, I'm right near your office. If you look outside your window, you'll see a Starbucks on the . . . where am I? . . . northeast corner of—"

"I know where you are, Rick." I went to the window.

"Can you see me? Shit!"

"I see a handsome young man with blond highlights dressed all in black, standing at a pay phone looking agitated. Is that you?"

"You can see my highlights from up there? Shit. They were supposed to look natural."

"I'm teasing you, Rick. I know you have highlights. We were on set together last night, remember? I was two feet from your face."

"They were still supposed to be subtle." I heard the pout in his voice. "Look, can you get away for a half hour or so? I need to talk to you about something really important."

The recorded voice of the operator cut in, demanding more money. I heard the clink of another coin. I covered the receiver with my hand and looked at my watch. "Do you think I'll be missed if I pop outside for a bit?" I asked Demetrius.

The art director's eyes were closed. He seemed to be meditating. "I'll cover for you, mahn," he said hazily, not opening his eyes.

I removed my hand from the receiver. My heart was thumping. I had no idea what Rick had in mind, but I wasn't going to miss my chance to find out. "Rick? I'll be downstairs within ten minutes."

"There's a table way in the back, as the coffee shop curves. Not the side near the restrooms. The other end of the store. I'll be there with a copy of *USA Today*."

"I'll be the one in the trenchcoat and fedora, wearing a red carnation in my lapel."

"Huh?"

"I'll meet you there, Rick. Be down in a few." I hung up the phone.

"So, is he gonna make you a big star?" Demetrius asked.

I shook my head. "I have no idea what he's up to, but he's making it sound highly dramatic."

"He's an actor, mahn. Dat's what dey do."

"Hold the fort, Demetrius. He said this would only take a half hour or so." For some reason, I felt like a kid at six A.M. on Christmas morning, knowing there's a really big present under the tree with my name on it, but that I have to wait until my parents are awake before I can open it. I grabbed my purse and tried to look discreet and nonchalant as I left the office, masking my intense curiosity about what Hollywood's Reigning Hunk wanted so desperately from me.

15/Rick's Pitch

Rick Byron was as incognito as any movie star gets, slouched in the curve of the wooden banquette, wearing aviator Ray•Bans and a Cape Fear Crocs baseball cap. He motioned to me to join him. "Want one?" he asked solicitously, pointing to his cup.

"I don't know yet. What is it?"

"Chai tea latte."

I shrugged. Rick took a couple of crumpled up bills from the front pocket of his black jeans and handed them to me. "Go get whatever you want. Ordinarily, I'd be a gentleman and go to the counter for you, but I don't want to run the risk of being noticed."

"I don't think it poses too much of a threat in that get-up." The visor of the minor league cap obscured his face well enough and the Ray•Bans took care of the rest. I complimented Rick on the coolness of his hat.

"Yeah, Harleys are my high-priced hobby, but I also like to collect minor league caps." He started counting on his fingers. "I've got the Asheville Tourists, the Lansing Lugnuts, the Mudville Nine, the New Britain Rock Cats, the Piedmont Boll Weevils, the Queens Kings—I guess that's a better name than the

Kings Queens—and probably the most famous because of the movie, a Durham Bulls cap."

I laughed. "Pretty impressive. Well, no matter what cap you were wearing, if you keep those Ray•Bans on, the counter girl would probably only know it was you if you went up there bare-assed." I was referring to a tattoo of Goofy on his butt that all of America and any nation in the studio's distribution package saw on glorious display in Rick's campy pseudo-horror flick *I Know What You Did with the Baby-sitter Last Summer*.

Rick grinned. If Con Edison were to harness the wattage in his smile, there would never be another blackout in Washington Heights. "I don't have a tattoo in real life. That was makeup. It looked pretty good though, didn't it?"

I nodded.

"If you don't believe me, Liz, you could ask your friend's friend. Kitty, the acting coach. She would know."

I knew that Kitty knew that too, but was shocked that he was letting that information slip. I took Rick's money and came back to our table a few minutes later with a mocha frappuccino. "So, Rick," I said, seating myself across the table from him, the better to shield his hard muscular superstar's body from the teeming female masses who might want a piece of it. "What's with all the hush-hush stuff?"

He took another sip of tea and lowered his Ray•Bans. His eyes were a bit bloodshot.

"Party hard after the show last night?" I asked.

He shook his head. "I'm allergic to my new cat." Rick leaned forward on his elbows. Our heads nearly met; our bodies formed a triangle over the tabletop. "What did you think of me last night? Be honest."

I wasn't sure I understood the question or where he was going with it. "Think of *you*?"

"Yeah. Was I funny? Did you think I was sexy?"

"Why are you asking me this, Rick?"

"Okay, then. One question at a time. Did you think I was sexy?"

"Any female over the age of ten and probably more than half the *men* in the world think that."

"But did you think I was sexy *last night*?" he insisted. "Be straight with me."

I took a deep breath and went out on a limb. "Yes, I think you're sexy, in general. Last night? I guess with the banter they wrote for you, you ... well ... you didn't come off particularly sexy, no."

I thought he'd be devastated, but he smiled ever so slightly. "Then how *did* you think I came off?"

"Brutal honesty?"

He nodded his head emphatically.

"I think you came off like a politically incorrect smarmy little dweeb. Personally, I wouldn't mind you being un-p.c., but the smarmy little dweeb part began to wear thin very quickly."

Rick's smile lit up the dark recesses of Starbucks. "Aha! I was right! Liz, can I tell you something? I hated every line they gave me to say. I felt like a total moron up there, except when I was talking to that Diz woman about her Harleys. Hey, you two could have a talk show. 'The Liz and Diz hour.' So this is what I want you to do for me. A major league favor. You're an advertising copywriter, right?"

I nodded, taking a sip of my iced coffee.

"I mean, you made up the 'site bytes' stuff." He removed his Ray•Bans, placed his palms on the table, and sat up straight, his gaze level with mine. "I want you to write some copy for me to say on the air. And instead of doing the crap the writers give me, I'll say your lines and make them look like ad-libs."

I couldn't believe what I was hearing. "Rick, you have to say the lines you're given. You can't bring in a new writer."

"I can do anything I want. If I walk off this show, it goes down the toilet. I don't mean to burst your bubble here, but people aren't tuning in to see you-all up there. It's me they're turning on the tube for."

"At the moment, anyway," I countered. "The stakes are still low and the nation hasn't had the chance to get to know us—and therefore truly despise us—yet. Why don't you just take your clout to Rob Dick and the writers and demand better material? Don't you see it's a conflict of interest for me to be writing dialogue for you and be a contestant on the show?"

Rick leaned in to me, dropping his voice to a whisper. "To answer your first question, I have a bit of a reputation for being kind of a bad boy. I was once referred to by a director as the only straight diva he'd ever worked with. My manager keeps reminding me that I've got to stop ruffling so many feathers or I'll end up in straight-to-video releases for the rest of my natural life. So I need to get my way by finding a back door, so to speak. You're that back door, Liz. C'mon . . . I'd make it worth your while."

I matched his pitch and prayed he wasn't wearing a wire and this wasn't all some sort of elaborate entrapment scheme set in motion by producer Rob Dick. "Then pay me a million dollars, Rick."

"You know I can't do *that*."

"That's the grand prize, though. All the marbles. That's the reason I agreed to do *Bad Date*. Why should I settle for less?"

"Because you'll probably get voted off the show long before you get to the million dollars, so what I'm offering you is considerably more than what you'll most likely end up with."

Although he hadn't put a dollar figure on the table, the offer was indeed a tempting one; but from what I'd heard about Rick's dealings with Kitty Lamb, his modus operandi was to get an attractive woman to help him look good professionally and then deny her the opportunity to derive any recognition for it. Now he was pulling the same stuff with me that he'd done with Kitty. If history was a good teacher, I wouldn't even be able to take my ghosting credit to the job bank, and it would be a gamble that I could leave my job at SSA, hitch my star to Rick's wagon, and thereby make enough money to start up my own agency. In any event, the deal amounted to a clear conflict of interest, whether or not I got credit down the line for ghostwriting Rick's banter. As I sipped my frappuccino I pondered the pros and cons of the scheme. I felt something graze my ankle and suddenly realized Rick was playing footsie with me. I looked over at him, completely surprised, and before I knew it, Rick had reached over the table and was kissing me. His hand traveled from my hair to my throat and down to my right breast. Because my body was essentially blocking his from view, unless someone was looking very carefully, they would not have been entirely sure what he was up to.

Is it really bad form to say that Rick's kiss was definitely not bad at all, but Jack Rafferty's were a lot better? And what is this current mania that seems to have struck New York men in the past twenty-four hours where they seem to feel the need to grab me and kiss me? Where have they all been? I broke away from the kiss.

"I *said* I would make it worth your while to write for me," Rick said, seating himself again.

"You must be pretty desperate then," I responded, "to offer me sexual favors. Or else you think I must be pretty desperate to accept them. Or your offer."

I continued to evaluate both sides of the issue. Who would turn down Hollywood's Reigning Hunk? Even my own mother would think I was crazy. But I wasn't ready to give up on *Bad Date* right away. I'd only gotten safely through a single episode. Jem thought Jack tried to deliberately poison me to prevent me from appearing on the show. Now, the very famous and very handsome host was asking me to compromise my integrity, to do something that would no doubt count as several violations of my contract with the show. Did these men know something I didn't?

To some people, the choice before me would have been a no-brainer: let the gorgeous movie star do whatever he wants to with your body while you pretend to be appalled, then take the pile of money he's offering you to ghostwrite for him.

I polished off my coffee. "I can't do it, Rick," I told him. "For . . . a number of reasons, it doesn't feel right. But I think you should sit down with Rob Dick and the writers and tell them that you don't feel comfortable with the material. Don't go in there and act petulant or throw a tantrum, but make some suggestions. If you want, tell them you've been polling people informally and they felt the banter you did last night didn't take advantage of your greatest attributes—the attributes that made you a huge star and the reason they signed you to host the show in the first place. Play the charm card." We rose from the table. "I've got to get back upstairs."

Rick caught me by the arm before I could get too far from the table. "You're not going to tell anyone about this, are you?"

I looked him straight in the eye. "Don't be silly. This stays between us. But take my advice and see what happens." Rick leaned over and gave me a gentle kiss on the cheek. "See you Sunday evening," I told him.

We parted company just outside Starbucks. I jaywalked across the street, while Rick headed uptown. It was hard to readjust to the pace of the office, and the combination of the waning buzz off of Demetrius's pot smoke and the recent caffeine blast wasn't helping. For the rest of the day, I pondered Rick's proposal and wondered if I had done the right thing after all.

16/Jem's Quest

After the third week of the show, it was becoming clear that we women had a much rougher time out on the dating circuit than the guys did. The audience bid goodbye to overgrown frat boy Chad Wilkins after the second episode. His dismay that a knockout date he'd taken to a New England Patriots playoff had spent the entire second half of the football game doing a crossword puzzle was a tale that failed to elicit much sympathy from the house.

The dumpee on the third episode was golden boy Travis Peters, the surfer dude with a million-dollar physique and a ten-cent brain. No one felt bad when he said he'd been promised a date with one of the *Baywatch* girls and was disappointed when a different one showed up for dinner.

This left all of the women, plus Milo, Double-E, Luke, and Jack as the remaining contestants. Candy seemed to have a never-ending supply of colorful stories. There was the date who ended up dead in the Meadowlands, the date who ended up dead off Coney Island, and the one she confided to me in our dressing room would be her Week Four story, the saga of the date who ended up doing the dead-man's float in the

Potomac on Candy's high school senior class trip to Washington, D.C.

Rick's on-show banter did in fact improve after the second episode. In the span of two weeks, he'd gone from obnoxious lout to charming, puppyish rogue. The image was certainly preferable and the show's ratings began to pick up speed. Each week Rob Dick gave the remaining contestants a pep talk in the hair and makeup room before each telecast. Some people didn't seem to care if they were caught doing anything that might be construed as "fraternizing." Rosalie Rothbaum, who I learned had never dated a Jewish guy in her life, kept turning on the brights for the laconic Luke Arrowcatcher, who seemed rather overwhelmed by her nonstop chatter.

Jack phoned me a couple of times between shows. At first, he claimed to be calling just to say hello. Then he asked me out. Then he went back to calling just to say hi. Nell and Jem remained adamant in their unwillingness to believe him or his motives. Their collective radar was usually infallible, so as much as I sort of did want to see Jack socially, if not romantically, I found myself trusting their judgment instead. From time to time, though—usually when I was sitting at my desk after digesting one of Gwen's weird lunches—praying for creativity to strike, I would take Jack's business card from my wallet and sort of stare at it, running my fingers along the embossed lettering of his name.

As for Jem, Nell, and I, we had started to adopt a cool cordiality toward one another, each of us playing our cards closer to our chests. At first, we'd been willing to confide in each other about which of our

old nightmares we were considering trotting out week
by week. Now, if one of us dared ask another which
humiliating experience she planned to share in the up-
coming episode, we were greeted with an abstract
"I don't know." Here we were, three of the closest
friends in the world and the possibility of winning a
million dollars was already altering our customarily
jovial interaction. The dinners I fixed for us were eaten
in near-stony silence. Nell got spacier. Jem clammed
up more than usual. She continued to concoct amazing
cocktails for us after work, which still made me horny
with nothing to do about it but privately fret that the
most (and best) action I had seen lately came from an
irresistible but possibly toxic bachelor who would
make his amorous interest in me quite clear and then
pull way back and claim he was just into some nebu-
lous getting-to-know-one-another-better b.s. I felt like
his damn red yo-yo.

"At least you've *had* bad dates," Jem said, with a
slightly jealous edge to her voice, as I was fretting to
them about the outcome of my dating experiences
being as predictable as summer reruns. This evening,
she had done something with Malibu rum, pineapple
juice, and a secret ingredient that was making me con-
template sultry nights in an airy Moorish-style villa
overlooking a blue-black sea. But this time, besides
the usual sensual cravings Jem's cocktails inspired in
me, I felt a sense of loss, of emptiness, of an aching
longing to be held. It was no fun standing on the ter-
razzo patio of my fantasy villa alone.

Jem lay down on the living room floor with a raw
silk toss pillow under her head. "I'm stuck, ladies. I've
spent my days focusing on getting degree after degree

and then teaching people whom I'm too old and too smart to go out with." She started doing slow leg lifts because Jem is incapable of just doing nothing. "I've spent my nights grading papers of the people I'm too old and too smart to go out with. The dating experiences I've had have not been fulfilling, but they lack the panache to be spectacularly disastrous in prime-time terms." She lowered her legs and inhaled. "Basically," she said, exhaling very slowly, "I've run out of things to say on the show."

This was quite an admission, given Jem's recent reticence about sharing anything.

Nell, inspired by Jem's dedication to a workout, began to do the yogic Sun Worship. "I could give you one of *my* dates from hell," she offered generously.

"I've got more than enough to go around, too, but you can't do that," I responded, deciding now was as good a time as any to flip through Nell's Victoria's Secret catalogues. I rationalized my slothfulness because there wasn't enough room in the living room for all three of us to exercise at once. I wondered if the slimfit London Jeans would make me look fat; they looked big in the ass. "Nell, you're supposed to tell the truth. Those little electrode things would register automatically as soon as Jem started telling your story."

Nell rolled up, vertebra by vertebra, and reached for the ceiling. "I bet there's a way to fool them. There has to be. If anyone can do it, it's Jem. She's got more self-control than anyone else I know."

"It's my blessing and my curse," Jem answered.

"I admire the hell out of it, Jem."

"Well, Nell, thanks for the compliment, but maybe I should have let go at least a little, lived a little more in the moment, taken spontaneous chances instead of planning everything out so methodically. But it's not the way I'm built. I'm so afraid to make mistakes."

I dog-eared the London Jeans page as a "maybe" along with a page of really cool sandals. "And yet, for all of us who can't seem to *stop* making them, for those of us who seem doomed to repeat the same mistakes until we've perfected them into an art form, *Bad Date* is our ironic reward. Where else can you get the chance to win a million dollars and a trip to Paris for being a doormat loser?"

"I thought my cocktails made you horny, not self-pitying, Liz." Jem finished her exercises and sat up. "I'm going to have to do what I always do."

"Which is . . . ?" Nell asked.

"Be proactive."

"That's such a ridiculous word," I said. " 'Proactive' is a redundancy invented by, well, probably by communications professors. It's Orwellian market-speak."

Jem rolled her head from side to side, stretching her neck. "Nevertheless. I am going to get myself a bad date, so I have something to talk about on the show. I've got about one more good story left in me, and then I'll probably end up getting booted from the show unless I come up with some more."

"What do you plan to do?" I questioned.

"Carl Foster."

"Who?" Nell asked.

"The Warlock."

Nell looked shocked. "No way!"

I laughed. "I never knew he had a name. In all the years I've known you, Jem, I've only heard you call him 'The Warlock.' No, wait . . . you once referred to him after a 4-C Christmas party as 'The Groper.' I thought you can't stand him."

Jem grinned. "Exactly. Though, for the record, he never groped *me*. And I think he'd had about seventeen cups of eggnog at the time."

"And you're planning to use this guy so you can chew him up and spit him out on live television and make money from it. At least another thousand dollars for surviving one more episode. It's kind of an underhanded plot, Miss Straight Arrow."

"Teachers are woefully underpaid, Liz," Jem said, still smiling like the Cheshire Cat. "I admit that I felt a little guilty right after I came up with the idea. And I'm not entirely sanguine about it now. But let's look at it this way: It's a win-win situation. The Warlock finally gets a 'Yes, I'll go out with you' from me after all these years of icky persistence on his part, and I'll have a dreadful date to talk about on the air."

"I think you should tell him you're using him," Nell said thoughtfully. "I mean, it's just not right if he's got these great expectations and you drag him along with you on the humiliation trolley."

"Woman, you're insane," Jem said.

Nell continued to protest. "He may be really icky as you say, but that's still no reason to—"

"Use him like one of my electromagnetic dust-rags?" I interrupted.

I've mentioned Jem's intractability before. Nell couldn't dissuade her. I didn't even try. Jem decided that she would remain the prey and allow The Warlock to continue to be the aggressor. That way he would feel a tremendous sense of victory when she finally, as she had it all choreographed in her mind, sighed and fretted and oh-so-reluctantly agreed—'But just this once, Carl'—to accompany him somewhere. This was the only item she was leaving to chance, banking on The Warlock's clocklike pursuit. According to her, he asked her out on a date a minimum of twice a week. This had been going on for upward of the seven years they'd been colleagues at 4-C. Her excuse had most often been something she never practiced when creating her magical cocktails: never mix, never worry, meaning that a department professor should not date that department's chair.

"Tell me, Jem," I asked her, "what is it about The Warlock that specifically repulses you?"

"Everything."

"I said *specifically*."

"*Everything*. Where I'm cool and controlled, he's persistent and passionate. Give me Tahari and Calvin Klein. The Warlock dresses like a straight version of Hamish Bowles, sort of fussy and neo-Edwardian, like he's a refugee from a road company of *Jekyll & Hyde*. Give me any exhibit at the Whitney; he visits the Cloisters practically every Sunday. Not that I'm high-tech; I hate that. But I do like clean, uncomplicated lines. And then there's the religious question. I'm a lapsed Episcopalian; he's a reaffirmed Pagan."

"His wardrobe sounds a bit eccentric, but none of what you listed sounds 'repulsive' to me, Jem. And I notice you've said zip about his personality," Nell said, sitting on the living room rug in a lotus position. "Is he kind? Funny? Compassionate? Is he the kind of guy who's afraid to kill spiders because he believes it brings bad luck?"

"*Kills* 'em? He keeps them as pets! The man owns a tarantula. Now there's a way to my heart. 'Hey, Jem, wanna come on up to my place to look at my hairy tarantula?' " Jem smacked her lips and went off to the kitchen to fix herself a margarita.

"She's said zip about his looks, too," I whispered to Nell. "Have you ever seen him?"

Nell shook her head. "Nope. But from stuff Jem has said I think *he's* a human melting pot, too. All sorts of mixed races and ethnicities and religions. I think the reason he became a Pagan is because everyone in his family is from a different culture and religion and they were all trying to get him to be what they were, so he rejected them all and became a neo-Celt or something. My guess is that he's probably pretty good-looking, but Jem has never said word one about it."

"I wonder if he's been seeking to convert her all these years."

"I don't know," Nell said. "Do Pagans proselytize?"

Jem returned to the living room with a tray of margaritas. "The more I've been thinking about this, the more I see it working out—I mean *not* working out—with me and The Warlock." She handed each of us a glass, smiling with beatific serenity. "It's a match made in the bowels of hell," she added, smiling. "It'll be absolutely perfect."

17/Charmed, I'm Sure

Wearing a black glittery sweater I'd knitted for her birthday last year (her "lucky sweater," she called it), Jem did make it safely through the fourth episode, during which Diz ran out of steam and rode her Harley into the sunset after the audience voted her off the show. I think Rick Byron was sad to see her go. She was the only contestant he related to on anything more than a superficial level. Rob Dick and the writers still wanted him to flirt outrageously with the pretty female contestants and Diz didn't fit the profile, which gave Rick a little leeway in his banter with her.

Episode four was where I told the whole story about this guy I went out with briefly when I was a college sophomore. This was the incident I alluded to in my initial audition for *Bad Date*. Essentially, it was a summer fling and he flung me over for my baby sister, whom he then ditched for his old steady girlfriend who had dumped him for asking me out in the first place. Of course I never knew he had a steady until his friends started asking him, in front of me, what ever happened to Beverly. "Beverly who?" I would ask, and he would shrug it off and say, "Oh, she was just some girl I knew." Oh, how many women are out there who are being referred to by men they've given their hearts to as "just some girl"?

As we "attritted" week by week, there was more time on the show for getting to know each remaining contestant better. Jack really did appear to be a magnet for toxic bachelorettes the way I seem to attract all the screaming babies and the people who fall asleep and drool on your shoulder during long cross-country flights. His episode four dating debacle revolved around an experience he'd had a few years ago when he was dating a realtor named Delilah who smashed the windows of his apartment with a baseball bat because he needed to take a business trip and was unable to bring her along. Maybe I'm naïve, but I had no idea that women could be so looney.

Jem was growing increasingly anxious because The Warlock, true to form and expectations, had asked her out—except they couldn't coordinate their schedules because Carl had department meetings after work, plus his coven's bowling league was in the finals at the Port Authority lanes and he had a 275 average and his team needed him. Jem taught Wednesday evening classes and also had to go visit her grandmother who was being placed in a nursing home somewhere out in New Jersey. Additionally, she didn't want to appear too eager after seven years of putting The Warlock off. That surely would have set off some bells and whistles.

Their date was finally scheduled for the Thursday before the fifth episode of *Bad Date*. Needless to say, it had to be an unqualified disaster for Jem to be assured of advancing any further on the show, unless, of course, another contestant's sob story that night would turn out to be even lamer than what Jem intended to share.

I had been cheering on her proposed dating failure, but not too hard. Although the whole idea had been a lark while we girls were auditioning for *Bad Date*, we hadn't been in the game for the fun of it since the first episode. Every week as we got closer to the jackpot it became more real. We were now a third of the way through the season. The brass ring was far away, but at least it was within sight. "Keep your eyes on the prize and strategize" was one of Rob Dick's mantras as well as his mandate to the contestants, which was how Jem rationalized her selection of The Warlock as a surefire disaster date. And I was curious as hell to see how she would manage to pull it off. So I decided to trail her and find out.

Jem told Nell and me that The Warlock had booked an eight P.M. dinner reservation at a restaurant named Pywacket, in the East Village. I laughed when I heard the name and was greeted with a blank expression from Jem; unlike me, Jem is not an old movie buff. I explained that Pywacket is the name of the cat that is the witch's "familiar" in the Kim Novak classic *Bell, Book and Candle*.

I stationed myself across the street from the entrance to 4-C and waited for the two of them to emerge. The Warlock kept trying to take Jem's hand. She kept moving away from him. I followed along at a discreet distance as they headed southeast, always staying across the street from them. My disguise took some getting used to. So did my long blonde wig. I'd thought about wearing a hooded sweatshirt and cargo pants, along with impossibly high, clunky black platforms that wouldn't be out of place in a *Franken-stein* remake, but realized that once I got to Pywacket I'd be underdressed. So I opted for a leather mini and boots, with a black leather carcoat and a crushed velvet slouchy hat that, even with the wig, was way too big for my head.

Boy, those two could hoof it. And my boots weren't made for walking. Jem and The Warlock strolled all the way to the East Side, chatting incessantly—and Jem is not an ebullient type—then meandered down-town, past Pywacket, a few blocks south into the heart of the East Village, where NYU theater students still dressed up like Morticia Addams; scads of young Asian women with bleached blonde or dyed red hair scoured the trendy boutiques; and chic wine bars and coffeehouses had sprouted amid the dope peddlers and winos. This is not Jem's kind of territory. I noticed The Warlock pointing out things of interest, stopping to talk with one or two people he seemed to know, and to whom he introduced Jem.

At Ninth Street and First Avenue, The Warlock steered them around a corner to the west, halting in front of a boutique. This was going to be risky; the stop wasn't on their itinerary. The Warlock held the door open for Jem. A set of windchimes crafted from silvery pentacles tinkled a welcome. After counting to fifteen, I followed them up the steps to Enchantments, a witchcraft paraphernalia boutique.

I felt like I often do on museum trips when I latch on to the middle of a guided tour and eavesdrop on the docent's lecture. The Warlock was giving Jem a run-down on the various kinds of candles, books, amulets, smudging wands, and other tricks and treats of the trade. I liked the way the store smelled . . . the faint aroma of wax blended with various essential oils I couldn't identify. While I kept one eye on Jem and the Warlock, I busied myself by playing with various vials of scent, rubbing them into the pulse points on my wrists, as though I were considering a custom blend.

The Warlock approached a counter at the back of the store, where a pale brunette was smoothing oil over a thick green cylindrical candle. Then she rubbed it in multicolored glitter. Jem asked The Warlock what the glitter was for.

"Evening, Raven," The Warlock said to the candle lady. "My friend here wants to know what the glitter's for." He turned to Jem. "The green is the money candle. Raven will carve certain totems into the candle and you burn it for seven days and pray over it for financial rewards."

Raven didn't look up from her work. "The glitter just makes it pretty," she told Jem. "It's the totems that are the key."

Jem looked fascinated. I can't remember when I've ever seen her so entranced by something, especially a world she's been openly mocking for years. The Warlock noticed her expression and asked her if she wanted a candle. He gestured to a colorful array on a shelf to their left. "Each one carries a significance. Pink for love, red for passion, and so on."

"Green for money," Jem smiled.

The Warlock selected a grass-green candle and checked it for nicks and scratches before handing it to Raven, who had just completed the other customer's money candle. "That's $14.95," she said. "Pay up front at the register. Did you notice we have the new

Pre-Raphaelite Tarot cards in? You can ask Melora to show them to you. They're right behind the counter next to the Harry Potter decks."

Raven explained how the money candle worked. Jem told her that she wanted to win the million-dollar jackpot on *Bad Date*. To maximize the effect of the spell, she asked for Jem's astrological sign, which she would carve into the candle, along with *Bad Date*'s logo.

"I never knew you were a Capricorn," The Warlock said.

"It's not on my résumé," Jem replied tartly. Then she softened. "And someone told me I have a Pisces moon, so what does that mean?"

"It means that you're a dreamer at heart." The Warlock selected a red candle and handed it to Raven who was busy turning Jem's money candle into a work of colorful sculpture. "Raven, carve Capricorn and Scorpio into this one for me, when you're done."

The shop was small enough for me to hear their conversation while I remained near the front of the store, now checking out the silver charms in the display case. Swiveling stand-alone racks partially obscured me from their view. In order to kill more time, I asked to look at the Pre-Raphaelite Tarot deck. Even though I have absolutely no idea how to read the cards, they were so pretty that I shelled out the fifteen dollars for the pack. I could always shellac them and make a découpage hatbox to give to Nell.

I realized that when Jem and the Warlock made their way to Melora the cashier with their candles, it would be nearly impossible for them not to notice me. I left the shop and stood by the curb, where I could continue to observe them. I pushed back my hat and removed a set of binoculars from the lined mesh-style purse I'd bought a day or two earlier on the street. I didn't want to carry a handbag that would be all-too-familiar to Jem in case she looked in my direction.

I peered through the binoculars. Melora was showing Jem some of the jewelry in the front case. I had admired it myself. The shop had just gotten them in—terrific amber pieces and ancient scarabs purportedly dating from the days of Cleopatra. I saw Jem's face light up when Melora showed her one of the scarabs. Jem is a huge fan of all things Cleopatra. I could see that my roommate, a woman who ordinarily wears very simple and elegant modern gold jewelry, was suckered. She drew her wallet from her purse, but The Warlock stopped her, and placing his hand on hers, guided it back into her handbag. He removed a Gold Card from his billfold and handed it to Melora, who wrapped their candles in clouds of purple tissue paper and placed them in separate shopping bags. The Warlock asked Jem a question that I obviously couldn't hear. Then Jem smiled at him—actually smiled—and he gently brought the charm around her neck and fastened the clasp. I shoved the binoculars back in my purse and had crossed to the opposite side of the street before they finished descending the steps from the store to the pavement.

I followed a safe distance behind Jem as she and The Warlock headed uptown to Pywacket. Jem looked like she had forgotten she wasn't supposed to be having fun. Then something strange happened. Jem stopped suddenly, grabbed the wrought-iron fence railing outside a brownstone and sat on the grubby stoop. She removed her right shoe and rubbed her foot. I heard her telling The Warlock that she'd gotten a sudden cramp and didn't think she could make it to the restaurant. Was she testing him, I wondered. If she bailed on him now, she wouldn't exactly have a tale of woe to share on *Bad Date* this Sunday. What could she say? That after seven years, she finally agreed to go out with this guy who took her to an eccentric little witchcraft shop and bought her jewelry? I think not.

The Warlock knelt on the sidewalk and started to check out Jem's aching instep. What a communications department chair at a community college knew about orthopedics was anyone's guess; the guy probably had a foot fetish. At any rate, he certainly was solicitous. He wiggled her foot around, ascertained that she hadn't broken anything—if I know Jem, she'd realized the date was going too well and had to do something about it—and he somehow managed to convince her to put her shoe back on and get into a taxi with him. Give Round One to The Warlock.

I couldn't wait to see what was going to happen next. I hailed the next passing hack and said something I've been longing to utter for over thirty years. "Follow that cab!" I commanded my driver.

Whew! Thank God The Warlock had convinced Jem to go to Pywacket after all. The hostess escorted me to a table from which I could have just the view I needed. I handed her a crisp twenty-dollar bill. Then I messed up the opposite side of my deuce so it would look like I wasn't dining alone.

The restaurant was very romantic and so dark that

I could barely see the menu, let alone Jem and The Warlock. It was illuminated entirely by candlelight. Votives dotted the cozy tables; tapers dripped from medieval circular iron chandeliers that would have been right at home in Errol Flynn's *Robin Hood*. The menu items bore Gothic-sounding names like bare breasts (grilled boneless chicken) with blood orange sauce and a sinfully rich flourless chocolate cake they called Nevermore.

Jem, obviously sensing that this dinner might go too well, complained that the cozy corner table was too dark to see either her menu or her meal. She flagged down the hostess and made an embarrassing scene, hoping, I suppose, that The Warlock would be mortified that his date had suddenly morphed into a latter day Joan Crawford. However, the hostess apologetically told Jem that there was no other table they could move to, so my line of vision luckily remained intact. I've mentioned before that when Jem gets really angry, she gets quiet. Therefore, these histrionics had to be an act. But The Warlock, unlike his white shirt, was unruffled. He got up from his seat and stood behind her chair with a votive candle, aiming it right at her menu so she could see every item clearly.

I smiled. Jem had just lost Round Two. There was nothing The Warlock, who seemed to have the very soul and manners of a perfect gentleman, had done so far to ruin the evening. So Jem had to do it for him. When their bottle of red wine came to the table, Jem managed to knock over The Warlock's goblet, so that the wine spilled all over his white shirt and brown velvet frock coat. While she pretended to be solicitous of both his feelings and his haberdashery—even to the point of telling him that she wouldn't be at all shocked if he didn't want to walk out on their dinner then and there—I heard The Warlock tell her that his jacket was Scotchgarded and he had a half dozen similar shirts in his closet. He ordered them in bulk, he said, laughing.

Round Three to The Warlock as well.

With the possible exception of Jem, no one was more surprised than I at how well this was going. Jem's plan was that dinner with The Warlock was going to be hell on earth, but I've never seen her as happy and as animated as she'd been for the past couple of hours. She practically glowed from within. In all the time I've known Jem, she's never been able to connect romantically with anyone and her chemistry with The Warlock was, well, magical. I refused to let her sabotage this chance for happiness. So I called over our waiter and asked him to deliver a bottle of Jem's favorite champagne to her table. When it arrived, she was nonplused. I heard her ask The Warlock how he could possibly have known how much she loved Bollinger.

The Warlock watched Jem melt and just smiled cryptically at her, which gave her the impression that he really cared. The truth, of course, was that he was entirely clueless as to how that bottle of Bollinger got to his table. He probably figured his red candle was working already and he hadn't even lit it yet.

I'd instructed the staff to add the bottle to my tab, and unfortunately, the waiter whispered something to The Warlock and pointed in my direction. When I saw what was happening, I rose and made a beeline for the ladies' room. If Jem and her date saw anything, they caught a miniskirted blonde heading to the opposite side of the restaurant. When I tried to return to my seat, I saw that Jem had angled her chair so that she would have a good view of my table. Knowing her as well as I do, she wasn't about to rest until she learned why the waiter had gestured toward my table. Where's a potted plant when you need one? I stationed myself behind a pillar, and peered through the darkness of the restaurant like a film noir detective, but I began to feel just a tad obvious. I didn't want the evening to turn into something out of a *Pink Panther* movie instead. So I sought out the waiter and told him I was going over to the bar and asked him to bring my tab over there, where I could more easily blend with the other minglers.

I paid my bill, left Pywacket, and stationed myself outside the restaurant. God knows what I must have looked like to passersby with the binoculars pressed to my eyes, as I tried to scope out Jem and The Warlock through the glare of plate glass and the duskiness of the ambiance inside. After about half a minute—and when I saw the rare beat cop heading down the street—I decided it was time to move along.

On the way home, I wondered how the rest of the evening would transpire for the two of them. I hadn't been able to hear what they'd been discussing all through dinner, but I can say that they certainly never ran out of topics. From my vantage point behind the Pywacket pillar, it seemed to me that after a slice of the Nevermore cake and white chocolate–dipped strawberries to complement the champagne, not only was the dinner a great success for Cupid, The

Warlock, and Liz Pemberley, but I would be shocked if it didn't lead to a second date. It just goes to show you that if you give someone half a chance, hellish expectations might turn out to be downright heavenly.

18/Blonde Attack

By the time Jem got home, I was sitting on the couch making another stab at last Sunday's *New York Times Magazine* crossword puzzle, with half an eye on the video Nell was glued to. She'd finally bought her own copy of *Notting Hill*, after renting it so many times our local Blockbuster started asking her if she wanted "the usual" every time she set foot inside the store.

"Nell, do you spell gecko with a *ck* or with two *k*s?" I asked her.

"I don't spell 'gecko' at all," she answered. "Words with icky scales, pebbled skin, or more than four legs aren't in my vocabulary. Shhhhhh, we're getting to the good part. Where she says she's just a girl asking a boy to love her." She wrapped herself more tightly in the granny square afghan, as though it were an embrace. "I'm loving this blanket by the way, Liz. I know I told you this when you gave it to me, but I think it's one of the best Christmas presents I ever got. I mean you made it all my favorite colors and everything. Even my sorority colors are in here. It's so much more thoughtful than something store-bought."

"I'm glad you're still so happy with it. It's always

such a roll of the dice when you make something for someone with your own hands. I mean, what if you work really hard to surprise them with something you think they'll find truly special . . . and they end up hating it?"

Nell wiggled her fingers through the gaps in the granny squares. "No one could hate anything you did, Liz."

I have a terrible feeling that might not be entirely true.

The apartment door slammed shut, rattling the framed prints that hung on the foyer walls. "Nell, you better dip into your trust fund and buy yourself a damn good explanation!"

Nell turned around to look at Jem. "It was only $9.95," she said, gesturing to the videotape box. "If you rent it three times, it already costs more than that."

"I'm not talking about the fucking video and you know it, Nell. You're one of the smartest women I know, so don't pretend to have a 'blonde attack' on me now." Jem marched through the living room, stopped the VCR, ejected the tape, and flung it at Nell's feet. "Why the hell did you do it?"

Nell clutched her precious videotape to her chest. "I honestly have no idea what you're talking about. I'm not kidding. I don't."

Jem paced the room like a caged panther. "Okay. If you want to derive the satisfaction of hearing the whole damn sordid thing from my own lips, I'll make you happy."

"What happened at dinner?" Nell asked ingenuously.

"You know what happened, Nell. If anyone knows, it's *you*!"

"Then what *did* happen?" I asked. "Didn't the date go poorly?"

Jem lit a cigarette. She knows we decided that the entire apartment was a smoke-free zone. Nell was afraid to say anything about it. I didn't want to say anything until I heard Jem's version of the story.

"Where's an effing ashtray in this dump?" Jem demanded.

I opened a drawer in our breakfront and extracted one for her, a pretty porcelain square. I'd liberated it from Claridges hotel some years ago on a trip to London.

Her video removed, Nell devoted her entire focus to Jem. "So was The Warlock as creepy as you expected him to be?"

"His name is Carl," Jem snapped at her. "And he's an absolutely fucking terrific guy."

I pretended this was news. "What?"

"I couldn't shake him," Jem told us. "I tried to pull a diva number and he didn't let me get away with it. He was just so nice about everything. He didn't lose his temper, didn't patronize me . . . and he didn't act like a doormat either. It was like he was waiting patiently, maturely, for me to run out of steam. I hate him," she wailed, stubbing out her cigarette in the ashtray.

Nell looked puzzled. "I'm missing something here. I thought you *knew* you were going to hate him. And that was supposed to be the best thing about it; it was why you picked him in the first place. So your date would suck."

"Exactly," Jem said, dissolving into tears. "But he didn't suck. He's sweet and fascinating and generous. The date was wonderful and we're going out again next week! No thanks to you, Nell."

I closed the magazine and let it rest on my lap. "What does Nell have to do with The Warlock—I mean Carl—being a nice guy?"

Jem leveled an accusing finger at Nell. "Ask her. She knows. She was *there*. She sent a bottle of Bolly over to our table."

Nell looked stunned. "Wait a New York minute, Jem. You think I spied on your dinner date? I've been here watching *Notting Hill* for hours!"

"She's seen it straight through twice already, trust me," I offered, trying to be helpful with Nell's alibi— well, the truth, actually. I wanted to clear Nell's good name, but I wasn't ready to confess my culpability until I'd figured out how to deal with Jem's inevitable attendant wrath.

"Hold on, Liz," Nell said, looking at me. "You weren't home until I was a quarter of the way through my second screening." She and Jem looked at each other. Then they looked at me.

"What?"

"Where were you this evening?" Jem leveled her gaze at me.

"I had to work late."

"Something doesn't add up," Nell said.

I felt my stomach churning. "Couldn't it have been a coincidence that Carl ordered your favorite champagne, of how ever many sparkling wines there were on the menu?"

"Carl didn't order the champagne. It just showed

up, and the waiter whispered something to him and pointed to someone behind me. By the time I could turn around in my chair, all I saw was Nell walking toward the ladies' room."

"Or someone who looked like Nell," I added. "You mean blonde and beautiful?"

"And leggy. Only Nell wears skirts so short a hooker mistakes them for tube tops."

"Jem, that's so unfair!" Nell protested. "My leather mini is a Dolce & Gabbana."

I have to admit it had looked really good on me, too. I had no idea my waistline was as small as Nell's was. And we all do borrow one another's garments from time to time; we just tend to ask first. I asked Jem about her plans for the next episode of *Bad Date*.

She went over and opened the living room window to release some of the cigarette smoke from the room. "What do you think?" Her tone was surly. "Unless someone gets bounced for lying, it looks like a sure thing that I'm going to be the next person off the show. Congratulations, ladies, you're both one step closer to a million dollars. Do me a favor and re- member me in your wills!"

Jem left the living room and removed a thick volume from her shoulderbag. "I finally finished the Katharine Graham bio," she said to me, "so you can have it back. What an amazing career she had." Jem headed off to my bedroom to deposit the book and, before I could stop her, she'd opened the door and en- tered the room.

"What the f—?" she said, staring, stunned, at a long blonde dynel tendril hanging from my underwear drawer. I had no place to stash the wig so I'd stuffed it in my drawer. My bedroom is near the front of the apartment so I didn't need to pass the living room to get there. Nevertheless, in my haste to get undressed undetected by Nell, I'd just sort of shoved away the elements of my disguise as quickly as I could. I managed to return Nell's D&G mini by sneaking past her with the leather skirt hidden under my bathrobe as I claimed to be heading to take a shower.

"Wait, Jem!" I cried, putting out my arm to try to stop her from opening the drawer. I wanted to say, "There's a good explanation for everything."

"You evil little witch," Jem said to me, quietly, evenly. "Some fucking friend. I'll just take this, if I may," she continued, even more quietly, removing the wig from my bureau drawer.

She left my bedroom without saying another word, just slunk out, feline, in control.

I sat on my bed and cried. A couple of minutes later, there was a knock on the door. Nell, still draped in the granny square afghan, pushed it open. She'd been crying, too. She looked at me with the saddest little tearstained face. I've seen her cry before, but this was the first time I'd noticed how bloodshot her blue eyes had become. "Why me, Liz?" she asked in a small voice. "Did I ever do anything to deliberately hurt you? And if I did, whatever it was, I'm really sorry." She slid the crocheted blanket from her shoulders and balled it up in front of her. "Here," she said, trying to throw it at me. It landed in an oddly shaped heap on the floor. "Take it back. I don't want it anymore."

For a moment we just looked at each other, huge, silent tears rolling down both our faces. I reached out my arm to her but she shrank back, still holding my gaze. After another few moments, she turned and left my room. I wrapped myself in the afghan and sat staring at the door. "Nell, wait!" I called to her.

I found her in the living room sobbing in front of *Notting Hill*. "I'm sorry, I didn't mean to hurt you. Or Jem either." I extended my hand to her. "Come with me. I want to talk to Jem."

I knocked gently on the door to Jem's bedroom.

"What?" came the muffled response. "You're not coming in."

"Then I'll stand out here. Jem, *I* sent over the Bolly. In fact I followed you from the time you and Carl left 4-C until just after you got the champagne. I did it— trailed you—because I was dead curious to see what this guy you've been deriding for the past seven-plus years was like in the flesh. And not only was he great-looking, with the manners of an angel and the patience of a saint, considering you tried to ruin the date every step of the way . . . but you were having so much fun it was breaking my heart that you were trying so hard to manipulate the evening into a disaster."

"It was none of your damn business, Liz."

"I know . . . but I saw how happy you looked this evening. Jem, you *laughed*! And you don't even laugh at the Marx Brothers."

"I hate choosing sides, Jem," Nell added urgently. "But I think we should consider forgiving Liz. She might have acted like a dodo bird, but at the time she thought she was doing a good deed."

I heard Jem sort of growl through the door. "What you decide to do is up to you, Nell. Now leave me alone."

Nell and I exchanged a glance, then a hug. I'd come clean, confessed, and at least Nell had understood and absolved me. But Jem? I had no idea where things now stood between us. All I could do was wait anxiously for the other shoe to drop.

19/The Roach Motel

For the first time in ages, I had actually been looking forward to coming into work. It got me out of the house and away from Jem who didn't teach morning classes, although I admit I spent the day having a mild anxiety attack wondering what she might be up to.

The dynamic duo, Jason and F.X., knocked on my door sometime around eleven and told me they had good news for me. At least they hoped it was good news. They were sending me to Miami for a couple of days to meet with the Numbers Crunchers clients.

"Why isn't F.X. going?" I was puzzled. Ordinarily, it's the account execs who interface with the clients; they don't send copywriters on road trips, especially when hotel accommodations and per diems come into play.

"His wife's family is in town from Madison . . . or someplace with an *M* in it," Jason said, responding for his corporate partner. "And she's throwing a hissy fit because every time her parents come in to the city, F.X. pulls a disappearing act."

"Liz, the client loved the stuff you worked up, but

he wants to make just a few changes. And at this point it makes sense to have you down there to work with him and his team, rather than postpone the meeting. You're the one who has to do the rewrites, anyway."

I wondered why the other account exec in the office wasn't anxious to go. After all, from what I'd heard of the demographic of the South Beach area lately, it was Jason's kind of town. So what the hell was Jack Rafferty doing living there?

Oh, shit. Jack Rafferty lives there. And yet he was the one person I most wanted to see. Maybe, away from my home turf and the tension caused by my roommates and the television show, we might have a chance to explore what was going on between us.

"Numbers Crunchers is F.X.'s account, not mine," Jason said simply. "And we've just landed a new account that I pulled the short straw on, so I've got to meet with the client on that one."

"It's a newly minted show for the Food Network," F.X. said. "Spiritual Chinese Cooking. Set to run on Sunday mornings. The show is called *Wok with Mee.* Don't give me that look, Liz. I don't make these things up."

So, I was being packed off to Miami. Land of sun, sand, and spring break. Land of prunes, plaid polyester golf pants, and early bird specials. Land of Tito's Famous South Beach restaurant . . . and Jack Rafferty. The meeting with the Numbers Crunchers folks was set for Friday morning. I was supposed to catch a flight back to New York that evening. Then there was the fifth episode of *Bad Date* to hurdle on Sunday.

Actually, it felt pretty good to have an opportunity

to get out of Dodge after the debacle of Jem's good-bad date. And I was getting an extra day and a half in the bargain that I could use to sightsee, or just veg out on a wicker chaise by a green-blue swimming pool and sip umbrella drinks with silly names in improbable colors.

F.X. handed me a thick envelope. I opened it and found my round-trip airline ticket, rental car voucher, and the hotel confirmation for the trendy new Palmetto hotel in South Beach. Attached to the Palmetto reservation was a splashy article from *Architectural Digest*, citing the hostelry as one of America's top ten newly renovated hotels, offering any number of quirky perks. For the life of me I couldn't imagine why anyone would want to name a four-star hotel for a cockroach the size of a Honda Civic.

"Look," Jason said, pointing to a paragraph of the article, "you can tell them ahead of time what your fantasies and pleasures are and they try to accommodate you—within reason, of course. Their motto is 'Just so long as no one gets hurt.' "

"In that case they can take the bugs out of my room," I said.

"Oh, come on, Liz, it'll be fun. To be honest with you, I really do wish I were the one who was going on this field trip. I hate my in-laws. They must be the only people from Wisconsin who consider Cheez Whiz a delicacy."

"Well then, F.X., if I get my fantasy treatment, tell them to float lavender rose petals in my bath water every day. Have a masseuse on call for me twenty-four hours—"

"Oh, that's so tame," Jason said.

"Yeah," I quipped. "You'd want a twenty-four-hour well-oiled cabana boy."

"And on that note, I think it's time we all got back to work," F.X. said. "After the client meeting, give us a call with a postmortem."

All during my flight to Miami the following day, I thought about Jack Rafferty. Did I want to initiate contact with him? Something drew me to him, yet managed to put me on edge at the same time. He was gorgeous, funny, fun to be with, but I couldn't yet figure out whether his romantic interest in me was genuine. One thing was for sure, I still didn't totally trust him . . . like when he told me he *did* want something and the something was simply to get to know me better. Although I couldn't forget his words, for the most part he just seemed too nice to be on the level.

Maybe I should track him down, I thought to myself. In the guise of saying hey, I'm in town on business for a couple of days and I sure would love a local tour guide. Whaddya say, Jack? Then I could scope him out a bit. If Jem and Nell were correct in surmising that he befriended me for a reason, my best guess was that it had something to do with our competing against one another on the show. Yet that kind of underhanded behavior flew in the face of the personality of the man I'd come to like so much. The Jack Rafferty who'd stuck it out in the Mount Sinai ER with me was not a manipulative guy. I was eager for an opportunity to cozy up to him and hopefully prove that my roommates' opinions had been all wrong.

* * *

The Palmetto was one of those newly renovated art deco hotels on Collins Avenue. It had been a long time since I'd been down to Miami. In the South Beach area anyway, the gay scene was indeed very much in evidence. I regretted SSA's not having sent Demetrius down here, too. A few doors from the hotel, I spotted an old-style Jewish deli called Ess SoBe and laughed. Yiddish flavor, modernized. I pulled into the semi-circular driveway and a valet materialized, wearing a white polo shirt with a golden bug insignia—a palmetto—over the left breast. I showed him my hotel room confirmation, he handed me a ticket, and after a similarly attired bellhop unloaded my luggage from the trunk, he disappeared with my rental car into an underground garage.

Imagine a science fiction/horror movie with a Midas touch. Everything in the otherwise all-white lobby was adorned with gold palmettos, from the design woven into the carpet runner on the marble lobby floor to—*ugh*—the service bell at the front desk. The *Architectural Digest* article Jason and F.X. had given me didn't begin to capture the ambiance. I guess they didn't want to freak out the tourists. Since there was no one around to help me check in, I tapped the bug-shaped golden bell. Its wings flew out and the bell emitted a noise that summoned the concierge. I nearly jumped out of my skin.

My bedroom, white on white on white, with over-stuffed sofa and armchairs and a fluffy white down-filled comforter on the king-sized four-poster bed, was accented with palmettos. They were everywhere, from the finials on the four-poster to the finials on the curtain rods, to—and this really grossed me out—the handles on all the water faucets in the bathroom. Even the house stationery and note pads were embossed with a golden flying cockroach. What I wouldn't have done for a can of Raid. I could predict having nightmares in this room. Who the hell did they think their target customers were? Entomologists?

I found a local phone book in one of the desk drawers and looked up Jack Rafferty. No listing. Then I checked for Tito's Famous under the business listings and found the restaurant. I couldn't figure out where it was in relation to the Palmetto and I didn't feel like getting back in the car and looking for it. It was probably a better idea to call the restaurant first anyway, rather than pop by on the chance that Jack was on the premises. I had no idea what his hours were.

I rang the number and was immediately put on hold. After what seemed like forever, a woman with a pleasant Latina lilt to her voice apologized for keeping me waiting. I asked her if Jack was there and told the woman I was a friend of his from New York who was in town for a couple of days. "Tell him it's Liz," I said. The woman apologized again for needing to put me on hold. About a half minute later, Jack picked up the phone.

"Hey there."

"Hey there yourself, Jack."

"So what brings you to our fair city? Weather to your liking?"

"A bit too hot, if you really want my opinion on the subject. Down here you may call it 'sultry,' but we Yankees just call it 'muggy.' "

"Well, let's see what we can do to cool you off. Had dinner yet?"

"Jack, it's three-thirty in the afternoon."

"Sorry, I've completely lost track of time. Things are crazy here today. The sous-chef called in sick, my hostess never returned from her lunch break, and the Easter baskets I ordered for my staff were just delivered a mere week and a half late. Have you got plans for dinner, then?"

"Not a thing."

"Tell you what. I'll swing by, pick you up around seven o'clock. Does that sound like a plan?"

"Sounds terrific. Are you clairvoyant?"

"Not the last time I checked. Why?"

"How can you pick me up if you don't know where I am?" I told him where I was staying, describing the bug motif in detail, including the mosquito netting–style draperies hanging from the four-poster that gave the bed a casbah fantasy sort of appearance. "I suppose it's to keep all the palmetto representations in the room from disturbing one's slumber. I have to get out of here, Jack; I'm beginning to itch. See you in the lobby at seven."

I hung up the phone and changed into my bathing suit, immediately thinking it was a mistake not to have brought my "slimsuit," having opted instead for the first two-piece I'd worn in decades. It exposed parts of my body I didn't even remember. I grabbed the complimentary bathrobe with its golden palmetto insignia embroidered over the left breastal area and checked the informational looseleaf (with a gold bug in relief on the book cover) for directions to the pool. I really hoped the swimming pool didn't resemble what I feared it might.

It did.

Hadn't these people heard of overkill?

I did a couple of laps in the belly of the bug, pausing momentarily to chuckle at the giant butterfly nets at the end of long, telescopic poles, poles that are usually used for scooping bugs and other detritus from pools. I had visions of a giant bug wielding the pole and scooping up all the humans from the pool in an extra-large net.

I toweled myself dry and summoned one of the roving staffers to ask about their drinks menu. I was swiftly handed a laminated card listing the usual "umbrella" cocktails: piña coladas, planters' punch, hurricanes, mai-tais, and the specialty of the house—a Jem-like concoction combining Cuervo Gold, Coco Lopez, pineapple juice, and Galliano, that yellow liqueur they use to make Harvey Wallbangers—called, what else? A Palmetto. *When in Rome,* I thought, and ordered one.

Two-thirds of the way through the second Palmetto, I was feeling no pain.

When the sun finally dipped past the horizon, I headed back up to my room to shower and dress. The creepy bug faucets didn't bother me as much now that I was comfortably anesthetized. I had no idea how women dressed for dinner in South Beach so I went with something I knew I looked good in, a princess-seamed silk dress in tiny turquoise gingham checks with spaghetti straps that had the habit of slipping off my shoulders. Bare legs. My only pair of Manolos, bought years ago on final sale.

At precisely seven P.M., I headed down to the lobby. Jack was waiting for me, looking damn fine. His white shirt set off his light tan, giving him a healthy glow. We embraced casually, his lips brushing mine in a friendly, unromantic kiss.

He pulled back to get a better look at me. "You look fantastic, Liz. That's a great color for you." He put his arm on my shoulder and steered us toward the front door.

"So, are you taking me to Tito's Famous?"

Jack gave me a "you must be mad" look and shook his head. "Nuh-uh. I don't mix business and pleasure. Besides, I've told you I'm not proud of our kitchen."

"I take it you and Tito aren't seeing eye-to-eye lately."

Jack sighed. "It's been that way for a while now. Call me madcap, but it just seems to me—speaking as a businessman as well as a chef—that the *food* should be a restaurant's main attraction." His look didn't invite further comment from me.

I couldn't believe the car that appeared a few minutes later, a deep midnight blue convertible with a right-hand drive. "Is this yours?" I asked, totally blown away. "It's gorgeous—and I'm no car connoisseur. What is it?"

"A 1964 Aston Martin." Jack pulled out of the driveway. "Lovingly restored and maintained by yours truly. I figured if I wanted to drive around in something like this, I'd better get to know it intimately. Try finding a good mechanic for a forty-year-old classic. Now, where shall we go for dinner? How about one of Miami's most celebrated restaurants for something you can't get in New York. C'mon, it's not fancy, but I'll take you to Joe's Stone Crab House."

"You must be joking." I looked over at him. "Jack? Do the two words *anaphylactic shock* mean anything to you?"

"Oh, shit, I'm sorry. You must think I'm a total idiot."

"Not totally," I teased. " Just nefarious." DEATH BY SHELLFISH, I could just see the *New York Post* head-line proclaim, with an article that began: "Gotham copywriter Liz Pemberley was found dead in the posh Palmetto hotel Wednesday night after dining with one of her competitors on television's hottest new reality show, *Bad Date*. Miami restaurateur Jack Rafferty, who once tried unsuccessfully to knock Pemberley out of the running for the million-dollar jackpot by cooking her a lobster dinner, finally succeeded in his mission by force-feeding her a local Miami delicacy, stone crabs."

"Tell you what," Jack said, interrupting my day-dream. "We'll go where there's nothing potentially lethal on the menu, trust me."

I wondered aloud how he expected to just walk in someplace without a reservation. Silly me. Because of Tito's, every major restaurateur in the city knew him; he could get a table at the last minute at whatever es-tablishment he chose. "Best Italian in the city," Jack said. "Gennaro's in Coconut Grove."

We toasted my visit with a delicious Prosecco and Jack recommended a homemade ravioli stuffed with porcini mushrooms and pignoli nuts. It was a particular favorite of his, as the dish was made without cheese. Jack was convinced that parmesan cheese was a plague visited on Italian cuisine that disguised the mundane and blighted the extraordinary. In between bites of the lightest pillows of pasta I had ever tasted, I summoned the courage to suss out Jack's strategy regarding *Bad Date*. "You really want to go for all the marbles, don't you?" I asked.

He smiled enigmatically. "It's quite a commitment to make—commuting to New York and back every week for a quarter of a year. It's not exactly as though the Urban Lifestyles Channel is paying for it." Jack took another sip of his sparkling wine and poured a second glass for me.

I took a sip, lowered my glass, and looked across the table at him, searching for something in his eyes. Humor, malice, something that could give me a clue as to how hard he was playing the game. His expression gave me nothing. He was probably a terrific poker player. "Would you do whatever it takes to win?"

Jack wiped the corner of his mouth with the edge of his white linen napkin. "You like old movies, Liz?"

I grinned. "Love 'em."

Jack smiled back. "Well, there's another thing we have in common. You know how you find yourself in situations sometimes where you think 'This is *just* like a scene in . . . ?' "

"You bet," I nodded.

"Well, Liz, in one of my favorite noir movies, *Out of the Past,* it turns out that neither the hero nor the heroine are playing by the most ethical rules in the book. There's a scene in a Mexican casino where

Kathy is betting wildly and losing money hand over fist, and Jeff turns to her and says, 'That's no way to win.' And Kathy says, '*Is* there a way to win?' and Jeff tells her, 'There's a way to lose more slowly.' " Jack raised his glass at me. "I told you that night of the first episode what I wanted to get out of being on the show. From where I'm sitting, a million dollars and a trip to Paris aren't the only prizes. Think about it," he said.

I did. But was Jack referring to me or to the little *ka-ching* sound he heard in his head every time he and Rick Byron bantered on the air about Tito's Famous South Beach Salsa?

Jack proposed a moonlit stroll after dinner. I figured walking off the pasta, and the tiramisu I'd eaten for dessert, was a good idea. We were driving toward the beach, past the Port of Miami, when I made a remark about all the cruise ships with their twinkling lights strung stem to stern like so many stars. The ships looked to me like giant skyscrapers lying on their sides. Jack said they reminded him of elliptical beehives, with so much activity swarming about inside them.

He pulled the car into a parking lot by the pier and we got out and walked along the length of one of the giant hulls, dwarfed by its pearly monstrosity. You couldn't really see inside, but the night air was so still that it was possible to hear calypso music wafting down from one of the decks and happy laughter mixing with the tinkle of clinking stemware.

Jack stood staring at the ship, then looked out at the dark water. "I've always loved the sea," he said, taking my hand. "Even if it meant running away from home one summer and lying about my age just so I could work as a busboy on one of these ocean liners."

I looked up at him. "A busboy? You really ran away to sea to become a *busboy*?"

"Herman Melville probably would have rolled in his grave, but it was the closest thing I could get to being a cabin boy. Besides, as a busboy on a ship I sure learned a lot about how a huge kitchen is run. I also learned a lot about the right way to treat people from the way I was occasionally dealt with. When you're on a low rung of the service ladder, you're sometimes regarded by your patrons as a nonentity or some sort of 'untouchable.' It was quite an eye opener for a pudgy American teenager who imagined the world lay at his feet."

"Were you good at it?" I asked Jack.

"Being a busboy?"

I nodded.

"I sucked. I told you I only excelled at cooking and chemistry—and the chemistry thing was a fluke. I was a dreadful student. I just didn't care about being in school, so I didn't bother to do the work. Have you ever seen the bumper stickers that say I'D RATHER BE SAILING? Well, you could have plastered one on my forehead." He bit his lip and looked thoughtful. "Then and now, actually," he added. "Although I'd like to think I've broadened my horizons somewhat since adolescence."

"Yo-yos?" I smiled.

"I said 'somewhat.' "

I confessed to Jack that I was just the opposite,

growing up—the A student whose parents wondered too loudly and too often why I wasn't working hard enough to merit an A+. I winced at the memory. "I cared so much about trying to be perfect that I lost sight of the forest for the trees. Things that should have been fun, weren't."

"Do you think you're still that way?" Jack asked me gently, intertwining his fingers with mine. "Liz? You look a bit rueful."

It was a tough question. I didn't answer him for a while. I stared at the ship and let the sounds of the party on the upper deck and the soft slap of the waves against the hull's waterline wash over me as I pondered what Jack had just said.

"Yes . . . ," I said slowly. "Unfortunately, yes. I want to ace *Bad Date*. I want to nail every ad campaign I'm assigned without suffering writer's block. I want whatever's going on between us to be perfect . . . whatever perfect is. No bumps or ruts, I guess. And just because reality doesn't work that way, it doesn't stop me from wanting everything I'm involved in— game, job, relationship, whatever—to be perfect."

"No wonder you're not having fun with the fun stuff," Jack remarked. "You've chosen to live in a pressure cooker. Sometimes you've got to relax, relinquish control, and let things take their course." He smiled. "You'd be surprised. More often than not, the 'go with the flow' result ends up happier than the one you end up with when you drive yourself so hard. Listen to this Miami boy." He looked into my eyes and brushed my cheek with the back of his hand. "That's my mission. To unwind you a bit."

I took his hand and gently kissed his palm, appreciating his advice, wondering if I really wanted to be "unwound" and whether it was possible to break my habits of a lifetime and give Jack's philosophy a try.

20/The Love Grotto

The following morning, Jack phoned me after breakfast and said he wanted to bring me to one of the most spectacular places on the south coast, something I absolutely couldn't see in New York.

When he arrived, the convertible top was down on the Aston Martin. Brown terrycloth towels were spread across the leather upholstery. Jack tossed me a bottle of sunblock and demanded, nicely, that I coat myself before getting in the car. I complied and after he kissed me on the nose, necessitating the reapplication of Bain de Soleil, we were on our way.

"We're going down to Biscayne Bay," Jack told me. "I take it you've never been to Vizcaya."

"Viz-what?"

Jack released a long passionate sigh. "Vizcaya. Only the most romantic place in Florida—in my humble opinion. I can't believe you've never heard of it. It was the winter home of James Deering, one of the two International Harvester heirs, a real Jay Gatsby type."

He continued his informal tour once we reached the museum itself, a fantasy estate that paid playful homage to both French and Italian architecture, although the red tiled roof and whitewashed façade reminded me of a Spanish hacienda. "I come down here a couple of times a month to get away from the twenty-first century, just to take a mental time-out, sit in the gardens, and write poetry," he told me.

"You write poetry, Jack?" I was impressed. "Can I read some of your poems? Or will you read some of them to me?"

"Absolutely not."

"Why not?"

"Because they're crap, that's why. Just because I find writing poetry therapeutic or cathartic doesn't mean it's art."

Jack couldn't wait to escort me inside. He was right. Vizcaya was indeed magical, ethereal, glorious. Emblems of sailing ships decorated an airy rotunda that looked out onto sparkling Biscayne Bay and Deering's private quai—a fantastical stone creation that looked to me like a Venetian interpretation of Cleopatra's barge. The air smelled "aqua": clean, blue, and a little briny.

"Check this stuff out," Jack whispered to me, taking my arm. We entered the banquet hall, filled with heavy Renaissance furniture. The late morning light streamed into the room. "Look up," Jack said. "On that wall." He pointed to a pair of tapestries. "This is why I think Vizcaya is the most romantic place around. Those were owned by the Brownings."

Wow. Double wow. "Robert Browning and Elizabeth Barrett Browning?"

"Yup. Theirs was one of the great romances of all time. After Robert whisked Elizabeth away from her tyrannical father and they eloped in Florence, these tapestries were displayed in their home there, Casa Guidi."

I felt Jack's gentle touch on my arm as I admired the wall hangings, then his hand slipped into mine. It felt warm and dry. "Jack? What did you mean last night in the restaurant when you were talking about 'a way to lose more slowly,' and the million-dollar *Bad Date* jackpot not being the only prize?"

He kept his hand in mine. "I want to share my life with someone. I actually *like* the concept of commitment. You always hear women talking about having rotten luck when it comes to dating—"

"I'm living proof of that," I interjected.

"—well, *I'm* living proof that it's just as hard for *guys* to find someone who isn't unhinged or has an agenda of some sort. You're a terrific lady, Liz. And every week that I manage to stay on the show is one more week of getting to know you better."

I found myself staring into his eyes.

"What's the matter?"

"You are, Jack."

"I'm afraid you've lost me."

"Don't think I'm some sort of man-hater for saying this, because nothing could be further from the truth, but I've kept you at arm's length these past few weeks because I've never known a really nice guy. I mean someone who wasn't being nice or good to me just because he wanted something: sex, copies of my term papers, an introduction to Nell. So I always believed that genuinely nice men with no ulterior motives were mythical beasts, like griffins or unicorns. My roommates were convinced I shouldn't trust you and I've found myself following *their* instincts."

Jack placed his hands on my shoulders and leveled his gaze at me. "Are you sure it wasn't just your own gut—or your heart—you weren't trusting? And not me at all?"

"Nope," I grinned. "I didn't trust you either. Trust me."

I moved my hands up to my shoulders and laced them into his. "Thanks. Though I'm starting to get used to the idea that you might actually *be* as nice as you seem. I just need to go slowly, okay?"

Jack leaned down and gently kissed my lips. "Take all the time you need."

I smiled. "I'm ready to move on, now. In more ways than one."

"In that case," Jack said, "when we're through touring down here, you've got to let me take you upstairs and show you my favorite thing in the whole interior."

I was curious, and feeling warmer by the minute in a most pleasant way. Jack led me upstairs and we stopped at the entrance to one of the bedrooms. "Another of the greatest real-life love stories." He pointed to the bed. "It's said to have been the property of Emma, Lady Hamilton. I have always been thoroughly convinced—with absolutely no scholarly research to back it up, mind you—that Emma and Nelson had some of their first trysts in this very bed."

"I have to let you in on a little secret, Jack. Being an old movie buff, my knowledge of Emma and Nelson is pretty much based on *That Hamilton Woman* with Laurence Olivier and Vivien Leigh, but I always stop the video before Nelson dies in the Battle of Trafalgar. I like happy endings."

Jack brought my hand to his lips and kissed it. "Do you?" he teased. He pulled me into an embrace. The scent of him mixed with his signature blue watery fragrance was wonderful. I made a split-second decision to stop trying to delve into any motives he had for wanting my company. Whatever was happening now was bound to be better.

"You know what I would really like to do right now?" Jack asked me before our mouths met.

What seemed like several minutes later, I shook my head.

"I want to make love with you right here, right now, in this room, on Emma's bed. The most romantic bed in all of South Florida! I don't think I can wait any longer to be inside you." Taking me with him, he gave a furtive look outside the door and up and down the corridor to the room. "Shhhh," he continued, placing a finger to his lips. Then he backed me up toward the bed so that my thighs touched the embroidered coverlet and he began to unbutton my white linen blouse.

"Jack," I whispered back, my heart racing, "I think that it would be deliciously erotic, but it's probably not such a good idea. . . . I mean, someone's got to play the grownup here." I really hated myself for behaving so damn pragmatically. Jack could no doubt have guessed how much I wanted him, too, when his hands brushed against my nipples through the fabric of my blouse.

We heard footsteps. Argument became moot. I blushed as I fumbled with my shirt buttons. Jack faced me and ran his hands through my hair. "The gardens," he said, kissing me. "I have an idea."

I struggled to keep up with Jack's pace as he practically sped toward Vizcaya's formal gardens, trotting past dozens of hedges and classical statuary to one of the estate's partially hidden grottoes.

"What happened to stopping to smell the roses?" I joked.

We reached the grotto, which was guarded by half-naked stone sentinels supporting a pediment shaped like the arch of a cockle shell, except that the design on the pediment, which looked like dripping seaweed from afar, was really dozens of carved heads resembling sea nymphs. The semicircular rear wall inside the grotto looked the same. Jack pulled me onto a bench with him. I felt like we were under the bay itself, in a dark, private, special little cave. The air was thick and damp and smelled of brine.

"I expect to see a mermaid in here," I began, but Jack stopped my mouth with a kiss. I realized I was trembling. "Remember when I said a little while ago that I needed to go slowly?" I asked Jack somewhat breathlessly.

He nodded.

I caressed his cheeks and cupped his face in my hands. "Well, that was then; this is now. I really want you, Jack. Very much," I whispered, and claimed his lips. They tasted sweet. I ran my tongue along his lower lip, savoring its taste and its softness. We kissed again, as gently as though a whispered secret were passing from his mouth to mine. Our passion intensified. We'd spent so much time apart, thinking about each other. Now, finally, desires were translated into action.

"I just want to be double-sure that it's okay that we're doing this," Jack said, pulling back slightly from our embrace. "And doing it *here*, too, instead of hunting for a bit more privacy and comfort. Because I've been thinking about this—making love, I mean—since the day we met."

"Me too," I said clinging to him, my own breath coming in shorter and shorter gasps. "I have a quick confession to make, Jack. I've been carrying around the business card you gave me every day as though it were a lucky sixpence. Call me madcap, but it sort of makes me feel like you're right there, for real, in my pocket. We could wait until we get back to the Palmetto, but to tell the truth, I don't really want to. I'm dreadful at delayed gratification."

"Put me in your pocket, Miss Madcap." Jack's hand slipped down to my waist, over my midriff and down between my legs. He slid one hand up under my skirt and let it play along my thigh. I could feel the energy coming off his palm, going directly into every cell in my body. I adjusted my position so that he was able to reach his ultimate destination, letting him slide first one finger, then two under my panties and inside me. I was almost embarrassed at how wet I was. I've never before wanted a man as much as I wanted Jack then. He was passionate yet gentle, adventurous yet dependable. Knowing him gave me a renewed faith in the possibilities of happily ever after. I moved my hands along his chest, unbuttoning his shirt until I could caress the broad expanse of skin, then allowed my hand to graze down to his belt buckle.

He was already hard when I first touched him, held him.

"Sit on my lap," Jack whispered.

I hiked up my skirt and did as he asked me, then

placed my arms around his neck, pulling him to my breasts as he entered me. It was a glorious moment of mutual fulfillment. Jack held my hips, easing me up and down as I rode him, moving his mouth from my nipples to my throat to my lips. We exploded together, rocketing with sensation like a pair of shooting stars.

Still feeling Jack deep inside me, we held each other for several minutes as our breathing slowed to normal, as, heart pressed to heart, our rhythms synchronized as one. I rested my head on his shoulder and he ran a hand through my tangled, slightly damp mop of hair, sending pleasant shivers down my spine. "I've seen these gardens by moonlight," Jack whispered, the first to finally speak. "And they are truly breathtaking. But I wish you could see your face now, Liz. It's so beautiful." A rush of warmth suffused my heart. I drew a lazy O with my tongue around his lips and softly kissed him.

Jack held me tightly. "I don't know what it is about you. I'm so drawn to you. I've said this before; it must be something chemical."

I nuzzled his neck and gave his ear a little nibble. "The feeling is definitely mutual. And . . . I think . . . now that I finally know how it feels to make love with you, I'm not entirely sure that I'll ever be able to get enough." My grin must have been a mile wide. "Unfortunately, I have to go back home in about"—I looked at my watch—"thirty hours."

Jack sighed. "Then we'll have to make the most of the time we have. So, if you wouldn't mind getting up . . ."

I rose and straightened my skirt, refastened my blouse. Jack restored himself and his clothing to a publicly acceptable state and took me in his arms for a kiss before we headed out into the sunlight again, our arms around one another's waists as we headed for the parking lot.

"Where are we going?" I asked Jack as we left Vizcaya.

"Someplace where we can remain blissfully undisturbed," he replied. "We're going sailing."

21/The Siren's Song

Carefree. I think that's the way I would have to describe the feeling . . . riding in Jack's convertible with the top down, wearing my Jackie O–style sunglasses, with a salt breeze blowing off Biscayne Bay ratting my hair as we skirted the coast. I felt warm, fuzzy, cared for, and was falling in love. To our left loomed fancy, monolithic hotels, and to our right, posh marinas, pristinely maintained, studded the shoreline.

Jack pulled into the gated driveway of the Bonaventura Marina and punched a code into the electronic sentry box. The arm rose to admit us and we hung a right turn into the parking lot. "They have a pretty decent restaurant here," Jack told me, as he swung the Aston Martin into a space marked "reserved." He turned off the engine and pointed to an outdoor café shaded by rush-covered rooftops and table umbrellas that gave the place a tiki hut feel. "They make a mean coconut shrimp with mango chutney. And as you might imagine, I'm pretty picky about other people's cooking."

"You *are* trying to kill me," I teased. "Either that or you really need to start taking ginkgo biloba supplements."

Jack slapped his palm against his forehead. "God-dammit, I did it again." He took my hands in his and kissed them. "I'm sorry, Liz. I must have some sort of blind spot about shellfish and you. Well, they also make a terrific barbecued pork tenderloin open-face sandwich." I saw him look at his watch, a fancy-looking thing with all sorts of dials on it. Probably a diver's watch of some kind. "I've set the bezel to re-mind me when the tide is up, so we should shove off pretty soon. Do you mind if we get the food to go? I've also got plenty of provisions on board, if you just want to eat there."

Great sex always makes me hungry. I opted for the takeout.

I figured Jack had some little, modest sailboat; I wasn't prepared for what I saw. We walked to the fur-thest end of one of the docks, with Jack propelling me gently by the elbow, cautioning me to watch my step in my heels, so I didn't get caught between the hori-zontally laid planks or trip over a stray line. A gull swooped over our heads with its lunch in its beak. We stopped in front of a gorgeous sailboat; it looked huge from where I stood.

"Here she is," Jack said proudly.

I read the name. "Circe."

"She was the Circe when I bought her fifteen years ago and it's bad luck to change the name of a boat, al-though since I'm a master chef, I *had* considered re-naming her the Galley Slave."

"So this is your . . . ?"

"My baby. My pride and joy. I spend as much time aboard her as I can. She's a sixty-seven-footer, an original John Alden staysail schooner built in 1930."

"Request permission to come aboard, captain."

"Permission granted. But first of all, you're not shod for sailing, so please take off those very sexy sandals before you hurt yourself and we end up spending another blissful night in an emergency room."

I gave him a dirty look, then sat on a white wooden step unit, unbuckled the straps, and removed the offending footwear.

"Here, let me take those from you. Seriously, Liz, if you're not used to running around boats, you could slip and turn your ankle . . . or worse. I love my teak deck, but I'm more concerned with your welfare."

I handed him my shoes, which he took in his left hand, offering me his right one for balance. "Step up, then step down," he instructed, as I mounted the step unit that brought me level with the bulwark, then I gingerly stepped down onto the deck.

Jack came aboard and stood close behind me, placing his hands on my shoulders. I relaxed my head back into his chest. He pointed at the masts. "Oregon spars," he said. "These are the original masts . . . over seven decades old."

Jack slid back the hatch leading below and suggested I descend the ladder ahead of him. I'm sure he got a great kick out of watching me from behind as I negotiated the narrow wooden steps. "The main salon," he said indicating the central area in which we were standing. I was surprised at how spacious it seemed for a sailboat; I guess I'd expected it to be dark and cramped and not at all conducive to spending too much time below deck. Jack pointed at the double skylight, the source of much of the sunlight flooding into the cabin. Light also streamed in from the bronze portholes.

My host placed our takeout orders on a counter in the galley and lifted the hook on one of the polished mahogany cabinets, unlocking it. "If you don't do this," Jack explained, pointing at the hasp, "the minute you hit rough seas, the cabinet doors will fly open and everything will spill out and roll all over the floor. Try cleaning up couscous or rice sometime." He retrieved plates, flatware, and glasses, as well as burgundy linen napkins from a drawer near the sink.

Once we'd eaten our lunch, we went back up to the deck and Jack showed me the ropes, so to speak. So *that's* where that expression must come from. "If you're going to be my first mate, you have to know the lingo," he told me. "So when I call out to you to do something you won't stand there looking at me like I'm speaking to you in Swedish." He taught me how to take in the rubber fenders that protected the hull from banging into the dock and to cast off the spring line first, followed by the bow and stern lines, and then, as we headed away from the pier, how to raise and trim the sails. I felt like a pirate lass.

We spent the entire afternoon on the water. It was wonderful—and gloriously romantic. My first experience sailing and I was hooked.

As the sun began to set, Jack headed for a quiet inlet and dropped anchor just beyond its mouth. "The sea always makes me hungry," he said, pulling me toward him. His kiss tasted of sun and salt. "What do you say to picking up where we left off back in the grotto at Vizcaya?"

"The 'love grotto,' " I giggled.

"Why, Liz, you're blushing."

"I have no doubt of it," I admitted. "And from now on, whenever I read the phrase *love grotto* in some work of erotica, I will silently grin like an idiot and remember this afternoon. I've never been so . . . spontaneous before."

We descended from the cockpit down the ladder into the salon. I started to laugh, then suppressed it. "What? What's up?" Jack asked me, smiling. "C'mon, Liz, you must be thinking of something dirty; the tops of your ears are turning bright red."

"It must be the sun," I lied. "Okay, if you insist, I was thinking that the word 'cockpit' was . . . well . . . we were just laughing at 'love grotto' and a cock pit would be a love grotto, wouldn't it?" My cheeks were burning up.

"Liz, how can such a smart-mouthed copywriter blush when she talks dirty?" Jack riffled through my hair; it felt magnificent.

"Because of *you*, that's why. I think about what we were doing just a little while ago, and—"

"—and it's an appetizer compared to what we're about to do." Jack opened a door aft of the main cabin. "*Voilà*," he said. "The master stateroom."

Damn if it didn't have a queen-sized bed.

What a wonderful oasis of elegance and sensuality. The well-appointed wood paneled chamber with its low ceiling and soft lighting was lushly intimate. Jack took me in his arms and we edged toward the bed as one, sinking onto the mattress without letting our lips part. Fully clothed, we lay enfolded in one another's embrace, our hips pressed together, continuing, deepening our kiss. Finally, Jack drew himself away from me. "What do you say we eliminate some of those garments," he whispered. "As in, all of them."

My heart began to race. This would be the first time we'd hold, touch, make love completely unclothed. Soon I would know what it would be like to feel Jack's skin touching mine. *Would it feel warm? Cool?* I sat up and began to unbutton my blouse, my fingers fumbling slightly. I realized I was nervous, even though we'd already been intimate. *Would he like my body?*

"No, here, let me do that for you." Jack stood facing me and one by one slowly undid each button. I looked at him somewhat expectantly. "Why rush?" he said. "We have all the time in the world." He offered me his hands, and when I placed my palms in his, he pulled me to my feet and slid the blouse off my arms, tossing it onto a nearby armchair. Then he reached around my waist and unzipped my skirt, sending it slipping over my thighs, grazing my calves, until it pooled at my ankles. I stepped out of it with as much grace as I could manage, given the fact that I was nuzzling my face into Jack's chest, inhaling his scent. His cool water fragrance now comingled with the aromas of the bay breezes, the sun, salt water, and sweat. Another moment later and my panties were on the floor; my Miracle Bra, unhooked, joined it. I stood entirely naked before the still-clad Jack. When he very gently touched my shoulders and seated me on the edge of the captain's bed, I felt a tiny shiver of anticipation.

I watched Jack as he undressed. He didn't rush that either. He seemed to enjoy the pleasure I derived from watching him undress just for me. I loved the light golden brown of his skin, the perfectly symmetrical thatch of dark hair on his chest. I couldn't wait to run my hands across its silkiness, to feel his strong, toned arms embrace me. Oh, what a lucky girl I was: This stunning, kind, fascinating man was my lover.

Jack joined me on the bed, easing me onto my back. Our lips met again and his hand traveled the length of my inner thigh. He paused to let his hand rest briefly on the juncture of my legs, his fingers pressed against me, feeling my heat, my moistness. I wanted him to explore me there with his fingers, but Jack delayed my gratification, smoothing his hands along my belly and cupping my breasts. He traced circles around my aureoles, increasing his pressure when he felt my hips arch up, seeking his. Then his tongue replaced his hands as he nibbled, suckled, until I felt as though I might implode from the sheer intensity of the sensation.

Our mouths joined once again, tongues exploring, never seeming to get enough. It thrilled me that Jack enjoyed kissing me as much as I adored kissing him. He brushed his lips against my cheek, then nuzzled my head to one side as he buried his face in my neck and behind my left ear, depositing soft kisses there that sent tingles up into my hairline.

Jack's mouth returned to mine and he began to travel down my body again with his lips and tongue. He gently parted my thighs and nestled between them, tasting me in long strokes, allowing the sensation to leave me wanting more, feeling my body quivering for him to satisfy my need; then he would touch me again. He slid his hands under my rear and lowered his face to me as though he were drinking from a goblet. He

ceased teasing me with his tongue and began to take
me with it. It felt freeing and wonderful to give myself
to him. To be his. I lost track of the number of orgasms he gave me. I'm pretty sure I stopped counting
after three. Then, when I could have sworn I was
floating, blissed out, a few inches above the bed, Jack
covered me with his body and entered me. Our
rhythm matched, then overtook, the gentle roll and
pitch of the sea beneath us as the current gently
rocked the Circe's hull.

Making love at Vizcaya had been so exciting because it was the first time we were experiencing, exploring one another, and because of the danger and
potential embarrassment involved in our being discovered. Our passion had outweighed the risk. That
would always be special. But our lovemaking aboard
the Circe was exquisitely beautiful. Jack was such a
caring, attentive, and generous lover. He understood
instinctively where I liked, needed, to be touched. And
for the first time in my life I experienced a mutual orgasm. It was the most incredible, urgent, powerful,
magical release.

We lay entwined for a while, then Jack got up and
left the stateroom, returning a few minutes later with
a pitcher of ice water and two glasses. Paper-thin slices
of lemon floated in the carafe. He poured us each a
glass, handed me mine, and sat back beside me on the
bed. "I'm so hot," I breathed.

"Me too. Let's remedy that, shall we?" Jack pushed
open one side of the skylight above our heads. I
hadn't noticed how dark it had become. "I'll be right
back," he said, kissing me on the lips before he left the
stateroom.

I heard his footsteps on the deck. "What are you doing out there?" I called up to him. "You're butt-naked!"

"Like someone's going to see me?" Jack peered down at me through the half-open skylight. "I'm cooling us off," he said. "Setting up an upside-down little headsail that will catch the night breeze and waft it straight down into our cabin."

While Jack worked up on the deck, I thought about what a celestial day I was having. Jack was just so . . . I don't know . . . gentlemanly. Competent. Loving. All of the above.

By the time Jack returned, his rigging was already producing a gentle breeze. He sat on the edge of the bed, dipped his index finger in his water glass and seductively traced my collarbone with a ribbon of cool wetness. I handed him my glass. "Thanks so much, Jack. I really needed that."

He smiled at me. "The sex or the water?"

"Both."

"We've barely begun."

"Good. I've got the energy and the desire for a marathon. This is our first day as lovers. If we've had enough of each other already, this relationship is in big trouble!" I reached for him and pulled him toward me. "This afternoon—the sailing—was fantastic. I think I'm hooked for life. I kept imagining you were Captain Kidd or something. I have a confession to make, Jack. In the throes of adolescence, I had this recurring fantasy of being kidnapped by pirates and forced to be the captain's sex slave. Totally un-p.c."

"Liz?" Jack's voice was husky.

I wondered if his reaction was a "yes," a "no," or

a "maybe." "Would you . . . can we . . . ?" I asked tentatively.

Jack kissed me deeply. "Is that what you want, Liz?"

I felt my pulse racing. "Jack, I've never, ever divulged this fantasy to anyone. I don't think I've ever felt so . . . vulnerable. For all I know, you may think I'm some sort of pervert." Embarrassed, I averted my gaze from his.

He asked me again. "Is that what you want, Liz?"

"Yes," I answered softly. "But do you?"

Jack opened the door to a wardrobe built into the wall of the stateroom and selected four silk neckties from a collapsible rack. He approached the bed and lit two candles, safely protected by deep globes of ruby-colored glass, then switched off the lamp.

"Lie back," Jack instructed gently. "In the center of the bed."

Jack took one of the neckties and deftly secured it around my right wrist with a slipknot, half-hitching the other end of the tie to the post above my right arm. He skirted the edge of the bed and fastened my left wrist in the same manner. "Open your legs, Liz," he asked softly. I complied, unbelievably aroused, bending my knees slightly. Jack secured my ankles to the posts at the far end of the bed with the two remaining ties. He stood at the foot of the bed, dead center, watching me. "Are you all right?"

"Yes," I breathed.

"Now. I get to do whatever I want with your body. And you get to squirm and wriggle and beg your captain for mercy." He lowered himself on top of me and began to feast—first along my hairline, gently kissing my eyelids, exploring my mouth for what felt like a blissful eternity. His fingers traced my face from my temples to my chin with fluttering caresses; his hands plunged through my hair, sending tingles across my scalp. I begged him to kiss me again.

"I wish I had more than one mouth to pleasure you with," Jack said, in between love bites to my nipples.

"I don't know if I could take it," I replied, arching my back in response to the intensity of his touch. He took me time after time with his tongue until I thought I was delirious. I longed to put my arms around Jack and hold him close, but I couldn't. I was caught between my romantic desire to clasp him to me and the increasing carnality the temporary captivity inspired. Each held its own special brand of passion.

Jack straddled my body, placing himself between my breasts, cupping them toward one another, pillows for his hardness, close enough to my mouth so that I reached for him with my tongue. He adjusted his position so I could more easily pleasure him, and slipped a damask-covered neckroll behind my head for support.

I loved being able to gratify him by taking him in my mouth, teasing, stroking with my tongue. Deprived of the use of my hands, I had to become even more creative. Jack seemed quite ecstatic with the results. When I felt him nearly ready to explode in my mouth, he switched positions and penetrated me, parting my legs wider than their tethered manner already rendered them. I wanted to bring my legs up and over his back, urging him closer, deeper, but the deprivation was somehow delicious in an altogether different way.

"You are so beautiful, Liz," Jack breathed.

We seemed to be developing a talent for having mutual, simultaneous orgasms. Jack rested on top of me, his head on my chest. "I'm listening to your heart," he said, as I inhaled the scent of his thick, dark hair.

"What does it say?"

"It says, 'Hey, Liz, this Jack guy thinks you're pretty wonderful. I think he's a keeper.' "

I laughed, and hugged him to my breasts.

"You make me so happy, Liz. Are you happy?"

I nodded. "Can't you tell?" I teased. "What's more important is that you also make me happy when we're fully dressed."

Jack ran his thumb along my lower lip. "You're a wonderful lover . . . and a terrific friend, as well. I enjoy your companionship immensely." He rose and released me from my sweet bondage. The four neckties looked a bit the worse for wear. I certainly had sweated and strained against them. "Well, that's why drycleaning was invented," he said, and tossed them into a small wicker hamper. He opened the mirrored door that led to the head and turned the tap in the sink, returning with two wet terrycloth hand towels embroidered "Circe." Jack sat beside me on the bed and handed me one of the towels, using the other to cool and cleanse me from head to toe, which in and of itself provided a sensual thrill. I used my towel to do the same for him. The terry went from cool to warm as it captured the heat coming off our bodies. When we were through, Jack hung the towels over a bar in the head and returned to bed.

We were both spent. My legs felt like Jell-O. My

brain, equally giddy with sexual satisfaction, felt like one big, happy, party balloon.

Jack blew out the candles and we pulled down the coverlet. We snuggled close, under the bedclothes. "Thank you," I murmured. "It's been a beautiful day."

Jack took me in his arms and whispered, "Sleeping together is great, but *waking up* together is even better. There's something I finally get to ask you, Liz."

"What is it?"

"How do you like your eggs?"

"Jack?" I murmured softly, feeling myself drifting off, "can you crack an egg with one hand?" His face was close enough so that the sliver of moonlight streaming through the hatch illuminated his puzzled expression.

"Of course I can, I'm a chef. I can even do two at once. Why?"

"Because . . . because maybe I'm silly . . . but I think that's one of the sexiest things a man can do." I kissed his lips. "Goodnight, my captain."

I fell into the deepest sleep I can remember in years, with my head resting against the soft hair on Jack's chest.

22/Pet Projects

Jack wasn't beside me when I rolled over, awakened by a shaft of sunlight that kissed my cheek as it came down through the open skylight. I sat up in bed, still feeling dazed. Wow, what an evening it had been.

He entered the stateroom with a wicker breakfast tray. "You never did say how you like your eggs, so I brought you some coffee and freshly squeezed orange juice." Jack placed the tray on the bed. "Good morning, cutie," he said, kissing me.

"When did you get up?" I asked, sipping the juice. Very little on this planet is better than the taste of "fresh-squozen" orange juice.

"Been up for a while," Jack shrugged. "Checked the anchor, spruced up a little of the bright work, listened to the weather forecast up on the deck, even wrote a poem. And no, you can't see it. It's a lovely morning, by the way."

"What time is it?" I'd put my watch in my purse when we were sailing yesterday because I wasn't sure how waterproof it really was.

"11:12 A.M.," Jack answered, looking at his watch. "And time to be heading back to port before that crunching sound you hear will be our hull against a rock."

Crunching sound.

Numbers Crunchers.

Oh, shit. Oh shit oh shit oh shit oh shit.

My meeting with the Numbers Crunchers client was supposed to have started on Biscayne Boulevard one hour and twelve minutes ago.

And where was I?

Off the coast of Miami enjoying the delightful and affectionate company of a new friend and lover, the afterglow of sensational sex, the first good night's sleep I'd had in months, strong coffee, and fresh orange juice. The Circe had earned her name. Lured the unsuspecting away from duty and into the arms of passion, delayed them so long with her charms that they forgot where they were originally headed.

"How long will it take us to get back to port, Jack?"

"About three hours."

"Where the hell did I leave my purse?" I jumped up and searched for it in the stateroom, finally locating it on the banquette in the salon. I fished for my cell phone and my little appointment book. Thank God something had told me not to take it out of my bag when I left the hotel yesterday to head off to Vizcaya. I started to go up to the deck to make a couple of rather urgent phone calls when Jack stopped me.

"You're naked, you know."

"Yeah, I know. In the immortal words of Jack Rafferty, 'Who's going to see me?' "

"When *I* went on deck naked it was around two A.M."

"Screw it." I grabbed my white linen blouse, slipped my arms through the sleeves, and went up top. Before I alarmed Jason and F.X. it made more sense to locate the client and see if we could move the meeting to sometime later in the afternoon. I phoned the client's office, fudged by telling the receptionist that I had gotten tied up—well, that was *true*, wasn't it?— and missed the ten o'clock start-time for our meeting. She very nicely informed me that my client Mr. Grossman had waited for me as long as he could, and that he had just left for his noon golf date with his local congressman, was heading straight from the course to his brother's wedding in Baltimore, and wouldn't be back in the office until Monday.

Shit and double shit. This wasn't good. I phoned SSA and got Jason on the line. The getting tied up line wouldn't work with him because he had sent me down there to do only one thing: meet with Grossman to finalize the Numbers Crunchers copy. What could I use? Kidnapped by a pirate captain to whose lustful desires I most willingly submitted? Food poisoning?

Good enough.

"I found out I'm allergic to shellfish, Jason. And I missed the meeting." Both sentences were true. They just had nothing to do with one another. So, technically, I wasn't lying.

"Liz, you're already on probation," Jason reminded me. *Now* I felt sick to my stomach. "Look, obviously there's nothing we can do about this now . . ."

"I *did* try to reschedule for later in the day. My flight doesn't leave until close to dinner time. I'm really, really, *really* sorry about this. It was just an . . .

extenuating ... circumstance." There was a long silence on the other end of the line.

"We'll talk about this first thing Monday morning," Jason said. Then, in what sounded like an afterthought, he added, "Fly safe."

Jack came up on deck, holding my coffee cup. He saw me fold up the cell phone and must have caught the look on my face. "What's up, pumpkin?" he asked, handing me the mug.

"Guess where I was supposed to be an hour and a half ago? And guess what couldn't be rescheduled? So, guess who's fucked?" I exhaled an exasperated sigh. "I blew my assignment. Only *one* goddamn thing I had to do down here in three days, only *one* brief meeting, only *one* place where I absolutely had to be at a specific time on a given day, and I blew it." I took a couple of sips of coffee. "I've never been like this, Jack. When it comes to assignments, I'm the fucking Rock of Gibraltar. It's only since I auditioned for *Bad Date*—since I met you, as a matter of fact— that I've been screwing up everything at work. I haven't always loved every product, but at least I did a good job with its ad campaign. In the past month, I have walked out in the middle of a pitch for one client *and* totally blown this meeting with another. If the Number Crunchers thing had been across town, it would have been bad enough, but this entire field trip—the airfare, hotel, per diem—is on the company dime. SSA can't possibly charge the client for it; I never showed up! I wouldn't be a bit surprised, and wouldn't blame them, if Jason and F.X. expected me to reimburse the agency for this whole debacle."

Jack stood behind me and massaged my shoulders,

then gently stroked my hair and placed his arms around my neck. "Tell you what; I'll take full responsibility for this 'debacle.' After all, I did whisk you off to a place where the only way back to shore on your own was by breaststroke. If reimbursement becomes an issue, I'll take care of it. Okay?"

"Thanks. That's very sweet of you." I stretched my arms overhead, reaching for his neck and pulled him toward me, kissing him fully, deeply.

"I wouldn't say it if I didn't mean it, Liz."

"But there isn't a snowball's chance in Havasu that I'd ever accept your offer. I don't want your money, Jack. It's noble of you, but I don't need rescuing."

I went below deck, got dressed, and we weighed anchor and headed back to Miami, taking turns at the helm. "I want to be sure you know this," I told Jack. "That despite the fact that I missed an incredibly important business meeting, despite my little tirade, despite the fact that I may not have a job to come home to, I would not have traded anything in the world for what we shared yesterday and last night."

"They won't fire you," Jack said reassuringly. "Trust me, you're too good to lose."

"I hope you're right, Jack, because if I really *do* lose my job, winning that million dollars is going to become more than a pipe dream." I took a deep breath. "And speaking of dreams, Jack ... What are we going to do about 'us' when we're both in New York for the show? Remember the no-fraternization clause?" I felt my heart pounding and realized I was terrified of what Jack might say. He certainly had given me no indication that what we just had was a mere fling ... but you can't always tell with guys. In my experience, it's always been safer never to assume anything.

Jack looked me straight in the eye. "Option one: We work very hard to keep 'us' a secret and continue to explore our relationship. Option two: It ends as soon as we tie off the spring line. Assuming I get a vote here, I think option two sucks."

"I agree," I said, breathing a tremendous sigh of relief. "But option two is risk-free."

"Option two is stupid. Is that where you're casting your vote?" Jack asked anxiously. "In fact, there *is* no option two, as far as I'm concerned. I only invented it so that it looked like you had a choice."

"It's not about 'I.' It's about 'us.' I don't do one-night stands, Jack. I play for keeps."

"Then why did you say that option two was 'risk-free,' as though you wanted me to strongly consider it?"

"Giving you an out, I guess. Just in case."

Jack shifted my body so that I was standing in front of him. He placed my hands on the wheel, and then rested his over mine. He nuzzled his face in my hair. "Then our course is charted, Liz. We take the risky route but, ultimately, the more rewarding one."

"Relationships are about risks," I agreed.

"*Love* is about risks," Jack said.

The "L" word. He mentioned the "L" word! I was soaring higher than the gulls. After Jack brought me back to my hotel, I took a walk and found a yarn shop where I bought several skeins of a nubby Irish tweed. Enough for a man's sweater.

* * *

I came home, with much trepidation, to a catfight. Jem's eyes were red. Nell's hair was green.

"She and that new boyfriend of hers voodoo-ed me," Nell wailed when I saw her.

"I've already told you twice that I apologize. It backfired." Jem couldn't stop rubbing her eyes. I realized the reason when I saw a tiny kitten brushing itself against Nell's ankle.

"Is that your familiar?" I asked Jem. "Do witches-in-training get kittens nowadays and they get full-grown cats when they graduate to perfecting their spells?"

Nell scooped up the cat. "She's mine. Some bone-head left this little baby in a Dumpster across the street; you know, where they're doing construction work in front of the brownstone just off the corner of Seventy-fourth Street. I was on my way home from the subway station and I heard this little pathetic whimper and so I tried to balance myself on the edge of the Dumpster and look over the top of it and there she was, looking all scared and hungry. How could I have left her there? It was a moral imperative to bring her upstairs."

Nell deposited the new arrival on our sofa. The cat immediately began to test the upholstery as potential scratch-post material.

"Nell!" I screamed, trying to grab the kitten without taking too much of my loveseat with it. "This was my grandmother's couch. You can't even begin to imagine its sentimental value to me, not to mention the fact that by virtue of its age, it's an antique. If your stray ruins it, I may have to kill you."

"Brutalize me all you want; just don't hurt Johnnie Walker," Nell answered.

"Who's Johnnie Walker?"

Nell pointed at the kitten. "Her."

"What kind of a name is Johnnie Walker for a female?" I asked.

"You're worried about a damn piece of furniture," Jem wheezed. "That stupid cat ruined my *face*! She knows I've got asthma." Jem leveled an accusing finger at Nell. Not only were Jem's eyes red and swollen, but so was her nose. It looked like she'd taken to tippling. "Liz, do you have any idea how many Seldane I've taken in the past three days?" She reached for her inhaler for the fourth time since I'd walked in the door.

Nell stood up, holding the kitten in the cup of her palm. "How could I leave this little pookie to die out there in the vast wasteland of Manhattan inhumanity? It would have been cruel. Besides, Jem, all bets were off once you made my hair turn green!" Nell bent down and released the kitten, who scampered off to explore new territory, i.e., my luggage.

"Jem, how did you make Nell's hair green?"

"First of all, it wasn't me; it was Carl. Well, he gave me an incantation to do, and I must have left out a step or something."

"And why did you want Carl to give you a spell?" I felt like a district attorney.

"To get back at *you*, Liz! For playing Cupid and sabotaging my bad date. So I took the blonde wig you were wearing that night and I showed it to Carl because he's always talking about spells needing strands of the person's hair in the recipe, and he told me what to do, and I did it, and the next thing I know, it looks like Nell has been swimming in a heavily chlorinated pool without a bathing cap for about five years running."

The color of Nell's hair was a sort of deep chartreuse.

"And I don't know how it happened, but the spell somehow ended up working on the *real* blonde and not on the fake one—*you*—who was the one wearing the wig."

"Jem, your spell might have had an effect on me after all. I ended up missing my client meeting this morning and couldn't reschedule. I dread the thought of Monday."

"Fuck your client meeting!" Nell shouted. "How am I going to go on *Bad Date* Sunday night with fucking green hair?"

Nell rarely cursed. But her hair was her crowning glory, and a matter of extreme personal pride.

"You can always dye it," Jem responded.

Nell switched from anger to indignance. "I have never colored my hair—not even so much as getting highlights—and I won't do it now. I'm probably the last natural blonde left on this island."

It's true that the pre-spell color of Nell's hair was gorgeous, made even more so by the fact that Nell was born with it.

"I'm holding you partially responsible too, Liz," Nell sniffled.

"I'm sorry, Nell. I'm really, really sorry. Jem, you have no idea how bad I feel about this."

"My haaaaair," Nell continued to wail.

"You could go on the show looking like a mermaid," I said, trying to be helpful. "Pick something flowy in sea colors. Allegra would love you for it."

Nell sneered at me.

"And what am *I* supposed to do?" Jem demanded. "Go on the show looking like Puff the Magic Dragon? As long as Johnnie Walker stays here, I'm going to look like this!" She pointed at her swollen face.

I turned to Nell. "Nell, can Johnnie Walker stay somewhere else for a while? Please?"

Nell shook her head.

"Jem, keep popping those Seldane and wear shades on Sunday night. Nell, I know you've got a big heart and want to take in strays, but you've got to remember that you don't live here alone and—holy—!"

I rushed over to the plastic bag that contained the yarn I had purchased in Miami that afternoon. I had made pretty good headway on a sweater for Jack while I was waiting in the airport.

"Nell, noooooooooo." I tried to pry Johnnie Walker from Jack's double cable stitches with little success. Already the eleven or so inches I'd done on the back of the sweater had become unsalvageable.

"Don't hurt pookie," Nell gasped, reaching for the kitten. "She's just curious. That's what you are, aren't you," she cooed to the cat, extracting lengths of imported Irish tweed from its sharp claws. "It's not her fault."

"No, it's not her fault," I agreed, though it was a struggle for me at this point to summon up much sympathy for the stray. "We three have had our squabbles in the past, but we've always managed to work things out and continue to live harmoniously. And now we've got green hair, red eyes, and a ruined sweater—"

"Not to mention bad karma all around," Nell interjected. "And we've all got to appear on TV on Sunday night."

"It's not Nell's fault. It's yours, Liz. You started it by ruining my date with Carl."

I wasn't going to let Jem make me feel guilty for my actions at Pywacket. "Jem? You and Carl were having the time of your lives before I decided to play Cupid. Even if I hadn't done that, you two were still having a fantastic date."

"Jem's right. It's still your fault, Liz," Nell chimed in. "Because even if you had good intentions, Jem believed you sabotaged her date so she voodoo-ed the wig, which turned my hair green."

This whole mess may have started with my behavior during Jem's date, but I was getting angry with the two of them for ganging up on me, assigning me the lion's share of blame. "Still, Nell," I said, "you brought home the cat, maybe out of your innate sense of rescuing a creature that might have eventually died out there on the street, but don't tell me you didn't see it as a great chance to get back at Jem, knowing she's asthmatic. And your pet project just ruined something that was important to me." I pointed to what was left of the sweater and the bag of yarn with half its skeins all ratted and snarled.

"So, ladies," I said, my heart pounding, "unless we can figure out how to patch things up between us, we've got a full-scale roommate war on our hands."

"Don't forget that last week when Nell took a bunch of clothes to the drycleaners for me, every garment somehow came back ruined and I couldn't find a thing to wear on the telecast," Jem said.

"It must have been a coincidence, then, that whatever I tried on, you told me it made me look fat," Nell shot back.

"And somehow all my powder eyeshadows turned to petrified granite practically overnight, an entire drawer of new pantyhose vanished into the ether, and none of the clasps on my necklaces will fasten anymore," I added. "But can we all apologize to each other for playing catty games—pardon the pun, Nell—and hug or something? What's happening to us? Has *Bad Date* warped our perspectives this much?"

There was a long stretch of silence as we regarded one another, first warily, then our expressions softened into ones of apology and acknowledgment.

"Yeah, we're turning into people we wouldn't even want to have lunch with, let alone live with," a teary-eyed Nell agreed, stroking Johnnie Walker. "The meanest thing I did to this pookie was to bring her home knowing that Jem is allergic."

Jem sighed. "I knew Nell had nothing to do with my first date with Carl. He warned me that getting back at Liz for it by using hair from her blonde wig might have an effect on Nell, but I wanted to do the spell anyway."

"Honestly, Jem, when I saw that you had a great guy right under your nose, I just wanted you to be happy. I'm sorry I didn't go about it the right way. If there is a right way." I held out my hand to Jem. She clasped it then turned to Nell and fingered a length of her hair. "You know, Nell," she said, starting to giggle—a rare thing for Jem—"it's kind of a pretty color . . . for a frog!"

" 'It's not that easy being green,' " Nell began to warble, serenading Jem. Jem's laughter was contagious. Nell's singing became interrupted with gasps. It was hard to tell if she was laughing or sobbing. The cat began to yowl in its shrill little voice.

Tremendously relieved, I draped an arm around the shoulders of each of my roommates, while Nell continued to regale us with Kermit the Frog's signature song. I was giggling, too, especially at Johnnie Walker's vocal contribution. "Everyone's a critic," I laughed. Jem sneezed.

23/A Night for Surprises

So for the next two nights, Johnnie Walker slept on Nell's chest and Jem carried her inhaler from room to room. Yet she no longer seemed concerned that she would more than likely get kicked off the show by the end of the taping on Sunday night. In fact, she began to walk around our apartment with a serenely inscrutable expression on her face, which became even more serene and even more inscrutable when Nell and I tried to pry a bit into what she planned to say when it was her turn to sit in the cone throne.

She opted to wear a pair of smoky-lensed sunglasses on the show, as they would hide her bloodshot eyes without entirely obscuring her face from the viewers.

To placate Nell, who was complaining bitterly that she owned nothing that would match her chartreuse hair, I suggested that she hide it, offering her the loan of my Hamptons Artists & Writers softball game cap. She could stick her hair in a ponytail and thread it through the back of the hat, put on a tight jersey top and an equally tight pair of jeans, slip into a pair of wooden-heeled mules, and pretend to be Casual Barbie.

On Sunday, the three of us didn't travel to the set together and I was late getting to the studio, so I headed straight for hair and makeup. Jack was already there, seated in a chair with his back to mine, but we could see one another through the mirrors we faced. He tipped me a wink when no one was looking. I can't wink for beans, so when I tried to return the gesture I probably looked like I had some sort of facial tic. When she asked what was wrong with my eye, I told Gladiola (whose hair this week was black except for a skunklike stripe of Halloween orange), that I was being bothered by what felt like a stray eyelash. I could see Jack across the room, trying very hard to suppress a laugh.

When we left hair and makeup to head off to our respective dressing rooms, our hands brushed against one another and Jack gave mine a little squeeze. "I don't dare risk doing any more than that here," he whispered to me. "Just believe that I want to." I looked up at him and felt my heart begin to race, thinking about our magical time together in Miami, and how much I wanted to hold him again, to feel him touch me. A mere caress would have sent me over the edge.

When I got to my dressing room, there was a bouquet of pink roses and a card in a pink envelope with my name written on it. *That sneak,* I thought to myself. I figured I had better open the card before Candy Fortunato walked in. Grinning like a lovestruck idiot, I tore open the envelope and read the card.

> *To my partner in crime, my wittier mate:*
> *Coffee? Or Champagne?*
> *You set the date.*

It was signed "Rick B."

Rick?

I felt the corners of my smile turning down. What was our host up to? Was he still trying to woo me to ghostwrite his onstage banter? Or . . . and this was pretty unthinkable . . . I mean the man was a major movie star . . . was he trying to woo me, period? He'd been leaving messages for me on my office voicemail for the past few weeks, but I never returned his calls. It had seemed, even from his behavior that afternoon in Starbucks when he tried to hire me under the table, that he wouldn't stop at seduction to get what he wanted, but until now, I hadn't taken his romantic interest even remotely seriously.

I heard a noise outside the dressing room and shoved Rick's card with the envelope into a zipper compartment of my purse, then quickly checked the roses for any little cards that the florists stick in with the arrangements.

Candy's "pleather" miniskirted rear end entered the room before the rest of her did. I heard furtive giggling. Candy and someone else's. The next thing that caught my eye were the pale, slender fingers exploring Candy's ample boobs—fingers that were adorned with several unusual Celtic rings.

Candy and Allegra almost fell into the room. Allegra, red-faced, shut the dressing room door behind her. "Don't tell anyone what you just saw!" she hissed. So much for that tinkly little speaking voice she used on camera.

"Allegra, everyone knows you're gay. By now, all of America knows you're gay." I did a double take and looked at Candy. "But I didn't know *you* were!"

"It's not about my lifestyle choices," Candy answered anxiously. "It's about the no-fraternization clause. Hey, Liz, why're you smiling? Wanna get in on the action?"

Did I really resemble the Cheshire Cat? "I'm not going to say a word, believe me," I assured the two of them. "I guess Candy surprised me a little because all her bad date stories so far have been about men. I mean most of your boyfriends end up dead."

"Yeah, well," Candy said, tracing the curve of Allegra's breasts right in front of me. "I figure I have such bad luck with guys that maybe I should try women. I'm not doin' it to be in vogue or nothin'. Ya know, a lot of strippers are bisexual or gay. I don't want to get into what gets some of us started in the business, but it's not surprising that a lot of us prefer women."

"I thought you were an *ex*-stripper, Candy."

She cracked her gum. The *pop* almost echoed in the dressing room. "Yeah, well, whatever."

"Just promise not to tell anyone about this," Allegra repeated, just as insistently, though more softly now. She kissed Candy full on the mouth. Then she opened our door very slowly and peered out, checking the corridor in both directions before gliding noiselessly down the hall to her own dressing room.

"So are you two a couple?" I asked Candy.

"Don't know yet. Want some gum?"

"No thanks. Maybe later."

"Hey, these are gorgeous!" Candy exclaimed, noticing my roses. "Got a secret admirer?"

I debated whether or not to share the information.

It might not be such a bad idea to have a witness with no stake in my personal life who could attest that Rick had been hitting on me, so that in the event the producers or the media somehow got wind of it and decided to treat it as a violation of *Bad Date*'s code of conduct, Candy could corroborate that Rick had been the aggressor and I'd done nothing to encourage him. After all, he was the big movie star host, and who was I in comparison? Without a confidante, my version of events might not be believed and I could end up booted from the show. "My admirer's not so secret," I told her.

"C'mon, tell me. I swear it won't leave this room. Besides, *you* got something on *me* now, so we'd be even."

I leaned over and whispered the name in her ear.

"You're shittin' me!" she gasped.

I showed her Rick's card, adding that only in his mind was *I* in any way his "partner" or "mate."

"Well, I'll be damned. He's certainly got a case of the hots for you." She plunked herself down at her dressing table. "Is my makeup okay? Allegra didn't kiss it all off, did she?" Before I could answer, Candy began reapplying her lipliner and filled in her lips with a dark berry shade that matched her midriff-exposing tank top.

There was a knock on the door and Geneva gave us our five-minute call. As we headed down to the set, I had the feeling that living rooms across the world were in for some wild entertainment.

We were definitely captivating our audience this week. Jack told the viewers a six-year-old story about what happened when a woman from Detroit with whom he'd been carrying on a long-distance relationship came to stay with him in Miami for the weekend. She'd combed through his closet and cut an Armani sportcoat and a half dozen Valentino neckties to ribbons because her father had once been arrested by a *carabinieri* in Rome for some traffic infraction, so she was determined to detest everything Italian from that point on. The fact that he didn't know this about her and had gone to great pains to make *osso buco*, one of his culinary specialties, only compounded matters. She threw the food, plates and all, into the neighbor's garden.

"Hey, Liz," Rick said, sauntering down to my chair after my ball popped out of the machine. "You look like you got a little color this past week. You look great. You're positively glowing. Or maybe you just got lucky. Where were you, Temptation Island?"

He'd cut a little too close to the bone, so he had to be stopped before the conversation drifted into more dangerous waters. "Gee, Rick," I replied, smiling sweetly, "I just love reality TV jokes. In fact, I rented a video of one of your movies last night and I'll be gosh-darned if you weren't the weakest link in the cast."

"Good-bye! Whoa there, girl."

I slipped my fingers into the electrode cones and told the world about a three-day weekend from hell I'd spent at one of the Club Meds with a lawyer I dated several years ago. The biggest surprise was that he'd invited his mother to join us—a fact I didn't learn until we actually arrived on the island. It got to the point where I tried anything to get away from them, including signing up for an off-shore underwater excursion to swim with sharks—probably my all-time biggest fear in the animal kingdom, trumping cockroaches and snakes by a two-to-one margin.

Candy discussed how a guy she went down on behind the P.C. Richards appliance store confessed to her that she had just given him his last blowjob before he got married. His nuptials, with a full two-hour Catholic mass, were scheduled to begin fewer than eight hours after Candy had entertained him. "So when the priest says, 'Has anyone got anything to say,' ya know, 'speak now or forever hold your peace,' I stood up and said, 'Yeah, Father Rizzoli, I got something to say. *I* was holding Frankie's piece at about four-thirty this morning, back behind the P.C. Richards on Flatbush Avenue. In fact, I was holding his piece in my *mouth*. So I don't know what youse wanna do about it, but I'm in a church here and I got the fear of God in me, and while I did some things in my past that I'm not too proud of, I don't want to go to hell for blowing a dirtbag like Frankie. So I gotta confess.' "

This was good. This was good TV! I could bet that right now, millions of mothers were clapping their hands over their children's ears while no doubt staring open-mouthed at Candy Fortunato. The kicker was that Candy hadn't said anything that was technically "beep-able." All of the contestants and the entire studio audience were in hysterics. No one in his or her right mind was ever going to vote this woman off the show; she was far too entertaining . . . and she was serious competition for the rest of us.

Still, as much fun as we had listening to Candy, the moment I was waiting for had yet to arrive. Jem had been wearing a beatific smile for the entire show. Even when she walked on set, she seemed to be gliding an inch or two above the floor. Her name was the last one to be called and she approached the cone throne with her customary regal dignity. Smooth, polished Jem.

She slid her fingers into the metal cones and began to speak. "I believe that I am the luckiest, happiest woman in New York today." The polygraph lines didn't wiggle so much as a hair. "I had the most wonderful date with a remarkable man. Believe it or not, we've known each other for more than seven years, working side by side; and ladies, I am here to tell you, to remind you, to *beg* you not to judge a book by its cover. Well, actually, my man has a damn fine 'cover,' it's just that he and I don't necessarily share the same religious convictions. Let's just say I was born and raised a Christian and he practices something else. Now I didn't believe for a moment that because of Carl's religion and his cultural and extra-curricular interests that we had a snowball's half-life in hell of being compatible. But something made me finally give him a chance . . ."

I looked at the television monitor that showed the polygraph screen to the other contestants. It still wasn't zigzagging. I guess it was because Jem had truthfully acknowledged that "something" had made her change her mind about Carl. She just didn't say what that particular "something" was.

"Uh, Jem," Rick Byron interrupted. "I thought you'd be one of the last people I'd have to remind that the name of the show is '*Bad*' *Date*."

"I know," Jem beamed. "Isn't it great! I am never going to have to go on another bad date again. Because I have found a good man. I am in looooove, ladies and gentlemen, and it feels sooooooo good. So I would be *proud* to be kicked off this sorry show tonight, and get on with my life! My happy life."

Jem removed her fingers from the cones and raised her arms above her head, as triumphant as Muhammad Ali after a knockout. The audience went nuts applauding for her. In fact, they gave her a standing ovation.

Then they kicked her off the show.

"Congratulations," I told Jem, on our way back to the dressing rooms. "You scored one for romance."

"I'm feeling very munificent after that little on-air revelation." She leaned over and whispered in my ear. "You don't have to apologize to me anymore for 'sabotaging' my first date with Carl, because if you hadn't sent over the champagne . . . I'll never know . . . maybe that was what clinched it for me . . . that he somehow knew what my favorite was. Get Nell and we'll go to Pinky's for a drink. My treat."

I really wanted to take her up on it, but I hadn't had the chance to see Jack one-on-one since Miami. "Tell you what," I said, checking my watch. "I need to talk to Candy about a couple of things before we go. How about I meet you over there? If I'm not there by eleven o'clock, don't wait; just go on home without me when you're done." I hugged her. She hugged back. Jem is not a hugger. At least she never used to be.

"I had been debating with myself whether to say something on live television about you playing Cupid. About how pissed off I was at you after my first date with Carl because I thought you were trying to screw up my chances on the show. Then I decided that would, to quote Nell, be 'really bad karma all around,' so I kept my mouth shut. There are some things not everyone, and certainly not a gazillion Nielsen households, need to know."

"Thank you. You know, I couldn't be happier for you, Jem. And I'm really glad you don't hate me."

"I could never hate you, Liz. Want to snap your neck in half on occasion, but never hate you. God, we all had these grand idealistic, altruistic plans about what we would do with the money, back when we auditioned for the show. But face it, as much as we really believe we'd do something noble if we won the million dollars, it was still a get-rich-quick scheme." Jem was brimming with "happy tears" I'd never seen her experience in all the years I've known her. "It stopped being about going for the money, Liz." She held out her hands, fists closed. "Pick one," she instructed me.

"Pick one?"

"Left hand is love. Right hand is money. Pick one."

I looked at her face. Talk about glowing.

Jem looked me straight in the eye. "You didn't pick a hand, Liz. Doesn't matter, though—you should already know the answer." She all but floated down the hall to her dressing room.

24/Animal Instincts

Candy and I hung around our dressing room for a while, allowing everyone to leave the building before us. She was waiting for Allegra. I was waiting for Jack, but Candy didn't know that. She thought I was waiting to speak with Rick. I didn't correct her.

I counted on Allegra and Candy being too wrapped up in one another to pay much attention to my business. We jumped when there was a sharp knock on our dressing room door. I went to open it. Jack stood there with his brown leather bomber jacket draped over his arm.

"I . . . uh . . . wondered if anyone was walking east." Clearly, he hadn't expected Candy to be in the dressing room as well.

She eyed him, on her guard. "I'm waiting for someone."

"Me too," I said. That should keep Candy off the scent and hopefully telegraph to Jack that I was punting. "But thanks anyway." I almost added, "Maybe another time," but bit my tongue.

"Okay, well . . . I'll be heading on out now. Got to get back to the Waldorf before room service packs it in for the night."

I picked up on his hint. "A posh place like that doesn't keep the kitchen open twenty-four hours?" I *tsk-tsked*. "I'm sure if you're hungry you can grab a McDonald's. Or meet Jem and Nell over at Pinky's. That is, if you're not concerned about that no-fraternization clause." Had I fed him enough clues about my roommates' whereabouts and my own plans to join him later, I wondered.

"I'm not into noisy bars tonight. But thanks for the suggestion, Liz."

"Have a good night, now," I told him.

"I fully intend to," he replied, waved at Candy, then walked away down the hall.

"Whew, that was a close shave," Candy sighed after I closed the door.

"Sure was," I agreed.

"He's real cute, ya know? And not an asshole like most guys I know."

I smiled. "If you say so." I knew she was right.

I made it to the Waldorf-Astoria about a half hour later. It was wonderful to spend time together without having to edit our behavior.

"How'd you ditch Candy?" Jack asked me, as he poured each of us a glass of champagne.

"Allegra showed up and they pretty much forgot I was there."

Jack arched an eyebrow. "Allegra?"

"Whoops! Oh, God, I promised Candy I wouldn't say anything. It just came out of my mouth like it was common knowledge. Let's just say that you and I aren't the only happy couple to have emerged from the depths of *Bad Date*."

"It's probably a good thing for us if more than one person knows about them. Knowledge is power." He held his glass aloft. "To us."

"To us." Laughing, I entwined our arms and fed him the champagne from my flute.

Jack took me in his arms. "Can you stay the night?" he murmured, nuzzling my ear. He took a sip of champagne and I licked the taste from his lips.

"Too risky. Nell and Jem still don't know about us. I told them I needed to hang around the dressing room to speak with Candy and would try to meet up with them at Pinky's if it didn't get too late." I smoothed my hands over his chest and slipped his blazer down over his arms. "But I might have time for a quickie," I teased. "I'll miss you tonight, though," I added softly. I would have liked nothing better than to have been able to awaken in the cozy warmth and security of Jack's morning embrace.

"I'll miss you too, Liz." Jack removed the champagne glass from my hand and put it on the bureau. "Turn around."

I complied and he unzipped my dress. "I've got another little bit of intelligence for you," I teased, as Jack slid the straps of my dress over my bare shoulders. I could feel his hardness against me as he stood behind me, his hands covering my breasts.

"Then say it quickly because in about fifteen seconds, the only vocal thing I want you to be able to do is moan."

I spoke as rapidly as I could. "Rick Byron sent me a bouquet of roses and a suggestive card. They were in my dressing room when I got to the studio this evening. A month or so ago, he invited me to a secret meeting where he tried to woo me to ghostwrite copy for him to say on the show because he hated what the writers were giving him."

"And . . . ?" Jack edged me over to the bed, giving his hands free rein over my extremely willing body. Words were beginning to fail me.

"And I refused. And now it seems like he was asking me on a date. Candy couldn't help but see the flowers when she came into the dressing room tonight, and I showed her the card, too. For insurance purposes. That's who Candy thought I was waiting for tonight after the show. Rick, I mean. He's also been phoning me a couple of times a week, both at work and on my cell, but I have no intention of returning any of his calls."

"Should I be jealous? Do I need to bust his jaw?" he murmured.

"You must be joking," I whispered, taking his lower lip in mine.

"So Hollywood's Reigning Hunk isn't turning my lady's head . . . is that what you're saying?"

I smiled ecstatically at him. "You bet that's what I'm saying. Your lady. Wow. That's the first time you've said anything like that, I think. Jack Rafferty, nothing makes me happier than being your lady."

"Good answer," he whispered, grazing his mouth over my midsection.

Moan.

Jack was nibbling at my panties with his lips and teeth. I could feel his warm breath through the fabric. He hooked his fingers through the waistband and slid them down past my thighs, over my calves, grazing my bare ankles. I kicked them onto the floor. I felt like

I was melting into the mattress when he parted my legs and buried his face between my thighs. His hands caressed my midriff and moved upward to my breasts, his fingertips lightly teasing my nipples. I exploded in shades of magenta and violet.

I reached out my arms for him. Jack moved his body up along the length of the bed and we held each other tightly. I burrowed my face into his chest, kissing the patch of hair that peeked out from the top of his white broadcloth shirt, then rested my head against him, allowing myself to drift off to a state of half-sleep, eyes closed.

A few minutes later, hungry again for my lover, I began to unbutton his shirt. "We still have time to get naked," I whispered in Jack's ear. I reached down and fumbled with his belt, trying to unbuckle it while he was still lying down.

Jack laughed softly, then rose from the bed. "Let me help you," he said, quickly divesting himself of his wardrobe.

When he slid inside me I felt like he was coming home.

Nell was the only one in the apartment when I unlocked the door as quietly as I could at around one A.M. "Jem went over to Carl's place for the night," she said. "I hope you don't mind that I'm using your computer."

I noticed that she was on the Internet. "I tried to call to say I was running late," I lied, "so you wouldn't worry. But I guess you were online. I figured you would have gone on home once it got past eleven o'clock or so."

"That was some long conversation with Candy," Nell said casually, waiting to access a Web site. She glared impatiently at the screen. "Come on, you slow-poke. Hurry up! Liz, we should think about getting DSL in here. You could cook breakfast in the time it takes this thing to connect. You smell like Moulton-Brown shampoo," she added, without missing a beat or changing inflection. "Are you sure you were with Candy?"

"Who are you, my mother?"

"Gotcha!" Nell said triumphantly to the computer monitor, as I reflexively flinched. She looked over at me and her eye fell on my knitting basket, where the unsalvageable tangle of Irish tweed, courtesy of Johnnie Walker, sat atop the still untouched skeins like a clump of cooked spaghetti. "You weren't talking to Candy at all, were you?" she said with a confident smile. "Miami . . . knitting . . . I seem to remember the three of us standing around in the kitchen on Valentine's Day, drinking some red cocktail that Jem had concocted, bemoaning our manlessness, and you said you were never going to cook another dinner or knit another sweater for an undeserving creep again as long as you lived."

I looked at the wicker basket. "How do you know I'm not making a sweater for myself? Or you? Or Jem?"

"It's not for Jem because the color wouldn't do a thing for her complexion. It's not for me because I don't wear sweaters you could swim in and what you were working on is clearly for someone who wears at least a forty-two, and it's not for you because you don't wear big sweaters either and you never keep what you knit for yourself. QED," she concluded, tapping a few keys.

"QED?"

"I may be a natural blonde but contrary to popular belief, I did a lot more than file my nails and pass notes during algebra. QED, something major is going on between you and Mr. Miami."

I felt my hand involuntarily fly to my mouth.

"Don't be shocked, Liz. I was the one who practically introduced you guys the day we auditioned. It's not exactly a total surprise."

"Jack's not an 'undeserving creep,' by the way. Though you and Jem were thoroughly convinced he was trying to get me off the show."

Nell shrugged. "If you want to know the God's honest truth, and maybe it's a bit mean to admit it, I was afraid that if you found a great guy, then we three—Jem and you and I—well, we just wouldn't be 'us' anymore. I always sort of thought of us as the Three Musketeers: all for one and one for all, you know? But now Jem has someone, so it's all a moot point anyway. And you seem really happy, too, so it's none of my business. I'd love to be half as happy as you and Jem seem to be. But if I were you and Jack, I'd be on high alert insofar as *Bad Date* goes. Someone catches you two and you're both off the show." She returned to the screen. "Speaking of getting kicked off the show, my number is pretty much up unless I can snag myself a disaster date in the next few weeks."

I stood behind her and looked at the screen. "What are you up to?"

"People are always meeting each other online. In chat rooms. And you always hear about how when they finally get together face to face, it's usually a recipe for disaster because it's so easy to misrepresent yourself when you're online. You know, it's like phone sex." Nell lowered her voice to a husky whisper. "Hi, Bob. How are you tonight? What do I look like? I'm five-feet-nine with a body like Pamela Anderson, only it's all real. Yes, I'm wearing a thong. It's red. Red satin. And I have a Ph.D. in astrophysics." She resumed her normal speaking voice. "Like they say, 'On the Internet, no one knows you're a dog.' "

"But you're not a dog, Nell."

"So maybe I'm one of the few people in cyberspace who isn't faking it when they're talking about how they look. But, okay, take *this* guy, for example," she continued, pointing at the screen. "What's his name?" She leaned forward to peer closer at the monitor. "A.J. something. Where did you go, A.J.? Hey, come back! Here we go. His full name is A.J. Stevens. Okay, A.J. Stevens," Nell said, talking to the screen, "the way you described yourself to me, you sound like you look like a Ken doll. No one looks like a Ken doll in real life, A.J. Liz, what do you bet this guy is like sixty-five years old and balding with a beer gut?"

"Sounds perfect for you," I deadpanned.

Nell broke into a grin. "Damn straight!" She raised her hand for a high-five. "And I found him in just the perfect place for a Park Avenue trust-fundette to meet Mr. Wrong."

I looked at the screen, watching her type a flirtatious sentence to her new cyber pen pal. "Where the hell are you e-mailing this A.J. guy, Nell?"

My roommate was laughing her ass off. "In a Future Farmers of America chat room! Isn't it the best!?"

She was right. Nell sprays herself with Deep Woods Off! before she watches the Nature Channel.

"Yee-haw!" Nell whooped. "Now this guy thinks I'm Ellie Clampett. Another day or so of this and he should be hooked." She crooked her finger at the screen. "Come on, big boy. Come to Momma. Momma needs a new pair of Manolos." She flashed me a million-dollar grin. "One step closer to the jackpot," she crowed.

I looked over Nell's shoulder and watched her fabricating fiction for the farmer. She continued to type furiously. "His family's dairy farm is upstate—less than three hours away—so he can just come on down to the big city in his Ford pickup and take me for a hayride. And it's going to be one helluva hayride, Liz." A few moments later, she stared at the screen, looking stumped.

"What's up?" I asked her.

"I don't know how to answer this one. Help me out here, Liz. Your brain works so much faster than mine does. A.J. wants me to tell him, in *rhyme*, how I feel right this moment. Jeez! What am I supposed to write?" Nell slid away from the desk, rose, and practically pulled me into the chair. "You write something, please," she pleaded.

"Nell!"

"C'mon, Liz. Just pretend you're me. A.J.'ll never know you aren't. Like I said, on the Internet, no one knows you're a dog."

I glared at Nell. "Oh, thanks a whole helluva lot."

Nell sank to her knees and pretended to beg.

"Which one of is—or isn't—the dog, here? You've got me all confused," I said.

"Me, too. I'll owe you big-time for this," Nell said, an urgent look in her eyes.

I looked at the screen and scrolled up to read the rest of Nell's chat with A.J. so I could get into character. I felt like a latter-day Cyrano de Bergerac, only with a considerably daintier nose. "How do I—you— feel right now? In rhyme? That's what I'm—we're supposed to tell A.J.?"

Nell nodded.

I typed, as Nell leaned over my shoulder:

I'm thrilled a guy from way upstate
Would want to take me on a date

"Ooh, I like that. This is fun," she giggled.

"You're right, actually, it is." I added a second couplet.

Oh, lucky me! What perfect karma
To find a hunky dairy "farma"

"Oh, Liz, that's a hoot. As corny as Kansas in August."

"Isn't that what you want? Should we add more to it or send it?" I was getting into this, almost wishing Nell would ask me to continue to "ghost" her for another few stanzas. I thought about Rick Byron's ghostwriting proposition and smiled to myself, still glad I'd declined it.

"Heck, let's send it now," Nell said with finality. "If we—I mean *I*—write too much, he might think this comes naturally to me, and ask me to send him dopey rhymes off the cuff all the time, and *then* where would I be?" Nell's hand flew to her mouth. "Oops, I didn't mean to say that your rhyme was dopey, Liz. And right after you did me such a big favor."

"You're right; it *is* dopey," I acknowledged. "Not the kindest reflection on you, though. Maybe I should have made you sound more like Emily Dickinson."

"I'm glad you didn't try. It wouldn't have fit with the Ellie Clampett act I was doing for him."

My second wind was now gone. I needed to switch off my brain and go to bed. Maybe the angels would be good to me tonight and send me a yummy dream about Jack. I missed him already. "I've got a big day ahead of me; if it's not too much trouble, can you sign off my computer in the next few minutes or so? I need to get some sleep," I told Nell.

Nell smiled at me, seated herself at the desk, and typed "Gotta say goodnight now, I need my beauty rest," then got off-line. "Thanks a zillion, Liz." She gave my shoulder a little squeeze and nodded at the computer. "I think you may have temporarily saved my *Bad Date* butt."

"Well," I sighed, "that's what friends are for. Goodnight, Nell."

She went into her own bedroom, happily humming the theme from *Green Acres*.

25/Moving On

I spent a sleepless night, dreading getting up in the morning to face the wrath of Jason and F.X. I really had no excuses to offer them. And I was sick of lying.

Coffee and prune danish—my all-time favorite breakfast food—were waiting for me when I got to work. My two bosses looked grim.

"Liz, you've been with the agency ever since you graduated from college," F.X. began.

"And we adore you—don't get us wrong," Jason said, completing F.X.'s sentence. "But you've managed to get two strikes against you within just a few weeks."

"In baseball, you get three strikes," I offered meekly.

F.X. tried to smile. "The only thing advertising and baseball have in common are pitches. Lillian was gunning for you after you walked out of the Snatch meeting."

"I blanked," I confessed. "Dried up. And I thought it would be the worser part of valor to admit that I had no third campaign to present rather than just walk out. That way, maybe my behavior could have been interpreted as a sudden stomach virus, like, I don't know, bad clams or something. I know it was unfortunate that Lord Kitchener happens to be Lillian Swallow's inamorata, but you have to agree that the product wasn't an easy one to come up with a campaign for, given its name."

Jason couldn't suppress his laugh. "Actually, that's why we assigned you the account. F.X. and I put our heads together before we asked you to do the copywriting and we couldn't come up with anything better."

"In fact, what we came up with was worse," F.X concurred, "but writer's block is no excuse."

I reached for another mini danish. At least I would be fed well this morning.

"So what happened in Miami?" Jason asked me.

"I missed the meeting."

F.X. adjusted his glasses on his nose. "Speaking of stomach viruses, Jason said something about food poisoning. You seemed fine on *Bad Date* last night. By the way, that was the most entertaining episode yet. Are you sure you can't get me a date with Candy?"

"Candy's not batting right-handed anymore, for the time being, if you catch my drift," I told F.X. "And as of last week, you were still married with children which is why you didn't go down to South Beach." I paused. "Uh-oh. We're talking about Miami again."

"So what did happen down there, Liz?" Jason sniffed the milk as though he smelled feet, decided it was still good, and poured about a quarter of an ounce into his coffee cup.

I decided to tell them the truth. Adding in enough specifics to keep them titillated, yet leaving out Jack's name. "My priorities used to be work, work, work.

So no wonder my relationships suffered in the bargain. I used to love my job, guys. Don't get me wrong. Maybe what I did in Miami, missing the Numbers Crunchers meeting, was some form of 'acting out.' I don't know. But I'm fully aware that I haven't been giving SSA a hundred percent for a while. My blood doesn't race with every challenging new ad campaign. Lately, I feel like a curmudgeonly 'what-do-any-of-us-need-this-for' Andy Rooney type."

I poured myself a glass of orange juice. "So maybe it's time for me to move on. God knows what I'd do, because this is the first and only job I've ever held. But obviously I'm not doing you any favors here anymore." I felt the tears start to come. I really, *really* hadn't wanted to cry. And I hadn't planned to say any of what I had just admitted to F.X. and Jason.

"I guess what I'm saying is that I quit."

I quit? How the hell could I say that? I didn't have another job. I didn't even have another *prospect.*

Jason and F.X. looked at each other. I couldn't tell whether their expressions were ones of relief or concern, or even of melancholy.

"You can't quit, Liz—" F.X. began.

"Because we're firing you." Jason completed his partner's thought.

Holy shit. I've just been fired from the only job I've ever had.

F.X.'s thick lenses were beginning to fog up. "You're the best copywriter we've ever had, Liz. But you've become more of a liability than an asset."

"Nevertheless, we both know that you can't collect unemployment benefits if you walk away. Which is why we're firing you," Jason added. There was a very long pause. No one knew what to say. "I guess it's probably a good idea for you to start clearing your stuff out of your office." He turned away and reached for a tissue. "Shit. This is like cutting off a leg or something. You're family, Liz."

"The leg has gangrene, Jason," I said, no longer able to control my own tears now that he had lost it. "You've got to do what you have to. Which is to save the body. SSA is better off without me right now and you and F.X. and I . . . we all know it." The tears fell silently down my cheeks. At least I wasn't bawling.

Jason took both my hands in his. F.X. came up behind me and put a hand on my shoulder. "I really hope you win that million on *Bad Date*, Liz. We're all rooting for you."

"I hope so, too," I sniffled, choking back a sob. "Because now I'm *really* gonna need the dough!"

It's amazing how much crap you can amass in a dozen or so years at a job. My two Clio awards, which for years had made impressive bookends in my office, would now make spectacular doorstops at home. Demetrius helped me schlep cartons of detritus down to a taxi; he even rode home with me and carried the boxes upstairs in our West End Avenue building's freight elevator.

"I don't know whether I'm coming or going, mahn," my former art director said, as he unloaded the last box into my apartment's narrow hallway.

I didn't need to ask what he meant. There were twice as many boxes lined up waiting to be removed from the apartment as Demetrius and I were bringing in. The stereo was blasting tunes from Madonna's *The Immaculate Collection*.

Jem was sitting cross-legged in the center of the living room, surrounded by more cartons, methodically inventorying their contents. She looked up at me, somewhat surprised. "You're not usually home this early."

"You're right, I'm not," I said softly. "I just got fired." I motioned to the boxes Demetrius was carrying into my bedroom. "I guess I'll be home a lot from now on."

Jem put down her pen and placed the clipboard on top of one of her boxes. "Then I guess now would be a bad time to tell you I'm moving out." She tried to make a little joke out of it, to coax even a tiny smile from my lips. I wasn't in a smiley mood. "Carl asked me to move in with him," she continued. "And it just seems to make sense, given that I've been over there nearly every night since we started seeing each other, it's only one rent for the two of us . . ."

"You don't need to come up with reasons to convince me why it's a good idea, Jem."

She came over and gave me a hug. Carl had turned her into a hugger. "I was pissed off at you for a while, Liz, but that's water under the proverbial bridge. It's not as though you're losing a friend."

"No, but I'm losing a roommate." I blinked back tears while we held each other. "Jem . . . I couldn't be happier for you. You really deserve it. I hope Carl realizes what a great catch he's got." I sniffled and pulled away.

Jem brushed a wayward strand of hair from my eyes. "Wish me luck," she said.

"I do." I smiled.

"Hey," she added, tugging on my hand like we were six-year-olds on the playground. "I owe you a bottle of champagne."

I went into my bedroom for a much-needed tissue, slamming the door shut behind me a bit more forcefully than I had intended. I burst into sobs. Johnnie Walker, curious about the sound, poked her furry head out from under my bed. I picked her up, held her to my chest, and silently forgave her for shredding Jack's Irish tweed sweater-in-progress.

There was a gentle rap on the door. "Come in," I said through my tears.

It was Demetrius. "Jemima invited me to stay for a farewell drink. She's going to whip up something she calls a Limbo. Dark Jamaican rum in my honor, and a coconut milk eggnog she make from scratch, plus a dash of fresh ground Grenada nutmeg on top. A hangover so sweet you won't see the floor coming up to hit your face." He smacked his lips.

"Tell her I'll have three," I said. "And see if you can find our other roommate Nell and tell her that her kitten was hiding under my bed." Demetrius made cooing noises at the tiny fluffball, so I brought Johnnie Walker over to him. The kitten developed an immediate fascination with Demetrius's dreds. *Better his hair than mine,* I thought.

I noticed that my computer was up and running. It was still online. Great. I hated to think this way, but I found myself with one less person to help with the rent, no job, and Nell had left the Internet connection on. "You and Jem start drinking without me. I'll be out in a minute," I said. Demetrius closed the door as he left the room, and curious to see what Web site was open, I wiggled the mouse, which "disappeared" the screensaver and brought up an instant message chat that had been running between Nell and A.J. for God-knows-how-long. "BRB," her IM had said. I wondered how long ago she'd told him she'd be right back. I didn't even know if she was in the apartment. Talk about leaving a guy hanging.

Intrigued, and having more or less received tacit permission from Nell to write whatever might be guaranteed to bring them together for a date, I sat down at my computer and scrolled up the length of the IM conversation. Nell had been so up front about sharing her initial chat with A.J., as though it was a game we were both playing with him, that I guessed she wouldn't be too particular about my reading the contents of this communication either.

Jeez, it looked like they'd been pouring out their hearts to each other all day. A.J. Stevens seemed like a genuinely nice guy—in cyberspace, anyway—anxious to please, eager to fulfill Nell's every wish no matter how insignificant, each desire no matter how slight. He told her he wanted to take her up to a mountain-top upstate near New Paltz, on the hiking trails adjacent to the Mohonk Mountain House property. He'd proposed a picnic on a plateau from which you could see something like five or six states on a clear day. Nell had assured him that she had a new pair of Timberlands that she was dying to break in. I don't think Nell even knows where to *buy* a pair of Timberlands. A.J. was tossing around nature-boy terms like "Gore-Tex," to which Nell had replied—in all earnestness—"I thought it was Bush who was the

Texan." He'd then written "LOL." This fledgling relationship needed help if it was ever going to fly once Nell and A.J. finally met one another.

Time to play Casper the friendly ghostwriter again. I sat down at the computer and flexed my fingers like a piano virtuoso might, just before attempting to play the Rach III. "Whew! Sorry that took so long," I typed. "I hope you haven't been waiting too long."

"Not too long," came back the immediate reply. "I figured it must have been something important. Don't worry your gorgeous blonde head about it. I wasn't afraid you'd abandoned me or anything."

I typed faster. "Believe me, A.J., I'm the kind of girl who plays for keeps. The last thing I would ever do is string you along." *Oh, God, I'm going to e-mail hell,* I thought, where you're chained to your computer in a hot, cramped room and are forced to IM with cyber-flashers to whom you never gave your e-mail address and who want to know how big your hooters are.

"I love the picnic idea," I continued. "Oh . . . but I should warn you, I'm a strict ovo-lacto vegetarian. So you can leave the curried chicken salad at home. Might I suggest we bring along some of my favorite foods? I could feed you with strawberries dipped in chocolate. If you bring them, I have a cold bag in my wicker hamper that can keep them the perfect temperature. And along with the strawberries you could bring me some Veuve Cliquot—it's my favorite champagne. Did you know that oysters are supposed to be an aphrodisiac? You did? I bet you did. Well, I wouldn't be eating them anyway. But guess what? You won't need oysters, because you'll have *me*."

A.J. took a few moments to read "Nell's" IM before

responding. "It sounds like a plan. I could get us a room at the Mohonk Mountain House for the night, or even for the weekend, if you're into it. I realize we really don't know each other, but the proprietors are good friends of my family. We've known them for years. Feel free to phone them and tell them you've been asked to spend the weekend there with me and ask them to be candid about the kind of guy I am. Do you like fireplaces?"

"Is that a question?" I fired back. Oops, I sounded more like Liz and less like Nell on that one.

"Well, do you?" he asked, followed by a :) emoticon. Smileys and everything. A.J. was simply precious. Nell would adore him.

"Fireplaces are sheer heaven," I wrote.

"I trust you have no objection to four-poster beds."

"Not so long as you're sharing it with me, A.J.," I responded, and followed it with a ;) which I hoped was an emoticon wink. "By the way, you know it's really bad karma to bring up our IM conversations when we're actually on our romantic getaway. Let's just promise each other to enjoy those moments and not rehash our correspondence, okay?" I heard a noise in the kitchen. "Oops, gotta run. Cocktail hour at the ranch. More later, sweetums. xxooxxoxoxo. Bye."

"Bye."

I signed off the Internet before being able to extract a promise from A.J. not to bring up the subject of our e-mail messages. I didn't want to risk him referencing all the things "Nell" had just told him and have her vehemently deny ever sharing them with him. If Nell wondered why we were disconnected, I planned to feign surprise that the computer had been online the whole time and suggest that maybe AOL had kicked us off for not responding after a while.

I found my two roommates in the kitchen, sampling the Limbo drinks. Jem handed me one. I tasted the frothy concoction. Delicious.

"We took you at your word," Jem said, pointing to two more Limbos lined up on the kitchen counter. "Demetrius said you ordered three."

"These are . . . wow . . ." I said, licking my lips. I looked at the two more glasses of elixir awaiting me. "The Limbo, huh? Gives new meaning to going on a bender."

Nell raised her glass. "Well. We have some things to toast this afternoon. Some good," she said, nodding at Jem, "some not-so-good," she added, looking at me, "and . . ." she hugged her glass to her chest. "And, well, who knows. To moving on."

I looked at the happy tears in Jem's eyes. She looked at the unhappy ones in mine. Demetrius watched us with extreme curiosity.

"Yes. To moving on," I agreed. "And may it be—where all of us are concerned—a good thing. A very good thing indeed."

26/Design for Loving

The following three weeks were weird. I felt root-less. I rose at seven-thirty every morning because that's what my body was accustomed to from years of being essentially a nine-to-fiver. I wandered aimlessly around the apartment trying to find something useful to do. The only way I could pry Nell away from my computer, where she spent the better part of every day sitting in her little blue Victoria's Secret bathrobe e-mailing A.J., was to dangle listings of sample sales in front of her face. "BRB" became her euphemism for "Prada is discounting shoes by thirty percent from noon to two P.M. only."

So when my computer became my own again, I took the opportunity to browse Web sites like Monster.com and scope out some places to send my résumé. I became the queen of the cover letter. But I didn't get so much as a nibble. In fact, I learned that the downside of being able to e-mail a résumé to a prospective employer is that they can e-mail you a re-jection that much faster.

I admit to being a smidge envious of Nell, because she could still afford to shop. For example, I would go into the Donna Karan store and try on an amazing pair of olive suede pants that looked like they were constructed just for me. Then I'd look at the price tag and realize it was the same as two unemployment benefit checks. Reality checkout time. The pants went back on the rack. My purchasing jones had to be satisfied with browsing for the time being. I had a closet full of clothes anyway, some of which had been there so long I'd forgotten they existed and they now qualified as "vintage." Maybe I could unload them and make a few bucks. Had I spent the past couple of years at my job hating most every minute of it and collecting a paycheck so I could clothes shop? *Ugh.* What had I become? At least being jobless compelled me to confront what was really important to me. And what I could—or be more or less forced to—do without.

I was surprised at how quickly I became used to only the two of us, Nell and me, living together. Jem's moving out seemed like eons ago, although it had only been two weeks. I missed her, but her residence seemed like something from the distant, rather than the recent, past.

Jack had been a real brick. He decided I wasn't eating enough now that I was unemployed, so he treated me to all sorts of wonderful restaurants I never in a gazillion years would have stepped foot in on my own. In fact I suggested he curtail his gastronomic generosity because I was afraid I was blimping out on French sauces and desserts and would look like a hippo on camera every Sunday evening. My darling's response to that was to enroll us in a gym membership.

Gee, thanks, Jack! I thought.

Well, it gave me somewhere to go during the day. I

would spend a half hour on the treadmill going nowhere and think about how my career was . . . going
nowhere. At least my love life was golden. Except that
we had to sneak around everywhere, which somewhat tarnished things for me.

On the Saturday evening before the seventh episode
of *Bad Date*, we were walking across town from
dinner at the Tapas Lounge, enroute to Serendipity
for dessert. Jack had never been there and I assured
him it was a real New York experience. Hand in hand
we had just crossed Second Avenue, when a sudden
realization made me stop in my tracks. "This is so
nice," I said, indicating our joined hands. "But if you
hadn't seen that cab speeding toward us, I don't think
you would have touched me."

"What are you talking about, Liz?" Jack looked totally confused.

"I don't like keeping our relationship a secret. I
don't want to feel like we have to dine in dark restaurants or order room service from the Waldorf's kitchen.
That's another reason I suggested we get dessert at a
bright, bustling place."

"We're recognizable now," Jack argued. "At
least by anyone who's hooked on *Bad Date*. If we're
caught . . . *canoodling* in public, we could end up at
the center of a quiz show scandal."

I sighed. He had a point, but I still didn't like it.

"Cheer up," Jack added, "maybe there's a way to
compromise. Maybe if you were sort of incognito, we
could indulge in public displays of affection."

"Incognito?"

"Yeah. You could wear your blonde wig from Jem
and Carl's Pywacket date."

Was he serious? Besides, it had been destroyed in Jem's attempt at a satanic ritual. "You're kidding, aren't you, Jack?"

He looked around, then caressed my cheek. "Of course I was."

"See, to me," I said, focused on the square of pavement beneath my feet, afraid to look him directly in the eye. "Keeping us a secret feels . . . I don't know . . . like we're less than legitimate. Being clandestine is losing its allure. It adds spice, but you can't make an entire dish with spice alone. We're both legally and emotionally available, and we hardly get to see each other since you're in Miami for most of the week. When we finally get the chance to be together, I don't want to have to keep my hands and lips away from you every time we step beyond your hotel room."

Jacked tipped up my chin with his finger. "What about the show, Liz? Answer me honestly."

"I'll always answer you honestly, Jack. I *do* have my 'eyes on the prize,' as Rob Dick says. Yes, I'd like to win. Who wouldn't want to win a million dollars, especially when they're more than halfway there? I've come this far. Don't you want to win?"

"Not as much as you do, I guess. But if advancing on the show is as important to you as it sounds like it is, then why tempt fate by trumpeting our relationship for the world to see?"

"I know you're right," I acknowledged begrudgingly as I trudged alongside Jack. "I'm so confused. I want to tell the world what a great guy I've got— finally—*and* I want to survive *Bad Date* 'til the end. I guess I've convinced myself of the possibility of a win-win situation."

We stopped outside Serendipity and I eyed the dessert menu posted in front of the restaurant like I was a kid in a candy store, enumerating all the mouth-watering options, each one more enticing than the last.

"One thing is for certain," Jack muttered testily, peering over my shoulder at the menu. "You definitely want to have your cake and eat it, too."

After week six, the studio audience had sent Luke back to the painted desert, and Feng shui'd Allegra back to Lala-land following episode seven. Candy was disconsolate over that. She started throwing her cosmetics at the mirror and cursing like a longshoreman. She admitted to me that she had fallen in love for the first time in her life but the "ass-kicker" was that now she was going to be in a cross-country commuter relationship. "It totally bites the big one!" she'd fumed. I suggested she wangle herself a business trip out there by making an appointment with the Frederick's of Hollywood buyers to take a look at her stripwear collection. "You're a household name now because of this show," I reminded her. "The sale should be a piece of cake."

Jack flew up after work on Thursday so we could spend more time together before the telecast of episode eight. "This is your day, Liz," he told me Friday morning. "Whatever you want to do, we'll do."

I looked at him kind of sideways. "Are you sure?"

"Totally."

"Then let's go Alphabet Shopping," I said.

"What the hell is that?"

"I made it up a few years ago, but I've never actually done it. Alphabet Shopping is when you go from store to store, A through Z. To make the sport more challenging, you can narrow down the merchandise categories. For example, fine jewelry: Asprey, Bulgari, Cartier . . . did you want something? A nasty cigar for example with a sterling silver thingy to clip the end off? We'll head to Davidoff."

Jack pretended to look queasy. "I know I told you we could do anything you want, but does it have to be jewelry? You'll bankrupt me."

"I didn't say we were going to *buy* anything," I teased. "Just *shop* for it. There's a difference."

He smiled. "I think it's more of a technicality."

"Besides," I added, "who said anything about my expecting you to take out your wallet?"

"You're on unemployment," he reminded me.

"*W* is for window shopping," I replied. "Okay then, I've got another category. With something for you in every store. Ritzy Italian designers: Armani, Bottega Veneta, Cavalli—those first three alone are within a few blocks from one another on Madison Avenue. I've always imagined going into Giorgio Armani, even to *pretend* I can afford to dress like Sharon Stone or Nora Roberts."

"Nora who? I know who *Julia* Roberts is." He drew me to him and kissed me on the nose. "Are you sure we can't just watch TV?"

"You're kidding, right?"

"Not really. There's a masters tournament on at four P.M."

"I thought you said this was my day."

Jack sighed and gave me a little squeeze. "Okay,

if that's what you really want, Liz, let's hit the pavement."

How can you not fall in love with a man who will—however reluctantly—give up watching golf to indulge your shopping fantasies?

We entered the Armani boutique and I asked Jack whether he minded if I tried something on. He agreed, as long as he got to choose the outfit. I had my eyes on an ultrachic black pants suit. Jack preferred a beaded cocktail dress with a plunging neckline and an asymmetrical hem. We compromised on both. I was tickled pink that he was being such a good sport. He really was a sweetheart.

When I emerged from the dressing room in the pants suit and a whisper-thin cashmere camisole, Jack drew in his breath. "You look . . . absolutely stunning," he said. "You could go anywhere in that . . . except one place." He placed his hands on my hips and pulled me to him so that, from where he sat, my breasts were nuzzling distance from his face. "Bed," he murmured into my chest. I could feel his warm breath filter through the cashmere to my cleavage.

"Gee, you really know what to say to a girl to make her get undressed," I teased, leaning over to nibble on his lip. I spun away and slipped back into the dressing room, returning to him a few minutes later in the cocktail dress. I started to laugh at his expression. "I never thought people's jaws really dropped. Until now, I assumed it was just a figure of speech."

"Looking at you, I've figured it all out," Jack said. "I don't know why guys put up such a fuss about going shopping with their women. I've just decided that it certainly isn't a waste of an afternoon to accompany my love on an excursion where she gets dressed and undressed and parades her body around in front of me, just for my approval."

"God, I love you, Jack." The words just flew out of my mouth.

His expression changed and he looked at me somewhat soberly. "Do you realize that's the first time you ever said that to me?"

"Wow. You're right." I felt myself grow equally serious.

"How does it make you feel, Liz?"

"Happy. Scared."

"Why?"

"It's hard to be the first one to say the word. I mean I just blurted it out; it wasn't an earnest take-your-hands-in-mine-and-look-deeply-into-your-eyes 'I love you, Jack.' But I certainly did say The Word. And yet it's still scary because, for all I know, you're not emotionally there yet."

Jack clasped my hands in his and looked me squarely in the eye. "Do you love me because I was willing to play your goofy shopping game, or . . . ?"

"I love you because you make me glad to be alive and so happy to be around you. I love you because you have a huge heart and an adventurous spirit. I love you because you're considerate of my feelings, even when I'll admit that on certain occasions they may not be entirely rational."

"Girl logic."

"Okay, girl logic," I laughed. "I love you because I find myself grinning from ear to ear every time I think of you, and one of the reasons I'm grinning is because *you* put that grin on my face." I was even grinning as I spoke the words.

"I love *you*, Liz Pemberley," Jack said softly. He brought our joined hands to his lips and kissed my knuckles.

"Wow," I breathed. I lifted my chin so our lips could meet in a kiss.

"You're very good at that," Jack said, when we broke the embrace.

I smiled. "It takes two," I whispered. I kissed him again, then went back into the dressing room and put my own clothes back on. When I emerged, I started to rush over to hug Jack, who was waiting for me near the center of the store, and found myself momentarily distracted by a familiar head of highlighted blond hair. "Oh, shit," I hissed, and grabbed Jack's arm.

"What the hell is the matter with you, Liz?"

I pointed at the blond man fingering cashmere blend T-shirts. "It's Rick Byron. We'll never sneak past without his noticing us. We'd better hide before he sees us together!" I pulled Jack into an alcove just beyond the menswear and tried the door handle of the closest dressing room. It was locked. "Shit, shit, shit," I muttered. "This is the last thing we need." I realized I was still holding the garments I had tried on. There weren't many people in the store. At any second Rick might turn around and spot us. The dressing room door opened and the gentleman who had occupied it walked past us, giving me a funny look. I hoped he wouldn't alert the staff to the anxious-looking woman lurking there. I poked my head around the corner to see what Rick was up to. He had an armload of garments and was headed our way.

"He's coming toward us," I whispered to Jack.

Jack pulled me into the dressing room with him. He had lodged one foot in the doorway as the suspicious previous occupant was leaving. The door closed behind us.

I looked around and started to giggle. Jack gently placed his palm over my mouth which only made me want to laugh harder, until I ended up with the hiccups. I pointed at our reflections. "Mi-rrors!" I hiccuped. "So-rry."

"Sorry for what?" Jack asked.

"My hi-hiccups. Oops."

"Hold your breath and swallow," Jack said softly in my ear. Then he darted his tongue in there and I was a goner. Not only couldn't I stop the hiccups, but he had just gotten me extraordinarily aroused. "Get undressed," he whispered. "Don't look incredulous. That's what dressing rooms are for!"

I stifled another giggle. The hiccups were almost gone. "Are you sure that door's locked?"

Jack went over and tested the handle. "It seems to lock from the outside as soon as it closes. But there's an additional button here." He depressed it. By the time he returned to the camel-colored upholstered bench, I was down to my bra and panties.

He looked at me with a mischievous glint in his eye. "Everything," he said.

"You too, then."

Jack removed every stitch of clothing and maneuvered the bench to the center of the room. We were surrounded on nearly all sides by illuminated mirrors. "I don't think I've ever made love under such flattering lighting," I joked.

"Shh." Seating himself, Jack touched a finger to my lips and with his free hand, pulled me onto his lap. Our lips and tongues met in a deliciously rapturous kiss.

I was ready for him, enveloping him, taking him inside me. I put my arms around Jack's neck and held him as close as I could.

"Look at us," Jack encouraged me as I rode him, rocking my hips slowly to take him deeper inside me. He cupped my breasts, teasing my nipples, then sucking them; his warm breath felt like a life force rippling through me.

I watched our images in the mirrors, admiring the way our bodies entwined, the way our rhythms became perfectly synchronized, the speed and intensity of our lovemaking increasing. I arched my back and Jack buried his face in my breasts as we came together, my softness muffling his sexual ecstasy; throwing my head back, I emitted a silent scream of pleasure. For several minutes we remained intertwined on the bench, holding one another. I nuzzled the side of Jack's neck and kissed away a sweaty rivulet.

"It smells like sex in here," Jack commented, as we began to get dressed.

I took a bottle of cologne from my purse and started to spritz it around the room.

Jack started to laugh. "This is supposed to be a *men's* dressing room."

"So sue me," I said, replacing the bottle of Trésor in my bag. I sniffed the air. "Well, at least it somewhat masks the unmistakable. Do you think Rick Byron is gone by now?"

"Either that or he's been trying to listen in at the keyhole." Jack poked his head out the door.

"There isn't a keyhole . . . is there?"

Jack looked at me and rolled his eyes. "Figure of speech." He stepped out of the dressing room. "The coast appears to be clear." He extended his hand and motioned for me to precede him out of the store.

I grinned at him when we reached the pavement. "Jack, do you think if we could see each other every day if we wanted to, instead of living in separate cities, that we wouldn't be so tempted to make up for lost time?"

"Like what we just did back there?"

I nodded.

Jack stopped walking and traced a fingertip along the length of my cheek. "I find myself wanting you all the time, Liz."

"Wow," I breathed. "I feel the same way, you know. . . . I guess you've already figured that out. And thank you for being such a sport and indulging my shopping fantasy."

Jack squeezed my hand. "The Armanis were spectacular on you . . . but when all is said and done, I think you look even better naked."

27/Animal Husbandry

Tensions were high in the studio on Sunday evening. Milo and Double-E weren't pulling any punches on their mutual dislike and disgust, each calling the other a misogynist. In the hair and makeup room Rosalie wouldn't shut up about the long-gone Luke, claiming that one thing Jewish girls and Native Americans have in common are reservations. "Haven't you heard that old joke about us? That's what we make for dinner," she turned and said to Jack, by way of explanation. Then she seemed to set her sights on him, which made me a little nervous. "What a catch you'd make," she said, dilating her pupils. "I mean you're a chef. A girl would never need to enter the kitchen."

"Thanks, Rosalie, but I need a woman who will cook alongside me. Even if it's only slicing lemons."

I cracked up when I heard this, almost doing a spit take with the swig of seltzer I'd just taken. Gladiola whacked me on the back.

"I wasn't choking!" I told her.

"Good. And don't mess up your makeup either," she warned good-naturedly. The skunklike streak of orange (which she'd later peroxided to a platinum white), that had been part of her hairdo a few weeks ago was now gone, in favor of a meticulously rendered American flag pattern all over her bleached, cropped hair.

Candy was glum. Ordinarily, she was the life of the party, making off-color jokes and creating a rambunctious atmosphere, which usually did much to alleviate the competitive tensions we contestants were feeling just prior to the telecast. This evening she was dressed in a leopard print catsuit with matching knee-high boots. Underneath the sleek jumpsuit, which was unsnapped practically to her navel, she wore a black lace bra.

"That's real 'prime time,' " I kidded her, when we were alone in our dressing room.

"You're confusing me with someone who cares," she shot back. "Look, Liz, I got a confession to make, and I figured it would help you if I said something about it now, in case you got a strategy about winning or something. 'Cause I don't care no more."

I was intrigued. "What's your confession?"

"I'm gonna bail tonight. I been thinkin' about it ever since Allegra went home." Candy started to tear up.

"Hey, hey," I consoled, offering her a tissue. "You don't want to spoil your mascara." I put my arm around her shoulder.

"It's like, it don't mean anything anymore," she sniffled. "Being here. I mean now that Allegra is three thousand miles away. I could try to stick it out 'til the show's over, 'cause God knows, winning the money would be great . . . but to be honest, I've told so many stories out of school that I got an anonymous letter a few days ago telling me maybe I should take a nice trip out of town for a while. So what am I still here for? To get measured for a coffin? For some dumb-ass prize money that I probably wouldn't-a won to begin with? For my design business? Shit, we've got the Internet. And I can do my drafting anywhere. I don't need to be in my Bay Ridge walk-up to do it. So I'm gonna bail. Get myself voted off before I get bumped off. Take the money I've gotten up to now and move in with Allegra in Benedict Canyon. That's near Hollywood, you know," she informed me. "Now I can even introduce my Stripwear to Frederick's in person," she added brightly.

"So what are you planning to do this evening that will pretty much guarantee that you'll get kicked off the show?"

Candy paused in the middle of lining her lower lip. She smiled. "A girl's gotta retain a little mystery, doesn't she?"

As we headed down the hall to the set, Rick stepped out of his dressing room and grabbed my arm, pulling me inside the door. "What's the matter, Liz? Why aren't you returning my phone calls?" he asked me.

"Because I think they're inappropriate, under the circumstances," I replied.

"And which circumstances are those?" He was practically pouting.

"One, it compromises our mutual and individual integrity while we're doing the show. Two, it seems to me you're already involved with someone. If the tabloids are correct, anyway."

"Never mind about my personal life. Are *you* seeing someone?"

"C'mon Rick. We've got a show to do." I opened

the door of his dressing room and started down the hall.

He practically scampered behind me, speaking under his breath. "You know, I've got an incredible crush on you, Liz. But I'm not sure I *like* you."

I turned back to him and smiled. "You'll get over it."

"Which one? Or do you mean both things?"

"Figure it out," I answered enigmatically.

No one much liked Double-E DuPree, but you had to admit that he was a character. On tonight's episode he talked about seducing his son's girlfriend and having the woman turn the tables on him by telling him that she'd laid down a bet with DuPree's son that his dad would try to make time with her—a bet which she told Double-E she'd just won, obviously—leaving him high and dry with the check in a high-class see-and-be-seen kind of restaurant in New Orleans. Double-E chuckled when he added that he and his son hadn't spoken since then.

"Gee, Double-E, isn't life kind of short for that?" Rick Byron asked. "I mean we're talking about your only son here, dude."

Rosalie Rothbaum shared the unfortunate experience of what happened when a date dared her to give him a blowjob on Coney Island's famous Cyclone rollercoaster. "The doctors in the emergency room couldn't stop laughing."

Milo, a perennial crowd favorite, who carried his costumed Chihuahua on his lap at every broadcast, told America about a neighbor who he'd seen nearly every day walking a Russian wolfhound. "They were both exquisite animals," Milo said of the canine and its owner. "I always made sure to admire his dog. And one day, Serge asked me to come up to his apartment for a cup of tea. He said he had something very important to say to me. And we had the loveliest afternoon. We listened to Brahms and we talked about books—we both love James Michener—and he was resting his arm over my shoulder the whole time. So, finally, I got up the courage to ask what made him ultimately invite me to his place, what was it he wanted to tell me." There was a long silence. "And he said he needed to be sure that he and I were simpatico before he asked me, because it was very important to him and to Vronksy."

"Vronsky?" Rick asked Milo.

"The wolfhound," Milo said sadly. "Serge said he was going off to see his lover in St. Louis for two weeks and needed someone he could trust to dog-sit. I was devastated."

Rick looked genuinely sympathetic. "So what happened?"

"Shnook that I am, I said yes. Do you have any idea how much a Russian wolfhound can eat?"

Jack talked about the trip he took with a former girlfriend to Las Vegas. This was Monica the cultural anthropologist who had done her Ph.D. thesis on the history of fairytales: "Goldilocks and her Forbears." He'd given her his credit card to "buy something nice for herself." The "something nice" she bought turned out to be a couple of buckets of hundred-dollar chips, which went right back to the house in games of roulette and blackjack. "She couldn't just buy a dress and some accessories, like a *normal* woman," he bemoaned.

"Do you know the definition of clinical insanity?" Rick asked Jack incredulously. "What kind of guy just hands over his credit card to some chick, especially in Vegas?"

"A generous one," I quipped. That was Jack's Achilles' heel. He was too damn nice.

"Monica and I had been dating for about eight months at the time and I hadn't a clue she had a gambling problem," Jack told America. "But let me tell you, when these guys in dark suits with earpieces come up to you and each one grabs an arm and pinches you in a way so that you know they mean business, it's a freaky deal."

"So why'd they come after *you*?" Rick asked.

"It was *my* credit card she'd just maxxed out. The only fortunate thing to come out of it—aside from the decision to end the relationship—was that I'd handed her a card with a preset spending limit. If I'd given her my American Express card, I'd probably be in some Dickensian debtor's prison for the rest of my life."

"Well, this gives added meaning to the phrase 'a fool and his money are soon parted,' " Rick said, as Jack descended the cone throne's pedestal and returned to his own chair. I wished I could have belted our Hollywood host in his perfectly white, perfectly capped teeth for taking potshots at my lover's insanely admirable, unflagging good nature and generosity.

"Liz Pemberley, come on down!" Rick announced. "Or rather, come on up! So, what's tonight's tale of woe, Lizzy?"

Did I ever mention that I really hate to be called "Lizzy"?

"Oh, I thought I'd contribute my variation on this credit card theme, *Ricky*. Actually it's a kissing cousin to Jack's experience." I discussed my less-than-idyllic Cancun vacation a few years ago when *I* ended up in credit card debt because my boyfriend at the time had more or less pissed away two weeks' worth of hotel accommodations through his generous, multiple contributions to the resort's bars and gaming tables. So I had to pay the bill or consider what life might be like in a Mexican jail.

The next name to pop out of the gumball machine was Candy's. She took her wad of gum from her mouth and stuck it to the underside of her captain's chair. When she sat down in the hot seat, she slid her fingers into the metal polygraph cones and took a deep breath. As she began to speak, I noticed that, uncharacteristically, she was keeping her boisterous, gravelly voice very even.

"I was going to tell youse tonight about this date I had where it was a Saturday morning and we were going to go watch a local little league game which my nephew PeeWee Fortunato was in—that kid's a great shortstop, by the way—and my date, Vinny, asked me to take my car and drive it 'cuz he had a migraine and couldn't see straight. He said he was seeing colors, ya know, so he thought he'd be a menace on the road. But he was real firm about not wanting to break our date. So I picked him up and we're driving along Fifth Avenue in Bay Ridge and we're just past Kleinfeld's Bridal, and he tells me he needs to stop at a bank to get some cash, 'cuz he's got none on him and what if we want to get a Coke or a coupla hot dogs or something. So I'm patting my pocketbook and telling him 'No problem, *I* got money. And we're gonna miss the first inning if we don't step on it.' And ya know, in little league, they don't play the full nine, so you get there late, you miss a good chunk of the game. But Vinny insists he's gotta stop at the bank. So I pull over to the curb and he goes inside, and whaddya know, maybe five, seven minutes later, he comes out with, like, this canvas bag, and he opens the passenger door of my Accord and says, 'Floor it!' and I says, 'What? You got a rabbit turd for brains?' And I kicked my leg out and he got a bootful right in the nuts. So he grabs his crown jewels and drops the bag of cash on the sidewalk, and then I hit the gas, with my passenger door still open and I leave Vinny there on Fifth Avenue, still clutching his balls. The good part of the story is that I got to see my nephew make a great play to end the first inning and I told my friend Laurie-Ann's brother Joe, who's a cop—and whose son Joey Jr. is the team's centerfielder—about Vinny's little trip to the bank."

Candy licked her lips. "Anybody gotta drink of water?" she asked. No one had ever made that request during the actual show. Geneva indicated that Rick needed to cut away to a commercial. He announced that Candy would continue when we returned to the air.

"So as I was saying," Candy went on, when we resumed broadcasting, "I was going to tell you all about my very brief date with Vinny—he wasn't a close friend or nothing, by the way—but I changed my mind. Instead, I just want to say that all of the stuff I've been sharing with all you out there for these past seven weeks, eight counting tonight, has been total bull—"

She was *bleeped*, but those of us on the set and in the studio audience heard the entire word. There was a collective murmur; people were unsure how to react to this bombshell.

"Yeah. I've been making it all up."

"Uh . . . Candy?" Rick said after what seemed like an interminable pause.

"Yeah, Rick?"

"The needle on the polygraph didn't move when you were talking about your date with Vinny. Or any of your other dates over the past eight weeks. But it actually went haywire when you just told us you'd been fabricating these anecdotes all this time. We've been watching the screen above your head. We can even run back the footage and show you, can't we, Geneva? Is Rob Dick around? Does anyone know what the rules are for something like this?"

From her position alongside camera two, Geneva shrugged. She made a hand gesture to Rick to move on.

"Well, Candy, unless you're a good enough liar to fool our expertly calibrated equipment, courtesy of the PrevariTech Corporation, it would seem to me, and to our studio audience—" Rick gestured to them, almost in supplication. "It would seem that you've actually been telling the truth all along and you're only lying now by saying that you invented all your disaster dates."

"But if you lie, you get kicked off the show, right?" Candy said.

"Well, that's up to tonight's studio audience. And I can't presume to vouch for what they're thinking at this moment." He raised his hand for quiet. "And, correct me if I'm wrong, but this show will be even more suspenseful if for the time being we don't let on our opinions about Candy's little performance this evening." He offered his hand to Candy, who rose from the cone throne and permitted Rick to escort her back to her seat. She recovered her gum and popped it back in her mouth.

"And now for the final *Bad Date* contestant of the evening . . . Anella Avignon!" Rick said, as the last ball of the night was ejected from the machine.

Nell sauntered up to the cone throne and installed herself. "A lot of you think that because I grew up on Park Avenue that I've led a charmed life. It's been pretty good, that's true. But I've had my share of ups and downs."

"You mean we shouldn't hate you because you're beautiful?" Rick quipped.

"Yeah, whatever," Nell responded. "And it's also true that I haven't had as many nightmare dates as a lot of my fellow contestants up here have had. That's mostly because I'm not as brave as they are. They just keep getting back on that dating horse, no matter how many times they get thrown, thinking that Mr. or Ms. Right is still out there waiting for them. And they'll never find them if they stop looking."

Nell adjusted her fingers in the metal cones. "And I'm here to confess that several days ago, I did something really nasty. And I've been really worried about my karma since then, so maybe if I share it with everyone tonight, then, you know, it will sort of wipe the slate clean."

I felt a knot in my stomach.

"Okay, I haven't had thirteen really bad dates. I mean, at least I can't remember having had them. So I decided to find a man and get myself a date that would be a real nightmare and tell everyone about it tonight."

Nell went on to explain how she had gone on the Internet and found a Future Farmers of America chat room. "So I started e-mailing this guy named A.J. whose family owns a dairy farm near New Paltz. And I made him think I was a real Daisy Mae type, so he would ask me out. And I don't know whether he saw through my bull or whether my country-bumpkin act was what made him invite me on a picnic, but I went. And I thought I would be telling you this evening about how this uptown girl arranged to meet this up-state guy, this hayseed who wore overalls and chewed on a stalk of wheat or something, and we'd all have a good laugh."

Nell leaned forward a bit in the cone throne. "So, honey, I just want to apologize for being a real twit and having, well, dishonest motives. Because I really love you. He's here tonight, ladies and gentlemen. My fiancé, A.J. Stevens."

Your what? I thought.

The audience strained to see who Nell was talking about. The size of the knot in my stomach doubled.

"Yeah, our first date was a fabulous, long romantic weekend upstate, and now we're engaged. Isn't that great?! A.J.'s family supplies most of the milk and other dairy products to Brooklyn, Queens, Nassau, and Suffolk Counties. And he's got a master's degree in business administration from Cornell's agriculture school, which we call 'Moo-U,' and he's *really* gorgeous . . ."

Camera one zoomed in for a close-up of A.J. Good God, he really *did* look like a Ken doll. Tanned, handsome, and blond. He and Nell would make an ostentatiously good-looking couple.

". . . and sweet and kind and generous and funny," Nell continued.

I found myself beaming. It may have been the quickest courtship of the century, but for Nell's sake, I hoped she'd have the same blissful look on her face forty years from now.

"Although, I have to say . . ." Nell paused dramatically, "that when A.J. told me that it was something that I shared about myself in one of our e-mails that really made him go for me in a big way . . . well, I don't really remember saying the things he was talking about. I mean, I can get kind of flaky sometimes, so maybe I did. I don't even know if you can print out an IM conversation on the Net, but I have a sneaking suspicion that A.J. got a little help from somewhere."

The knot in my stomach felt like it was the size of a watermelon. Since Nell had invited me to help her snag A.J., would she now cleanse her karma, expose me as her ghostwriter, and suggest that I might have been responsible for the mysterious push her romance had received?

"A.J. says that I shouldn't worry about remembering exactly what I told him about myself and my interests and all that," Nell continued. "He just says we should be grateful that God brought us together. And I think that is so loving and so sweet. But I have a feeling the intervention was maybe slightly less than divine and a little closer to earth."

Please don't look at me, Nell. Please don't look at me.

She didn't.

Whew! Double-whew!

"Anyway, I'll be moving upstate to live with A.J. And we're going to open a little petting zoo on his family farm, so that kids can understand how to be kind to animals and learn to love and respect and appreciate them. And there isn't going to be any charge for that; it'll be free. In fact, the very first animal to live at our new zoo is Johnnie Walker. Sweetie, show them the kitten."

The camera panned over to A.J. who held up the furry creature.

Nell told everyone how she had come to rescue the cat. One or two audience members spontaneously pledged financial support for the zoo venture. *Bad Date* was turning into a Paws telethon. *I love the magic of live—or at least seven-second delay—television. The show's producers and staff had totally lost control of their program. Or had they? I bet they banked on the beauty part of these reality shows being that sometimes you never know what's going to happen next.*

When it came time for the audience to vote someone off the show, *I'm not sure anyone had a clue how things would turn out. Ordinarily, Nell would have been the obvious choice, but Candy had so openly and flagrantly dissed the rules of the game. Maybe they would punish her. On the other hand, if they* didn't kick Nell off the show, then what was the point of any of the rules to begin with? She hadn't shared a bad date story.

It was a nail-biter for a minute or so as tabulated votes seemed to trickle in. People were having a hard time making up their minds. Finally, Rick Byron made the announcement that all the votes were in and Nell had emerged the winner, or should I say the loser. She shook hands with Rick Byron, then held out her arms to A.J. From God-knows-where A.J. had managed to produced a cellophane-wrapped bouquet of two dozen long-stemmed American Beauty roses, which he presented to Nell.

Bad Date's house band played the Mendelssohn wedding recessional as the two of them, Barbie and Ken, walked off the set and out the stage door reserved for the losing contestant of the week.

Back in the Green Room, I gave Nell a huge hug, spent a few moments chatting with A.J., who it seemed couldn't do enough for his new fiancée, and the *Bad Date* contestants, staff, and crew toasted their future.

Jack and I went back to his hotel where we ordered Monte Cristo sandwiches from room service, made love, and then he just held me close until I figured I ought to be heading home. When he began to gently cajole me into staying the night, since Nell had A.J. with her this evening anyway and wouldn't be wasting time wondering where I was, I readily agreed. The last time Jack and I had awakened together had been aboard the *Circe*, and I'd been missing the embrace of his warm morning arms.

It was hard to fall asleep, though. My eyes

remained wide open. I was thinking about Jem moving in with Carl and prenuptial Nell about to head off into the woods with A.J. My overwhelming happiness that both of my roommates had found true love was somewhat dampened by my anxiety about being able to make do with no job and a big, rambling, old-fashioned New York apartment, which had been rendered affordable by splitting the rent three ways. In Manhattan, if you've got a great deal on an apartment, as we ladies did, there is no moving to a smaller place if you find yourself strapped for rent money. New leases on smaller apartments are just as high, if not higher, than renewing a long-standing one on a bigger place.

It was sort of a moot point anyway. With all the recent events in my life, I was looking at not being able to afford to live *anywhere*. Jack enfolded me in his arms, I pressed myself up against his chest, and drifted off to sleep enjoying the next few hours of protection and solace his love and companionship would bring.

28/Taking the Bull by the Horns

When I returned to the apartment the following morning, Nell, whose feet had heretofore only been comfortable when her stiletto heels were tapping against the asphalt, was squatting on our living room floor in a pair of faded jeans and a plain cotton T-shirt, tossing her spiky footwear into a suitcase and waxing rhapsodic about things like alfalfa.

I've always envied Nell because she's so damn sweet you forgive her for being so drop-dead gorgeous. But now I had new reasons for my Venus envy. Nell had the guts to accomplish what few women would do in real life—jettison everything she'd ever called familiar for the lure of true love. I told her that the Jill Clayburgh character in *An Unmarried Woman* should have taken a leaf from Nell's new gamebook.

"What?" Nell looked at me quizzically.

"City mouse Jill Clayburgh's got this opportunity to have an incredible life with Alan Bates, a gorgeous, sensitive, artistic guy who wants to do nothing but adore her. Except that the trade-off is that she's got to move to the bucolic mountains. And what does our intrepid model of feminism do? She passes up her best chance at happiness in favor of bouncing around in a jog-bra and looking across the East River at Queens every morning."

"I think she's an idiot," Nell sniffed dismissively. "By the way, do you think I can get married in white?"

"Apart from the standard objection, why not?" I asked her.

"Dirt, silly. I always dreamed of a white wedding dress with a long flowing train. Something Grace Kelly might have worn, you know? But it's probably not appropriate for an outdoor wedding."

"Probably not one in the Great North Woods," I teased. "Although all the little woodland creatures from your petting zoo could come and sit on your train like you're Snow White or some other Disney heroine who camps out in the heart of the forest."

"A.J. and I decided to exchange our vows on that plateau where we had our first picnic. But Mummy would have had kittens if we tried to have the reception up there, so we've already managed to snag the Mohonk Mountain House for that. I told you, A.J.'s family's very well connected up there."

I admired Nell's surety. She can be a supreme flake, but once she makes up her mind about something, she is as decisive as Jem. We'd both accepted Nell's offer to be her bridesmaids, just so long as we didn't have to wear Timberlands or Birkenstocks with our backless gowns. "Nell?"

She looked up from her packing. "Yeah?"

"Remember what you said on *Bad Date* last night about A.J.'s divulging what clinched it for him . . . in terms of his really falling hard for you . . . that it was something you'd told him in one of your IM conversations?"

Nell nodded, held a royal blue pullover up to her chest, surveyed it, then decided to pack it.

"You're not a flake. I mean, not that time, anyway. I played Cupid again. Or Cyrano. I put words in your mouth and sent them off to A.J."

Nell stopped packing but didn't look up. The room grew very quiet. "I had a funny feeling that might have been the case," she said finally. "And I can hardly blame you for it. I mean, we started out, you and I, as partners in crime, which was a pretty low thing to do to A.J. So I don't know what 'we' told him when I wasn't looking, but it sort of doesn't matter in the grand scheme of things what you wrote to him about me, because what you wrote to him on your own was at least the truth. When you and I started out writing him those e-mails, I didn't want him to know the real me, so I could have a bad experience on our date. I mean, how dishonest is that?"

Nell had a heart as big as the Adirondacks. I threw my arms around her. "Nell," I sobbed, "I'm going to miss you so much."

"Oh, honey . . ." Nell was crying, too. We dried each other's tears with our fingers. "You've been so busy playing Cupid for me and Jem that you can't get your own house in order. I think you should make sure Jack knows how much he means to you. Don't let him get away, Liz."

A couple of days after she had moved out, I began to feel extraordinarily lonely.

*   *   *

Jack bristled at my idea. "I told you this could end up worse than the quiz show scandals of the 1950s," he insisted firmly.

Over the phone, we were rehashing our major issue: I adamantly wanted to "go public" with our relationship, expressing again to Jack that because we had to sneak around like we were conducting some hole-in-the-wall backstage intrigue, despite our declaring our mutual love for each other, the relationship somehow didn't seem entirely "real" to me. The situation was becoming exasperating.

"Liz, you've got to know that it's potential *Bad Date* suicide. We even kept our relationship a secret from Nell and Jem for weeks. What's the big deal about waiting a little longer? Soon, we can get on with our lives. If you want to make out on every street corner in Manhattan, then deliberately bail out of the show, like Jem and Nell did," he urged. "If not, what's the real harm in waiting another month or so? Five more Sundays, to be precise. The time'll be gone before you know it."

"I hear everything you're saying," I acknowledged, "but I can't make my head and my heart see things the same way. As each other, I mean."

"Liz, you're driving me crazy here." Jack sounded like he meant it. There wasn't a trace of humor in his voice.

I tried to explain the conflict raging around inside me. "My head says, 'Pragmatic Jack makes perfect sense,' but my heart keeps . . . well, the best way I can think of to describe it is that it's sort of throwing a temper tantrum, saying, 'I want what I want when I want it . . . and I want it *now*!' "

"I think you should tell your heart to stop acting childish and 'Snap out of it!' as Candy would say. If you want to get to the final episode, keeping 'us' a secret is for your own good, Liz." I could hear the rising tension in Jack's voice. It practically crackled through the phone lines.

"It's like what I said to you out on the sidewalk in front of Serendipity about wanting a win-win outcome—to have things be the way I want them with us and also to turn out the way I want them to on *Bad Date*. Remember what I told you that night on the pier in Miami about always feeling that I had to ace everything or be 'perfect' all the time?"

"Fine. If that's how you feel, I'm not going to let you fuck it up."

"Since when do you call the shots?"

"When I think you're being unreasonable," he said edgily.

"I'm so confused. And so frustrated. And I know I'm in danger of making a mess of things all around, because I want it both ways. This much I know: It's driving me nuts for us to be in love with one another and have to worry about where we go, who sees us, and what it looks like when we converse in front of people. It's crap, that's what it is. It's unhealthy for the relationship, and I don't want to live like this anymore, Jack. Not for one more minute."

There was a long silence on the other end of the line. I mean a *really* long silence.

"Then you don't have to."

"What?" I wasn't sure whether my heart should rise or sink at his response.

"I'll make it easier on both of us. You don't have to

be in a relationship that's a secret," he reiterated, his voice sounding tense and strained. There was another nearly interminable pause. "You've created an untenable situation and you're asking the impossible of me. The way I see it right now, I'm standing between you and your pot of gold. So, I'll help you by removing a major obstacle. I think we should call it a day, Liz. At least until you get to the end of that *Bad Date* rainbow you're so sure you'll arrive at."

I felt like I'd been slammed in the solar plexus by an Olympic heavyweight. The air had suddenly become strange around me. I looked dizzily down at the floor to see if my guts had reached the parquet yet. "Wha . . . ? But I love you, Jack. I love you so much."

"Yet you won't walk away from the show the way your roommates—excuse me, your *former* roommates—did when they fell in love. And they weren't even in love with a guy on the show. You know that if we got discovered, we'd get kicked off and likely have to forfeit everything we've won thus far. Frankly, I don't give a shit, but you seem to." Jack sighed deeply. "You've made your bed. And I am incredibly sorry I won't be lying in it with you. See you at the studio on Sunday. I . . . do love you, Liz." He hung up the phone first.

I sank to the floor by the wall phone and sobbed as hard as I had when my grandmother died. I don't know how long I was there for. I was desperate for someone, something, to hug and hold close, and there was nothing readily available but a tapestry-covered throw-pillow from the living room sofa. I clutched an image of an eighteenth-century rustic idyll—a marzipanlike shepherd and shepherdess—to my chest, staining the blue watered silk around the image with my tears.

When I finally pulled myself to my feet and padded into the bathroom to inspect my face, my eyelids were as swollen as though I'd gone ten rounds with that prizefighter who'd slugged me in the solar plexus when Jack dumped me.

My thoughts were so jumbled, banging around in my brain with such zigzagging speed that I couldn't harness any one of them and try to get them to make sense.

No job, no money, no roommates, and now no lover. I poured myself a glass of really dreadful chardonnay and wished that the apartment had a baby grand like the one my parents had when I was growing up. Whenever I was miserable, I would grab a glass of apple juice and curl up on the giant faded red silk pillows under the piano until the pain went away.

In my head I kept replaying the conversation I'd had with Jack. He'd made so much damn sense, and I'd behaved like a selfish baby. Why was fighting so hard to have everything my way worth it if the result was losing Jack? Was I nuts?

Tonight I vowed not to wallow too much in my misery and assured myself, like Scarlett O'Hara, that tomorrow would be another day. A better one. It had better be.

29/An Offer I Could Refuse

The phone rang Sunday evening as I was getting ready to head over to the television studio for episode nine. I let the machine get it. Whoever it was could wait. I was anxious enough about the show, as I was every week, and I was anxious about seeing Jack for the first time since he'd decided to put the brakes on our relationship.

When the answering machine beeped I could hear Jason Seraphim's singsongy voice chirping away, while I was deep in contemplation about what would look terrific on television that I hadn't already worn on the show.

"Hi, Liz, Jason here. Just wondering how you're doing . . . what you're up to." He paused. "Liz . . . something's come up here at SSA and I wondered if you . . . no, F.X. and I are asking you to come in for a breakfast meeting tomorrow morning. Say, eight-thirty? Tell you what, I'm sure you're probably getting ready for tonight, so don't call me back unless you *can't* make it in the morning, okay? Really hope to see you. Bye." Jason hung up before the answering machine was ready to cut him off.

He'd certainly piqued my curiosity. I had nothing to

lose by strolling down to SSA for a free breakfast, which reminded me . . . I headed into the kitchen for a caffeine fix, pouring myself a large glass of black iced coffee to energize myself for that night's broadcast.

Once at the studio, it was like the famous Yogi Berra line "déjà vu all over again," insofar as Jack's behavior toward me was just like it had been more than two months prior when we'd appeared for the very first episode of *Bad Date*—in other words, aloof. I tried very hard not to look at him, not even to make eye contact, because I was so sure I would start to cry all over again. I missed just looking into his eyes and trying to read his soul. I missed kissing him. I missed the way our bodies melded together. I missed his sense of humor and his thirst for fresh adventures.

Tensions ran high that evening. Looking around, I realized that the three remaining women—Rosalie, Candy, and I—were, of all the women who had been cast on *Bad Date*, the ones most likely to behave like firebrands. The three remaining men—Double-E, Milo, and Jack—couldn't have been more different from one another. Jack was above the fray, but Milo and Double-E carped at one another once again, like some politically incorrect interracial version of *The Odd Couple*. Rosalie kept glancing at Candy and me, as if she were continually sizing us up. Every time either one of us said something, Rosalie would realign her body and strain to listen, just in case we were talking about something we might plan to say on the air.

I tried to ignore her, but Candy got annoyed with being stared at. "Fuhgeddaboutit, cookie," she said sharply. "I know something you don't." This made

Rosalie shiver and finally go back to minding her own business.

What Candy knew was what she had been planning for the past two weeks, which was how to get herself kicked off the show so she could move out to LA and spend the rest of her life in Allegra's lithe, alabaster arms. "I shoulda remembered," she confided to me in the dressing room, just before we went onto the set. "My strategy last week was all wrong. Never fake it; it only comes back and bites you in the ass." Nevertheless, she refused to divulge this week's game plan to me.

When it was her turn to ascend to the cone throne, she told a story about how she'd gotten stood up once by a blind date. Compared with many of her tales of woe wherein her dates invariably ended up whacked, iced, or otherwise liquidated before they reached dessert, this was about as vanilla as a date could possibly get, particularly for a woman with as colorful a life as Candy Angela Fortunato. The audience, visibly and audibly disappointed by her little performance, made it the swan song she so gleefully coveted.

And so, for the sake of her new true love, my greatest female competition on the show removed herself from the running.

With four of the fourteen of us pairing up with a co-contestant, *Bad Date* was becoming a bit like Noah's Ark.

I had no idea what to expect from my ex-bosses at SSA. I showed up ten minutes early, poked my head around the place, and felt my heart plummet when I saw that my former office was now occupied by a young woman who barely looked old enough to be out of college. Was that how young *I* looked when I'd started working there? She had a cute little plaque on her door that read JACKIE'S OFFICE. WELCOME TO MY WORLD.

I couldn't walk in there and introduce myself. I didn't have the spirit for it. I was feeling an odd mixture of relief and regret and was afraid I would do something inappropriate in front of this total stranger.

Jackie looked up when she noticed me sort of lurking in her doorway. "Can I help you?"

I wavered for a second. "N-No. I'm okay."

"Are you here to see someone? Are you a client?"

"Yes, I'm here for a breakfast meeting with F.X. and Jason and no, I'm not a client."

Jackie studied me for a few moments. Then it looked like a light went on behind her eyes that soon zoomed up to full wattage. "I know who you are!" She leapt to her feet and came out from behind my—I mean her—desk. "You're Liz Pemberley! My God, we studied your ad campaigns in school. I've always wanted to write like you."

I started to laugh. "I'm just a former hack."

"I can't believe I'm actually getting to meet you. I mean, you've won Clios."

"They're not the Nobel Prize," I told Jackie. "I'm using them for dust magnets at home now." I felt flattered, yet at the same time I felt silly. Although it's true that I had been rewarded by my peers for what I did, I was neither a Hemingway nor an Edna St. Vincent Millay. Meeting Jackie this morning reminded me of the love-hate aspect of my work that had so torn me apart to the point of not being able to do it capably anymore.

"I'll run and tell Jason you're here," she said, practically sprinting down the hall to the conference room. A few moments later, she dashed back. "They're all waiting for you," she reported. Jackie returned to her desk. "I shouldn't be keeping you," she added. "The client is really cute, by the way. I wish *I* were in there," she said a bit wistfully.

I hadn't the vaguest idea what Jackie was talking about. Why would Jason and F.X. bring a former employee in to meet with a client? We'd parted on the best of terms, but still . . .

I opened the door to the conference room. F.X. and Jason were sitting near the far end of the long table, facing me, with a number of jars arranged in front of them, stacked like a brick-red pyramid. Seated opposite them was Jack Rafferty. When our eyes met, I couldn't decipher the inscrutability of his expression. Jason waved his arms at me. "Welcome back, Liz!"

"That is, if you want to be welcomed," F.X. added quickly. "Have a seat."

I wasn't sure whether to sit next to Jack or alongside my former bosses. "What's this all about?" I asked them. I could feel myself growing edgy.

"First, let me say," F.X. began as I squeezed into a chair at the head of the table, with the SSA partners on my left and Jack by my right elbow, "how sorry I am to see Candy Fortunato get kicked off *Bad Date*. What was up with her? I mean, she's got this wild life and last night she talks about a busted blind date that wouldn't have made the Virgin Mary blush."

I looked at Jack. He was never privy to Candy's

strategy, although her trying to get kicked off the week that Nell did had been no secret to anyone. Besides, I'd told him about her and Allegra. Jack didn't answer F.X.'s question. "I have no idea what her deal was," I lied.

"Did you ever check out her Web site?" F.X. asked the rest of us excitedly. "It's fantastic! You sign on and the first thing you see is an image of a big pink pussy—"

I shot him a dirty look.

"—cat. And it says 'Welcome to Candyland.' " His glasses were already beginning to fog up.

"He has a thing for Candy, in case you couldn't tell," I said to Jack. Then I turned my head back to Jason and F.X. "Okay, guys, why am I here? Aside from the prune danish, which I love but which I didn't need to pull myself out of bed for. And what's *he* doing here?" I added, pointing at Jack.

"Obviously, you two know each other," Jason began. "And you know about the restaurant in Miami where Jack is part-owner."

"In fact, you guys did a whole riff on this product on the very first episode of *Bad Date*," F.X. said, picking up the thread. "Remember when Rick Byron asked you to come up with an instant ad campaign for Tito's Famous South Beach Salsa?"

"I don't even remember what I said at the time."

Jack smiled at me. It was his old warm smile. "It took you all of about three seconds before you fanned yourself somewhat seductively and purred, 'Is it hot in here or is it Tito's Famous South Beach Salsa?' "

"I think I was just trying to extricate myself from an

embarrassing situation, being put on the spot on national television and all."

"Well," Jason said. "Jack approached us last week and told us that he's been working on plans to launch his salsa in a big way in the northeast."

I recalled running into Jack in the Chelsea Market, when he'd told me the same thing, obscuring the competitor's product with jars of his own. My mind flashed to a series of images as to where this chance encounter had led. Had he contacted SSA before or after he'd broken up with me? Either way, it was an enormous gesture.

"Are you okay, Liz?" F.X. asked me. "You look a little glazed."

"I'm . . . I'm fine. Thanks."

F.X. leaned toward me. "Jack has been working on marketing the product up here, in mass quantities—not just in specialty shops like Balducci's and Zabars, and he came to us to do his advertising campaign."

"With one proviso," Jack added.

"That you be the copywriter," Jason said.

Jack looked over at me. "You're the only one I want to handle this, Liz. Otherwise, it's a no-go."

I took a deep breath. "So you're getting me my job back?" I studied the faces of all three men.

"You're an ace," Jack replied. "From Tito's perspective—the restaurant, not the man—it's a sound business strategy."

"It's a *freelance* assignment," Jason said, making a steeple with his fingers. "Work here. You've got the run of the shop. Whatever you need."

"Whatever I need?" I asked, forming the words slowly and carefully.

Jason and F.X. nodded.

"I need . . . to say no."

"What?" Jack looked incredulous.

My former bosses looked confused.

I spoke very softly. "F.X., Jason, you're not out any money that you didn't have yesterday. And if you think I screwed you out of a new client, I'm honestly sorry. But I can't do this. It's a kind gesture, but no thank you. I've known these guys for years," I said, nodding at Jason and F.X. "So there's probably very little personal dirty linen we don't feel relatively at ease airing in front of one another. Jack, I don't need you to play my White Knight. I don't want to be rescued by you, or want you to be the sole reason I have a source of income."

I rose from the table. "So, I'm taking a pass. Thanks for breakfast. Enjoy the rest of your day." I picked up my purse and walked toward the door, touching Jack on the shoulder as I went by. His scent made me miss him all the more, and I noticed, in the tiny glimpse I took as my hand rested ever so briefly on his jacket, that there was a small rip in the weave.

I wanted to take Jack's face in my hands and turn it toward mine, kiss him fully and deeply, not giving a damn that Jason and F.X. would be watching. I wanted to take him by the hand, bring him home with me, slide his blazer off his shoulders and mend it for him . . . after we made love.

Instead I walked out the door.

30/The Revelation

Later in the afternoon, as I was rinsing shampoo out of my hair and wondering if my decision to reject the offer of temporary employment wasn't one of the dumber things I'd done lately, I thought I heard the downstairs buzzer. I turned off the shower, squeezed as much water as I could out of my hair, threw on the terrycloth robe that Nell had given me, and tracked squishy wet footprints all the way to the intercom. "Who is it?" I called into the speaker.

"Me. Jack. Can I come up?"

I didn't know exactly what to say, so I just pressed the buzzer and let Jack into the lobby.

"These are for you," he said, when I opened the door. He sort of thrust a box of Belgian chocolates into my hands.

When he tilted my chin so I could meet his gaze, there were tears in my eyes.

"I don't want to break up, Liz. I didn't in the first place; I thought it would be easier on your psyche—and mine, too—if I weren't in the picture for a while. But I've missed you like crazy this past week."

I choked back an ecstatic sob. "Oh, God, Jack!" I threw my arms around him and pulled him to me, kissing him, while I led him in a sort of backward dance over to the sofa, never relinquishing his lips.

"I know how many résumés you've sent out in the past few weeks. I was just trying to help this morning," he said, when our mouths finally parted. He attempted to run his hand through the wet tangle that was my hair.

"I know you were. You know why I couldn't accept, don't you?"

"You said as much in the conference room."

"Besides, I still have very ambivalent feelings about the work I was doing for SSA."

Jack lifted my bare legs onto his lap and began to gently stroke them. He looked over at me and smiled. "I was equally serious about hiring you because you're top-flight. And I would have hoped that *my* product isn't one of those you couldn't promote because it's something you think consumers don't want or need!"

I laughed. "Not at all. Though I've never tasted Tito's Famous South Beach Salsa, and since I pride myself on my integrity as a copywriter, I would have to try it before I wrote a single glowing syllable. But there's a lot more operating here, Jack. Jason, F.X., and I agreed that SSA wasn't the best place for me right now. And I'm not drowning in debt yet. My unemployment check sure as hell isn't a living, but I'll eventually have several thousand pre-tax dollars coming to me from the Urban Lifestyles Channel for surviving at least the past nine episodes of *Bad Date*."

"You know, you make me crazy sometimes," Jack said.

"Yeah. I know. But isn't my asylum a wonderful place to be committed to?" I teased.

When Jack ran his index finger along the underside of my knee, it was very hard to concentrate. "You know, I meant what I said about not wanting you to jump in and rescue me. I was so demoralized when I left SSA that F.X. and Jason would not have called me in to the office just a few weeks later to freelance on a project. You made that happen. You created a situation that wouldn't have existed otherwise. For me to accept the assignment to write the advertising copy for Tito's salsa was tantamount to your taking out your checkbook and directly writing me a draft for thousands of dollars."

I raised myself to my knees and stayed in this semi-squatting position on the sofa so I could focus on what we needed to talk about without the distraction of Jack's caresses. If I couldn't make my point comprehensible and acceptable to him, then all the touching in the world wasn't going to make us effective communicators as lovers.

Jack reached over for my hand. "First of all, I respect any decision you make about your professional life. But the salsa does need an ad campaign. I will have to hire an agency to handle it sooner rather than later, given the timeframe of my mass market northeast launch. So why not ask you to do it?" Jack stroked the top of my hand. "That's what I was thinking when I contacted Jason Seraphim . . . that's all," he added softly.

"I don't want to be thrown a bone."

"That's one way to look at it," he conceded. "You

know, you're not doing *me* any favors by rejecting the offer. Now I'll have to find a second-tier copywriter."

I turned my hand over and slipped it into his. "I see your point of view, but I'm not going to change my mind about why I think it would be a bad idea for me to accept the job. I will, however, change my mind about insisting on bringing our relationship into the open while we're both on *Bad Date*. I spent sleepless nights kicking myself in the butt, realizing that you were right; there was no way to have it both ways no matter how much I wanted it. And I guess I was too mortified to admit my obtuseness to you before now. After all, I'd made such a huge deal out of my perspective on the situation. I'm so unbelievably sorry, Jack, for putting you through all that nonsense. Our relationship is more important to me than anything—and you need to know that. I screwed up before, okay? Can we just kiss and make up now?" I asked, squeezing his hand.

Jack leaned over and stroked my face. He grinned. "I think that's a swell idea."

"Then can we go to bed?" I asked provocatively. "I need to feel your arms around me . . . need to feel your skin against mine. When's your flight back to Miami?"

"Not 'til tonight. But why waste any more time than is absolutely necessary?" Jack playfully pulled me onto his lap. "Mmmm," he murmured into my wet hair, starting to slip his hand under my robe. "What'cha got under there?"

"I want you to find out," I purred back mischievously.

"Warm," he said, his cool hand locating my right breast. "Did I ever tell you I love you with wet hair?"

"You don't think it makes me look like a drowned rat?"

"Nuh-uh. I think you look incredibly sexy. But if you did look like a drowning rat, I'd want to rescue you."

I smiled and touched his lips with my index finger.

"That's right," he added. "You don't want to be 'rescued.' " He tugged at the terrycloth belt, pulling open my robe, slipping it down over my bare shoulders. "I want you so much," Jack whispered, taking my breasts in his hands, gently pushing them together, bringing the now closely spaced nipples to his lips. The touch of his mouth sent shivery, silvery ripples through my spine.

"My God . . . feel how wet I am for you, Jack."

He moved his hands to the warmth between my legs and slipped a finger inside me. "I love the way you're always ready for me."

I moved against the rhythm of his finger. "I may not always agree with your way of doing things . . . but it doesn't stop me from wanting you . . . all the time." My words came in short, breathy exhalations.

Jack slid me off his lap and began to undress, placing his sportcoat, tie, shirt, and pants over the back curve of the couch.

"You have a tiny rip near the left shoulder, by the way," I told him, conscious of a soft maternal quality to my voice. "I'll try to fix it for you later."

In his magnificent nakedness he was as ready for me as I was for him. That was another thing I loved about Jack. It took no urging for him to get aroused for me.

He was always already there. He was standing, erect, in front of me, while I lounged back against the sofa cushions. "Come here," I whispered to him. He was level with my lips and I took him into my mouth, enjoying pleasing him, reveling in how he felt in my hand. I liked the way he moaned softly when I tongued a certain spot or generated a particularly delicious sensation.

"You know what I love?" he asked me, his voice gentle and subdued. I wasn't exactly in a position to respond, so he answered his own question. "I love the way you take pleasure in pleasuring me." He ran his hands through my damp hair, grabbing fistfuls of it, making my scalp tingle. Then he lifted my face away from him and joined me on the sofa, covering me with his body, entering me effortlessly, holding me so close I could feel his heartbeat as though it throbbed within my own breast.

We made love slowly, savoring each new sensation our bodies visited upon one another. He discovered that the sweat trickling down my neck tasted salty, and that my freshly shampooed hair still smelled of the sweet fragrant juices of mandarin and papaya. I brought my lips to Jack's forehead, inhaling his own aroma, finding it made me feel calmly secure as much as it aroused me. The scent of his skin was one I could grow old with; it was masculine without being in any way overpowering. It was just . . . Jack.

This time our mutual orgasm was a simultaneous melding of souls as well as a festival of carnal cravings. My blurred perspective on so many aspects of my life in that moment came into focus with crystalline clarity.

I could get all corny about the transformative power of true love, but as Jack and I made love, I realized how amazing that power can be. I thought of how finding the right lover had proven little short of an epiphany for Jem. For Nell. For Candy. And now, for me, too. For the sake of love, my friends had been willing to accept change, appreciate compromise, and celebrate the differences between themselves and their partners instead of making those contrasts into obstacles to their future happiness together. This was how I wanted things to be for Jack and me.

"Why are you smiling?" Jack asked me, his voice soft and dreamy. "You look like the Mona Lisa."

If my smile had been subtle, it widened into a full wattage grin. "Because I think I figured it all out." I placed my palms against his cheeks and pulled his face to me, tracing his lips with my tongue, then kissing him with all the ardor of the happiest, luckiest woman on the planet. The vows I had previously made about not giving too much, because I always ended up emotionally devastated by the man I so favored, I could rethink now.

"Jack? How would you react if I repaired your jacket for you?"

"What a silly question."

"Why?" I looked at him.

"I'd be very appreciative. What, Liz? Were you afraid if you sewed up the hole in my sportcoat that next week I would bring you a suitcase full of sweatsocks to darn?"

I laughed. "Kind of. Maybe."

"Not going to happen. I think your offer to mend my jacket is very sweet."

We were lying side by side on the sofa. God knows how we both fit without falling off. I snuggled against Jack's chest. "On Saturday night, when you're back in town, I'm going to make us one hell of a dinner. I'm taking quite a risk to cook for a professional chef."

"Hey, you told me way back when that you couldn't cook."

"I never said that."

"Sure you did. I could swear that the day we met, you said you didn't cook."

I kissed the broad expanse of his chest. "What I believe I said to you was that I *don't* cook—which isn't the same thing as saying I *can't* cook. I just decided I wasn't ever going to be taken advantage of again by an undeserving guy. I can indeed cook—although I wouldn't even presume to concoct the recipes I imagine you can throw together without a second thought."

"Your hair is almost dry," Jack observed, gently running his fingers across my brow. It felt lovely. "Liz, I'm going to let you in on a little secret about Jack Rafferty. I'm not going to rush out the door and yell 'Taxi!' No matter how much you want to give, I can promise you that you're going to get just as much from me in return. No hidden agendas. No ulterior motives. I just want to love you."

Wow.

I'd never felt so cherished. I wanted to bottle his words and spray my naked body with them every morning after I stepped out of the shower.

Jack wrapped a length of my hair around his hand. "Did you ever look at your own hair?" he asked, his face all boyish curiosity. "There are so many colors in here, it's like fine-grained wood." He turned his gaze from the hank of hair in his hand to my face and looked at me thoughtfully. "Okay . . . here's how I think we should handle things from now on. I'm putting a compromise on the table here, even though I know you said a little while ago that you were willing to shelve the idea of going public until the show ends. I don't want you to feel like you're—or we're—a secret. So let's just not flaunt our togetherness in the immediate vicinity of the Urban Lifestyles studio building. How does that grab you?"

I moved his hands to my breasts, offering them to him. "I don't want to talk about it anymore, my love. We've discussed it to death. I'd rather *you* just grab me, okay?"

31/Risky Business

I may have gone a bit overboard with the menu for my homecooked meal for Jack that Saturday night. We started out with vichyssoise, then moved to filet mignon with orange béarnaise sauce, and finished the meal with a baked pear pancake with gingered maple syrup. It wasn't at Jack's cordon bleu level, but I didn't embarrass myself. He brought the wine. A different variety for each course. Needless to say, we had a lot left over and still I felt toasted by the end of the evening.

"Well, Julia Child," Jack said, getting up from the table to recline against the cushions on my sofa. "You've really done it."

I beamed like a little kid. "I did? Thanks. This was a major deal for me, I hope you realize. I broke my promise to myself. Not only are you the first man I've cooked a meal for in ages, which is in itself a testament to how much I love you and want to do things for you, but as I said to you before, I was scared shitless about attempting a major production number for such a pro. Cooking you a meatloaf, for instance, just wasn't what I'd had in mind, and I was terrified, actually, that

I'd screw something up and you'd make fun of me and I'd never get over it for the rest of my life."

"Not a chance."

"Not a chance that you'd mock me, or that I'd never psychologically recover?"

He shook his head and stifled a laugh. "Come here, you." He held out his arms and pulled me over to the sofa to snuggle against him. "What I meant when I said that you'd really 'done it' is that I think I'm too full now to make love."

I went for his midriff to pretend to pinch his non-existent spare tire. "Get over it," I teased.

He did.

At the television studio on Sunday evening, preparing to go on the air with episode ten of *Bad Date*, Rob Dick gave the remaining contestants his usual producer pep talk in the hair and makeup room, reiterating, as he did every week, that "we're the most honest show in reality television," and then mentioned that there had been a rash of thefts from the dressing rooms lately. Therefore, as a security measure, cameras were being installed that would monitor comings and goings on closed-circuit television monitors at the security desk in the lobby.

Milo looked anxious. "You mean we're going to have cameras in the dressing rooms?" His face was three shades paler than usual.

Rob Dick set the record straight, explaining that the cameras were being installed outside the dressing rooms and consequently would be able to pick up any activity outside the door and in the publicly traversed areas of the building; no one was going to install cameras in the dressing rooms themselves. "Besides, I'm sure that's probably illegal," Rob added.

When we got to the dressing rooms, there was a printed notice that provided the same information about the new security measures. It was the first time I'd had the room to myself, now that Candy was gone. It felt stark and lonely, very industrial, without her colorful presence. I realized that I missed her. I hoped that she and Allegra were blissfully happy in Benedict Canyon.

There was yet another floral arrangement from Rick Byron on my dressing table. I hadn't given our hunky Hollywood host the time of day, but I had to award him points for persistence. Still, I couldn't figure out what it was he wanted from me. I had neither wealth nor fame, and while people have told me they think I'm very pretty, I could certainly never compete with the kind of starlets and models men of his ilk customarily squire around town. How flattering it might have been had he been enamored of my mind, but he didn't know me well enough to qualify for that. I decided that he just simply didn't know how to take "no" for an answer.

On set, even in the middle of the telecast, I found it very hard to focus on the show; I kept thinking how much I would rather be with Jack instead. My mind and tongue didn't feel as razor-sharp as they had during previous episodes, when I would just let a few well-aimed zingers fly at Rick Byron without a second thought. I was working at it tonight. Even my bad date anecdote was nowhere as entertaining as my previous tales of woe had been. I barely remember what I said. I think I told America about José, my ninth-grade crush. I was dreadfully afraid he wouldn't dance with me during the class weekend trip to the country because the day before we left I had gotten slammed in the forehead with a wooden tennis racquet, when my friend Diana and I were hitting tennis balls against the wall of the gym. Diana went for a backhand and her racquet went straight into my head. A lump formed that immediately turned the color of midnight and swelled to the size of an extra-large egg. In fact, I still have the bump. I'd tried to disguise the disaster with Max Factor pancake makeup to look pretty for José, which only made the lump more obvious. But the sweet thing was that he really didn't seem grossed out by my ghoulish appearance. And he did dance with me.

So, when the studio audience voted Double-E DuPree off the show, instead of feeling elated that I was one step closer to the million-dollar jackpot, I had a tinge of regret for the first time that it wasn't me saying goodbye instead.

Week eleven went by and this time it was Rosalie Rothbaum who failed to ignite the prurient interest of the studio audience, so she became *Bad Date* history.

For the past two Sundays, Jack and I had waited until we figured everyone had left the building, dawdling in our respective dressing rooms to kill time. Then we'd walk along the deserted corridors as close to one another as we thought we could safely get away with, though after week ten, I didn't have a free hand because I brought Rick Byron's ostentatious floral display to the guard at the front desk (I'd removed the card, of course), and suggested that he might like to bring it home to his wife, since it wasn't doing anyone any good sitting in an airless dressing room for days. When he asked me why I didn't just take it home myself, I lied and told him that I had a kitten at home who liked to chew on the blossoms. The truth was that I didn't want to be seen accepting Rick's gifts. I didn't want them, either in my dressing room or in my home.

Jack and I were getting ready to leave the studio after the week eleven telecast, walking down the hall past the row of dressing rooms. I'd perfected the technique of walking so close to him that my breast brushed against his arm while we both kept our eyes facing forward, looking as if nothing untoward was going on. It was our secret signal to let Jack know I wanted him, but the body language was so subtle that an unsuspecting eye would have discerned nothing out of the ordinary.

"It's so quiet here," I marveled. The sound of my heels against the linoleum floor practically echoed. "I need you, Jack. I want to kiss you," I whispered to him. "Right now."

"Here?"

"No." We'd just passed an emergency exit door that led to one of the stairwells. "There." I stopped walking and turned back to face the door.

"Do you think . . . ?" Jack seemed rather intrigued by the idea. "It's pretty risky."

We both looked up and down the long corridor to see if there was anyone within either sight or earshot, and determining that it was safe, Jack cautiously opened the heavy door to the stairwell. It made a very discomfiting creaking sound as it swung toward us. We slipped through the doorway into the stairwell and Jack guided the door closed, afraid it might slam.

"Now, you were saying . . ." Jack placed his hands on my breasts and steered me so that my back was against the wall. I could feel Jack's heat everywhere: flickering on my tongue, dancing in my mouth, searing through my sweater and penetrating the hollow between my thighs.

I'd just been angling for a kiss, but when he slid his hand along my leg, I accommodated his progress by bending my knee and resting my leg, storklike, with the heel of my shoe pushing against the wall about two feet or so off the floor. Any consideration of common sense became totally lost in a flood of sensation. All I could think about was how much I wanted to give myself to Jack—heart, soul, and body.

"Well, aren't you a naughty little girl," he whispered, a lascivious little glint in his eyes. "Did you go without panties on national television?" He pressed his body against mine as his hand sought the source of my heat.

"On prime-time, baby," I said playfully, gently biting his lower lip.

"And such a short skirt, too. No wonder they didn't dare kick you off the air. What possessed you to do this, sweetheart?"

"Fantasizing about what you're doing to me right now," I gasped, in between moans.

"Shhhh," Jack cautioned.

"Or maybe I was just feeling wicked," I whispered. "Jack?"

"Yes, love?"

"I want to feel you inside me."

"Now?"

"Now." I reached for his belt and managed to undo it with my right hand, then unzipped his trousers, reached through the flap on his briefs and drew him out, guiding him into me. As I leaned back against the wall for support, Jack lifted my legs so that I was straddling him as he stood. The urgency of our passion and desire enabled us to maintain our contorted position and yet enjoy the most luscious sensations as I wrapped my legs tightly around Jack's waist, pulling him deeper and deeper inside me with each thrust. I wondered if the look in my eyes was as glazed as his. We climaxed together in a sort of silent scream, then practically devoured each other's mouths, using our tongues to fill the void from which no sound dared escape.

My thigh muscles had received quite a workout. My legs felt like mush. I slowly lowered them to the floor and found I was too wobbly to stand. I reached one hand back and placed my palm against the wall, and grabbed Jack's forearm with the other to steady myself and regain my balance. With his index finger, Jack smoothed a few beads of sweat from my brow and kissed me where they had rested. Then he dressed himself and made sure my miniskirt was no longer in a compromising position.

"Well, that was quite an adventure," I said, catching my breath, my hand still grasping Jack's arm. I had yet to fully regain my equilibrium. "Wow. It seems like the stairwell is spinning." I looked up at Jack. "Was it good for you, too?"

He took my face in his hands and kissed me tenderly. "Need you ask?"

I reached for the doorknob and turned the handle. "Jack?"

"Yes?"

"Either the fantastic sex we just had sapped me of all my strength, or this door is locked."

"It can't be locked." He tried the handle. "It's locked. Shit."

"I don't remember seeing a sign on the door saying we couldn't get back in, do you? Otherwise, we wouldn't have gone through the door in the first place."

Jack tried the handle again, unwilling to believe that it could possibly have locked behind us.

"Uh-oh," I said. "This is a no re-entry stairwell."

Jack surveyed our surroundings. "Okay, Liz, we can either go up or go down and try to get into one of the corridors on another floor. Got a preference?"

"I'd prefer to go down. Of course."

"Of course." He took my hand and we descended to the next landing. That door, too was locked.

"One more flight and I think we're at street level," I said, remembering that *Bad Date* is broadcast from Studio 3B. At the foot of the stairs, the door was clearly marked EMERGENCY EXIT ONLY and instead of a knob or a handle, had one of those rectangular metal bars across the width of the door. Affixed to this bar was a red and white sticker, warning that an alarm would sound if the door were opened. "Where do you think this leads?" I asked Jack.

"Beats me. Outdoors, I expect."

"Do you think we should open it, Jack?"

"I don't see any alternative. Unless you want to snuggle up here on the staircase and call it a night. Maybe some nice janitor will let us out when he comes around in six or seven hours or so."

"Okay. You've convinced me."

Jack pushed against the bar and the door opened easily, immediately triggering a deafening, wailing siren. As we stepped into the night, I noticed that the alarm was just above our heads, right on the outside wall of the building. We were on an alleyway. I grabbed Jack's hand. "I say we make a run for it."

"Good idea."

Hand in hand, we ran down the length of the alley and out onto a side street, feeling like convicts escaping the state penitentiary. I had hoped it would seem more like Bonnie and Clyde, but wasn't nearly as glamorous. We kept running until we reached the corner, turned it, and once the studio was out of sight, panting like crazy, we stopped in the vestibule of a coffee shop to catch our breath.

"I need a drink," Jack wheezed. "Want to stop for a quick one at Pinky's?"

I shook my head. "Whatever you want, I've got it at home." My heart must have been pumping a million beats a minute. "Let's take a nice hot shower and finish what we—"

A police car, gumball flashing, siren blazing, screeched to a stop near the coffee shop. Both cops jumped out of the car like they'd been ejected by a magic button.

I looked at Jack. "You don't suppose they're looking for who busted out of the studio?"

"Somehow I doubt it."

One of the cops had a two-way radio, and I could hear someone's voice crackling through the static about the TV studio located at . . . the address of the Urban Lifestyles Channel. I didn't think it prudent to continue to eavesdrop any longer. "Let's go," I hissed under my breath. Trying to look as unassuming and nonchalant as possible, we trotted to the corner and grabbed the first cab we saw. I told him to head straight up Eighth Avenue—and, until we got out of the immediate vicinity—to floor it!

32/When the Shoe Fits . . .

"What time is it?" I grogged into the phone.

"Ten A.M. Do you know where your former bosses are?"

"Oh, God, I thought it was dawn." I rolled over and reached for Jack. His side of my bed was empty, but still slightly warm. Oh yeah . . . it was all coming back to me. He had to leave insanely early to make an eight A.M. flight out of LaGuardia back down to Miami, and had insisted, in the still-dark, predawn hours, that I stay in bed and not accompany him out to the airport, as was my wont. I rubbed my palm against the sheet, imagining that it was a magic lamp that could grant me the wish to return my lover to my arms.

I cradled the phone to my ear. "Liz? It's Jason and F.X. here. We've got you on speakerphone. Are you there?"

I looked over at the digital clock. It was indeed ten o'clock in the morning. I must have fallen back asleep soundly. That's what great sex will do for a girl. "Yes, I'm here. I'm in *bed*," I grumbled. "What do you guys want?" I tried really hard to focus, to wake up. I reached for the half-glass of water on the night table and took a swig. It was lukewarm.

"Liz, we really need you back," Jason began. "We've got a major project that only you can handle. A big new client."

"What's wrong with Jackie?"

There was a pause on the other end of the line. "We had to let her go," F.X. said. "She just couldn't cut it."

"Face it, she was as green as Kermit the Frog," Jason added apologetically, as though he felt somewhat guilty for attempting to fill my job with someone far less experienced. "Don't get us wrong; she was a very bright girl, eager to learn . . . but SSA is just too small to be a training ground. At the level we work at, our clients expect top-notch performances from seasoned ad veterans across the board."

"Like Jason said, we really need you back, Liz. We've thought long and hard about it and we think you're the right person for the job—so much so that we're willing to give you another chance here."

I continued to listen to their pitch.

"F.X., back me up on this. It's a fabulous client, Liz. Trust me, you'll love creating the campaign. And we can all but promise that you won't think it's something consumers never knew they wanted or needed until you got hired to force-feed them with ad copy that makes the merchandise seem utterly irresistible."

"Liz, you'll love the product," F.X. continued. "On Nona's grave, I swear it."

I took the bait. "Okay, I bite. What is it?"

"Shoes!" they said in gleeful unison.

I looked back at the clock: 10:03. "Shoes, huh? I'll be down there in an hour."

By noon, I was standing over several shoeboxes in the SSA conference room, fingering the fine quality materials and admiring the workmanship. God, the new leather even *smelled* good and it was buttery soft and supple to the touch. I bet shoes like that didn't even give you blisters the first time out.

I couldn't resist the urge. Boy, do I love having sample-size feet. I slipped off my own shoes and lifted a nut-brown slingback with beige topstitching and a high, conical heel from one of the boxes and slipped it on. I wiggled my foot. I can't remember when I've tried on a more comfortable shoe. I limped around for a bit, with only the right shoe on.

Jason started to laugh at me. "That's ridiculous! How can you get a proper idea of how they fit if you only put one shoe on?" He lifted the left shoe out of the box and held it out to me. "Here, try the mate."

I slipped into the other shoe and started doing laps around the conference table. My hunch was correct; they really didn't need breaking in.

"The company prides itself on its product lasting forever," F.X. told me as I continued to circle the room. "Remember how Coach leather used to promise to repair its products for you *for free* for as long as you owned the bags? Well, these guys stand behind their goods in the same way. No matter how long you own a pair of their shoes, you can ship it to them from anywhere, they'll pay the freight, and return them to you good as new."

I looked at the array of shoes. "They're gorgeous, that's certainly true." Then I looked at the prices marked on their boxes. "And they're not cheap."

"They're more high-end than the average purchase for a pair of good shoes, that's true; but the cost is no higher than, say, Charles Jourdan or Bruno Magli," Jason commented.

"And they're supposed to be environmentally friendly, or something," F.X. added.

"What the heck is that supposed to mean?" I asked. "Like, if you accidentally stepped in dog shit, the shoes will automatically compost it?"

Jason laughed. "I haven't a clue. Call the client and ask. Or wait until he comes in here on Friday afternoon and ask him then. We're as curious about that claim as you are."

"Cute logo," I mused, turning over the shoe to see a picture of a jungle bird carved into the leather sole. The same bird graced the shoebox top. "It reminds me of the Froot Loops cereal bird."

"I think it's supposed to be a toucan," Jason said. "Did you know that those exotic jungle birds—well, I don't know this for a fact, I heard it on the Discovery Channel or something—they mate for life! Isn't that cool?"

I could feel myself suddenly grinning like a blithering idiot.

"What's with you, Liz?" F.X. asked.

"Ask Demetrius to come into my office in an hour," I replied, trying not to feel too smugly triumphant. I had my ad campaign.

"I think it's the easiest one I've ever done," I told Demetrius, two days later as I admired his rough sketches for the Sole Mates print campaign. "It's like everything conspired at once—in a good way—to give me just the angle I needed. We've captured the beauty and durability of the product, and the manufacturer's corporate culture, though I'll be damned if I can figure out why a pair of pumps is eco-friendly."

Demetrius shrugged. "I dunno. Maybe the box is biodegradable, mahn. Or they think there'll be less waste when your shoes last forever." Demetrius looked down at my feet. "Nice. Very sexy. How do they feel?"

"They're the most comfortable open-toed purple suede pumps I've ever worn."

I looked at our brainstorming list. The Sole Mates "Mate for Life" campaign was taking shape with record speed. In just two days' time, Demetrius had dashed out collectible-quality posters. In lush, exotic, colors, against a luxuriant South American landscape, he'd rendered a pair of tango dancers so seductive you could feel the heat emanating off the page. The woman's perfectly shaped calf entwined about the man's leg; on her foot was a black leather Sole Mate's shoe not unlike the style I was wearing, except strappier. It looked entirely appropriate in that milieu. I'd asked him to sketch in the phrase "Toucan Tango" above their heads. I hadn't yet decided where to place it on the poster, or simply to replace it with the "Mate for Life" phrase that I'd originally intended to be the tag line for all the print ads, as in "Sole Mates: Mate for Life." There was also the briefest explanation of the product's lasting durability, and a word or two about the company's loyalty to its customers. I'd come up with a bunch of slogans for different ads, all with different images, batting wordplay around in my head. I finally settled on "A Lasting Relationship" as a catch-phrase that might work.

This "Mate for Life" campaign was the best fun out of bed I'd had in years. In addition to the hot tango poster, I asked Demetrius to work up artwork for a Cinderella and the Prince ad, in which he's slipping a Sole Mates slipper pump on her foot. I had him provide recognizable images of Clark Gable and Carole Lombard stepping with their Sole Mates–shod tootsies into the cement outside Hollywood's famous cinema, Grauman's Chinese. Even the company's less-than-sexy shoe styles had an arousing look to the ads. For the heavy, lug-soled hiking boots, Demetrius had rendered an exceptionally attractive couple trekking through a lushly verdant rain forest, two toucans perched in a tree overhead, with the words "Rubber Soul" underneath the graphic.

And the client was a joy. The owner of Sole Mates, Domingo Peres-Arroyo was a tall, elegant Argentinian who gave new definition to the word *courtly*. His family had been Sephardim from Spain who emigrated to Argentina in the early nineteenth century. His barely accented English was tinged with a slight lilt that made his speaking voice soft and musical. I was enchanted. Upon learning that I was an inveterate shoe shopper, Domingo assured me that from now on, I could have any pair of shoes in his catalogues free of charge, whenever I wanted something.

It felt like Christmas in July.

"Please. If you should ever need anything, I want you to call me," he said after our first meeting at SSA. "You do have my number?"

"It's in the paperwork somewhere."

"No. You should never have to search for any-thing." He retrieved a wafer-thin card case from his inside breast pocket and removed his business card. "I must tell you again, Liz, how delighted I am with the 'Mate for Life' campaign and the mock-ups you showed me. Your concept is so sensual, the ads seem . . . almost fragrant. I hear *music*."

We shook hands. It was the beginning of a beautiful friendship.

For the first time in ages, I wanted to grab life with both hands and give it a big wet kiss. I had my boy-friend back. SSA had given me a second chance and I was back in the groove, in the zone, in the saddle again, in every corny cliché I could think of. And two days after my client meeting with Sr. Peres-Arroyo, after episode twelve, sweet, lovably eccentric Milo Plum was voted off *Bad Date*, leaving nothing standing between me and a million dollars, plus that all-expense-paid trip for two to Paris, except the personal opinion of 253 members of the studio audience and . . . Jack Rafferty.

"You know we get your *Bad Date* show in Ar-gentina," Domingo told me over the phone, after I'd FedExed him the mechanicals for the print campaign to solicit his final approval. "I'm sorry such a lovely woman as yourself has had such terrible encounters with such a beautiful thing as romance. My wife tells me that you are not so unusual." Domingo paused for a moment. The air on the phone line felt strangely thick.

"I would like to share something with you, Liz, because I think you should know it," he continued.

"Before Seraphim Swallow Avanti was recommended to me, I entertained a pitch from two account executives at another agency. I would prefer not to mention the name, because I was not terribly pleased with their concept. And we were chatting about what sort of programming to run a hypothetical Sole Mates commercial on, and one of the men mentioned *Bad Date*, because of the female contestants on the show who seemed to be shoppers and the audiences who related to them. In fact, they referred to Rosalie Rothbaum by name because she is a professional personal shopper. I reminded them that the show would soon be off the air unless we could agree on a concept and get a commercial up and running in time."

I wondered where this was going. Domingo spoke slowly and deliberately in his customary gentle tone, his voice as soothing as if he were singing me a lullaby. "This particular agency had a major client who was running spots every week on *Bad Date*. According to this prominent client's account rep, who was a guest of the sponsor at one of the broadcasts, and was sitting in the producers' 'skybooth' at the time . . ." Domingo's voice faltered a bit. "Perhaps I shouldn't continue. After all, I don't know this to be true from any firsthand knowledge."

"Domingo? Please do," I urged him, not wanting to seem too edgy or anxious about what he might have to share.

"Well, then. According to that advertising agency executive, you were supposed to have gotten voted off the show after episode ten."

"Which was . . . ?"

"The one where the studio audience voted off the jazz musician instead."

"That was the night I talked about José, from my ninth-grade class."

"Yes. I remember that. I remember being flattered that you favored a Latino." I could almost hear a smile in Domingo's voice.

The magnitude of what Domingo had just imparted was beginning to become manifest. "How did the sponsor and his account rep know that I should have been kicked off the show?"

"Right after the votes were tabulated and they went into their final commercial break—which included the third spot of the episode for this particular client—mind you, they're a primary sponsor of the show—there was a hasty meeting between the producers and the sponsors who were present. The sponsors maintained that to lose you would translate into losing audience share, which translates into wasted advertising dollars. The producers acknowledged that your interplay with the host provided the sort of banter that raised the show a notch from its competitors, and made for highly entertaining television, since no one knew what you might say and when you might say it. Apparently, the agency responsible for this major sponsor's ad campaign had conducted several focus groups, and their research determined that you were one of the viewers' favorite contestants and your presence was good for business all around. The jazz musician scored far lower than you did. Even viewers in his own demographic didn't like him. The producers didn't want to risk losing their key sponsors who are their major source of revenue."

"So, what exactly are you saying?" I felt breathless.

"Liz. Please remember that this is hearsay. I can't report it to you as fact because I was not there in the studio when this 'confab,' if you will, took place. What I am saying is that the producers manipulated the results. So that someone else was voted off the show, instead of you. As an ordinary viewer of the show, I can tell you that they show the home audience no graphic, for example, that looks like a skyline with bars of light of varying heights to indicate how many votes each contestant received. The audience votes electronically, the results are allegedly tabulated, and the loser is then announced. That's what we see at home."

I found myself gripping the edge of my desk. Call me naïve, but it was hard to believe what Domingo had just told me. *Boy oh boy oh boy.* I distinctly remember my three interviews and auditions for *Bad Date* when Rob Dick told me that the show was scrupulously above board, not to mention his litany about it being the most honest show in reality television. "Why did you tell me this?" I asked Domingo.

"Because I felt . . . after I met you . . . somewhat *avuncular* toward you, Liz. I would not use the same word had I been twenty, maybe even ten years younger and a bachelor."

"That's very elegantly put. I'm flattered."

"Don't be. I can be a very fond fool sometimes."

"You are too kind, Domingo."

He laughed. I was surprised at its sound, like the bark of a seal. "That's what my wife always says to me. So I am too kind. I had not yet met you when I heard about this incident. Once I did, I felt I could not keep the story to myself. Enjoy the rest of your day, Liz. It's the only June twenty-fifth we'll have all year."

After I hung up the phone, I stared at the receiver for what felt like eons. Then I grabbed it from its cradle and dialed up Jack in Miami.

33/Circling the Wagons

He was on his cell phone. I'd caught him polishing the railing on the *Circe* and applying putty to some unfamiliar-sounding part of the vessel. "I take it you got a call as well," Jack said the moment he heard my voice on the other end of the line.

"What are you talking about?"

"You didn't get a call from Rob Dick's office?"

"No. Not yet." Suddenly, I felt a bit queasy. "Why? What's up?"

"I'm not sure. His assistant called and just said that Rob wanted to see me in his office tomorrow afternoon. I need to take care of some business things down here and if I can get them done in time, I'll come up this evening and spend the night with you. How's that sound?"

I laughed. "What do *you* think?" I found myself tapping the end of a ballpoint against my desk blotter.

"What's that clicking?" Jack asked me.

"Nervous energy. Jack? You don't think something's up, do you? I mean I haven't heard from them yet. You're making me anxious."

"Sorry, honey, I don't mean to. Tell you what. Call

me if you hear from them and we'll take it from there, okay?"

I mumbled some vague assent. "For what it's worth, Jack, I did receive a rather interesting phone call from my new client." I shared the major details of Domingo's conversation. Jack wondered if there might be a connection between what Domingo had accidentally learned and the phone call from the *Bad Date* producers. I doubted it. "They why would they be calling *you*?" I asked him. My intercom buzzed; Jason needed to speak to me. "Gotta run," I told Jack. "I can't wait to see you tonight. Love you!" I blew him a kiss through the phone before hanging up.

Within fifteen, maybe twenty minutes I had received a call of a similar nature to the one Jack had gotten. I can obsess nearly anything to death, and needed to permute every possible scenario or I wouldn't be able to concentrate on anything between now and our meeting with the *Bad Date* producers the following afternoon.

For the next twenty-four hours, I couldn't eat a bite. I noticed that my arms would develop uncontrollable goosebumps even though I wasn't cold. I couldn't wait to get the thing over with.

Jack surmised that if the meeting had nothing to do with Domingo's revelation, then it was more than likely some kind of informational session regarding the ground rules for the final episode of the show. I wanted very much to believe that it would turn out to be nothing more than one of Rob Dick's usual pep talks; nevertheless, I still felt like a seventh-grader being summoned to the principal's office for cutting gym class and smoking in the bathroom. Jack thought this might be a bit of an overreaction on my part.

I rushed over from SSA, arriving at the Urban Life-styles Channel's reception area at two minutes to three and was scarcely kept waiting. Tara, the sweet, peppy young woman who had helped run the *Bad Date* auditions, escorted me down the now-familiar corridor to Rob Dick's office. The blinds were closed, obliterating anyone inside from my view. Tara rapped on the glass door, then slowly pushed it open and poked her head in to announce my arrival. She allowed me to step into the room, then let the door close behind me.

Jack was already there, seated on Rob Dick's beige leather couch. In addition to Rob, there were three other men I had never seen before. Two looked like tanned, buffed, groomed, graying LA types. The third stranger was an Asian man in an impeccably tailored suit.

Rob Dick motioned to me to sit beside Jack on the couch. He looked at the two of us, his expression indecipherable. "Jack, Liz. Before I make the introductions, I would like to show you an audition tape for a new reality TV show we're considering for next season's fall lineup." He popped a black videocassette into his VCR and pushed the "play" button. It ran for a few moments, the image on the television screen a blank. The image then became a cross-hatch of scratches, which metamorphosed into grainy black-and-white footage.

When I saw what was on the video, I blanched and reached out to take Jack's hand, finding it cold.

Rob Dick rewound, then replayed the tape. "So," he began, his lips set in a thin, unamused line. "How long has this been going on?"

I opened my mouth to say something but Jack squeezed my hand. I took the hint and kept quiet.

"You certainly startled the front desk guard with your performance," Rob said. "I'd bet a thousand bucks it's the first time in his employment history that he's paid attention to anything the security cameras were filming."

"Doesn't Liz have great legs?" Jack asked in an attempt at levity.

"You do realize that *fraternization*—and this sexual escapade goes well beyond the definition of the word—is strictly prohibited by the terms of the contract you both signed with the Urban Lifestyles Channel?"

Jack and I continued to look at Rob and tried to give nothing away. We certainly did not nod our agreement with the producer's statement, although we were over a barrel and we knew it.

Rob introduced the other gentlemen in the room. "This is the president of the network, Ronald Ebsen, and the attorney for the Urban Lifestyles Channel, Ken Benson."

That covered the two Caucasians in the room. The men could have been fraternal twins. They moved to shake hands with Jack and me, which seemed a ludicrous gesture at best.

"And this is Gregory Sakamoto. Mr. Sakamoto is the lead attorney for Sakura Media Enterprises, the Urban Lifestyles Channel's parent corporation."

Mr. Sakamoto inclined his head politely.

Mr. Ebsen took over the conversation. "I'll cut to the chase here, Mr. Rafferty, Ms. Pemberley. *Bad Date* is facing what could be a remarkable scandal of the magnitude of the 1950s quiz show debacle. Couldn't you two have restrained yourselves until the show went off the air? I mean for Chrissakes, it only runs thirteen weeks!"

"I wasn't aware that love had a timetable," Jack responded smoothly. How he could appear so unruffled was beyond my comprehension.

"Are you two dating?" the attorney Ken Benson asked us. "And if so, when did you begin?"

"I don't think we need to answer that," Jack said. "The fact of the matter is that you have a tape, the contents of which might create something of a problem for your show if a scandal were to erupt just a few days before the final episode is broadcast. So the issue at hand is: What are you going to do about it?"

"I don't think *we* need to do anything about it," Benson said. "At issue is your willful and flagrant violation of your contract, which clearly states"—he flipped over the legal-size pages of our *Bad Date* contract, until he found the one he wanted—"Item Twelve, paragraph one, subsection A: 'Contestants revealed to be fraternizing with one another in a social context beyond the parameters of collegial acquaintanceship, or in any other way consorting, including but not limited to sexual encounters between the parties, may be construed to constitute collusion on the part of the fraternizing contestants which will result in automatic dismissal from The Show and disqualification from receiving any monetary compensation therefor.' " He leaned forward in his chair to pass the copy of the contract to me to peruse. I held it between Jack and me so we could both review the passage for ourselves.

"You guys crack me up," I said. "First of all, you make *us* sign all this stuff, promising to be as clean as a baby's conscience. *You* signed the contracts, too. Rob says that *Bad Date* is the most honest reality show on television, yet from the get go, your brass selected three contestants who were roommates, in violation of your own no-fraternization clause, all the while keeping it from the viewers that Jem, Nell, and I were sharing an apartment; you've got more coupling going on backstage than aboard Noah's Ark; you've got a host, who, after the very first episode, tried to hire me under the table to ghostwrite his banter for him because he so detested what your writers gave him to say—the same host who has been sending hundred dollar floral arrangements to my dressing room every Sunday and phoning me both at work and on my cell phone several times a week to ask me out, while he's rather publicly engaged to Nastasia-Basha-Tricia—whatever the name of that Belgian supermodel is; and, to top it off, the 'most honest show in reality television' manipulated the results after at least one of the episodes. I was supposed to get voted off after week ten. I can get a witness who'll verify that, if need be. Let me tell you, Rob, Diogenes won't find his honest man among you guys."

The room was quiet. I looked at Jack who squeezed my thigh, encouraging me to continue. "Jack and I are not the first 'couple' to have met and fallen in love on *Bad Date*," I told the suits. "Allegra and Candy became an item, too. Candy even went to extreme lengths to get herself voted off the show so that she could hurry up and get on with the rest of her life, which included moving to LA to live with Allegra."

Rob Dick looked at his colleagues, as if requesting them to back up his version of events. "We didn't know why Candy was trying to get kicked off the show, and by the time we learned of her relationship with Allegra, they were both long gone. So it's apples and oranges, really."

"Did Candy and Allegra get paid for their weeks on the show?" Jack asked.

There was a moment of hesitation. "Yes. They did," Benson admitted.

"So you didn't think, for whatever reasons, that it was seemly for you to hunt them down and demand that they make restitution of the winnings they received? In case you're considering asking us to forfeit any money already due to us for the dozen weeks Liz and I have been on the show."

"That's right, Mr. Rafferty," Benson said. "But in this case, we've discovered your 'illicit'—in terms of your contract—relationship while you are still on the show. Your conduct is clearly in violation of the rules of the production, your behavior clearly inappropriate."

"Now, with regard to Mr. Rick's conduct . . . excuse me." Mr. Sakamoto smiled. It was the first time he had spoken up during this meeting. "Mr. Byron's conduct is something for which he should be personally ashamed, but, with the exception of his offering you money to write for him while you are a contestant on the show, the other 'infractions' are not much more than the behavior of a spoiled young man who wants to have everything. His cake and eat it too, you say." He took a wrapped confection from his pocket, and offered a handful 'round the room. "Plum candy?" Rob Dick was the only taker. Sakamoto carefully unwrapped his candy and popped it in his mouth. The way he folded the discarded wrapper was so intricate it reminded me of origami. He carefully placed the tiny paper in the inner coin pocket of his suit jacket.

"So Rick Byron's attempt to bribe me counts for nothing?" I asked.

The lawyer wouldn't answer my question. The producers looked uncomfortable. "Let's revisit the notion of a quiz show scandal," I said. "I don't know whether the FCC is the right entity to review ethics violations on the air, but I think your manipulation of the audience votes will make *The $64,000 Question* debacle look like *Mister Rogers' Neighborhood*."

"How do we know your supposed 'witness' is reliable?" Rob began to counter, but he was interrupted by Benson, who made the "cut" slash with his hand across his throat. Benson put a firm hand on Rob's shoulder, leaned toward him, and whispered loudly enough for me to hear, "Shut up, they've got us on this one."

Jack must have heard it, too. "I suppose we could go to the media with that," he suggested quietly. "But it wouldn't really do anyone much good. Audiences will wonder what else on the supposedly squeaky-clean, scrupulously truthful show has been manipulated for any number of possibly nefarious ends. They may be so pissed off at you and feel so betrayed that they tune out in droves to the final episode. Which should make your sponsors very cranky."

The suits looked like they were trying hard not to squirm; I noticed beads of sweat on Rob Dick's brow. "This show is my livelihood . . . my job," he breathed. "If it fails . . ." he made a throat-slitting gesture across his own. "I'm history," he concluded.

Jack looked straight at Ronald Ebsen, the station president. "We're the last two contestants left. If you kick Liz and me off the show today, then you don't even *have* a final episode to air, do you? Which should make your sponsors even crankier. Which one of you gets to tell these major advertisers, your prime source of revenue, that America won't get to learn who finally wins the million-dollar *Bad Date* jackpot on Sunday night because you got caught manipulating the results of the live audience vote, and therefore the Urban Lifestyles Channel will be airing a rerun of *Rhoda* instead?"

Ebsen looked over at the lawyers. "Well? What are our alternatives?"

"Keep everything as quiet as possible," Benson counseled.

"Sakura does not wish to become embroiled in scandal," Sakamoto contributed. "Our conglomerate does not wish you to bring shame upon it by engaging in corrupt business practices."

Ebsen looked around the room. "It seems to me that none of the parties concerned exactly kept their noses clean on this one."

"So, how do we fix it?" Rob Dick asked.

"I see things unfolding two possible ways," Jack said. "One: We all shut up about everything that was discussed in here this afternoon. But that doesn't take into account that the security guard viewed the video-tape of Liz and me, and also doesn't account for the possibility that he may have shown it to several of his closest friends and relatives before giving it to you. The knowledge of this footage goes beyond this room." He smiled ever so slightly. It was an expression I had seen before. His I'm-up-to-something partial grin.

"Which brings me to option two: We run with the scandal insofar as it applies to Liz and me. If that's okay with you, Liz?"

I nodded my assent.

Jack continued to reveal his plan. "I say you 'leak' this video to *Hard Copy* or a similar program. Expose and exploit our backstairs tryst as colorfully as you wish; hell, have Liz ghostwrite the copy! For the next three days, plaster the airwaves with commercials for *Bad Date* that show a glimpse of the footage."

"God, that's brilliant, Jack!" I chimed in. "Run a voiceover of a sonorous-sounding man saying something like 'Has this clandestine tryst tainted America's hottest new reality TV show?' Your ratings will go through the roof for Sunday's telecast, market share will soar. I would go ahead and tell the usual spot buyers that you're raising your price for commercial airtime on the final episode."

Rob Dick removed a white handkerchief from his desk and mopped the beads of sweat from his brow.

Jack picked up the thread of our now collective idea to salvage the show. "Remind the viewers that any-thing can happen on live TV. Episode thirteen is some-thing they'll hate themselves for missing."

The suits looked visibly relieved. They voted to run

with our spin and thanked us for our time. Sakamoto suggested that we each sign a confidentiality agreement. Rob Dick removed a copy of a boilerplate agreement from a file in his credenza and handed it to Benson to review. Benson determined that with a few minor word changes that could be handwritten in and initialed by each of the parties to the agreement, the document would work. Within another half hour, it was signed, sealed, and locked away within Rob Dick's files.

So this is how Jack came up with the initial plan to save our butts by exposing them (more or less); this was the plan I honed, and which was finally agreed upon, with just the tiniest tinge of guilt, by all concerned.

What would happen on Sunday night would be anybody's guess.

After the meeting over at Urban Lifestyles, I used my cell to phone the office and retrieve a message from Jason. They needed to talk to me about something ASAP. I returned the call, explaining that I had just retrieved the message and it would be practically the close of business by the time I got downtown. No problem, F.X. assured me. Just get back here as fast as you can. I felt like I'd been dodging bullets all day already. Now what did they want from me? Was I in trouble with them again?

When I got to SSA both of my bosses were on a conference call, so I closed my door and took a moment to dial South America. "Domingo? I want to thank you," I told him. "Yes, you were very helpful. You have no idea what you did for me. Now, I've got an order to place with you . . . four pair . . . let me grab your catalogue." I gave him the style numbers I wanted. "No, not a size 6 . . . they're not for me . . . the first two style numbers I gave you—the slingbacks and the hiking boots—should be in a size 7; and the t-straps and the open-toed pumps should be in a size 8½. I don't want these to be a freebie, Domingo . . . because they're gifts, that's why. Let me give you my credit card number. . . ."

After I got off the line with Domingo, I rang both Jason and F.X. on their extensions and informed them that I was back. "Great, we'll be right in," F.X. responded. Seconds later he and Jason entered my office and closed the door.

"We'll get right to the point," F.X. said.

"We're going to be making some significant changes around here," Jason added.

I didn't like the way he said the word *significant*.

Jason continued. "We've been taking a look at our business model, both in the long term and vis-à-vis short-range goals. First of all, if you honestly think you can continue to deliver as well as you did on the Sole Mates account, we're offering you your old office back full time, although for the next six months your work for SSA will be done on a freelance basis. If everything is still stellar after that, you'll be back as a permanent staffer."

I was nonplused. "I don't know what to say, guys . . ."

"Don't say anything until we've finished talking to you," F.X. said. "We're also going to begin to branch out a bit. To that end, we're floating a sort of trial balloon, initially taking on only a few clients. If it flies, we'll be looking over the next couple of years or so to creating a new division of SSA, geared entirely toward development and production of public service campaigns. At the moment, we'll want you to handle these PSAs, in addition to the campaigns we assign you, with for-profit clients. But you still have to share Demetrius."

"Take a day or so to think it over before you decide—" Jason said.

I cut him off. "Yes. It's a yes. I accept." I could feel my face getting stuck in an idiotic grin. "But why did you decide to do this now. This week? This afternoon, in fact?"

F.X. removed his glasses and began to clean them on the front of his shirt. "A couple of reasons, Liz. First of all, we're thrilled to pieces with your 'Mate for Life' Sole Mates campaign. You're back in the groove and we couldn't be happier, personally and professionally. And we want you to be aware of how much we value you."

"And secondly," Jason added, "we know you've got the final episode of *Bad Date* coming up on Sunday and . . . well . . . just in case you don't win that million, we want you to know that there's a place for you here that will allow you to be as creative as possible, as long as the work meets SSA's usual high bar when it comes to standards. And if you *do* win the jackpot, we want you to know the same thing . . . so you don't get tempted to take the money and strike out on your own or something."

"Yeah. We'd really hate the competition!" F.X. said.

"What else can I say? It's a 'yes,' guys. I accept."

They shook my hand. The handshakes turned to hugs.

"Good," Jason said. He looked at his watch. "Because you've got a six P.M. appointment with your first PSA client, who should be in the reception area right about now." He walked out of my office and returned about a half-minute later, followed by a tall, thickset man of middle-age, with a shock of blond-gray hair. "Liz Pemberley, meet Deputy Chief Maguire of the New York City Fire Department."

I extended my hand to the fire chief, who gripped it firmly. "A pleasure," I said, feeling unprofessional tears well up in my eyes. "You guys have always been my heroes."

F.X. jovially clapped his partner on the shoulder. "Jase? She's back!"

34/The Final Episode

When the Urban Lifestyles Channel blitzed the airwaves with the type of provocative commercials we had suggested, all sorts of creatures came crawling out of the woodwork of my past. My answering machine was deluged with messages from people identifying themselves as someone I'd met once on a checkout line at Fairway or with whom I went to second grade. I could have filled up a subway car with the number of male callers claiming to have gone out with me at one time or another, who felt compelled to either compliment or criticize my performance in the stairwell. My relatives, on the other hand, unsurprisingly, refused to acknowledge my existence.

At around four P.M. on Sunday afternoon, hours before the limo was due to whisk me off to the studio, a delivery guy bearing a huge box from Giorgio Armani materialized on my doorstep. I thanked him, tipped him, then brought the box into my bedroom to survey its contents. Tucked inside the crisply folded white tissue was a notecard. For a split second my heart skipped a beat, fearing that the gift might be from Rick Byron. After all, we'd determined that he was an Armani man.

The card read:

Let's go out in style, love.
Wear whichever one you want tonight.

Surprise me. J

I carefully slit the sticker that held the pristine tissue closed, savoring the moment. Inside the box were the pants suit and cashmere camisole I had tried on at the Armani boutique on the afternoon Jack and I had gone alphabet shopping; folded beneath them was the beaded cocktail dress that had been Jack's initial preference.

After devoting nearly forty-five minutes to changing back and forth several times (including accessorizing), I settled on the cocktail dress. It was overdoing it a bit, perhaps, but what the hell. As Jack and I had agreed that it would be a good idea if he went back to staying at the Waldorf for his last *Bad Date* weekend in town, I started to ring him there to thank him, but halfway through dialing, I replaced the receiver. We'd agreed to keep as low a profile as possible before the telecast.

I arrived at the studio, feeling deliciously glamorous in my new dress, and Ethan and the now-saffron-haired Gladiola pulled out all the stops, fussing so much with my hair and makeup that I felt like a movie star. Their extra dose of attentiveness went a long way toward taking my mind off the broadcast . . .

although there was a major issue I hadn't thought too
much about until I got to the studio and observed the
behavior of those around me.

See, I hadn't really minded zillions of total strangers
I'd never met, nor ever would, seeing the stairwell
footage splattered all over *Hard Copy*, but I did feel a
bit awkward about this exposure in front of people
I'd been in close proximity with who were little more
than acquaintances. For example, while Gladiola
didn't act any differently—she was invariably in her
own world most of the time anyway—Ethan congratulated Jack on his good taste and good fortune,
and seemed to let his fingers linger in my hair perhaps
a bit too long when he was working his styling magic.

Rob Dick seemed slightly edgy when he stopped by
to give his usual pep talk—minus the "We're the most
honest show in reality TV" line. I was listening for it
and when he didn't say it, I looked in the mirror to try
to catch Jack's reflection. He had a poker face, while I
was suppressing the giggles at the silliness of our
trying so hard to pretend that everything was status
quo when we'd been all over the air in a sort of *fla-
grante delicto* for the past half a week.

After the staff had beautified me, I went down to
my dressing room for the final time. It was hard to
relax and prepare for the broadcast. The butterflies in
my stomach were worse than they'd been before the
very first episode.

I stared into the mirror, feeling suddenly rudderless.
It's true that both Jack and I were working hand-in-
glove with the Urban Lifestyles studio brass in terms
of how to spin a near-disaster into a potential gold

mine. But when it came down to the outcome of the final episode and how we might feel if the other one of us walked away with a million dollars in prize money, Jack and I had barely touched on it. It was like the proverbial elephant in the living room. Everyone acknowledges it's there, but no one wants to be the first to comment on it. You'd have to live in a fantasy world to attach zero importance to the money. Sure, he'd like to win, Jack agreed, but winning wasn't everything.

"Well, if someone offered me an either/or choice: Jack or the jackpot, I just want you to know for sure that I wouldn't hesitate about picking you," I had told him the night before the final episode. "Would you . . . ?"

Jack gave me a loving kiss. "Of course I'd pick you, silly. You had to ask?"

"I've been thinking about this a lot lately," I said, gazing into his eyes. "Whatever happens tomorrow night, our lives will never be the same again."

I was jolted back to the present when Geneva announced our final five-minute call over the speakers in the dressing room, then knocked on my door to escort me to the set. She'd already collected Jack. We walked the length of the corridor in silence. I can't presume to speak for what Jack might have been thinking at the time, but I was still wondering how to behave during the telecast. Competitively? Affectionately? Jovially? What were the viewers expecting? And did I care?

Geneva gave her countdown and the house band struck up the now-familiar *Bad Date* theme music for the last time. Rick Byron came bounding onto the set, to a burst of tumultuous applause, already acting like he was revved up on a couple of extra latte grandes.

"Wow-weeeeeee! What a week it's been!" he roared into his hand-held microphone. The audience hollered and whistled. Just as the sound was dying down, someone let out a piercing wolf whistle, followed by the words "Go, Liz!" The studio audience crested another wave of shouts.

"You've got *some* thigh muscles there, girl," Rick said to me.

"I've been working out," I quipped back.

"And, Jack, there's certainly something to be said for the strong, silent type, huh? Aren't you the luckiest devil in this ring of hell?"

Jack sat in his director's chair, giving the appearance of being so cooly laid back that if I didn't know him better, I would have guessed it was a put on. "Let's get on with this farce, shall we, Rick?"

"Great idea, Jack!" Rick said, "but before we do, just in case anyone out there has been living under a rock for the past week, we've had some very, shall we say *titillating* developments between our two remaining *Bad Date* contestants. In fact, Jack and Liz have revealed more of themselves in these few minutes we're about to share with you than in the past dozen episodes of our program. So, what do you say, sports fans? Let's go to the videotape!" Rick made an "away we go" sort of gesture upstage to the big polygraph screen above the cone throne. "What a game of truth or dare, ladies and gentlemen!" The security footage of the sexual escapade in the stairwell was shared in its raw, unedited entirety—except for judiciously placed blue dots where necessary. We had, after all, remained basically clothed during the adventure. I suppose the only thing to have been grateful for was that Rob Dick and his Urban Lifestyles cohorts hadn't seen fit to interpose underscoring and subtitles.

Following the screening, which was incredibly embarrassing because I was sitting on live TV watching people watching me—and some of them were more interested in my reaction as I watched them watching me watching myself onscreen—Rick segued to the first commercial break. When we returned to the air, Rick said, fanning himself, "Well, what could have been viewed as a scandal of monumental proportions has only served to increase the intrigue surrounding our show, which, the producers tell me, has suddenly become, according to audience surveys, the hottest reality TV show *ever*. So without further ado, as they say, let's go over to the gumball machine and see who's up first tonight."

Rick fairly leapt up to the machine, was given a dramatic-sounding drum roll, and pressed the ejector button.

Nothing happened.

He tried again.

Nothing happened.

Then Rick turned to the drummer. "Best two out of three?" He hit the button and for the third time the machine froze on him. Rick gave Geneva a deer-in-the-headlights look. This had never happened before. Camera three panned over to Geneva. Our quick-thinking stage manager took a coin from her pocket and tossed it on set to Rick, who returned center stage.

"Good thing there are only two of you," Rick said, scrutinizing the coin as though he was amazed that it only had two sides. "Who'll make the call?"

"Ladies first," Jack commented.

Rick started to head toward my chair. "That's no lady, that's—"

"Watch it!" Jack interrupted. He wasn't kidding. It was the first time I'd really seen him genuinely pissed off at someone. I saw Rick respond with a little shudder, also genuine, I imagine.

"My hero," I said, turning in my chair so I could face Jack. *I* wasn't kidding; I was very touched by his chivalry.

Rick approached me. "Heads or tails, Lizzie? You call it."

"You know I hate to be called 'Lizzie.' Tails."

With a great degree of bravado, our host spun the coin into the air. It landed with a clunk somewhere downstage of him. He looked at the floor in the immediate vicinity and couldn't locate it. "Shit," Rick muttered under his breath. I tried not to laugh. He gave a little un-hunklike wail. "Geneva," he whimpered, stretching out his hand for another coin.

"Get over here," she commanded. She fished in her pocket and with a maternal gesture, pressed a second quarter into his palm.

"Don't spend it all in one place, Rick," I cautioned.

Rick flipped the coin and slapped it on the back of his hand. "Heads. Jack? Do you elect to give or receive?"

"Offense or defense?" Jack asked wryly. "I'll let Liz share her story first. Do your worst, kiddo."

"Kiddo" always annoyed me and he knew it, so I wondered why he'd said it. I shot him a look designed to make him believe that my "worst" was pretty damn lethal. In fact, Jack didn't know it, but I still wasn't a hundred percent sure what I was going to say once I got to the cone throne. I had about another three seconds to make up my mind. The house band played dramatic tension music as I ascended the polygraph platform and slid my fingers into the metal cones for the last time.

"You know," I began, "most of us who consider ourselves hopeless romantics, or in my case hope*ful* ones, pick ourselves up out of the mud after we've been thrown over, wash the stench of the partners from hell out of our hair, and continue our quest for The One. This is the story of the worst dating experience I ever had in my life. In fact, it was so bad that my lover didn't even break off our relationship in person. He rejected me over the phone."

I could hear a painful "ooooh" from some of the members of the studio audience.

"That was just one element that made this particular dating experience so dreadful. At the moment he chose to walk away, I wasn't able to look in his eyes, couldn't reach for his hand, had no opportunity to try to explain myself face to face. But the kicker was that I was finally, totally sure that *this* man *was* The One. At first, this guy was very easy to get to know, but for certain reasons, far less easy to trust. What did he want from me? Why did he want to get to know me so quickly? Why was he being so damn nice to me? It didn't help matters any that my two closest female friends in the world tried six ways from Sunday to convince me that he was bad news."

From the cone throne I could see some of the faces in the front few rows of the audience. There sat Jem in her t-straps, holding hands with Carl, and Nell in her slingbacks, with A.J.'s arm draped affectionately over her shoulder. I wondered what they were thinking.

My right index finger began to itch inexplicably. "The hardest part of being involved with this guy was that, because of certain conditions, we had to sneak around and avoid getting found out, even though we were both legally and emotionally available. So here I was—am—head over heels in love and didn't want the most special relationship I'd ever had to remain a secret; but the catch was that if I wanted the whole world to know that I had finally met The One, I would most likely lose every opportunity to reach *Bad Date*'s million-dollar jackpot."

I suddenly found myself fighting back tears. "My boyfriend tried to convince me that we should fly below the radar, as it were, as long as the contest was so important to me. But I wanted it both ways. He felt my response meant that the grand prize was more important to me than our relationship, and, therefore, he wasn't going to do anything to stand in the way of what I seemed to want most."

Although I was successful at stifling my tears, I had started to sniffle a bit. Instinctively, I reached for a tissue, but realized I had no pockets and my fingers were still in the metal cones. I saw Jack remove his handkerchief from his breast pocket and wave it at Rick, who brought it up to me and awkwardly dabbed my eyes with it. "Anyway," I continued, when

Rick had returned to his downstage position, "after that conversation, my lover pretty much said he was removing himself from the equation ... and said good-bye to me over the phone. I admit that eventually we did reconcile, but I know our relationship suffered for it. Anyway, I just wanted to tell everyone about the stupidest mistake I ever made and what the consequences were."

I laughed softly. "I mean, it's pretty cut and dried, isn't it? It's like that Beatles' lyric 'money can't buy you love.' It's true enough in my case, anyway. Money can buy someone sex, even great sex—so I've heard—but without love, in my humble opinion, how great can the sex really be?" I pointed a metal-tipped finger toward an audience member who was a fraction of a second away from becoming a heckler. "Don't answer that," I warned collegially. "I just want to add that while this has been a scintillating thirteen weeks, nothing you folks up there in the control booth can offer me will come close to the greatest treasure I have: my precious, wonderful man."

I had nothing more to say. I slid my fingers out of the cones and returned to my seat. The house was quiet. A somewhat subdued Rick Byron introduced the next commercial break.

We returned to the air. "Well, Jack," Rick said, his energy doubled, thanks to a huge jolt of lukewarm black coffee imbibed during the station break, "can you top this, as they say?"

Jack rose from his chair and took his final journey to the cone throne. He installed himself, paused, then furrowed his brow. "This is certainly my unhappiest dating experience in recent memory," he began. "Nearly every Sunday evening for the past quarter of a year, you have heard me talk about all these wacko, toxic bachelorettes I have encountered during my decades of dating. Invariably, in every story I shared, one of these women did something off-the-wall to me. This story is about something *I* did to one of them. When I first met her, what most intrigued me about her was her brain. She had the fastest wit of anyone I've ever known, and a glib sense of humor that she wore as defensively as a suit of armor. That's *armor*, Liz, not *Armani*."

"I noticed the polygraph lines didn't do anything on the screen when you mentioned how attracted you were to this woman's mind," I said. "Hmmm. Cool! Wait a minute—what about her hair?"

"Are you supposed to editorialize here?" Jack asked.

Rick looked at Geneva, then toward the mezzanine-level, glass-enclosed booth above the studio audience at the back of the theater, where the producers sat. He lifted his hands to them in a question, then shrugged. "I think all bets are off at this point," Rick said. "Just keep telling your story."

"Right. So here's this incredibly lovely woman with her angular New York edges," Jack continued. "And I'm from Miami. We've got sun and sand and salsa and, face it, we're technically in the South, where women—I'll shoot straight here—conceal their steely cores with a cloud of ultrafeminine gentility that comes from centuries of carefully cultivated behavior modification. Well, I was determined to pierce this

New York lady's armor and discover what truly lay beneath. What I found was that this amazing woman I fell for turned out to be the inside-out version of these other women. She's a marshmallow underneath. The hard veneer she's developed to protect her soul is as consciously crafted as the other women's seeming softness."

I watched Jack's face in the monitor. He appeared utterly composed.

"You have no idea how happy I was when this woman finally felt comfortable enough to drop her guard with me . . . how excited I was to discover what was beneath her shell, and how fantastic I felt when she began to realize that I had no intentions of hurting her, that it was okay to trust." Jack splayed his fingers and wiggled them as though they were cramped.

"Liz, I promised myself I would never hurt you, and by walking away from us the way I did, I broke that promise. I was at such a boiling point of frustration at the time, but I'm not a quitter when it comes to relationships. Your wanting things both ways was making me nuts, but if someone cuts and runs at the first sign of trouble in Paradise rather than doing their damndest to work things through, then how much did they care about their lover in the first place? I hope you're glad I wasn't such an ox about it to stay away, because I couldn't be happier . . . I don't need to win a million dollars. You're all I want."

"Whoa, there! Hold it!" Rick Byron rushed up to the cone throne just as Jack was releasing his fingers from their metal confinement. "Did we all just hear what I thought we heard?" Rick escorted Jack back to his captain's chair and stood between us. He looked back and forth from me to Jack. When he finally spoke again, Rick's tone was at once accusatory and incredulous. "Liz? Jack? Did I miss something here, or did you two just tell the same story?"

35/The Real Jackpot

They went immediately to a commercial. The hulla-baloo on the set was something to behold. When the live telecast resumed, the circus atmosphere prevailed. A third chair had been brought onstage for Rob Dick, who introduced himself to the world as the show's producer, quipping that the strands of gray in his hair had been brown at 7:50 P.M., when he and his colleagues at the station entered their glass booth to view the final episode.

"This is what's called 'winging it,'" Rob told the studio audience. "Our attorneys and researchers are checking for precedent, but at this point it's safe to say that nothing like this has ever happened. *Bad Date* is the Urban Lifestyles Channel's maiden foray into reality television production. So, all I can ask you to do," Rob continued, "is to vote the way you have been doing—well not you specifically, since our studio audience is a new one every week—but just use the electronic box in front of you to record your vote the way you were instructed to do during the pre-broadcast."

I have to say that some of the audience members looked confused. One of their number, a woman in her thirties, stood up and asked, "Well, how can we say who had the worst time of it, if they pretty much told the same story?" A man about ten years older than her stood and faced us. "I mean, you two were talking about each other, right?"

Jack nodded and reached for my hand.

"Did you plan to do that?" I asked him.

"Not until you were in the middle of your story," he said. "It just made sense to me to set the record straight and go completely public. Besides, if you were watching the monitor, you'd have noticed that the polygraph lines didn't wiggle and wriggle as I was talking. It *was* my unhappiest dating experience in recent memory. I wasn't breaking any rules by sharing it."

"I think the studio audience should vote, just as they've always done," Rob Dick said. He gestured to someone in the wings. "And at this juncture, I think we should remind the voters what's at stake here."

Bad Date's announcer reiterated the prizes via voice-over. A man and a woman came onstage. The woman was your typical bony fashion model, dressed in a tasteful navy evening gown. She bore a gigantic check in the amount of one million dollars, with the payee left blank. A stagehand came running out with an easel, which he quickly set up center stage, so that the super-size check could rest on it. The man, who carried a gilt-edged envelope, was introduced by the announcer as the publicity director of a major airline, the company that was sponsoring the rest of the grand prize: the all-expense-paid trip for two to Paris-the-Romantic-City-of-Lights. The airline was also a major sponsor of *Bad Date*, running at least two commercials over the course of the half-hour show each week. I wondered if this was the influential advertiser Domingo had alluded to.

Then it was time to vote. The band struck up the suspenseful theme music that it had played each of the dozen previous Sunday evenings.

"And now . . . it's time for our final vote," Rick Byron intoned somberly. "For the past twelve weeks, Jack Rafferty and Liz Pemberley have shared their stories about the worst dating experiences in their lives and have squared off against one another and the other dozen *Bad Date* contestants." He turned to the audience. "In fact, some of them are here tonight."

The house lights, which ordinarily remained on during the show anyway, came up a little brighter. Rick moved downstage. "We've got four of our former challengers right here. I trust you all remember Jemima Lawrence, to whom we bid a fond farewell after week five; Anella Avignon, who waltzed off after episode eight; and, together again, Allegra McGilli-cuddy and Candy Fortunato. Candy, as you folks may recall, outstayed Allegra by a few weeks, but found she just couldn't stay away!" Rick made an appeal to the audience. "Let's have a big hand for them!" The women smiled and waved at the cameras and the crowd responded enthusiastically. I saw both Jem and Nell point to their footwear and then to me. Jem blew me a kiss. Nell touched her heart.

Rick walked back to the center of the stage with his right hand behind his back. "Folks, it's time to vote. I know it's going to be a tough decision, given that they've both more or less told the same story, but rules are rules and it's up to you. Which of our two final contestants has shared the worst experience tonight? Ladies and gentlemen: Cast your votes!" Rick raised his hand with great fanfare, as though he were waving the green starter flag at the Indy 500.

For the next thirty seconds or so, all we could hear was the sounds of people shifting in their seats, muttering to themselves, looking like they were trying to make up their minds. The band resumed playing its suspenseful-sounding score.

Then, the oddest thing happened. The verbal rumblings in the audience began to build. "The thing's jammed," someone said. "Yeah," another agreed. "The system won't let me cast a vote."

"Oh shit," Rob Dick muttered. He grabbed the handheld microphone from Rick Byron. "Well, folks, that's the magic of live TV, isn't it." He tossed the mike back to the host and went over to talk to our stage manager.

"Geneva, I'm at a loss here," I heard Rob say between his teeth. "What the fuck are we supposed to do now?"

Geneva motioned to him to incline his head toward hers so she could whisper something in his ear. Something people should know about stage managers and wardrobe mistresses: a great one of these pros is worth his or her weight in gold. They also carry so much stuff on them that they'd be an easy bet to win a few quick bucks on the old *Let's Make a Deal* game show, or survive *Survivor*. From somewhere on her person, Geneva produced several packets of index cards. I think she normally used them for pre-telecast audience surveys. She handed the cards to Rob and suggested he distribute them to the studio audience.

When I saw him question what they were expected to write with in case they had no pens or pencils with them, she pointed to a box at the foot of the stage.

Rob retrieved the box, which contained hundreds of little yellow pencils. I turned to Jack and pointed out with some relish how much fun it was to watch the producer taking orders from his stage manager. "What are we supposed to do while they're all writing out the cards?" I whispered to him.

"How well do you sing?" he answered.

"Better than most contestants on *The Gong Show* but not as well as Judy Garland."

While Rob and Geneva and a couple of stagehands hastily handed out the cards, Rob instructed the members of the audience to write down the name of the person who they felt had the lesser story of the night. "I know, I know," he commiserated with those who remained confused, and still hadn't a clue how to answer that question.

"Can we write stuff in?" someone asked.

Rob Dick looked momentarily confused himself. "Like what? I mean, don't write 'Mickey Mouse' or 'Mata Hari' or your vote won't count, but you're welcome to write a comment, I guess. If you invalidate your card by writing in a name other than one of the two contestants, tonight's winner and loser will be based upon the number of correctly filled-out cards. Tell you what—we'll go to another commercial break, and as soon as we're back on the air, we'll collect the cards and count the votes. As always, a representative from the accounting firm of Tilzer and Durant will oversee the tabulation."

I leaned over to Jack and whispered, "This should be very interesting," but he seemed miles away. I'd never seen him like that.

Back on the air, the index cards now collected, Rick Byron was told to banter for a bit—"vamp," as they say—to fill the time while the cards were being read and sorted. "So, you two, how are you feeling?" he asked us.

What a question. "A bit tense," I replied. "And very curious."

Jack shifted in his chair. "Rick, as long as we need to do something to pass the time while the ballots are being counted, I have something I'd like to share." He rose from his chair. "And if those cones are still plugged in, you can verify, if you choose, that what I'm about to say was not something I planned ahead of time to say on the air tonight. I'll repeat that phrase under your polygraph if you want me to."

"Does it have anything to do with the million dollar jackpot?" Rick asked him.

"Not particularly. Not remotely, in fact."

"Then just say it, Jack," Rick replied.

Jack looked over at me. "A lot of guys pride themselves on being loners. They guard their independence as fiercely as a lioness protects her cubs. That's never been who I am. I think the most natural thing in the world is coupledom; it's loner-ism that seems like an imposition to me. I see my woman not just as my lover, but as my helpmeet, confidante, full-time partner, and lifelong best friend. How ironic that I had to get cast on a show that focuses on disastrous relationships to find the love of my life."

Jack took a small box out of his jacket pocket. He

held up the jewelry box and grinned at the camera. "Liz Pemberley, get over here."

I arched an eyebrow. "A command, Jack?"

"Yes, actually."

I descended from my captain's chair. As I headed over to join him center stage, Jack looked at me. "You know, you're better dressed than I am tonight," he quipped appreciatively.

"I imagine that will frequently be the case. Especially if you keep buying me Armani cocktail dresses." My heart was pounding a mile a minute, and here I was spouting nervous nonsense.

Before I knew it, Jack was down on one knee, clasping my left hand. "Liz, I'm not doing this to vamp for time and I will never take back these words. I just want to add that I decided to do this now because I don't want the outcome of tonight's episode to have any bearing on either my question or your answer. We have no idea what the audience vote will be and in any event, I don't care. For you, Liz, this Miami boy would sail the *Circe* up the inland water route and dock it permanently at the Seventy-ninth Street boat basin. For you, I'll open my own restaurant in SoHo instead of South Beach. What I want to say to you is not a publicity stunt . . . it's as spontaneous as I can be, given that I had intended to ask you this question pretty soon anyway."

We looked in each other's eyes. I can't remember when I had seen his sparkle with such depth. "I love you, Liz Pemberley . . . will you make me the luckiest, happiest man in the world and be my wife?"

The entire studio fell silent, save for one happy yelp from someone in the audience whom I was quite sure was Nell. I couldn't swear to it, though; my eyes were brimming over with tears.

Jack opened the box and slid a stunning emerald onto my ring finger. "Liz? Will you marry me?" For a moment Jack looked worried that I might say no.

I grabbed both his hands in mine and pressed them to my breasts. Well, that's what he could reach, from the position he was in. Besides, holding his hands to my heart helped keep it within the confines of my body. I thought I was going to burst with joy and exhilaration. "Yes, of course I'll marry you, Jack!" One of my tears plopped right into the well made by our joined hands. "Oh, my God . . . I love you so much," I murmured into his hair.

Jack rose, took me in his arms, and kissed me—a long magical kiss full of love and promise. The world went away, leaving only the two of us touching, holding, hugging, so exquisitely connected, so safe, so loved. For a while we just stood there holding one another. I think I was sobbing happy tears into Jack's chest. When I finally opened my eyes, I couldn't help but see that the screen upstage of us was displaying a montage of our embrace from every angle. The audience was cheering and crying, the entire carnival atmosphere of the evening now even more in full swing. I ran over to hug Nell and Jem who were carrying on so loudly, you'd think they just won the Publisher's Clearinghouse sweepstakes.

Rick Byron waved his arms to try to quiet the house. "The magic of live television!" Rob Dick kept yelling triumphantly. Finally, the audience settled down, when Rick brandished a sealed envelope, which, we all assumed contained the results of the voting. "I guess it might be a bit of an anticlimax, given the events of the past five minutes or so," he began, "but here we are . . . the moment half the civilized world has been waiting more than a quarter of a year for. May I have a drum roll, please?"

The band obliged.

Rick slit open the envelope. "Ladies and gentlemen . . . the winner of the million dollar jackpot on *Bad Date*'s very first season is . . ." Rick read the result on the card. *"No one,"* he said very slowly. Suddenly, it looked like his salon tan had faded completely. He walked over to Rob Dick with the card and showed it to him. "It really says the words *no one*," he told him, a bit panicked. "What do I do? I'm only the host!"

"Can we have our CPA out here, please?" Rob Dick asked. A tall, strawberry blonde was escorted onstage. "Folks, this is Audrey Tilzer, a partner with the accounting firm of Tilzer and Durant. Audrey, what happened here?"

"Well, Rob," said Audrey, shaking her head, "first of all, there were a vast number of cards on which people elected to write some version of 'neither should win because they told the same story, so we couldn't arrive at a fair vote.' And we couldn't count those cards, of course, as they're ostensibly an abstention. There are two hundred and fifty-three people in the studio audience and a hundred and fifteen of them 'abstained.' The remaining hundred and thirty-eight votes were split exactly. Fifty-fifty. Which translates to sixty-nine for each of them."

"How ironic," Jack whispered in my ear. His warm breath sent a tingle through me.

The audience had no idea why I started to laugh so hard. "How mutual," I whispered back.

"So what does that mean in terms of a winner?" the producer asked Audrey.

"What do your show's rules say, Rob?"

"Audrey, *Bad Date*'s rules are that the audience has the final vote. It can't be manipulated or changed." Rob looked nervously at Jack and me. I nodded my head toward the polygraph equipment and smiled as seraphically as I could manage. Of course, we weren't supposed to know that the producers could probably do what they wanted to with the money, when push came to shove, but no doubt if they didn't pay out the jackpot, *Bad Date* would never see another season, assuming anyone would want to assemble another cast of the haplessly lovelorn.

Rob approached us. "Well, Liz, Jack. Of course each of you will be sent a check for thirteen thousand dollars, representing the thousand dollars per week for the past thirteen weeks you've been on the air. But about the million . . . what can I say?"

Jack placed one hand over his own lavalier mike and put his other hand on Rob's lapel. "You can say you're one lucky son of a bitch. But you're confusing me with someone who cares." Jack released the producer. Rob immediately made a beeline for the airline's publicity VP, who had been frantically semaphoring to him for half a minute.

After a brief confab with the VP, Rob grabbed Rick Byron's microphone. "This is great, folks. That's what I love about live TV—you never know what's going to happen next. Ralph Drucker here from Trans•Global

Airlines, one of *Bad Date*'s major sponsors, and the corporation that is providing our winner with the all-expense-paid luxury trip for two to Paris, is quite adamant that his company's prize be awarded. Ralph?" Rob handed the mike to the airline executive.

Mr. Drucker took the gilt-edged envelope from his pocket. "Jack, Liz. We at Trans•Global are proud and pleased and honored to present both of you with this luxury vacation in the hope that you will use it for your honeymoon." He shook our hands, kissed me on the cheek, and pressed the envelope into my palm. "From all of us at Trans•Global, *bon voyage*."

We thanked him warmly. The studio audience continued to behave as though they were at a college pep rally.

While Mr. Drucker had been making his on-camera presentation, off-camera Mr. Ebsen, Mr. Benson, and Mr. Sakamoto had materialized and were onstage in a huddle with Rob Dick. When they broke, Rob tried to quiet the crowd and finally had to beg the band's brass section to get everyone's attention. The trumpeter played "Reveille."

"Well, folks, it's been a real rollercoaster ride tonight," Rob said. "And it ain't over yet. The executive producers of *Bad Date* have just had a conference on the mound, so to speak, and we all feel that owing to the audience vote, which resulted in a tie, and given that the contestants themselves played fast and loose with the rules regarding their anecdotes, and since there appear to be no clear rules governing an even split of the jackpot in the event of a tie on the final episode, it's been determined that *Bad Date* must uphold its reputation as the most honest reality show on television and respect the sentiments of our studio audience by not awarding the million dollar prize."

Rob Dick covered the microphone with his hand. "Shit," I heard him mutter to Geneva. "Now we'll never get renewed for a second season. My career is over. In the toilet. I might as well prematurely retire to Phoenix and play golf all day."

The rest of the broadcast became a blur. I remember my engagement ring flashing like a beacon under the stage lights. And I remember hugging Jem and Nell several times. I recall embracing Candy and Allegra. At some point, I know Rick Byron and I patched up any misunderstandings between us; I must have thanked Rob Dick—for what, I'm not entirely sure—and said a few nice words to the accountant and to Mr. Drucker.

I practically skipped down the corridor to my dressing room. I was packing up the sundries I had left there since the first episode of *Bad Date*, feeling like I was cleaning out my locker on graduation day and preparing to venture forth into a thrilling new life, when there was a knock on the door. "Come in. It's open."

Jack poked his head inside my dressing room. "Ready?"

"Just about." I shoved a blue terrycloth hand towel into my bag. "That's it." I took a last look around. The cinderblock walls looked especially uninspiring now that there were no flowers on the dressing table, no notecards shoved into the mirror frame, no vibrant personality such as Candy's to warm up the room. For a moment, I felt just a little tinge of sadness.

Jack held out his hand. "Let's go, love."

"Yup." I took a last look under the dressing table to see if I'd left anything behind, then I flicked off the light switch and closed the door. We started down the corridor, our arms about each other's waists. "You know," I murmured, "I'm glad you didn't dredge up our lobster-dinner debacle tonight."

Jack winked at me. "It wasn't a 'date,' remember?" He pulled me close, and as we walked, I inclined my head toward his shoulder.

We slowed down just a bit as we passed the door leading to the now-notorious stairwell. "Are you sure you want to take the traditional route?" I teased, glancing back at the door.

"I think the guard is a bit more vigilant these days," Jack said. With his right hand, he gave my midsection a little tickle. "After all, we became his favorite show!"

Just before we got to the security desk, Jack stopped and took me in his arms. I lifted my chin and gently bit his lower lip, turning the gesture into a deliciously long kiss. "I can only speak for myself here," I ran my hands through his hair, "but I *did* win the jackpot tonight. You're all I need to make me happy for the rest of my life, Jack. You and your smile." I looked at him, full of love, and kissed him again.

"Winning you is the best thing that's ever happened to me, too," Jack murmured. He grinned down at me. "But we did come away from the show with something else, the memories of which, like our marriage, will no doubt last forever."

We left the studio and walked out into the warm night air. I regarded him quizzically.

Jack tapped the gilt-edged envelope from Trans•Global that was sticking out of my purse. "Liz, my love, we'll always have *Paris*."

Don't miss this delightful
romantic comedy by Leslie Carroll!

MISS MATCH

Everyone from her happily married sister to her
meddling neighbor thinks it's time for thirty-five-
year-old Kitty Lamb to take drastic action to find
herself a wonderful man. So she enrolls in New
York's premier matchmaking service. If Walker
Hart, the gorgeous entrepreneur of the company, is
any example of the men who will be parading to her
apartment, then Kitty will definitely be a satisfied
customer. But as each promising encounter turns
into a disaster, Kitty realizes that the only guy who
has captured her romantic heart is the one who
doesn't believe in happily ever after.

Sexy and sassy, *Miss Match* is a hilarious first novel
that delves into the anxieties of the mating game,
where every now and then one has to bend the
rules. . . .

In paperback from Ivy Books.
Available wherever books are sold.

Subscribe to the new Pillow Talk
e-newsletter—and receive all these
fabulous online features directly in
your e-mail inbox:

♥ Exclusive essays and other features by major romance
writers like Linda Howard, Kristin Hannah,
Julie Garwood, and Suzanne Brockmann

♥ Exciting behind-the-scenes news from
our romance editors

♥ Special offers, including contests to win signed
romance books and other prizes

♥ Author tour information, and monthly announce-
ments about the newest books on sale

♥ A Pillow Talk readers forum, featuring feedback
from romance fans...like you!

Two easy ways to subscribe:
Go to **www.ballantinebooks.com/PillowTalk**
or send a blank e-mail to
join-PillowTalk@list.randomhouse.com.

Pillow Talk—
the romance e-newsletter brought to you by
Ballantine Books